The Curse of Sekhem Ka

Matthew J. Messina, D.D.S.

Keep Smiling!

Printed in the United States of America.

The Curse of Sekhem Ka

    ISBN 978-0-9852208-0-8

    Published by:
    Mathew J. Messina, D.D.S.
    20390 Lorain Road
    Fairview Park, OH 44126

First Printing 2012

About the Author

Dr. Matt Messina is a practicing dentist who shares an adventurous nature and Mid-western heritage with his fictional hero, Mike Murphy, DDS. Like Murph, the author graduated from The Ohio State University College of Dentistry at the top of his dental class and frequently sports the Block O baseball cap of his beloved Buckeyes.

Messina has been the Editor of the Ohio Dental Association since 2003, receiving numerous awards for his writing. He has been a national spokesperson for the American Dental Association since 1996, appearing on ABC TV's *Good Morning America*, National Public Radio (NPR), CNN, and in *USA Today, The Wall Street Journal, The New York Times, The Washington Post, Men's Health, Cosmopolitan*, and *WebMD* to name just a few. Messina's professional research and publications have focused on ethical decision-making processes in patient care. He is a member of the Visiting Faculty of The Pankey Institute for Advanced Dental Education in Key Biscayne, Florida. He currently lectures nationally on temporomandibular joint (TMJ) dysfunction and treatment, dental emergencies in sports, and the development of leadership qualities in professionals.

Messina lives in Cleveland Ohio with his wife Denise and three children. *The Curse of Sekhem Ka* is his debut in the action adventure genre. Given the rousing support for this novel and Messina's propensity for writing, Dr. Mike Murphy will return soon in another action-packed novel titled *The Black Swan Event*.

Dedication

For the loves of my life:
Denise, Caitlin, Michael and Brian

Acknowledgments

For the caring profession of Dentistry – a noble group of friends and colleagues much maligned in books and film over the years. This one is for you!

For my fellow faculty members at The Pankey Institute – Pankey is a community of encouraging colleagues, learning and training together for today's challenging practice environment. To all of you, especially George Platt and Mike Rogers, thanks for going on the journey with me!

For the Jesuit educators at Cleveland Saint Ignatius High School – A.M.D.G. Everything you do is for the greater glory of God.

For my classmates at The Ohio State University where it all began – Go Bucks!

For my editor, Deb Bush – you always make me speak with clarity. Thanks so much!

Most of all, I would like to thank my children, Caitlin, Mike, and Brian, for their enthusiastic support and encouragement, especially Brian, who was my first editor. My parents, Charles and Shirley Messina, and my in-laws, Burchard and Lois Sheehy, read the manuscript early and urged me to continue writing.

Finally, for Denise, the love of my life. Your belief in me allowed me to be committed enough finish the book and be brave enough to allow it to be read by others. With love, this book is dedicated to you!

Chapter 1

A heavy mist was falling from slate grey skies, and the clouds themselves seemed to be crying. A long dark snake of mourners, hunched against the cold, passed down the stone steps and out onto the street. Dampness seeped into their souls, in spite of their best efforts to ward it off, as they waited in quiet perseverance for their turn to pass by the casket lying in state in the rotunda of the Capital.

Such a dreary day to be out, but the Senator from New York had been much beloved. His death, while it saddened his many supporters, could hardly be considered unexpected. Edwin Shafter had, after all, just last year become the longest serving Senator. He had seemed robust and vigorous even to the end. His doctors had not thought much of it when he was admitted with abdominal pain, but the next day he was dead of an undetermined illness. Now he laid in peace in the halls he had so recently roamed as the Majority Whip, bullying other legislators with the force of his "in your face" style of politics.

After the crowds had fled to the warmth of their homes and darkness had fallen on Washington, his casket was removed from the bier and wheeled into an antechamber. The family paid their last respects, his daughter kissing his forehead for the last time. In preparation for sealing the coffin, the personal effects of the Senator were removed. His wedding band and class ring were given to his children, as his wife had passed years ago. The lid was closed, and the somber party in black moved quietly out to the waiting limousines for the trip home to Long Island. The body was to follow tomorrow for the public funeral on the weekend.

Before the lock on the chamber door had clicked fully shut, Billy stepped smartly out from behind a pillar and moved purposefully to the casket. Clad in a black windbreaker and dark jeans, no one had noticed him lingering in the shadows. Pulling a key from his pocket, he quietly undid the latch and lifted the lid from the coffin. He began his usual ritual of removing the ornate pillows and lining from around the body. It wasn't ghoulish, he always told himself. It was like recycling. Why bury something that could be used again for the next stiff? His boss at the funeral home always paid him well for this job, since no one else had the guts to do it. With practiced efficiency, he packed the contents of the casket into the cardboard box he had brought along.

As he tugged the last bolster out, the Senator's head rolled back and Billy saw a flash of gold reflected in the dim light. "What have we here?" he muttered softly. As if preparing the lifeless body for CPR, Billy arched the neck back and peered into the Senator's mouth. A shiny gold tooth stared back at him, the last tooth on the upper right. "This is too easy!" Billy crowed, discovering the tooth was in a removable denture. "It's in a friggin' plate! You won't be needing it anymore! Let the Halloran Funeral Chapel have the stinking pillows. This gold is *mine!*"

Billy pulled the rubbery lip back and hooked his thumb under the edge of the plastic flange of the denture. He expected it to pop easily, but it held fast. Damned adhesive! Grabbing the nose of the corpse with his left hand for more leverage, he tugged again at the denture. With a crunch, the Senator's jaw snapped shut, holding Billy's little finger in a vise. Swearing now, Billy fought to pry open the mouth with his left hand, but the more he struggled, the more the corpse bit down, wreaking its vengeance for this desecration. With a crunch, Billy screamed as the bone in his pinky fractured, but no one was around to hear his agony.

Panic set in, and Billy flailed around, beating the corpse with his left hand, but nothing would release the death grip. He forced himself to calm down and used his free hand to pry open the jaws. The pain in his fingers subsided slightly, and he withdrew the denture, the gold molar beaming in the half-light. He let out a shout of triumph, but it was short lived. An icy cold hand closed around his throat, and Billy's cries became a strangled sob. Unable to break free, the pounding of the blood in his temples became a roar and then blissful silence as everything faded to black, and Billy gave in to the void.

Chapter 2

With a spring in his step that belied his advanced age, Willi bounded up the brick walkway from the street and entered his home. The neat, trim building on the outskirts of Nordlingen was nothing to rate the slightest of attention, looking for all the world like so many others in this little German hamlet. That was just the way he liked it! Never being one for ostentatious displays, it suited him just fine that few would know that this small house was the home of one of the richest men in Germany. That's what made the day's events so maddening. He had hurried home to get away from all the fuss.

Walking into his study, he crossed quickly to the buffet, removed the stopper from the crystal decanter, and poured himself a generous portion of cognac. Rolling the amber liquid around the glass, he sighed and tossed the plaque he carried onto the leather sofa. Much to his chagrin, the village had felt compelled to have a day in his honor. Now that he was the "oldest living veteran of World War II", the mayor had convened a ceremony in the town square to wave the flag and present their "favorite son" with an award. So much fuss for an old man!

Willi Schultz looked every bit the Prussian gentleman. Stout, but erect of bearing, he cut a proud figure, exuding the boundless energy that had made him such a success in life. Before the war, he had been a simple toymaker. His factory was taken over by the Reich for munitions manufacture, and he was pressed into the Wehrmacht. Serving in the German army was difficult for one who was not a member of the Nazi party. There had been no promotions, and he served out the war as a simple prison guard, never leaving Germany.

After the war, he returned to his love, making the finest toys in the world. His bears were known everywhere, but he remained the faceless leader of the toy empire. Never one to seek the limelight, his company had always seemed to make the right decisions. People called him lucky, but he had always maintained that if you do what you love, it would be a success. His sons now ran the company, but he still remained the force behind the business, even if he had been largely forgotten. That was how he liked it! Until that cursed reporter had discovered that he was the oldest veteran. She had forced him out of the shadows.

His sons had never understood his reticence to talk about his past; he was a war hero, after all. This publicity would be great for the company, they reasoned. How could he pass up the chance to be on TV? You couldn't pay for this kind of exposure! Against his better judgment, he had agreed to the interview. It had seemed to go well. She asked fair questions, and he was as gregarious as always. His charm came through on the report, and his sons were thrilled when it became an international Internet success, picked up around the world by news outlets interested in a happy story. The ceremony today was only the latest public recognition of his history, but he had grown weary of all the attention.

Willi relished his peace and quiet. He loosened his tie and slumped into the leather armchair that was his favorite refuge. Another sip of the cognac, and the day's events were finally beginning to fade. Gladly, this should be the last of this foolishness. He closed his eyes and relaxed, breathing a deep sigh of relief.

He never noticed the two shadows that detached themselves from the heavy curtains flanking the windows and strode toward him. The figures crouched low, one reaching around the back of the chair to his throat. Willi awoke to a sharp pain in his neck and a gloved hand closing over his mouth. With surprising speed for a big man, Willi rose and flung his attacker across the room. Taken aback, his other assailant dove at his chest and forced him back into the chair. It toppled over backwards with the weight of the attack. Willi rolled over and jumped to his feet, throwing the man off, but his legs refused to work properly. Swaying more with each passing second, he became unstable and collapsed, lying on his back unable to move.

Using the sofa for support, a tall man dressed in black slacks and track jacket stood up and walked over to the prostrate toy-maker. A balaclava hid all but the eyes of his face. He dusted himself off and straightened the crease in his pants. Holding a syringe up for Willi to see, he bent down and waved it in the face of his now frozen victim.

"Willi Schultz, I have been looking for you for such a long time!" His voice dripped with malice. "The drug is Vecuronium.

4

It's such a potent paralytic that it works within 60 seconds. Sadly for you, it only took you 30 seconds to throw me across the room. For that, you will be very sorry, I assure you!"

Turning to his accomplice, he ordered, "The bag, quickly! … And tidy things up!"

The second man went to the window and opened it. Reaching to the ground outside, he grabbed a black leather medical bag and handed it over. He then proceeded to set the armchair upright and arrange the papers on the coffee table so nothing appeared out of the ordinary.

The leader opened the bag and removed another syringe. He uncapped the needle and expressed a few drops of the clear liquid, letting them fall menacingly on Willi's cheek. He bent down and whispered into Willi's ear, "Adrenalin." Willi's eyes widened as his assailant aimed the hypodermic at his chest.

The man pulled down the balaclava and smiled, his white teeth flashing like a wolf. "No, not straight into your heart. That would leave a mark that could look suspicious," he commented flatly. "This will be much better." He opened the German's mouth and pulled out his tongue. He jabbed the needle deep into the base of Willi's tongue and drove the plunger of the syringe home.

Calmly recapping the hypodermic, the man settled back on his haunches and chatted casually with his immobilized victim. "Few people realize that the tongue is a muscle that is filled with blood vessels. In an emergency, if you need to give a drug quickly, injecting a dose into the base of the tongue will work every bit as fast as an IV."

Willi tried to cry out, the adrenalin surging through his veins, but it was a futile effort. He could already feel his heart starting to race. With the paralytic drug still in effect, Willi was powerless to move as the tightness began in his chest and radiated down his left arm. *So, this is what a heart attack feels like,* he thought. *This is the end.* Willi began to sweat profusely, and the edges of his vision began to blur.

As Willi said his final prayers, his assailant reached into the leather bag again and drew out a pair of dental forceps. Forcing open Willi's mouth, he fixed the pliers around a gold molar on the lower left jaw and began to twist back and forth. As the crunching sound of breaking bone rang in his ears, Willi gave in to the crushing pain in his chest. His eyes rolled back in his head and he drifted away.

Chapter 3

NATIONAL GEOGRAPHIC NEWS
NATIONALGEOGRAPHIC.COM/NEWS

Egyptian Dentists' Tombs Found by Thieves
Stefan Lovgren for National Geographic News

Thank thieves for an archaeological discovery with some real bite. The recent arrest of several tomb raiders led an Egyptian archaeological team to graves of three royal dentists who had been buried in the desert for 4,200 years. Zahi Hawass, chief of Egypt's Supreme council of Antiquities, told reporters touring the site yesterday, that the thieves had launched their own dig in Saqqara, the ancient, pyramid-rich royal cemetery just south of Cairo.

"It seems for the first time that the ancient Egyptians made a cemetery to the dentists, and they are buried in the shadow of the Step Pyramid," said Hawass. Built for Pharaoh Djoser and named for its staircase-like construction, the circa 2630 B.C. Step Pyramid is believed to be Egypt's oldest pyramid.

Respected Profession

The dentists' tombs date back to ancient Egypt's 5th dynasty, which lasted for 153 years and ended in 2345 B.C. Archaeologists say the tombs were meant to honor a chief dentist and two others who treated ancient Egypt's pharaohs and their families. The engraving of an eye over a tusk is the symbol for dentists, and this hieroglyph appears frequently among the symbols decorating the tombs. One tomb also includes a curse proclaiming that a crocodile and a snake will eat anyone who violates the grave.

The ancient Egyptians "cared about the treatment of their teeth," Hawass told reporters, according to the Associated Press.

Cathleen Keller is an Egyptologist at the University of

California, Berkeley. "Saqqara is probably the single most important private cemetery of the 5th dynasty," she said. The fact that the tombs were built there reflects the prominent status with which dentists were held in ancient Egypt. "These are people who on a fairly regular basis would actually touch the person of the king," Keller said.

False Door

The tombs, built of mud brick and limestone, did not contain the dentists' mummies — leaving at least one mystery to be solved. Hieroglyphs on the tombs give the names of the chief dentist as Iy Mry and the others as Kem Msw and Sekhem Ka.

Hawass said the dentists were not related but must have been partners or colleagues, given that they were to be buried together. Wall figures also depict the chief dentist and his family playing games and presenting offerings to the dead.

It's fairly common for ancient Egyptian tombs to be decorated with colorful scenes depicting their inhabitants in their daily lives. "I wouldn't expect there to be any depictions [of the tomb owner] working in the royal mouth," Keller said. "We'd love to see him applying those ancient drills," she said. "But what he's interested in is showing how he conforms to accepted standards of elite representation."

Around the corner from the chief dentist's tomb's entrance, archaeologists found a false door, which tomb builders may have constructed as a gateway to the land of the living for the deceased.

Hawass has said he believes that only 30 percent of what lies beneath Egyptian sands has been discovered. Likewise, archaeologists say they expect to find more tombs in the area.

"There are vast expanses of areas [at Saqqara] that have simply not been scientifically investigated," Keller said. "The fact that local looters found the tombs is an index to how much more there must be out there." She added, "Just about every expedition I know of that has gone out to Saqqara to look for tombs has found something."

Chapter 4

THRUMMM. The low pitch of the sound was just irritating enough to intrude on his dream, but not long enough to cause any response. He stirred slightly, rolled over, moaned a bit, and just kept sleeping. Two minutes later, THRUMMMM. There it was again. Pushing up on his forearms, he looked over at the dresser across the room from his bed. Still lit up was the face of the offending object. The screen on his iPhone winked out, returning his room to complete darkness, but there was no denying he had received a text. Climbing out of bed, he padded over, pushing the auburn hair out of his eyes. *I'm awake now, let's see who is texting me at... 4:30 in the morning??*

He tapped the screen on the iPhone, and the message glowed up at him.

Carli Chamoun
Thinking of you!!
Call me ;)

Carli? Haven't heard from you in more than a year! He pushed aside a pair of jeans thrown over the back of the leather armchair next to the dresser and settled himself onto the chair. His apartment in Georgetown was small. Big enough for his bachelor lifestyle, but not much more than the temporary home that it had been for him over the last year. He clicked on the desk lamp and tapped his phone again. Pulling up his contacts, he scrolled down to Carli's name and touched the screen.

Instantly, her face smiled up at him. Her shoulder-length auburn hair was pulled back into a ponytail, as usual. Her smile was full of mischief, as though she knew something you didn't. And the eyes, those green eyes, a little too large for her face were somehow just right for her. He expected the photo to wink, wrinkle her nose and laugh. That was the Carli he knew!

But after more than a year, why a text in the middle of the night?? He would rather text her back, but she hated texting. She always preferred to talk! That's what made her different... special.

There was no one else he would wake up for and call back at this time of night, he decided. With a sigh, he tapped the screen. Settling back into the soft leather, he waited for the phone to ring, his smile broadening as he closed his eyes.

"Michael Patrick Murphy!" came the perky voice he knew so well. "How are you?"

"Sleepy!" he rasped, a bit too harshly, catching himself and changing tone, "How are you? I thought my favorite Egyptologist was supposed to be in Cairo?"

"I am silly! That's why I waited to call!"

"So you waited until it's 4:30 in the morning?"

"Oops! Sorry! I always mess that up. It's 11:30 am here and already really hot. I can call you later if you want…" Disappointment sounded heavy in her voice.

"No. No. It's OK. I'm up now, and I'm really glad to hear from you." He tried to recover quickly. "What did I do to make you think of me?"

"Oh, Murph, you didn't do anything." Now it was his turn to frown a bit. "I was out at the dig and we found the tomb of the pharaoh's dentists. Of course, I wanted to call and tell the best dentist I know."

"I'm the only dentist you know!" he deadpanned, hoping secretly that was still true. "I remember reading something about that on the Internet. I didn't know that was your project."

"Yes!" she said excitedly. "Saqqara has been our dig for the year, but only recently we were allowed to see the tombs of Iy Mry and Sekhem Ka. The main tombs had been raided by thieves, but just two days ago, I found an undisturbed side chamber. It's *amazing*!" Her passion for archaeology was palpable, even across thousands of miles.

That passion for long-dead mummies is why she's there, and I'm here, he thought with a wry smile. Stretching out his legs, he made himself more comfortable. *This could take a while!* "What did you find?"

"There's a series of hieroglyphics on the wall that tells a story so fantastic, I can't wait to figure it all out. I'm working on translating it, and I think this discovery will finish my degree. There's enough new here for my whole thesis!"

"That's great! I know how much your Ph.D. means to you."

""It's going to be huge! I can't wait to show someone, and I really want it to be you. Why don't you come to Cairo? Can you get away for a week? There's something about all this that is a bit weird and I need to talk to someone on the outside."

That's a bold idea, but Carli always was one for jumping quickly. Murph was rather between things all of a sudden, but he still would have to get permission to leave. "I'll have to check if I can get away..." At least, he knew his passport was current. This would take some planning, but it could be done.

"Super! I really miss you!" There was a voice calling her in the background that he couldn't make out. "Hey – I gotta go! I'll call you later! Please say you'll come!"

"OK, Carli. I'll try." It sounded weak, but she bought it.

"You're the best! Gotta run!" And she was gone.

That's Carli, he thought with a laugh — 5'1" and a ball of energy... always running somewhere. That's even how we met.

Chapter 5

Murph and his volleyball teammates had been leaving the RPAC, Recreation & Physical Activity Center, at The Ohio State University. Walking out the door after practice, he ran into Carli... literally. She always claimed he ran into her, but she was the one jogging. He just got in the way. While his buddies tried to stop laughing, Murph went over to help her up. He touched her arm, looked into her stunning green eyes and froze.

"Are you going to pick me up, or are you just going to stand there like a statue?" she teased.

"I'm so sorry! Are you OK?" he stammered while helping her to her feet.

Brushing off her slightly skinned knee, she quipped, "It's nothing that a beer won't cure. Why don't you buy me one?" She stretched out her leg and bent her knee a couple of times to make sure it was working well. "For now, why don't you run with me? I've got a couple of cold ones at my apartment, and you can buy the ones after that."

She started to jog, looking over her shoulder, grinning, "Well? You coming?"

The laughter of his friends stopped immediately. As they stood there with their mouths hanging open, he settled his backpack on both shoulders and trotted off after her.

They were a striking couple. At 6'2", he towered more than a foot over Carli. Of Egyptian ancestry, though she had been raised in suburban Cincinnati, her olive skin, chestnut hair, and expressive eyes always turned heads. With such an Irish name, people expected Murph to be red haired and freckled. Nothing could be further from the truth. Though his Dad was Irish-American, Murph favored his Mom and had inherited her Sicilian complexion. The Irish white came out in the winter, but add some sun, and he bronzed deeply.

His auburn hair was thick and wavy, but he kept it trimmed off his ears and collar. When it got too long, he would play with it, twisting it with his fingers while concentrating. Where she was open and outgoing, he was more reserved and quiet. His teammates had teased him, but they were all jealous that they hadn't run after her first.

Carli was training to run the Columbus Marathon, and she talked Murph into running with her. He had been an all-state volleyball player in high school at Saint Ignatius in Cleveland, running cross-country in the fall for conditioning. He was never a natural runner, but he could hold his own as far as stamina was concerned. Speed, however, was another thing. Carli slowed down so he could keep up with her when they ran together. She could see that his knees were killing him after years of junior Olympic volleyball, but he was too proud to let it show. She was secretly flattered and quietly tried to let him be the tough guy.

For over a year, it had been nearly perfect. He was in dental school, and she was beginning her Ph.D. program in Egyptology. Both were so busy that they cherished their time together, which seemed to be meals, working out, an occasional movie, and studying, lots of studying. Their friends assumed that they would always be together, but Murph was coming to the end of his time in dental school at Ohio State and looking at residency programs.

They had just begun talking about a future together when Carli had been invited to participate in the Saqqara expedition.

That meant two years in Cairo. It was the opportunity of a lifetime. She had earned the chance through her hard work, being one of the few experts on the Third Dynasty in the U.S. Her prior study of the Pharaoh Djoser made her a natural choice for this dig, as Djoser had built the great Step Pyramid at Saqqara.

Murph and Carli decided to put any future plans on hold and go their separate ways while she was in Cairo. It was a case of right person, wrong time, and they both knew it. They agreed to make the most of the end of the spring quarter together and let things go after that.

As Murph approached graduation, he had completed his clinical requirements early, so he was invited to take an Advanced Esthetic Dentistry course at The Pankey Institute in Key Biscayne, Florida. Only 20 dental students had been offered the opportunity to fill the class. Murph wondered if his father being on the visiting faculty had something to do with his good fortune, but whatever the reason, the course was too good to pass up. Lasting five days, the course allowed him to sharpen his skills and learn from some of the best in the country.

Carli had flown down at the end of the week, so they could enjoy a long weekend together before she left for the Middle East. Murph had booked a three-day cruise to the Bahamas, on which they relaxed and soaked up the sun, as well as a few pina coladas, while saying a long good bye.

Tanned and tired, they relaxed as Delta flight 1860, from Miami to Atlanta, rolled down the runway and into the afternoon sky. Not 20 minutes later, there was a commotion in the back of the plane. A flight attendant, visibly shaking, made an urgent announcement, "Is there a doctor on the plane?"

Murph raised an eyebrow at Carli. "I thought that only happened in the movies!" She shrugged her shoulders. Murph reached up and pushed his flight attendant call button. The BING had barely finished when the flight attendant ran up and knelt beside him in the aisle. Murph informed the agitated young woman that he was a fourth year dental student, and he offered to help in any way he could. She squeezed his hand and quickly accepted his assistance. He unbuckled and she hurried him to the back of the plane.

A young man sat in the window seat of the second last row,

his head leaning on the Plexiglas window. He was unconscious and drooling out of the corner of his mouth. His seatmates had clearly bailed out of the row and were packed in the aisle in front of the lavatory. As if he had the plague, no one wanted to approach him. Even the couple in the seat in front of him was leaning forward, pressed into the tray tables in the row before them. Suddenly, the victim began to writhe and convulse, classic signs of a seizure. While not particularly dangerous, a full-blown seizure is a scary sight for those not familiar with it.

Taking charge, Murph worked to protect the young man, laying him gently down on the floor. His head extended out into the aisle, but Murph supported his head and cradled his torso to minimize the violence of the tremors and the bumping of the plane. Murph's arms got banged around a bit against the unmoving legs of the seats, but he kept his patient free from additional injury. It may have been only a minute, but it seemed forever, and his patient eventually relaxed.

Without warning and to the horror of the flight attendants and passengers nearby on the full flight, the guy began to struggle to breathe, turning a sickly shade of blue. Realizing he was choking, Murph opened his mouth and pulled his tongue out of the way, opening his airway. As regular breathing resumed, Murph positioned him so he could breathe. The patient's condition had improved, but Murph was bent over, balancing on the seats, like something from Circe du Soleil. *This isn't the most pleasant way to fly to Atlanta!*

The lead flight attendant was on the phone with the cockpit. Looking at Murph, she relayed that the pilot would do whatever Murph wanted. They could return to Miami, divert to Orlando, or push on to Atlanta. It was his call. Feeling that the situation was stabilizing, Murph recommended that they continue to Atlanta, but declare a medical emergency to land quickly and have paramedics meet the flight at the gate.

His patient gradually regained consciousness and remained groggy for the rest of the flight. Murph had to straddle a seat to hold his head to keep his airway protected. The pilot never climbed to the planned cruising altitude, keeping the plane at their current level. It was the fastest route, but this altitude was the one filled with every bump between south Florida and northern Georgia. It was a flight that no one onboard would soon forget. Those in the front of the plane had no idea what was going on in the back, and they seemed to be alternately praying and cursing for the next hour, as they were tossed around the sky.

Landing safely in Atlanta, the passengers cheered, but were startled to see two EMT's with their gear board immediately and move to the back of the 737. Murph transferred responsibility for his patient to the local EMS and gave his report on what had happened and how he had treated it. They gave the victim a quick assessment, and everyone relaxed, as the emergency seemed to have passed. The EMT's and the Delta flight crew got Murph's business card and information. They all had paperwork to do, as this would require a full incident report. The guy had come around and was now able to talk a bit, though he still sounded drugged. He told them his name was Eric Reardon and that he had been in Nassau with friends, probably partying a bit too much. The EMT's grinned and assured Murph that the guy would be OK, once he sobered up a bit more.

Murph looked up and realized that the passengers up front had all left the plane, except for one. There she stood, leaning against a row of seats, arms folded, shaking her head and smiling. He walked up to her and she punched him lightly in the arm. "Show off!"

Murph looked hurt, but all he could do was laugh. "Did you have a pleasant flight?" She punched him again, harder this time.

They came out of the jet way to a smattering of applause in the gate area. The pilots shook his hand, and the flight attendants ran up to give him a big hug. They walked through the airport and boarded their next flight without further incident.

It was only when they landed in Columbus and were met by TV cameras in the airport concourse that they realized something was up. "Didn't you know?" a reporter asked, "You saved the life of the Governor's only son, Eric!"

Murph described what had happened as simply as possible. As much as he tried to say that he hadn't done anything more than anyone else with first aid training could have done, Murph was an instant celebrity. It was a story that was too good not to run with… good looking guy saves life of politician's only son… while on an airplane… and he's a dentist!

Murph was called to the statehouse to meet Governor Reardon and personally accept his thanks. The public ceremony was covered extensively, and the Ohio State University media people were quick to capitalize on a Buckeye hero. NBC's *The Today Show* brought him to New York and interviewed him as part of a segment on emergency treatment for seizures. Delta Airlines publicly thanked him and sent a fruit basket with a note of thanks from the entire flight crew. Then came the really strange call.

"Hello, Dr. Murphy. My name is Dr. Manesh Farouk." The speech was clipped, almost European in formality, deeply voiced, and silky smooth. "I have read of your experiences and I feel you would be an ideal addition to our project. A man of your talents would be welcome here. I want you to come to Washington, D.C. I have twelve candidates, but I am looking for thirteen. You will be the last one to join me… You see, I am looking for an Apprentice!"

Chapter 6

It was Murph's first thought that this was some sort of practical joke, but there was something in Dr. Farouk's tone that seemed deadly serious. In search of more details, he was directed to contact the office of the producer. As he suspected, this was to be another reality TV show, in the style of Donald Trump's successful show *The Apprentice*. The financial offer was attractive, and Murph arranged to delay the start of his residency program by one year. My penchant for adventure will get me in trouble some day, he thought. But the next thing he knew, he was moving to Washington, D.C. and having his publicity photos posted on the Internet and a profile created and printed in *People Magazine.*

Manny Farouk was a wildly successful esthetic dentist, with a clientele of the rich and famous from around the world. The contestant's first meeting was held in the Washington Center for Esthetic and Restorative Excellence. The Center was a limestone edifice just a block off the National Mall. The upper floor was an open clinic with 15 dental chairs on three walls around the perimeter. On the remaining wall, two rows of stadium seats looked down on a single dental unit, for the demonstration of techniques. It had an elaborate video system that permitted recording, making it an ideal setting for teaching purposes, taping technique videos and webinars.

The aspiring apprentices were shown to the gallery and instructed to be seated. Thirteen of the dental chairs around the room each had an 11 x 14 photo, a head shot of one of the contestants, placed on the back of the chair, illuminated by the overhead light of the dental unit. All other lights in the clinic were out, except for the ceiling mounted spotlights on the theater unit in front of the young dentists. They were all apprehensive anyway, but sitting in the relative darkness added to their general unease. No-one spoke, and the silence weighed heavily on them all.

With a soft click, the heavy fire door to the clinic opened, admitting the man of the hour. Walking briskly into the light, Dr. Manesh Farouk moved beside the dental chair and bowed slightly to the assembled crowd, extending his arms slightly from his side, palms upward. The spotlights reflected off the highly polished leather on his black Italian loafers, as the rest of his attire of athletically tailored black suit jacket and trousers with a black silk shirt seemed to absorb any light. His olive complexion confirmed his middle-eastern heritage, together with his dark hair, tightly styled back off his angular face. His smile was warm and inviting, with the large white teeth expected of a man who made his career in esthetics. His dark eyes were cold and hard, however, transfixing each contestant and seeming to bore into their innermost thoughts.

He opened his hands again. "Welcome, my friends!" Clasping his hands behind him, in the small of his back, he announced, "It is time we discussed the nature of the challenges you will face. At the end of each task, we will return here to the clinic and face *the examination*." The contestants would come to call these sessions "The Drilling."

"After the examination, the one of you found wanting will be asked to leave the group. To be *extracted*, if you will." A soft chuckle made this seem all the more ominous. "Then your dental light will be extinguished, and you will leave the house."

"You will find this much different than your dental school experiences. Not only will you have to perform clinically as a master dentist, but your every move and comment will be recorded by cameras, and be subject to examination. Unlike other programs, there will be no silly text or Internet voting. I will be the sole judge and jury, and will personally determine your fate. There will be no discussion. My word is absolute!"

"It is time for you to be off. Your first task awaits you. Return here tomorrow morning, packed for travel. Dress warmly. My sources tell me that it is still cold this time of year... in Alaska!" With that, he spun on his heel and left quickly through the door from which he had come, leaving the crowd murmuring. Murph was wondering what he had agreed to, but he had to admit that he was excited! All of his life, he had thrived on competition. He had never imagined competitive dentistry, but here it was. Time would tell how it would turn out, but he was determined to give it everything he had.

Chapter 7

The thirteen had been whisked away in the pre-dawn mist, traveling in a series of black Chevy Suburbans that would have made the Secret Service proud. The convoy entered the grounds of Reagan National Airport. But, rather than approaching the passenger terminal, it veered off to a private hangar on the edge of the tarmac. The SUV's entered the hangar and stopped in front of a pair of Gulfstream G550s. The long range, high speed jets were the pinnacle of executive transportation. The contestants marveled at the opulent display and thought privately, not for the last time, that this esthetic dentistry gig of Dr. Farouk's must be pretty good! Boarding the aircraft, the candidates settled in for the long flight to Anchorage.

Murph found his colleagues pleasant, but a rather shallow, self-centered bunch. They were the pretty people of the dental profession. There was entirely too much drama for his liking, but that was the nature of reality TV. Over the course of the show, he found it much more interesting to talk to the staff. He became friends with the camera crew, the pilots, the production assistants, and in general, everyone other than the dentists. He was to find out later that it was that appearance of being just a regular guy that endeared him to the TV audience, making him a fan favorite to win.

After seven hours in the air, they landed tired and cranky, but in the land of the midnight sun in June, the day was still very young. They had barely deplaned, when Jeff Stanley, Dr. Farouk's right hand man, called them together to explain the task. With a wave of his arm, he indicated the thirteen floatplanes and the bush pilots standing before them. "There are 13 Inuit villages that haven't received dental care in a long time. You are their lifeline to better health. Everything that you need will be waiting for you. What you do is up to you. We'll see you back here in a week. Good luck!"

There was a brief commotion as one of the contestants objected to flying in the small Cessna. Murph suspected that guy was about to be the first one *extracted*, so he shouldered his travel bag and walked over to the nearest plane and extended his hand to the pilot. "Mike Murphy. Glad to meet you!"

Accepting the firm handshake with a wide grin, the pilot tipped his worn baseball cap, revealing ginger hair tinged with grey. "Call me Red," said Lyman 'Red' Briggs as he ducked under the wing and opened the door to the Cessna 185. "Where do you want to go, Doc?"

Murph tossed his backpack and duffel bag in the back seat and didn't have to think before replying. "I'm always one for an adventure. Let's go all the way... as far from here as we can go! I want to see as much country as I can while I'm here. Don't know when I'll ever get back!"

"Capital idea!" Red walked Murph over to Jeff Stanley and the group of production assistants. "He'll take Nunapitchuk."

Stanley nodded. "Roger that!" Reaching into his briefcase, he pulled out a file folder and handed it to Murph. "First one to choose. I like that!" He shook Murph's hand. "Get to it!"

They went back to the blue and white floatplane and climbed in. Red motioned Murph into the right seat. "Might as well co-pilot. Can't see nearly as well in the back!"

Murph grinned, pulled an Ohio State ball cap out of his bag and set it firmly on his head. Red laughed and handed Murph a set of headphones. The propeller began to turn, then the engine barked to life and they were ready to fly. The other candidates were still milling about as Red's Cessna rolled out and lifted off the runway. With a wag of its wings, Murph's floatplane roared over the G-550s, turned and headed northwest.

Chapter 8

"Nunapitchuk is a Yup'ik Eskimo village located on the Johnson River in western Alaska," Red narrated casually as he flew. "It's on the Kuskokwim River Delta... THERE!"

Taking in the scene, Murph was struck by the beauty of the landscape. Blue water, green tundra, and white buildings scattered about, seemingly at random. It was inviting, but the harsh nature of the remote village was apparent even in the summer.

"There are four villages within sight of Nunapitchuk. The area is known as Akulmiut. Pronounce it *a-gool-me-yoot*, and they will love you from the start!"

"Thanks for the tip! I'll need all the help I can get."

"Ahh, Doc! You'll be fine. I can tell!"

As Red circled the village a few times, people began flowing out of the buildings, and a crowd predictably moved to the wooden jetty extending into the river. Satisfied that he had an appropriate audience, Red banked over the silver ribbon of water and settled in to a smooth landing. He taxied up to the dock, cut the engine, and drifted in perfectly. Two local men tied off the pontoon and Red jumped onto the dock with a flourish. Murph gathered his bag and climbed out after him. Red clearly knew this village well. He was their link to the world, and they greeted him warmly.

Red was telling them about his passenger as Murph walked up. Red clapped him on the shoulders and introduced him to the tribal elders. "I've brought you the best dentist in the States, my friend Dr. Murphy!" The recommendation came across in such glowing terms that Murph was inwardly worried that he now had a lot to live up to, but he was glad for the vote of confidence.

Murph shook hands with the elders. "Mike Murphy. Thanks so much for inviting me to Nunapitchuk. I'm glad to be with you in the "*a-gool-me-yoot.*"

They all laughed, and Murph joined in the fun. It was clumsy, but the Eskimos clearly appreciated the effort. Like all the Inuit villagers, the leader was short and stocky, with light brown skin and straight black hair. His wide face was dominated by dark eyes set over high cheekbones. The corners of his eyes were lined with playful wrinkle as he smiled and reached out to Murph. He clapped Murph on both arms and welcomed him like a long-lost brother. "I am Agloolik. Welcome to our village. We are honored that you are here." The others with him nodded vigorously in agreement. "This calls for a celebration!"

That evening, the whole village turned out for a feast in Murph's honor. As tired as he was, Murph knew how to work a crowd and make friends quickly. All the villagers wanted to meet the dentist, since most of them had never seen one before. He let his Irish charm come out, and it was late into the night when Murph fell exhausted onto the cot that would be his home for the next week.

The old wind-up alarm clock Murph had been given rattled across the floor next to him, its arm chattering back and forth between the bells on top of the face. He reached down quickly to swat it off, fearing he would wake the whole village. Murph held the clock and considered the battered face, the shorter hand pointing more-or less toward the six, since it had long ago been bent by some former owner angered by its loud ringing. Murph sat up and scratched his head, considering his situation.

He turned the key on the back of the alarm clock to wind it, reflecting on what he had learned from the villagers the night before. Nunapitchik had a population of 466. The village was without electricity, and 93% of the homes lacked running water and complete plumbing. There were no roads, and buildings were connected by a network of boardwalks. The Inuit men were fishermen, working at the difficult and often dangerous task of catching salmon and herring roe.

His arrival had been cause for celebration, Agloolik had told him, because the people were in dire need of help. Forty-two percent of the population was under the age of 18 and had never seen a dentist. Murph was cut off from civilization with no phone or electricity. His clinic had one portable dental chair and battery operated lights. The best he could offer was extractions and sealants, but he would have to make the best of it. He dressed quickly and stepped out of his hut into the morning mist.

Murph walked out and made his way around the boardwalk to where he could see the building set aside for his office. He stopped dead in his tracks at the sight.

20

Red came up quietly behind him and placed his hand on the back of Murph's neck, shaking him slightly. "Pretty amazing, ain't it!"

Murph let out a low whistle, and they both studied the line of people that extended from the door of the clinic down the boardwalk and around the General Store.

"Red, I'm not sure what I can do for them?"

"It's OK, Doc. You're here. That's all they want. Just do the best you can!" Red left Murph with a handshake of encouragement, "I'll be back in a week to get you."

Murph thanked the pilot and got right down to work. With only one dental chair and literally hundreds of patients, he had to work quickly to assess the situation. The most immediate concerns were with the children where decay was rampant. He had learned some hand magic in high school, which he put to good use now. Nothing fancy, but making a coin appear behind a kid's ear or a quick card trick put them at ease. A good laugh relaxed everyone and let him do the needed dentistry.

Placing sealants to protect teeth from decay was pretty easy, but many of the people had teeth that were so badly decayed that taking out the teeth was the only option. Murph did some of the most difficult extractions of his career, but after a couple of twelve-hour days, he felt he was making progress. The smiles on the faces of kids who were out of pain for the first time in years warmed his heart in spite of the cold.

He quickly realized that while fixing problems was important, preventing future cavities was better. He spent some intentional time communicating the value of caring for their teeth. Once people began to be free of pain, they were ready to listen to his suggestions on how to stay that way.

Agloolik returned late in the week with several other men from the village and "kidnapped" Murph. Laughing all the way, they took him to their skiff on the river and showed him how to catch Alaskan salmon like a native. They returned late in the night with coolers full of fish and empty of beer, They had accepted Murph as one of them. He knew how to work hard and enjoy the simple pleasures of the harsh land.

The week flew by, and when Red returned, Murph was exhausted but felt fulfilled like he had seldom been before. His pack was filled with drawings and carvings from the children and he would always have the memories of their smiling faces. The women of the village presented him with a leather necklace of polar bear teeth, which he proudly wore around his neck.

It was with a heavy heart that he hugged Agloolik and waved farewell to his new friends as the Cessna lifted off from the river and began the long trip back. Murph's backpack was stuffed, and he had a cooler filled with enough salmon to cook for weeks. Life was good!

Red made a low pass over the field as they arrived, and the crowd milling around the G-550's let Murph know that most of the others were back already. Red, showing off as usual, made a picture perfect landing and taxied over to the crowd.

Murph jumped out of the floatplane and shouldered his backpack. The week-old growth of beard gave him a comfortable woodsman look, and several of the dentists scoffed at the bear-tooth necklace around his neck. Murph smiled at them and pushed through the group, walking over to Jeff Stanley, *The Dental Apprentice* coordinator.

Murph handed Jeff his packet of records from the week. "Nunapitchuk was great. I wish I could have stayed longer!"

Stanley laughed, "Well you certainly look native enough! First one out, and last one back in. That's the way we like to see it done!" Stanley shook Murph's hand warmly. "Just grab your gear and get on the plane. We're leaving right away."

Murph turned to find Red and found the old bush pilot walking over carrying a giant Styrofoam cooler. Murph took the cooler from Red and set it down next to the Gulfstream jet.

Red gave Murph a giant bear hug, slapping him heartily on the back. "Doc, I'm gonna' miss you! …. And I know the folks up there will too. You really made a difference."

"Thanks, Red! That's the best complement I could ever get. I learned a lot and had a great time. I'll miss you, too."

A clipped voice interrupted Murph from behind. "Dr. Murphy. What is in that cooler?"

He turned to face the stern eyes of Dr. Farouk, who stood in the doorway of the jet.

Murph stood tall and smiled. "The cooler is full of salmon, which my Inuit friends taught me how to catch. It shouldn't smell too much on the plane."

"No, Dr. Murphy. Your competitors may turn up their noses now, but it is not the smell of salmon. That cooler is filled with *immunity*! Your hard work brought health to the village and their appreciation is obvious for all to see. You have earned immunity in this challenge. *Immunity* has a sweet smell indeed!" He turned and entered the plane. "Please join me as we return to Washington."

Red clapped him on the back, and Murph climbed the stairs into the Gulfstream as his smile stretched from ear to ear.

Chapter 9

The next weeks passed in a blur. Visits to the clinic for *The Drilling* came and went, and the number of contestants continued to dwindle. They were sent to perform extractions at the Free Clinic in Cleveland. They flew to Miami to each perform an esthetic smile makeover for a victim of domestic violence. They did more pediatric dentistry in Appalachia and geriatric dentistry in New York City. Murph continued to survive. He proved himself to be an excellent dentist but an even better people-person. His ability to interact with "the little guy" made him special.

Making the final four, he arrived at the "Center for Dental Stress, as they now called it, to see where they would go this time. Manny appeared, as always, out of the shadows into the spotlight, to congratulate his finalists. "There are only two tasks remaining," he warned them. "Two of you will be extracted this week."

That had their attention. "Being part of the Washington Center for Esthetic and Restorative Excellence involves public speaking on our behalf. This week, you will be required to teach oral health care to one of the most difficult audiences in the world... elementary school children! You will each present to a class here in Washington. I have in this bowl four slips of paper. Please choose your school now."

Manny took a crystal punchbowl from beside him and passed it to the group. Murph was offered the bowl last, and when he unfolded his note, the broad strokes of calligraphy revealed *Sidwell Friends*. Not only would Murph have Manny and the TV cameras watching, but also he would potentially have the children of the President and many members of Congress!

With only two days to plan, Murph considered his options. He had been assigned the Lower School of Sidwell Friends. This meant his audience would be kindergarten to fourth grade children and their parents. He expected them to be a bright group, and if all he did were talk about brushing and flossing, he would bore them. They would tune him out immediately and never hear his message.

He had done these programs before while in dental school at Ohio State and had found that it worked best to tell stories and then weave in his important points. Planning his PowerPoint presentation, he carefully scripted each detail. He even planned music to energize them prior to his beginning. Murph chose khaki linen slacks and an open collared chambray shirt under his blue jacket to project a casual, but professional image. He was surprised to see that Manny Farouk himself was in attendance as Murph set up and tested equipment.

The students filed in and were seated around him. The closest row sat on the floor, and several rows of chairs followed behind them. Parents stood along the walls in the back. It was a large group of about 350, but it felt like a more intimate gathering. Over the buzz of 5- to 10-year-old kids, Murph's rich voice rang out clearly.

"How old is the profession of dentistry? How long have people had teeth? Since the *beginning* of time, but the first recorded dentist was the Egyptian Hesi-Ri, with his tomb dated to approximately *3000 B.C.* He was the dentist to Pharaoh, and Pharaoh was the most powerful person in the world, except Pharaoh had *really* bad teeth!"

Murph had them. This was not what they expected at all. He showed them the hieroglyphics where the symbol of the eye over the tusk represented dentistry. He told them the Egyptians were the first to use toothpaste, made of wine vinegar and powdered stone. The Romans made toothpaste of honey and crushed eggshells. The wealthiest Romans even had slaves to brush their master's teeth for them. "Now *that* was a job you didn't want!"

"Noo!" they all said.

Murph told them about Hippocrates, the Greek physician, who wrote about how baby teeth came out, and the sequence in which teeth developed. He described using forceps to extract teeth and how the ancient Greeks filled cavities. He even talked about the ancient Greeks using wire to hold teeth together, just like braces.

Murph told them the Romans whitened their teeth by rinsing with urine. (Eewwww!) But the first scientific pamphlet on how to whiten teeth was written in the 16th century in France by... *Nostradamus*!

He told them that Paul Revere, the patriot, was a dentist, as well as a pewter smith. He also was the first recorded forensic dentist, kind of a CSI. He identified a decomposing dead body by recognizing the denture he had made for the man.

He told them George Washington's dentures were not made of wood, like many people think. The individual teeth were carved out of the finest ivory from a hippopotamus tusk and then held together with a gold base and golden wire. Each arch of teeth were hinged in the back with springs to push one arch up onto the roof of his mouth and the other down onto his lower jaw. "If he relaxed his muscles, then his mouth would spring open. That's why, in portrait paintings, he always has his mouth closed with a sour expression on his face. He was trying to keep his mouth shut!"

George Washington had two sets of teeth. One is in the National Museum of Dentistry in Baltimore. The other was loaned to the Smithsonian here in Washington for the bicentennial in 1976, but it was stolen and has never been found.

Murph emphasized the value of having a full set of teeth. "And you know what? The Egyptians felt that having a full set of teeth was so important that they conducted a whole ceremony when a body was made into a mummy. They called it the 'Opening the Mouth Ritual.' If you were missing any teeth when you died, they would use gold wire to secure teeth from other people or animals in the open space. If you were really wealthy, like the Pharaoh, they would make gold teeth to replace your missing ones, so that when you woke up in the afterlife, you had a full set of teeth to eat with."

Then, he transitioned from the Egyptians to cavity prevention. "Now we're smarter than the Egyptians, so we know how to prevent cavities so we don't lose any teeth." Murph went on to talk about why bacteria cause cavities and how to prevent problems by brushing, flossing, eating the right foods, and seeing a dentist. He even worked in a discussion on sealants and why it was important to wear a mouthguard when playing sports.

As he finished, the kids and adults applauded. Every hand shot up when he asked if there were questions, and it felt like the event was a great success. Murph received the highest praise he had ever received from Manny Farouk, as the tall Arab inclined his head, made a slight nod of his chin, and walked out of the back of the room. Murph left with a satisfied grin, feeling confident that he would make it another week. And indeed he did.

Chapter 10

The final challenge pitted Murph against Claire Summerville. A tall blonde from Southern California, she had made it through all the prior tasks, not by being exceptional, but by just not doing anything wrong. As a contestant, she was completely unremarkable, which Murph realized as he was trying to remember anything she had said or done. They had been together for over four months of taping, and he couldn't say he knew anything about her. She was pretty, but they had nothing in common. It was a struggle to have a conversation. She didn't like sports, so she wouldn't sit and watch a game. It had been winter, and all she seemed to want to do was work out.

Claire was the house yoga expert, and finding her inner peace was a solitary process for her. So the dental house had become increasingly quiet as the numbers dwindled. Murph had all along refused to become caught up in any of the drama that is inherent in these reality shows, with people scheming and back-stabbing all day. But that conflict is what gets people to tune in each week, so the producers worked to encourage it. With only two left, there was no stress now, primarily because Murph didn't want to be bothered with it.

To receive their final instructions, Claire and Murph returned to the clinic on the third floor of the Center. The yellow dental lights brilliantly illuminated the two remaining photos on the dental chairs. The other 11 were dark, creating a gloomy feeling of loss, made worse by the lack of any other lighting in the perimeter of the room. They took seats in the front row of the theater chairs and waited. In spite of himself, Murph was nervous. Throughout the whole experience, he had done his best not to allow the stress of the others to get to him. He was confident in his ability and always tried not to take himself so seriously.

To come to the last task, however, was a different thing. He really didn't want to come this far and not win, so he felt the tension rise. He realized he was turning the Claddah ring on his right ring finger, a nervous habit that he always tried to stop. Unclasping his hands and stretching his arms over his head, cracking his knuckles, he stole a glance at Claire. She was fidgeting with her ponytail, not really making any attempt to hide her discomfort. Murph smiled and offered, "I guess it will all be over soon. I wonder where we are going this time?"

Claire swallowed hard and tried to smile. Failing miserably, she grimaced and just shrugged her shoulders. They both looked up as there was the ominous click of the door across the clinic and Manny Farouk burst into the room.

"Indeed, it all will be over soon." As if he had heard their every word, which in fact he had. Manny smiled like a serpent as he entered the spotlight that bathed the center of the clinic amphitheater. He bowed at the waist while keeping his head up and eyes on the two. Opening his arms, he nodded. "I congratulate you on reaching the final task." He was in his customary dark slacks and black silk t-shirt, but today he wore a starched white lab coat. The stark color contrast of white on black, and the length of the coat served to make Manny appear taller and more angular than usual.

"Dr. Murphy!" His tone softened, but he fixed Murph in that icy stare. "Your work has been exemplary. You have earned the trust of your patients and co-workers. Every member of my staff would enter into your employ if you just asked. It has been a pleasure to follow your progress. It will please me to offer you the opportunity to join me if you successfully complete this final task."

Shocked by this sudden praise, all Murph could do was nod, turn red, and mumble a reflexive "Thank you" but Manny had already moved on.

"Dr. Summerville! You also have performed well. Your work is excellent, and you do not make mistakes. You, however, do not take any risks. It remains to be seen if the safe path is the correct choice in this endeavor. It will also please me to offer you the opportunity to join me if you successfully complete the final task. Only one of you will become my Apprentice. Please listen very carefully to my instructions. They are most explicit, and I will not repeat myself."

"In his presentation to the grade school children, Dr. Murphy spoke eloquently about the advanced nature of the ancient Egyptian culture. Your task involves the ancient art of the lost-wax technique of casting. You will be introduced to a patient, upon whom you are to prepare, wax, cast, and cement a gold crown. Everything you require will be available to you in the laboratory in the basement of this building. You will have five hours to complete this task."

Manny snapped his fingers and waved toward Murph and Claire. Out of the shadow, a dental assistant walked over and handed each of them a sealed container, roughly the size and shape of a pill bottle. It was surprisingly heavy, so Murph shook his, and as he had suspected, there was the clinking of a solid lump of metal rolling around the vial. Murph smiled in spite of himself.

"You are correct." Manny nodded approvingly. "The vial contains the gold that you are to use for the crown. Please retain any unused gold, and return it in the vial provided. The gold has been marked so there is no way that anyone other than you can perform this task. I must be away during this trial, but rest assured that I will be following your every move. There will be an examination upon my return, and an accounting will be made. One of you will become my apprentice. The time here will be ended for the other one. Return tomorrow at 8:00 a.m. sharp, ready to work. Good luck to both of you!"

He turned on his heel, and with the tails of his lab coat flying, he disappeared into the dark, leaving Claire and Murph to ponder his instructions.

Chapter 11

Murph stood up and stretched to his full height, arms over his head, cracking his knuckles. Shaking the vial again, he pocketed the gold. "Well, that was fun!" he said to no one in particular. He reached out his hand to Claire and touched her shoulder lightly. "We should get going. I don't know about you, but it's been a while since I cast gold, and I need to review how!"

Claire awoke from a stunned trance and blinked several times. "Thanks. I haven't done that since freshman year. It wasn't a big deal in school. The faculty at USC assumed we all would have lab technicians doing our crowns." She was definitely distressed.

Murph grinned, trying to break the tension, "Well, there's this thing called the Internet, and I hear that there's a YouTube video for anything these days. Let's go find out!"

The task was to perform dentistry as it had been done throughout history.

1. Prepare a tooth to receive a crown.
2. Take an impression of the prepared tooth.
3. Make a dental stone model of the prepared tooth.
4. Use wax to design the crown to cover the tooth and return it to normal form and function.
5. Make a cast of the wax pattern in dental stone.
6. Heat the stone to melt away the wax and leave behind a cavity in which to pour the molten gold.
7. Heat the gold to molten form and pour it into the stone mold, called an "investment."
8. Open the mold after it has cooled to reveal the gold crown in the exact shape of the wax crown.
9. Polish the gold crown.
10. Fit the crown in the mouth, and cement it onto the tooth when perfected.

Together, they studied and watched the process being performed on the Net until they felt proficient again. Murph realized that helping Claire was not going to help himself, but he still felt it was the right thing to do. He slept contentedly and arose early on the day of the challenge. After a quick run to clear the cobwebs, he showered and dressed for the task. Khaki slacks and a green polo shirt would look good under his clinic jacket, he thought. When they arrived at the center, they found the normally dark clinic all brightly lit and bustling with activity. Each of them had a dental assistant, and where their photo had been the day before, their dental chair had a patient eagerly waiting.

Murph went over and introduced himself to the stout woman with steel-grey hair in his chair. Though she was 74 years old, Mary Kay Steinmiller gave off the robust energy of a woman who could get things done. Her handshake was firm, and her eyes bright as she appraised the tall young man who would be her dentist. She gripped his hand tightly and pulled him a bit closer.

"I know what is at stake for you today," she whispered in his ear. "I'll do everything I can to help you!"

Murph squeezed her hand back and patted her arm. "We'll do this together, and I promise I'll take good care of you. It will all work out perfectly!" He sat back on his dental stool and smiled at his dental assistant. "With support like this, how can anything go wrong?"

Murph proceeded to examine the tooth in question, a broken lower right first molar. He numbed up the area and proceeded to prepare the tooth. The fracture and old filling were quite deep, but he built up the tooth and got a perfect impression. Excusing himself from Ms. Steinmiller, he hustled to the elevator, closed the door and hit the L button. *Could this elevator go any slower?* he thought as he paced irritably around the metal box. Time was of the essence here. Then the elevator settled to a stop, and the doors opened.

Murph was struck by the massive space of the lab, containing all manner of dental lab equipment, as well as a number of things he had never seen before. But he had no time to look around and feed his curiosity. A lab bench had been set up with his name on it, and all the materials that he would need to pour the model, mount the case, and wax up the crown were waiting for him. He set right to work, whistling as he waxed, just like in dental school. The blue wax flowed easily in his hands and carved into the exact representation he envisioned for her tooth. He placed the wax pattern on a sprue and mixed the liquid dental stone to pour around the wax crown. After the stone had set, he burned out the wax in the oven.

This is now the moment of truth, he thought. Cast the gold perfectly, and the end is near. Screw up, and it is back to square one!

Murph took the vial of gold from his pocket and placed the ingot in the reservoir of the casting machine. Lighting the torch, he began to heat the gold. Gradually, the surface began to glisten, looking wet and shiny and then almost suddenly, the solid lump of gold came to life, pulling together into a round droplet of molten gold… shimmering... radiating warmth. This was what had captivated men for centuries! Not waiting for the gold to oxidize or become contaminated, Murph poured the gold into the mold, saying a silent prayer that it would run smoothly and not develop any voids. When the mold was filled to the top, Murph lifted the red-hot mold with tongs and placed it into the cold-water bath. There was a hissing protest of steam as the hot metal met cold water.

He broke open the mold, half afraid to look, and found a perfect crown, although the gold looked dark and lifeless. Polishing the crown now, he cleaned off the oxidized layer. The gold was malleable, and he found it easy to shape the crown to perfection. As he worked the gold, it came to life again, gleaming with a deep, burnished hue that projected permanence and value.

Proudly taking the crown back up to the clinic, Murph and his assistant, Cheryl, marveled at the excellent fit. Everything was working perfectly except that the numbness was wearing off, and Mary Kay was becoming sensitive. Try as she might to hide the fact, every time the tooth was touched, she would wince and cringe. She was trying to be brave, and told Murph to just cement the crown. Manny's instructions were to cement the crown with zinc phosphate cement. It was an old-style cement, but one that worked well, having stood the test of time.

Unfortunately, Murph knew that, for all her trying to be helpful, Mary Kay would probably need a root canal because the decay and fracture had been so deep that the nerve was compromised. If he cemented the crown with zinc phosphate as ordered, the tooth would be more sensitive, and it would be impossible to remove the crown to do the root canal. The endodontist would have to drill a hole in the new crown, which would ruin it. With a sigh, he asked Cheryl to get him a eugenol-based cement.

Her eyes widened as she realized what he was going to do. "But the instructions are very specific. Use zinc phosphate cement," she warned.

Murph shook his head. "Ms. Steinmiller, your tooth will

probably need a root canal, and I don't want to cement the crown with a permanent cement if we need to take it off to do that. The cement I'm going to use smells like oil of cloves. It will make the tooth feel better now and make the crown easy to remove if you need a root canal."

Mary Kay nodded. "Thank you for thinking of me. I'm going to Miami for a couple of months of warmer weather. I hope this will last, and we can take care of it when I get back."

Murph stressed that he couldn't be sure it would last that long, but he had dentist friends in south Florida to help her if the tooth became uncomfortable. They exchanged cell numbers, just in case. Having made his decision, he attached the gold crown with temporary cement.

As soon as it was on the tooth, Mary Kay felt relief, and her smile returned. "That feels so much better!" She gripped his arm and then gave him a hug. "You will go far, young man!"

He thanked her for being such a supportive patient and let her go. Cheryl gave him a hug, as well, and said how nice it was to work with him. She told him good luck, but they both knew his decision to use a different cement would be an issue at the examination. Dr. Farouk was ruthless. Murph's defense would be that he had done what was in the best interest of the patient, and that's how he had practiced from the beginning. He wasn't going to change now.

The call came from the producer that Manny had been held up in Germany for another day after his lecture, so the examination was delayed. Murph was left to go back to the condo, twisting in the wind and wondering how it would work out. Trying to get his mind off the day, Murph cooked dinner, penne pasta in a vodka cream sauce, just like his mom used to make. Everything always seemed clearer while drinking Chianti and sautéing shallots and garlic.

Claire wandered in looking dazed and sat down, drawn into the kitchen by the aroma. Murph poured her a large glass of chardonnay and kept cooking. Like a good bartender, he knew that quiet presence has great value. She would talk when she was ready. As the wine began to work, she explained her day. She had completed her crown and cemented it, but she hadn't been pleased with how it looked. She never liked working in gold anyway, preferring porcelain for crowns. And she had always hated lab work!

The final exam couldn't come soon enough for both of them, so they sat in the dental house enjoying dinner. Half a bottle of wine later, Claire confessed that she had really sent in an audition tape to be a contestant on *The Bachelor*. She had not made the cut for the reality dating show, but the producers had offered her *The Dental Apprentice* instead. Murph smiled at the irony in that, since she was close to winning the dental apprentice, yet teeth were only a job for her, not her passion. As she neared the end of the bottle, she drifted off to sleep on the couch. Murph covered her with an afghan and turned down the lights.

He cleaned up the dishes and went to bed. Morning came without any contact from the producers or Manny, so Murph went out for a run around Washington to pass the time. He was relieved to be summoned to the Center as soon as he returned. After a quick shower, he was ready to go. Claire was nowhere to be found, so Murph went alone to face the examination.

Murph was surprised, when instead of going to the third-floor clinic, he was led down the long, carpeted hallway to Manny's private office. The thick hardwood door was guarded by a stern-looking receptionist, glaring at Murph over her half glasses, set low on her nose. He had tried to engage Margaret during his time at the Center, but Murph had never managed to get so much as a smile from her. Her expressions seemed as tightly controlled as the ponytail holding her dark hair neatly against her temples.

He sat uncomfortably squirming in a padded chair, feeling like a high school freshman about to meet the principal. Murph forced a grin and mouthed "Cameras?" jerking a thumb at the imposing hardwood door to the inner office. Margaret's features softened ever so slightly and she nodded "Yes." The phone on the desk buzzed, and she answered it immediately. Replacing the handset in its cradle, she silently said "Good Luck," inclined her head at the door, and indicated for Murph to let himself in.

He waved as confidently as he could and said, "Thanks! It's been nice knowing you!" Murph walked to the door and grasped the handle. There was a buzz, and the lock clicked. He straightened his back and twisted his neck until he heard the satisfying crack. Taking a deep breath, he turned the handle and pushed open the heavy door.

Chapter 12

No one would ever accuse Dr. Manesh Farouk of being afraid to show the fruits of his labors. Murph stood dumbfounded in the doorway of the inner sanctum of his benefactor as the oak door snapped shut behind him with an ominous clack. The teak floor upon which he stood now gave way to a series of ornate Persian rugs leading across the room to the foot of a massive desk. It seemed to be made of black stone, possible obsidian, supported by four obelisks. Each limestone leg was a miniature monument in itself, seeming to sprout from the carpet, the sheer weight of stone crushing the fabric into the floor.

Manny sat behind the desk, resting his elbows on the dark surface, his fingertips touching, forming a pyramid. His immaculately tailored brown herringbone jacket and black silk t-shirt shone in the TV lights that transfixed him, casting a pair of shadows on the wall behind him. There was no mirth in the hard black eyes, though he seemed to be playfully tapping his index fingers together. He opened his hands, waving two fingers of his right hand to indicate that Murph should approach.

A spotlight in the ceiling was angled to create a pool of light just in front of the desk. Murph took the hint and walked forward to stand centered in the limelight. The camera crew made formless shadows in the corners of the room, as they moved the boom mike in over Murph's head and focused the cameras. He was sure that they were angling for the close-up to get his reaction to what he now knew was coming. His throat suddenly dry as the desert, Murph forced a swallow, settled his legs comfortably at the width of his hips, balancing on the balls of his feet, and readied himself. He clasped his hands behind his back and stood tall. *It's OK,* he told himself. *I'm proud of what I have done. I wouldn't do anything differently. Let's get this over with!* Murph took a deep breath and forced himself to smile!

Manny's grim countenance wavered, and he smiled back, almost in spite of himself. "You were always my favorite," he began with a sad shake of his head. "I had great hopes for you, and you did not disappoint me. Always questioning and learning from each task. Applying each lesson to the next problem. Earning the loyalty of your co-workers and staff. You will achieve great things... but not as my apprentice!"

Murph's head sagged a bit, in spite of all he had done to prepare himself for those words. "Thank you for the opportuni-," he started to say, but Manny cut him off with a wave of his hand.

"I told you all at the beginning that my word was absolute and that my orders were to be fulfilled to the letter. Perhaps you did not understand when I told you to complete the crown and cement it?" Murph shook his head slightly, and Manny continued, "No, I think not!"

Manny rose from his chair and began to pace around the room detailing the virtues of obedience and attention to detail. Murph's attention began to wander and he examined the contents of the shelves behind Manny's desk. There was a clear ancient Egyptian motif to the room, with gold head masks from sarcophagi and from segments of stonewalls with colorful hieroglyphics. There also were historic dental instruments and an exhibit of partial dentures throughout the ages, made with pewter and even a few shining like gold in the spotlights.

Manny slammed his open palm onto the desktop and shouted, "Do you understand me?" His face was now inches from Murph's. He grabbed a dental chart from a pile on his desk, "It is not safe for your patient to be walking around with that crown cemented temporarily... It is unsafe for her!!" Slamming the chart down with a slap, he returned to his position behind the desk.

Murph couldn't understand the crisis here, but Manny clearly was obsessed with precision in following his orders. *I guess I should be glad I'm not his Apprentice!* Trying to present a solution, Murph offered, "I'll just call her and have her back to cement the crown. I have Ms. Steinmiller's phone num..."

"Silence," Manny hissed. "No names on camera!" Calling to the producer over his shoulder, "You will edit that out!" he turned back to Murph. "You're responsibilities here are over. As stipulated in your contract, you will remain in a condo provided until this episode airs on television. You will have minimal contact with people outside of the production, so it will not become apparent who has been dismissed. Your confidentiality will be absolute! I will care for your patient. You are not to attempt to contact her in any way."

His anger faded. Seemingly drained, Manny continued in a softer tone; "It has been a pleasure working with you. I wish you the best of success in your future. You will always have my support." Manny walked around the desk and shook Murph's hand warmly. "It is time for you to go into hiding for a while. I will contact you when it is acceptable for you to be seen again." With that, Manny grasped Murph by the shoulder and ushered him from the room, the oak door closing behind him with a heavy *thud* of finality.

Chapter 13

Murph realized he had been daydreaming. With more than two months of boredom since his dismissal, it had become something of a hobby. It was only 5:00 a.m., but Carli's phone call had him awake and alert. *Guess I might as well get up.* He eased himself out of the armchair and walked toward the bathroom, scratching his tousled hair, trying less than successfully to smooth out the bed-head. *I need to go for a run.* That always helped him think clearly.

His circuit measured just over five miles, and it was a brisk morning for a jog. The sliver of a moon was settling low in the sky as he crossed Pennsylvania Avenue off the National Mall and ran into John Marshall Place Park. Approaching C Street, he was contemplating his time on *The Dental Apprentice*, as the Washington Center for Esthetic and Restorative Excellence appeared on his left. His reverie was interrupted by the squeal of tires, and he narrowly escaped becoming a hood ornament on the Aston Martin convertible turning into the parking lot. Murph planted his palms onto the hood and vaulted over the fender, landing lightly on his feet. "Who the hell do you think you are? James Bond?" he growled.

"Ahh. Dr. Murphy," came the silky voice he knew in an instant. "You are out early this morning. Restless perhaps?"

"Dr. Farouk," Murph struggled to regain his composure at being surprised in the pre-dawn twilight. "I wanted to talk to you later today, but I was just out for a run. I'll get a shower and come down to see you when it's a better time for you."

"Nonsense. No time like the present!" Manny parked the car in his reserved spot and took his time putting up the top, giving Murph a chance to catch his breath. "Let's go up to my office and have a drink!"

Manny collected his leather briefcase from the back seat and they walked to the rear entrance of the building. Tapping the screen to awaken the security system, Manny entered the code (*Dee-Dee-Dee-Daah*) and the latch released with a click and the door opened with a muffled hiss of air pressure releasing. *Odd pass code — Beethoven's Fifth,* Murph thought. *Not much security there!* Murph hustled to keep up with Manny as he climbed the narrow stairs, pausing to open the door at the top. They entered Manny's office from the corner behind the desk. It was a door that Murph had not noticed the last time he was there.

Manny switched on the lights and the room burst into color, as the halogen lights illuminating the perimeter of the room bounced off all the gold and bronze artifacts which adorned the shelves in the perimeter. Manny walked to a wet bar across the carpets and opened the mini refrigerator. He selected two water bottles and tossed one to Murph. "How can I be of service to you?"

Still sweating in a t-shirt and shorts, Murph felt unprepared in comparison to the always-immaculate dentist before him. Manny was the picture of sophistication as he settled onto the leather sofa and took a sip from his water. Murph really didn't know where to begin, but he detailed the phone call from Carli and the reason for her stay in Cairo.

Manny seemed genuinely interested in the tale. "I was raised in Cairo, and I have a great fondness for Egyptian culture, as you can see!" Manny indicated the amazing array of artifacts with the wave of his hand. "You're time of confinement here is nearly over. I see no reason why you cannot leave and spend the remainder of your exile in the land of the Pharaohs."

Murph stood gaping in surprise. "Thank you for letting me off. I'll go back to the condo and start working on flights and a hotel." *That was way easier than I thought!*

"No need for that. You just go and pack. I'll arrange for the Gulfstream to take you. I'm not going anywhere for a few days, and the pilots are getting lazy just sitting around. I'll have my driver meet you when you arrive in Cairo. I have just the hotel in mind. It is truly a five-star experience and will certainly impress your young lady," he added a sly wink. "You prepare and I will have Margaret make all the arrangements."

"Carli will be thrilled. I don't know how to thank you! You're being too kind."

"Nonsense. All I ask is that you tell me what you learn from her research. I find all of these discussions of Pharaohs and ancient tombs fascinating."

Chapter 14

Life as an Apprentice had prepared Murph to pack quickly and travel light. The cab picked him up and negotiated the late afternoon traffic across the Potomac River and out of D.C. It was early evening when he pulled in to the parking lot behind the corporate hangar at Reagan National Airport. A light rain was starting to fall as he took his grey roller travel bag out of the back seat and tossed his backpack over one shoulder. He trotted over to the rear door and entered the hangar. The familiar scents of jet fuel and oil greeted him as he walked out from the back entrance toward the light of the open hangar door. The Gulfstream sat facing the runway, poised to fly into the gathering dusk. Derek Whitman, the lead pilot, looked up from his paperwork and waved. "Well, aren't you the *favored* Apprentice!" he taunted. "A G-550 all for your own private joy ride!"

"All you and Salas ever do is sit on your ass and make the big bucks, so you might as well work once in a while."

Ed Salas, the co-pilot, had come round the nose of the jet just in time to hear the exchange. He stopped long enough to flip Murph the bird and continued his pre-flight walk around.

"You don't care about us. I'm hurt," Derek whined. "Just for that, Tami won't be going on this trip!" Tamio Suzuki was the cheerful flight attendant who always made *The Dental Apprentice* excursions so pleasant.

The staccato click of high heels on the cement floor of the

hangar cut short their banter. "Ms. Suzuki wasn't ever going on this flight anyway. Just finish your trip documents so you can get out of here!" Margaret, Dr. Farouk's administrative assistant, had come out of the hangar's private office. She looked like she was on her way out for the evening. Gone were the glasses and tight ponytail. With her hair down and contacts in, she was stunning in a tight black dress and white cardigan. Derek caught Murph's eye and mouthed "Wow!"

Margaret walked over to Murph and smiled. "I always knew you were the most talented apprentice, but it wasn't to be. Dr. Farouk also thinks very highly of you, as evidenced by all this." She encompassed Derek and the Gulfstream with the wave of her arm. "I have your travel documents here."

She placed a manila packing envelope on the table in front of Murph and opened it. She spread out the documents. "Here is your entry visa, difficult to get in less than a day, but Dr. Farouk has connections that go very high in the Embassy. I assume you have your passport with you?"

Murph nodded and patted the pocket of his jacket.

"Good." Clipped and efficient, as always, Margaret continued, "Upon landing, you will be met by Saleh al Rahman. He is a long-time employee of the Farouk family and will act as your driver and interpreter while you are in Cairo. You will find him to be a useful friend. Reservations have been made for you in a suite at the Marriott Cairo Hotel & Omar Khayyam Casino. It is in the heart of the city and walking distance from many sites. However, Cairo can be a dangerous city for foreigners. Use your head, and stay with Saleh. Do as he recommends, and you will enjoy your trip without incident."

Reaching deeper into the envelope, she withdrew a satellite phone. "When you go out to the pyramids, phone service is irregular. This phone will allow you to contact Saleh. His phone number is programmed in for you, as well as the numbers for your friends Derek and Ed here. Since you have used your idle time over the last month playing golf and relaxing by the pool, your current tan will help you in the desert sun, but you will not blend in well with the locals. Be careful!"

"And I thought this was going to be a vacation!" Murph joked. *This is beginning to sound like a CIA briefing.*

"Listen to me!" Margaret's smile vanished. "Cairo is not to be underestimated. Since the 'Arab Spring', Egypt, like the whole Middle East, is an unstable place. In this part of the world, intrigue is a national sport. Do not become entangled in any local issues! Enjoy your visit. See Ms. Chamoun, and get out. I have included travel documents for her as well, in case she would like to leave with you."

"Toto, I don't think we're in Kansas anymore!" Murph's falsetto Judy Garland impression seemed to break the tension.

Margaret's eyes softened, "I don't want to worry you, but I need for you to be aware of the situation. Dr. Farouk has provided everything to make this a smooth trip for you. I think it is a better reward than Claire will get for winning. While you are enjoying Cairo," she winked, "just remember, click your heels together three times, say 'there's no place like home," and we'll get you out. I hope you remembered to pack your ruby slippers!"

Margaret packed up the envelope again and gave it to Murph. With a warm hug, she bade him farewell. "Gotta run. Opera tonight!"

Murph and Derek watched her every move as she walked out the back door and climbed into her Jaguar. The XJ sedan roared to life and swept out of the parking lot, breaking the spell on Derek and Murph.

Derek shook his head. "Next time you see her, ask her how she can drive in those heels!"

"Hey!" Ed called from the hatch of the Gulfstream, "Whenever you two are done debating who's going to ask her out… let's go… while we're still young!"

Murph gathered up his things, and they boarded the jet. He tossed his backpack onto a couch and took out his laptop. He plugged in his Mac and opened it to allow it to connect to the satellite communications system of the Gulfstream.

Derek looked back at the lone occupant in the cabin. "Make yourself at home! You know the drill by now, but there's still no Tami to take care of you." Of *The Dental Apprentice* cast members, Murph had been the only one to engage the flight crew. He had always been interested in flying, but had never had enough time to get a pilot's license.

While traveling, Murph had bought Derek, Ed, and Tami a

beer after hours on several occasions. He always seemed to be able to find a nice Irish pub, no matter where they were, and they had become good friends. Murph was closest to Derek, as they both shared the same love of old movies and traded cinema quotes like bad inside jokes.

Even though night was falling, Derek put on his aviator sunglasses for effect, flashed his best Tom Cruise smile and drawled, "I feel the need... the need for speed!"

"OK, Maverick," Murph laughed, "It's time to go do some of that pilot shit."

Murph went back to the bar in the galley, selected a crystal tumbler and poured a generous three fingers of Jameson. Adding a bit of ice to the Irish whiskey, he swirled it around and savored a sip. *This is going to be a long flight. Might as well enjoy it!* He brought the bottle with him to his seat.

Setting the drink in the well on his desk, Murph walked forward as the engines began to whine. "Hey! Can I fix you guys a drink? Oh, that's right, you're flying!"

"PISS OFF!" came the duet from the flight deck, and they slammed the door shut in his face.

With a satisfied smirk, Murph went back and settled in. As the Gulfstream began to roll, a tinny voice came over the intercom, "Welcome to Air Apprentice. Please fasten your seatbelt. We intend to make this as bumpy as possible... So sit back and relax for our 11-hour, 39-minute flight to Cairo."

Murph looked at his watch. It was 8:05 p.m. *Twelve hours flight time, plus a six hour time difference, means an arrival around 2:00 p.m. Cairo time.* He had been trying to call Carli all day to let her know he was coming, but she had not answered her phone. It was rather unusual for her, but Margaret had said that cell service was sketchy near the pyramids. He had to leave a voice mail again, but this time he added the ETA of early afternoon.

While they were still taxiing to the runway, his phone chimed with a text.

So glad u are coming I need u
Really weird here
Text when you land DO NOT CALL
love u

Murph sat rubbing his chin, savoring the Jameson as the pitch of the engines rose to a scream and the Gulfstream raced down the runway and into the gathering clouds. *That's odd... but I'll get the answers soon enough.*

Murph clicked the Mac to life and began his research. He had twelve hours to learn enough about the Pharaohs to impress Carli. It was going to be a tall order.

Chapter 15

The G-550 rose smartly from the runway and banked over the Potomac River. The Washington Monument glowed orange in the light of the setting sun. Ironic, Murph thought, *I'm flying past the largest obelisk in North America in order to go and see the originals. Where to begin? Start with what I know.*

Carli's group was going to excavate the Step Pyramid at Saqqara. A few keystrokes later, his screen filled with the image of a rough-hewn pyramid. *Looks like my weak effort at a sand castle on the beach in Miami.* The Step Pyramid was constructed between 2677 and 2648 B.C., stood 203 feet high, and was clad in polished white limestone. It was built for the burial of Pharaoh Djoser. Considered Egypt's oldest pyramid, it was the most important cemetery of the 5th Dynasty. The complex was designed and constructed by the grand vizier Imhotep, the architect and high priest credited with the innovative nature of the Pharaoh's tomb.

Imhotep! Murph rubbed his chin. *Why do I know that name?* He smiled as he remembered. *I bought Carli those dumb "Mummy" movies as a present. Imhotep was the Mummy!* Murph had given Carli DVD's of *The Mummy* and *The Mummy Returns* on her birthday the first year they were dating. He knew she was into the ancient Egyptians, and it seemed like a great idea at the time. As stupid as it was, she laughed at them anyway, and he knew their relationship was special. If she could appreciate a silly gift like that, then they had a future together. He would have to do better in choosing a present next time.

Thinking he had better bring a gift now, he walked back to the galley and selected a bottle of El Tesoro de Don Felipe tequila.

That Dr. Farouk certainly lives well. A bottle of this aged Blue Agave would make a fine gift indeed! Where Murph preferred the Irish whiskey or a good beer, Carli's taste ran to tequila, and he would make an exception this time. He carefully wrapped the bottle in a bar towel and placed it into his backpack. With a peace offering in place, Murph felt more content. He refreshed his own Jameson and returned to his seat to continue his research.

By the end of Djoser's 19-year reign, the step pyramid had risen to six layers and was the largest building of its time. As in earlier mastaba tombs, the burial chambers were underground, hidden in a maze of tunnels. In spite of the defenses, the tomb was plundered, and Djoser's mummy was moved to the Egyptian Museum of Antiquities in Cairo. The mummy is not on display, but a famous statue of Djoser with his nose broken off was placed in an antechamber near the grand hall. *Poor guy. Sitting there for eternity without your nose.*

The remainder of the Djoser complex was surrounded by a Tura limestone wall more than 30 feet high. Its paneled construction contained pillars imitating bound bundles of reeds. Fourteen doors interrupted the wall, but only one of the doors was functional for the living. The others were false, meant for the use of the Pharaoh in the afterlife. It was believed by the Egyptians that the Pharaoh would continue to perform the duties of a king after death, and so he needed his tomb to function as a palace.

Outside the enclosure wall, the complex was completely surrounded by a 120-foot wide trench. The walls of the trench were originally decorated with niches to make access to the area more difficult. Between the wall and the step pyramid, a massive courtyard was filled with stone pillars, creating a roofed colonnade. Under the courtyard, a tunnel-like corridor connected the blue chambers of the Pharaoh's throne room, the inner palace, with the South Tomb.

A staircase descended over 90 feet to terminate in the pink granite burial chamber, with its walls decorated with finely formed reliefs of the King. It was clear that the most skilled artisans were employed in these inner chambers. Their artistry was not meant for the living, but meant to ensure that the Pharaoh had the necessary regal bearing for his duties in the afterlife.

The architect was a master. Construction took advantage of

moving materials the least distance, since no heavy machinery was available at that time. The stone for the step pyramid was quarried from the external trench, with ramps created to raise the heavy rock to the higher levels as the pyramid grew.

The substructure of the step pyramid was a labyrinth of more than four miles of tunnels, some up to 20 feet square. The tunnels connected the rooms of the funerary apartment, which mimicked the palace and were meant to serve as the living place of the royal KA, or spirit. On the east side of the pyramid, eleven shafts were constructed to connect with the annex that housed the royal harem and the storerooms, in which over 40,000 stone vessels were found.

The tunnel out of the burial chamber ran north to the funerary temple, which was on the side of the pyramid facing north. This was an important element of ancient cosmology, as Pharaoh's afterlife ambition was to become one of the north stars, never setting for all eternity. The funerary temple provided a place in which the daily rituals and offerings to the dead could be performed.

To the east of the temple was the serdab, a small enclosed structure that housed the ka statue. The Pharaoh's ka inhabited the ka statue, in order to benefit from daily ceremonies performed by the priests. The most important of these ceremonies was the opening of the mouth, which the Egyptians believed allowed the Pharaoh to breathe and eat, and to benefit from the burning of incense. The Pharaoh was to witness the ceremonies through two small eye holes cut in the north wall of the serdab.

Off the north wall of the pyramid was another courtyard, flanked by the remains of two groups of chapels, which housed the priests who cared for Pharaoh in the afterlife.

That Pharaoh certainly lived well, even after death.... It's good to be the King! Murph could see Carli crawling around those musty tunnels, fascinated by every broken piece of ancient pottery and drawing on the wall. She would be in her element, smiling from ear to ear. He could see it now, as he remembered her excitement before she left... on the adventure of a lifetime, like Indiana Jones, without the bullwhip and hat. *Maybe if I tried the fedora and leather jacket?* He chuckled to himself, *Nah...*

Murph was still smiling when Derek poked him in the shoulder. "Wake up, sleeping beauty! Cairo is coming up in less than an hour. Make yourself pretty... if you can!"

Chapter 16

The sun was rising fast as the Gulfstream crossed from the azure blue of the Mediterranean onto the parchment yellow of the Egyptian desert. Looking out the window, Murph marveled at the vast expanse of sand and the narrow ribbon of green along the path of the Nile. The lush fertile valley gave way suddenly to the harsh reality of death in the burning sands. It was early afternoon when they touched down, and the heat waves rippled off the tarmac as they proceeded to the private jet terminal of Cairo International Airport.

Murph had time to change and freshen up, but missed *The Dental Apprentice* staff being on the plane to provide breakfast. This trip was strictly self-serve, so he grabbed a handful of granola bars and put them in his bag. He gulped down a glass of orange juice and put two water bottles in his backpack as well. He was sure Manny would have arranged a fine hotel, but he had learned never to take anything for granted.

Entering the hangar, the Gulfstream came to a stop and the engines ceased their whining. Murph readied his passport and entry visa, expecting a lengthy interrogation from the local authorities. Much to his surprise, he looked out the cabin steps to see a black Mercedes sedan, driven by an older Arab in a black business suit and open collared white shirt.

As Murph stepped out, the Arab rose from the driver's seat and moved to greet the startled dentist. Guessing his age would have been impossible, as his face showed the worn features of one who has experienced a great deal, but his eyes sparkled with a youthful vigor and his smile was warm and welcoming. Murph pegged him at about 60, but it could have easily been 10 years either way.

Bowing slightly, he extended his hand and said, "Dr. Murphy, it is a pleasure to meet you. I am Saleh al Rahman, at your service." His grip was firm. His English was excellent, with a hint of a British accent.

Where Murph was tall and lean, with the lithe grace of an athlete, Saleh was powerfully built and a good head shorter than his American guest. He moved easily, but appeared constrained by the suit jacket. Murph smiled, feeling immediately comfortable with Saleh. "Thank you. The pleasure is mine. I expected Egyptian customs and immigration officers, so this is a pleasant surprise."

"You will find that Dr. Farouk has tremendous, shall we say, 'capability' to help you here. He has made smooth your path. The authorities are aware of your arrival, but will pay you no heed during your stay. We simply need to visit the immigration office in the terminal. It is a mere formality. I am tasked with attending to your needs and making sure that you have an excellent stay in Cairo. My family has served the Farouk's for generations. A friend of Dr. Farouk is a friend of mine."

Murph then bowed slightly and said, "I am honored to have you as my friend and exceptionally pleased to have a friend as my guide."

Saleh returned the slight bow and smiled broadly. "It is my pleasure. Allow me to carry your bags." As he collected Murph's bag and backpack, he placed them in the trunk of the Mercedes.

Murph quickly stepped back up on the stairs of the plane and poked his head into the cockpit. "Thanks for the lift, guys. Are you heading right back?"

Derek looked up from his clipboard. "We have a pile of paperwork to file, then we have to spend the day sleeping off this red-eye. We were working while some of you were dreaming! We're supposed to go back late tomorrow or on Monday, depending on where the boss needs us." He rubbed his eyes and sighed. "I suppose you will want us to take you back, too. How long are you staying?"

Murph shrugged his shoulders. "I don't really know. It depends on Carli, I guess."

Derek allowed a sly grin, "With as much as you have been smiling, she must be pretty special. Just call me when you get tired, and we'll come and get you. You can tell us the stories, but no gloating!"

Murph grinned, his face reddening, "Yes, well, a... I'll probably call you in a few days! Let me know if you're going to be in town more than overnight. I'll buy the beer!"

"You're on!"

Murph jumped down and walked over to the car. Saleh

opened the rear door and held it for him.

Shaking his head, Murph said, "I mean no disrespect, but I would prefer to ride up front with you, so we can talk. I can't wait to see your city"

"Then we shall ride as friends! Come, let us see the beauty of the jewel on the Nile!"

Chapter 17

It had been as simple as Saleh had described. A quick stop at the terminal building led to a brief visit with Immigration. The stern faces of the armed customs officers softened noticeably when they read the letter that Saleh had provided them along with Murph's passport and entry visa. While he couldn't read the language, the note clearly spoke volumes and offered a "friend of Dr. Farouk" the express pass into Egypt. Without so much as a cursory exam of his luggage, Murph was handed his paperwork and waved back to the waiting Mercedes.

Saleh had been talking quietly on his cell phone while Murph was finishing with the Customs Officers. He snapped his phone shut and smiled. "Very easy... yes? Just as I said!"

Murph nodded, still amazed at the process. *I could get used to this treatment!* He settled into the taupe leather passenger seat and fastened his seat belt. "Let's go!"

Saleh shifted into gear and charged off into the traffic. His Mom had always accused Murph of being an "aggressive driver" and he was used to going fast, but he was not prepared for the trip into downtown Cairo. Saleh merged onto the highway, and Murph was horrified to see that, while there were lines marking four lanes, there seemed to be six lanes of cars hurtling into the city. Brakes were used at a minimum, with the horn as a substitute. Through the chaos, Saleh chatted away. Murph combated the adrenalin now surging through his body by focusing on Saleh's story and by turning his eyes away from the road.

Murph was surprised to see so many "unfinished" buildings that appeared close to completion but were missing major architectural features such as a roof. He asked Saleh why there were so many like this and why these buildings were inhabited prior to the roof being finished. Saleh informed him that buildings were taxed when the roof was put on, and so many of these structures were intentionally left unfinished to avoid the taxes.

Murph closed his eyes tightly as Saleh weaved through a particularly tight patch of traffic then suddenly lunged for the ramp into the downtown area.

"Almost there! But first, I take you to Tahrir!" The events of the "Arab Spring" of 2011 had captured the attention of the world. Over night, Tahrir Square become a name known around the world and a must-see stop for everyone visiting Cairo. Tahrir Square was really a circle and as packed with traffic and people as the rest of Cairo. On this Saturday afternoon, the area buzzed with activity.

On the northeast side, they passed a plaza with the statue of the nationalist hero Omar Makram, who was revered for his resistance against the invasion of Egypt by Napoleon. Behind it stood the imposing facade of the Omar Makram Mosque. Saleh noted the crowd outside the mosque and told Murph this was the location of the funeral prayers for any prominent Egyptian public figure. They then passed the Arab League headquarters and the ruling party's offices.

Murph tried more casual conversation, "After the Arab Spring, how has life changed for average Egyptians? Do they feel more free now?"

Saleh sighed, "For the people, little has changed. Since the time of the Pharaohs, the powerful live well, and the people endure." He whistled softly, "Lately, there are just new people in power." He turned into Abdel Monem Riyad Square heading toward the 6th of October Bridge to cross the Nile.

They passed the massive Egyptian Museum of Antiquities on their left and Saleh waved at it with his hand. "In there you will find the treasures of centuries. Then as now, the rich and powerful write the history. For us living, everyday remains the same. Power rests in the hands of very few. Only the names have changed." He shrugged his shoulders and said no more. Murph respected his silence and looked out at the dark waters of the Nile as they crossed onto Zamalek Island and covered the last five minutes of the drive.

Saleh broke from his silence as they pulled onto the carefully manicured grounds of the Marriott Cairo Hotel and Omar

Khayyam Casino. "One of the finest in all Cairo!" Once again, Dr. Farouk had provided well for his former apprentice! Saleh seemed well known to the staff and was waved over to park. As they exited the car, Murph's bags were taken by the Bellman, but Saleh escorted Murph to the registration desk.

The clerk waited patiently for them to approach, his Marriott nametag introduced him as Ahmed. A quick comment in Arabic from Saleh and Ahmed's smile broadened. With a slight bow, he accepted Murph's passport. "Welcome to Cairo, Dr. Murphy. We have been expecting you!" His English was excellent. "We have one of our Diplomatic Suites reserved for you. It has a beautiful Nile view. I know you will find it to your liking, but if there is anything you need, please call me. I am at your service." He waved to the Bellman and handed him the room key.

Murph turned to Saleh and shook his hand. "Thank you for your kindness in showing me the city."

Saleh pulled Murph toward him and clapped him on the back with his left arm. Meant as a gentle hug, the power of the blow almost took his breath away. "I am here at your service. Simply call me, and I will be there, anytime you are in need, day or night. My phone number is programmed into the phone you were given. I would like to meet Miss Chamoun and it would be my honor to guide you." He let Murph be led away by the Bellman and headed out of the lobby, opening his cell phone as he went through the doors.

Murph walked to the elevators thinking quietly, hardly aware of the Bellman leading him. *Saleh is exceedingly well informed. I don't remember ever mentioning Carli. That Dr. Farouk thinks of every detail!*

His room was immaculate with tasteful decorations in gold and blue tones, a king bed, a private balcony overlooking the Nile, and a separate living room with a small kitchenette area — five-star accommodations courtesy of Dr. Farouk. Murph tipped the Bellman and surveyed his room. Taking a water bottle from the refrigerator, he drank a long gulp and considered his situation.

Officially, he was soon to be unemployed. When the final show aired this week, his contract with *The Dental Apprentice* would end. He was in Cairo, as the guest of his former boss, and he had been provided first class travel and hotel. He had a driver at his disposal and was about to meet a beautiful woman that he hadn't seen in over a year. For now, life was pretty good. The future would have to take care of itself. Time to relax and enjoy!

Murph quickly sent a text to Carli to let her know he was in Cairo. He tossed his bag on the bed and headed for the bathroom to take a shower. It would feel good to relax and get the grime of the overnight flight off. He had slept in his clothes, and it felt like it. He had barely switched on the bathroom light when his phone buzzed. *That was fast!* The text was urgent.

Thank God u r here. They're after me!
Come to the Egyptian museum and I will find u
I'll be with the mummy like the movie
HURRY

The shower would have to wait. That was a different Carli than Murph had ever heard before. He drained the last of the water and took a quick look at himself in the mirror. He saw dark jeans and loafers with a black polo shirt and a day's growth of stubble, although with his tan it was barely noticeable. *No time to shave.* He grabbed another water bottle and tossed it into his backpack. *Time to find out what this is all about.*

He went down to the desk and inquired of the concierge about the Egyptian Museum. Informed that it was about a 20-minute walk, he set off with a map of Cairo and a rough sense of direction. The streets were busy but it was an easy trip back across the Nile to the edge of Tahrir Square. He was sweating in the heat as he approached the red brown edifice that is the Museum of Egyptian Antiquities. After passing through the security checkpoint, Murph was confronted by the atrium, with the rear of the building off in the distance. Light filtered in through the skylights, but overall the museum was dimly lit. Sarcophagi, glass cases with pottery and golden masks, and enormous statues blocked his view of the nooks and passageways that led off the main hall. This was going to be harder than he thought.

A quick glance at the museum guide he had picked up as he entered told him that there were 136,000 items on display, beginning with the Object of the Month, placed at the base of the steps. Murph looked closer at the stone statue facing him, with its grim face frozen for all time. The nose was broken off, making it look familiar somehow. Murph went down the marble steps and looked at the label. Djoser! Of course! He looked back up and remembered seeing the statue online yesterday. So much for all that last-minute study! At least this was some progress.

The Museum was a maze, so he would have to make a plan. No one else seemed to be interested at all in Djoser. People were brushing into him, as he stood in the entrance next to the imposing figure. He stepped aside and considered the museum guide again. The lower floor progressed through time in a clockwise direction from where he now stood. Since he had no idea where in time he was looking, this seemed to be a slow way to find the mummy and Carli. A tour guide led his charges past Murph, and he caught a bit of his spiel "...and we'll go upstairs to see the treasures of Tutankhamun's tomb. If King Tut is too crowded this morning, we'll stop and see the Hall of Mummies, then the tomb..."

Hall of Mummies! That's the ticket! Murph put away the map and joined the tail of the group, moving with purpose now through the rows of antiquities. Climbing the steps, he had passed through more than 3000 years of history, without paying the least bit of attention. The Tutankhamun exhibit was fairly quiet so the tour group went that way. Murph detached himself from them and headed in the opposite direction.

Upstairs in the museum, there were countless coffins, amulets, ushabtis, and other household items. Some of the Middle Kingdom tomb replicas included models of armies, boats and landowners surveying their livestock. The human figures seemed to almost come alive in the filtered sunlight. Passing through this, Murph entered the Mummy Room and came face to face with some of the great rulers of ancient Egypt.

Even with his sense of urgency, he stopped and stood open-mouthed in the presence of history. Looking around, the room was not crowded, but there were a fair number of people milling about. Small groups of tourists, some ordinary Egyptians, even a number of women in full burqas. Murph began to study the mummies more closely, looking for names of the Pharaohs that might sound familiar.

What was the name of the mummy in the movie? I can see him, but I remember being more interested in looking at Rachel Weitz... Carli frowning at me in mock irritation. He turned around to see a group of the women in black shuffling past. Tall, short, squat, they came in all shapes and sizes. They gathered around him as he looked at the plaque identifying the sarcophagus as Imhotep, the great priest and architect. *Imhotep! That's it!*

Murph looked up and all around. He wanted to ask the women if they had seen Carli, but how to know what they are thinking. Are they even approachable? Might they speak any English? How do you know? *All you can see is their eyes! Black eyes and heavy eyebrows, frowning, disapproving — except the short one — huge eyes — green eyes!*

The most beautiful green eyes I have ever seen! Her eyes opened wider, and he knew she was smiling under the veil. She inclined her head to her right. As the group of women moved on, chatting amongst themselves, Carli went around the back of the mummy into a shadowed alcove filled with pottery from the 5th Dynasty. Murph followed her, and she touched her finger to her lips, urging silence. He stood at the entrance to the passageway, his form blocking the light and deepening the darkness. She quickly shed the black garment, tucking it deeply under the last support for a case filled with a golden death mask.

Carli stepped out of the shadows, and Murph was startled. The green eyes were large and smiling, but she looked small and frightened. Dark circles sat under those eyes, and her hair was greasy, pulled back in a tight ponytail. Her face was stained with dust, and her jeans and t-shirt were worn and wrinkled. All told, she was a mess and the most beautiful thing Murph had ever seen!

He opened his arms, and she collapsed onto him, burying her head into his chest. With a sob, she began to cry quietly. Looking up, her tears streaked the dust on her cheeks, and he wiped it away with his thumbs, cradling her chin in his hands. He kissed her on the forehead and held her tightly.

"I missed you so much!" he whispered.

He could feel strength returning in her. Her muscles tightened, and she straightened up. "I love you too!" and she kissed him lightly. "Not here. We have to get away!" She stepped back and brushed off her clothing as best she could. She took the backpack off his shoulder and opened it. Rummaging around like she knew what to look for, she pulled out a grey baseball cap. Snapping it open and smoothing out where it had crushed slightly in the packing, she looked at the Ohio State scarlet and gray Block O logo on the front. "Some things never change," she said with a wry smile.

"I'm a creature of habit!" He shrugged.

"That's why I love you!" Her smile lit up her face. Suddenly, she didn't look as tired anymore. She put on the ball cap, pulling her ponytail out the back, and took a granola bar out of the bag, tearing it open and biting half of it at once. "Chewy bars, too!" she mumbled with her mouth full. She grabbed a water bottle and gave it to Murph, then zipped the backpack and put it on. She ravenously ate the last of the granola bar in one more bite and then took a giant gulp of the water. She hugged him again and led him by the arm to the entrance of the alcove. Looking both ways, she only popped her head out. The Mummy Room seemed quiet, so she struck out at a brisk pace for the exit, with a stunned Murph in tow.

They passed the dioramas, pushed their way through the gathering crowd waiting to see King Tut's treasures, and worked their way down the stairs. Looking back, Murph squeezed Carli's hand and pulled her to a stop. An Arab man with a full black beard and moustache was talking to the pack of women in burqas. He was easy to spot in the crowd, wearing black slacks and a black windbreaker, in spite of the stifling heat. Another taller man in similar slacks and jacket came over at a run, shouting. He waved a handful of black cloth, just as the leader of the burqa pack, a portly woman with black bushy eyebrows, extended her arm and pointed right at Murph.

"That's not good!" he said quietly. *And I don't even know what's going on!*

"RUN!" Carli sprinted down the rest of the stairs and began moving through the crowd in the main hall, heading for the Djoser statue at the entrance. The larger Murph had a tougher time moving people out of the way and was a good ten steps behind Carli as they approached the information desk near the main steps. Out of the corner of his eye, Murph caught a flash of black moving laterally to cut off Carli at the door. Murph ran over to the museum desk and swept up an armful of the Museum guides, sprinting after Carli.

She pulled up short of the security checkpoint, as she finally noticed the third black clad goon walking purposefully at her. The smug smile on his face broadened with each step closer, and he reached out his hand to grab her arm. Carli pulled back, just as Murph ran up behind her. He acted like he had tripped on the last marble step and threw the armload of brochures into the smiling face, aiming right for the beard. As he leaned back to avoid the blast of flying paper, their assailant missed a marble step and fell backward, crashing into another tour group coming in.

As general commotion ensued, the crowd of offended people pushed and shoved at one another, pinning the bearded goon to the ground. The security guards ran over from their posts and attempted to restore order. Murph grabbed Carli and led her quickly through the vacant checkpoint and out the doors into the bright sunlight of Tahrir Square.

Chapter 18

They knew they didn't have time to let their eyes adjust, so they ran blindly into the crowd. It was a faint hope that their pursuer would lose them while blinded as well. Carli pulled off the ball cap and undid her ponytail, stashing both the cap and her hair elastic in the backpack as she ran. Tahrir Square was full of people, but the crowd was not enough to hide them.

"The Metro!" Carli shouted and waved Murph after her. At a dead run, they crossed the street and went down the stone steps two at a time. Murph was now completely lost, but Carli's Arabic was fluent and she quickly got them onto the platform with her pass. The Tahrir Metro station, named Sadat in honor of the assassinated President of Egypt, was the crossroads of the two lines of the Cairo Metro. If only they could board a train without being seen, they would be almost impossible to follow. They melded into the crowd and tried not to call any attention to themselves.

Looking around, Carli was exasperated. "Try not to be so tall!"

She was right. At well over six feet, Murph's head stood out over the crowd. He tried to bend and slouch down, but it was too late. He saw their black clad friends coming down the stairs, starting to fan out onto the platform. A train was coming, but too late!

"I have an idea!" Carli pulled Murph toward the center of the platform. "The 4th and 5th cars are reserved for women who don't want to ride with men. We're foreign, especially you. Try to look like a dumb American tourist who doesn't know any better. With any luck, the women won't let our Arab friends onto the car and we can get away."

"OK. I'm right behind you!" They pushed into the crowd, which became increasingly female, and raised the ire of rather indignant women covered with head scarves and burqas. Their pursuers followed, as well, and though they tried not to look, both Murph and Carli could feel the noose tightening.

The westbound train pulled into the station and slowed. Its white cars with blue and red bands were so sun faded that the bands looked purple and pink. Murph now took the lead and plowed into the tightly packed mass of women, pushing open a path and pulling Carli after him. Glancing down the track into the tunnel, he thought he saw the glimmer of the headlight of an eastbound tram. The fourth car of the western train had stopped in front of them. Murph saw the doors open on the far side to allow passengers to depart onto the narrow cement walkway between the tracks. He stole a look behind them, and the bearded man was the nearest. There was that smile again, the leer of a wolf closing in on its prey. Murph made eye contact with the man, hardening his expression. *Not if I can do anything about it!*

Murph grabbed Carli by the wrist as the door opened in front of them. He pulled her onto the car, shoving another stout woman in a burqa out of his way. She shouted angrily in Arabic at him, but he shrugged his shoulders, palms upward in the universal sign for "I don't understand a word you're saying." Murph stole another glance down the tunnel to confirm the oncoming train. He turned and grabbed Carli around the waist, lifting her slight frame under his right arm.

Realizing the doors were closing, he lunged for the door and jammed it back open with his left arm. He stumbled a bit, wincing with pain at the shock to his shoulder but successfully made it onto the center platform. Free of the contact with his body, the tram door closed quickly behind him. The three Arabs closing on them were now fully engaged with a carload of women, shouting and waving at them to get out of their car. Murph smiled at the chaos. Carli had been right!

Murph's smile turned to horror, as the bearded man pulled a handgun from his pocket and fired two shots into the roof of the subway car, shouting commands. Screaming, the women dove for the floor, opening a clear path for the three. All of them were now brandishing weapons, and panic had begun on the far side of the train.

Without another thought, Murph jumped down the four feet from the platform onto the tracks. The horn of the oncoming train blared and he looked up. Jesus, that's close! All he could see was the light… and the wide eyes of the driver as he slammed on the brakes. Murph covered the distance of the tracks in four steps and threw Carli onto the opposing platform. Fortunately, passengers waiting for the eastbound train had heard the gunshots and were racing for cover. She slid to a rolling stop as he planted his palms on the cement platform and leaped from the tracks just as the train came skidding into the station, its brakes screaming in protest. Several cars of the train passed them, blocking the view of the other train, though Murph knew that the gunmen could have crossed to the center platform by now.

Not waiting to find out, Murph swept up Carli again and sprinted around the corner of the station. His luck still held, as they came to the last car of a northbound train. The doors were closing, but Murph forced his way onto the train. If the other riders were surprised by their arrival, they paid Murph and Carli no attention. Murph knelt and put Carli down gently. He peeked over the window sill long enough to see the gunmen run up the stairs to the station exit, never noticing the train leaving up the tunnel to the north.

Gasping for breath, he took the backpack from Carli. "Where does this train stop next?"

"What?" She seemed confused. He shook her lightly to break the shock of their near escape.

"WHERE DOES THIS TRAIN STOP NEXT?" That sounded harsher than he really intended, but it worked.

"Oh, Nasser station." She still looked like a startled deer, but he couldn't really help that now.

Murph opened front pouch of the backpack and pulled out the satellite phone. He snapped it open and punched the contact simply labeled as "Saleh."

The phone didn't even pause to ring when Saleh's voice

boomed, "Where are you Dr. Murphy? You left the hotel without calling me!"

"Never mind that, Saleh. I need your help! We're being chased by armed men. Can you help me?"

"Yes. Where are you now?"

"We're on the Cairo Metro from Tahrir Square to the Nasser station. We should be arriving in minutes."

Saleh didn't seem to be surprised about the armed assailants. "I will be there for you as you exit. Look for me!" and he cut off the call.

Murph shut the phone and put it in his pants pocket. He packed up the bag and shouldered it. Standing up, he lifted Carli to her feet and looked down into her eyes. There was fear there, so he tried to mask his own.

"Help's on the way. Once we get to the Nasser station, Saleh will meet us and get us out of here so we can figure this out!" He tried to sound as calm and reassuring as he could, while his heart was racing.

"But they were shooting! I didn't think it would come to that." She still seemed dazed.

"We'll talk about that later. For now, we need to get away when the train stops."

She nodded but was less sure than before. Her face looked tired and worn, made worse in the fluorescent light of the subway train. Murph squeezed her arms and smiled. That strengthened her resolve, and the color returned to her face. It warmed noticeably as the train neared the station and began to come out of the tunnel. The Metro entered the Nasser station and slowed to a crawl as the platform came alongside. Instead of the customary recorded voice announcing the station name, the tram driver's abrupt Arabic crackled. Murph didn't know what he said, but quickly reasoned by Carli's frown that it wasn't good news.

"He wants everyone to stay on the train when we come to a stop. He says there is a problem with the doors."

"If we stay here, we're trapped. When the train stops, scream that there's a bomb onboard and I'll pull the emergency door release. Stay with me and run for the stairs when the stampede starts!" He squeezed her hand, and she nodded agreement. Murph mouthed, "Love you!" and moved near the lever. Carli knelt down, so it would be less obvious who was shouting.

The tram jerked to a stop, and Carli began wailing. Murph didn't know the Arabic word for bomb, but the results were exactly as expected, regardless of the language. Murph pulled the emergency release and heaved against the doors. They crashed open and the panicked riders poured out. The rout was on, and once again Murph cradled Carli and moved with the flow off the platform and up the stairs into the sunlight.

Murph pushed into the open street. Police sirens wailed in the distance, but were beginning to converge rapidly on the area. He quickly scanned the corner, and there was Saleh in the black Mercedes, right where he said he would be. Saleh got out and calmly waved Murph over. Crossing the street, he carried Carli while Saleh opened the rear door. As Murph and Carli got into the back seat, Saleh hissed, "Get down!" and covered them with a worn grey blanket. They heard the back and front car doors slam and the Mercedes engine roar as they sped away. Several sharp turns later their speed dropped to a more normal level for Cairo. The sirens had long died away before Saleh advised them it was safe to get up. They turned onto a narrow street and passed under an ancient archway into a quiet courtyard. Saleh stopped the car and let them out.

They stretched, marveling at the cool oasis in the middle of the stifling city. The sound of water trickling in a fountain masked the presence of any residual street noise. All was peaceful and calm.

Murph was the first to find his voice. "Saleh, what is this place? It's wonderful!"

"Allow me to welcome you to my home, the safest place in all Cairo and the refuge you need today."

"We don't want to be a burden. The Marriott will be fine."

"No, Dr. Murphy. I'm afraid that is the first place they looked, once they lost you in the Metro. I'm sure they are waiting there for you now, and it would *not* be a pleasant thing for them to find you."

"But Saleh, who are they… and what do they want with Carli?"

Carli couldn't look at Murph, but started to speak.

"Tut tut!" Saleh interrupted. "Miss Chamoun has made some powerful enemies, but that is a story better told inside, over a strong drink. And something to eat, perhaps." He took Carli's hand

and led her toward the deeper shade of an inner courtyard. "You must be famished, my dear!"

Chapter 19

Saleh led them into a garden, lit by sunlight filtered through vines and palms. It was set in the traditional Egyptian style, with low cushions around a table. He bade them to sit, and he took off his suit jacket and loosened another button on his shirt. Clapping his hands twice, four young children appeared, taking his coat and bringing iced water with lemon and warm towels to wipe their hands and faces. An array of food was brought, as Saleh introduced his wife and children. Carli was clearly starving, and Murph quickly realized how hungry he was as well.

Saleh's wife, Ami (pronounced ah-Mee), smiled broadly and was pleased. "It makes my heart proud to see guests enjoy my cooking."

Carli complimented her in Arabic, which added to her pleasure. When they had eaten their fill, Saleh and Murph savored small cups of strong coffee and Saleh sent away his family. He returned them to the business at hand. "My dear," he began sweetly, "I think that you owe Dr. Murphy an explanation. He is involved now."

Murph was shocked. "Carli, have you met Saleh before?"

"At first, I wasn't sure. But you were involved with the dig from the beginning? Weren't you?"

Saleh nodded, "Yes, my dear."

"I didn't recognize you, since you didn't have on your robes and kaffeyeh." Seeing the blank look on her partner, she clarified, "His head scarf, Murph. He was my favorite helper. Such a hard worker!"

Saleh smiled broadly, opened his arms and bowed. "It was my pleasure to be of service. Miss Chamoun, you bring honor to our culture, unlike so many in Egypt today." He filled the coffee cups again from a silver urn. "For the good doctor's benefit, let us start at the beginning!"

She nodded and began her tale…

Chapter 20

"The new excavation of the step pyramid of Saqqara was a massive effort," began Carli, as she related how the American component of the dig was headed by Dr. Cathleen Keller, an Egyptologist and professor at the University of California at Berkeley. It was an honor for Carli to be selected to join the group and it afforded her the opportunity to work toward her Ph.D. while studying under one of the leaders in her field. She was thrilled at the opportunity and had headed to Egypt full of excitement.

Upon the Americans arrival, she recounted, they were shown to the site by the Director of the Egyptian Supreme Council of Antiquities, Dr. Zahi Hawass, and his assistant, Dr. Tanen Narmer. They found Hawass to be an intelligent and kind man, but Narmer was the quintessential nosy bureaucrat. His short stature was worsened by a perpetual forward bent to his neck. He looked as if he had spent his life crouched over in small spaces. Even his pasty complexion was at odds with the sunny desert climate. He was always mopping his brow with a dirty handkerchief that he kept in his pants pocket, and his eyes darted from place to place as if he expected something to jump out and bite him. His khaki pants and linen shirt were forever wrinkled, and the members of the scientific team loathed the time he spent poking his crooked nose into their affairs.

As was common in the world of antiquities, Egypt needed the help of outside groups to come and investigate its sites but was jealously guarding the treasures of its history. In the past, many of the treasures of ancient Egypt had been taken from the country and could be found in the collections of major museums around the world. It was difficult for the current Egyptian government to reclaim their lost artifacts, so they were careful not to let any more leave the country.

"Members of our expedition were careful not to show excessive excitement over any discoveries until they had all the facts, but when something the least bit interesting was found, Dr. Narmer always appeared, nosing around. Clearly some of the local laborers working with us doubled as informants for the Department of

Antiquities. Egypt is a land of secrets — and not just in ancient times.

"My invitation to the expedition was due to my area of expertise concerning the god *Ptah*. In Egyptian mythology, Ptah is the one who called the world into being. Having dreamt creation in his heart and speaking it, he brought it about. In art, he is portrayed as a bearded mummified man, often wearing a skullcap, with his hands holding the symbols of life (*ankh*), power (*was*), and stability (*djed*). Since Ptah had called creation into being, he was considered the god of craftsmen and the god of regeneration. Over time, he became considered an underworld deity, with power over the passage from life to death, and from death into the afterlife.

"From earliest times, the ancient Egyptians denied the physical impermanence of life. Their religious beliefs and rituals were focused on the quest for immortality. Egyptian theology, as well as the authority of the king, rested on the concept of *Maat*, which translates as truth, justice, or natural order. Maat was personified as a goddess with a feather on her head, or sometimes simply recorded in hieroglyphics as the "feather of truth." The natural order created by Maat governed the universe, causing the sun to rise and set every day, the Nile to flood its banks and deposit nourishing soil every year, and the dead to be reborn into the next life. Egyptian religion was an examination and explanation of these cycles of death and rebirth.

"In Egyptian culture, these cycles were not guaranteed natural events. The sun did not simply set and rise again the next day. The setting sun signaled the death of the sun god, *Ra*, and his descent into the nocturnal realm of the underworld. His progress toward rising again the next morning was aided by a host of protective deities to help him overcome dangers placed in his path toward rebirth. The walls of royal tombs are inscribed with elaborate descriptions of the sun god's nightly travails, and the Pharaohs believed that it was their path after death to mirror Ra's journey. Egyptians believed that in the afterlife, kings became one with the sun god, with whom they were reborn at sunrise. The ancient Egyptians simply did not believe their own rebirth in the next life to be an absolute given. For them, magic, force of will, morality, and some obscure knowledge, maintained by the priests, enabled human resurrection. Elaborate rituals and ceremonial objects were thus designed to provide the deceased with the essentials needed to reach the afterlife."

Murph shifted on the divan and refilled his coffee, and Saleh's cup as well. Carli would make a fantastic professor, he thought. Her knowledge was extensive, and her passion took a dry subject (he remembered napping through most of his History 181 class) and made it compelling. He noticed that Saleh's children had crept into the room and were sitting on the floor around his chair in wide-eyed wonder at her presentation. Saleh sat there smiling and nodding occasionally, his hands folded in his lap, fingers up, tips touching. Murph was on the edge of his seat, with no danger of falling asleep in this lecture. Carli stood up and began to walk around, becoming more animated as she continued.

"The dangers that Ra faced during his voyage at night were believed to be the same ones that all Egyptians faced after death, regardless of social class. The journey through the underworld was not only perilous but also full of possibilities. There was the potential for resurrection and immortality at its end. The elaborate funerary rituals associated with mummification and burial can be thought of as providing multiple layers of protection to aid the deceased during the dangerous crossing to the afterlife. The body was protected by physical coverings, amulets, and magical deities that together preserved the body and provided the deceased with the knowledge required for entering the afterlife.

The effort was to ensure safety for the *ba*, roughly the soul, of the person. The mummification process, which prevented the body from fully decomposing, was the first protective layer. The organs of the deceased were removed from the body, dried in natron salts, wrapped in cloth bandages, and placed in jars with lids depicting guardian deities. The body was desiccated in a similar manner, using soda ash salts treated with perfumed oils. The body was then swathed in linen.

"The ritualistic wrapping of the body emulated the myth of Osiris, who was the ruler of the netherworld. The myth says that Osiris was murdered and his body dismembered. His body parts were later collected, wrapped together in cloth, and reborn with divine assistance. It was believed that to be resurrected, a dead Egyptian needed to imitate the form of Osiris, and that once mummified, he or she would be reborn in the same magical manner.

"The mummies of royalty and nobles were adorned with elaborate attire, which included beaded clothing, jewelry, and even golden masks. The dressed body was then placed in its magically protected coffin. The Pharaoh's mummy would have been set in a massive sarcophagus that rested in the burial chamber of his tomb. Craftsmen would have been commanded to create an elaborate statue of the Pharaoh, which would stand at the entrance of the tomb, as a residence for the *ka* and *ba*, body and soul, of the Pharaoh."

Carli then went on to explain that the ancient Egyptians believed that the deceased had contact with this world as they journeyed toward and into the afterlife. Rituals were performed to allow the deceased to be able to see, smell, breathe, hear and eat. The re-animated mummy would then be able to partake of offerings of food and drink brought to the tomb each day. Through his statue, once the dead had been rejuvenated of his senses, he could watch over family members, affecting their lives. In the case of the Pharaoh, he could continue to survey the progress of his kingdom, and future pharaohs could seek his guidance.

Turning to Murph, Carli said, "You know the ritual! You always mention it when you do your history of dentistry talk to kids. It's the Opening of the Mouth Ritual. The tomb of Djoser at the step pyramid has a huge temple relief with one of the most extensive records of this ceremony. It was my responsibility to document and accurately translate those hieroglyphics."

"The first references to the actual process of the ritual are on the wall of the tomb. They indicate the rite should take place in the House of Gold and describe the Opening of the Mouth ceremony as using the foreleg of a bull and an iron two-sided woodworking adze. The two blades of meteoric iron, the *ntjrwy*, are said to open the mouth. The spell translates as 'O Osiris King, I split open your mouth for you — with God's iron of Upper Egypt and Lower Egypt.' The ritual seems to have been performed with a common wood carving adze or chisel, which was touched to the lips of the mummy or statue by the officiating priest. This hieroglyph is unique in that it actually describes the tools used for the ritual!

"The ceremonial adze was made from the metal of heaven,

some sort of meteoric metal, I guess. It must have been resistant to rust and made incredibly sharp. The drawings show it to be an arched metal blade fastened across the top of a wooden handle with leather thongs. I later saw it referred to as the *psh-kef* knife, in writings in the tombs of the dentists."

She stopped pacing and fixed Murph with her gaze, imploring him to understand! "Don't you see? Dentists in ancient Egypt were priests!" She clapped her hands together and turned, pulling her hair back. This reflexive move was followed by whipping a rubber band off her wrist and over her ponytail. She whirled around and stared off into the distance, her pupils widening as her eyes concentrated on the image in her mind of a bound papyrus.

"It says in THE BOOK OF THE DEAD, 'My mouth is opened by Ptah. The bonds that gag my mouth have been loosed by my God. My mouth has been parted by Ptah with the psh-kef with which he has parted the mouths of the Gods.'"

Murph had always been amazed at her photographic memory. His memory was good, but she put him to shame. His learning was more auditory. Once he heard a narrative and grasped the big-picture concept, then he could go back for the details. He had been taught by his mentors that stories are the pegs upon which we hang the facts. Carli was clearly a visual learner. If she saw something, she could reproduce it exactly in her mind. From remembered images (or pieces), she could put together the concept. *We do work well together,* he thought. *As Jerry Maguire said, "You complete me!"*

Now Murph was grinning, staring off into space. "Murph! Will you pay attention?" she scolded. "I did a paper on the ceremony at OSU, and you proofread it for me. That's where you got started with the Egyptian dentistry stuff for your history of dentistry lecture!"

"Oh Yeah! That's right. I kind of forgot." He looked up sheepishly.

"Descriptions of the Opening of the Mouth ceremony have been cataloged from the tombs of many Pharaohs, including Seti, Tuthmosis, and Amenhotep. I saw them myself at the temple of Amun-Ra at Karnak and the temple at Deir-el-Bahri. The ceremony should be carried out in the House of Gold. Once the deceased has arrived at his tomb, the priest performs the ritual to bring about the transformation and free the ka and ba from the mummy. The mummy is set up on a clean mound of sand, facing south. The Pharaoh should be purified with water and his mouth especially purified with water from the Nile — from both Upper and Lower Egypt, poured out of golden bowls. A bull is butchered and the heart is presented to the mummy. Its foreleg is severed and pointed toward the deceased. That hieroglyph for the foreleg is complex and denotes strength. I think that they believed the foreleg served as some sort of conduit to focus the transfer of the life-force of the bull to the mummy."

She faced them and pulled her lips back from clenched teeth with her left hand. "Then, the mouth was opened with the psh-kef knife." She acted like her right index finger was a blade forced between her front teeth, prying her teeth apart. "Then the mummy was presented to Ptah."

She put her hands on her hips. "An ostrich feather was presented, which symbolized the presence of Maat and indicated that the natural order had been restored by allowing the mummy to journey to the afterlife and be reborn. Incense was burned. Dates, grapes, bread, and other foods were offered, and the sarcophagus was closed. The image of the Pharaoh was anointed with oils. Green and black eye paints were applied to the face of the statue. It was then dressed in white clothes that were adorned with green, blue, and red. The red protected the pharaoh from his enemies, while the blue hid his face from those who would do him harm. The green ensured his good health.

"At this point, the ceremony was done. The newly animated mummy was left in his resting place, and his body and spirit (*ka* and *ba*) were now free to roam the world. The priests fed and communicated with the Pharaoh using his statue as the conduit. The mummy now remembered what had been forgotten and could eat bread and fruit as he desired. In a show of deference to the power of the Pharaoh, when the priest left the room after honoring and feeding the statue, he dragged a broom behind him to wipe out his footprints in the sand on the limestone floor."

Chapter 21

"I had just finished with these hieroglyphics," continued Carli, "when Dr. Hawass came to us with the news that thieves had plundered the dentists' tombs. Dr. Keller had been impressed with my work, so she asked me to assess how much damage had been done by the grave robbers and to begin cataloging the site. Unfortunately, Dr. Hawass assigned that weasel Narmer as well." Carli sniffed in disgust and shuddered. "What a vile little man! Ugh. He still makes my skin crawl."

Murph felt his blood pressure rise a bit. "Did he touch you?"

"No. It's not like that. He just stinks of sweat and cigarettes. He's a little rodent, always scurrying around, underfoot and into everything."

"Tanen Narmer is annoying, but not really that dangerous," Saleh offered. "Unlike others you may have met. Yes?"

Carli nodded and shuddered again, as if a chill wind had passed through the room. "Yes," she whispered, "I know whom you mean. I'm almost there." She rubbed her arms to shake the sudden case of goose bumps. She paused to sip some water and regain her composure.

"Dentists in ancient Egypt commanded a great deal of respect. The practice of dentistry was limited to the royal court and the extremely wealthy. Dentists were involved in research, and they kept their observations documented with a high degree of accuracy. Where you focus today mainly on treatment, in the past it was a really hit or miss system; curing wasn't really their specialty. If one thing didn't work, they would try something else, keeping close records of what happened. Failing with treatment, they would call upon their magic to destroy what they referred to as 'the enemy, which is in the tooth.' In the hieroglyphics from the tomb of Sekhem Ka, I found the recipe for a filling material. It was resin of terebinth, Nubian clay, and green eye lotion crushed together and applied to the tooth."

Murph thought for a moment. "I don't know what terebinth is, but that stuff could be like something we would use today as a temporary material to numb a sensitive tooth with a big cavity until we can do a filling or root canal."

Carli nodded. "Sekhem Ka also had a cure for bad breath. His 'breath sweetener' was to take frankincense, myrrh, cinnamon, bark and fragrant plants and then boil them with honey and shape the concoction into pellets, which the person chewed."

"Sounds fairly advanced." Murph laughed. "Four out of five Egyptian dentists would have recommended it!"

Now, she's getting off track, Murph thought. He tried to keep her focused, "The dentist's tombs were near the step pyramid, right?"

"Oh yes, sorry." She blushed. "The tombs of the three dentists are across the courtyard from the tomb of Djoser, the Pharaoh. Their close proximity is due to their role as priests, who would need to tend to the Pharaoh daily. There were three dentists. Dr. Hawass publicly reported Narmer's theory that the chief dentist was named Iy Mry, and that his two assistants were Sekhem Ka and Kem Msw. I'm not so sure that's correct, as it was a rather hasty conclusion. The story was easy for the media to grasp and was widely reported around the world."

Saleh nodded and Murph agreed, "I even saw it in Washington."

"Once it hits *National Geographic,* it's accepted around the world as scientific fact," lamented Carli sadly.

"What makes you think that story is wrong."

"When we got to the tombs, the grave robbers had taken out all the precious metals and jewelry, but had not damaged any of the walls. It was pretty common tomb construction. The doorway was covered with the standard hieroglyphics, warning of a horrible death to any who should violate the tomb. Unfortunately for the dentists, today's thieves can't read ancient Egyptian. These warnings were most specific. There was a crocodile and snake motif, and the phrase 'Rif Ich Er Chey Her Shut Moo'... Loosely translated as 'If you enter this tomb, you will be bitten by a snake and eaten by the crocodile.'"

"Well, that would keep me out!" chuckled Murph.

"The outer chamber of the tomb showed Iy Mry tending to Pharaoh and his family doing the things that rich Egyptians of the period did. Narmer simply looked at this and assumed that Iy Mry had such a high position and close relationship to the Pharaoh that he must be the chief dentist. I couldn't put my finger on it, but something was wrong. I went about my task of cataloging the information and recording the hieroglyphics. This was the most complete depiction of the Opening of the Mouth ritual. It was a great breakthrough by itself. Everyone was excited and falling over to claim credit for the discovery. But then…" Her voice faltered.

Murph started to get up, but she waved him back. Taking a deep breath, she continued, getting stronger and more determined with each word. "Everything changed… when I found the secret passage."

The children let out a gasp. Carli giggled. "It's like telling ghost stories at bedtime!"

Saleh began to reprimand the children, obviously some Arabic form of "be seen and not heard," but Carli smiled and knelt down in front of the children. Taking the hands of the smallest, a girl of about five, she patted her hand and reassured them it was OK. She led them around the foot of her chair and sat down, pulling the little girl into her lap. She held her close and continued.

"I found a false door, which led to a small chamber, about fifteen feet square. By the writings on the wall, this was the lab of Sekhem Ka. The pictograms of the life of Iy Mry were bright and broadly done, indicating a busy public life and presence at court. In contrast, Sekhem Ka's work was small and simple, without the gold inlay and vibrant colors. I found a masonry jar that was tightly sealed. It contained a number of papyrus scrolls. I had barely begun to examine them when Dr. Narmer swooped in. He took a quick glance and left immediately, cackling excitedly to himself.

"There was one larger bundle of bound papyrus and then several smaller scrolls. I took the bundle and unrolled it. It seemed to be a form of notebook or medical case record. Each page was the discussion of the illness or injury of a patient. The presentation of each was done systematically: title, examination, diagnosis, treatment, and glossus — a dictionary of the terms used. The amazing part was that each description of the symptoms ended with one of three statements: one, an ailment which I will treat; two, an ailment with which I will contend; and three, an ailment not to be treated."

"It was all cold and matter of fact. Each treatment offered ended with the instructions that it be used 'until he recovers,' or 'until the period of his injury passes by,' or 'until thou knows that he has reached a decisive point.' This reflects a level of medical knowledge that is not documented to have existed prior to the writings of the Greek Hippocrates, more than 2000 years later. The dentist who wrote these was not only an experienced man, but a very wise one."

"That is a significant find!" Saleh seemed impressed. "Can you tell who the author was?"

"I would assume it was Sekhem Ka, given where the scrolls were found and also the other documents that accompanied them. But then *HE* came." Carli darkened again. "I was making notes in my journal when Dr. Narmer came back. He said that since the project had uncovered information of a dental nature, he had consulted with the foremost dentist in Egypt, and he introduced me to Dr. Hamid al-Said. He's a very dark Arab — tall, thin, and athletic. He dressed all in black, strangely robed like a Bedouin, despite the fact that his English was perfect. He spoke pleasantly enough, clipped but polite. His handshake was like iron, nearly crushing my fingers. He complemented me on my work, looking briefly at the scrolls in my hand. The rest of the scrolls had scattered on the floor when they had startled me coming in. He was nice enough, I guess, but his eyes were black holes, and my heart froze when I looked him in the eye. He commanded Narmer like a servant to pick up all the scrolls and take them away. He turned on his heel and left the room. Narmer regained his mean composure, swept up the scrolls and ordered me back to our quarters to wait on the permission to proceed."

"Saleh, do you know this al-Said?" Murph was curious.

"Alas, I do." Saleh rubbed his brow and looked tired. "He is indeed the most famous dentist in Egypt. He is the local dentist to the rich and powerful here in the Arab world. Much like your friend Dr. Farouk, he was trained in England, educated at Oxford. His star is rising rapidly with the ascendency of his political party. He has the ear of powerful men in the government. He is a dangerous man to have as an enemy."

Saleh inquired about the men who were chasing Murph and Carli. When they gave the description of the three, especially the bearded smiling one in the dark windbreaker, all Saleh could do was sigh and shake his head.

"Those men may serve Dr. al-Said, but I cannot be sure. The bearded one is Omar Bengdara. He has been linked to the disappearances of several men critical of his party. Bengdara is an enforcer, and by all accounts, he truly enjoys his work."

Carli told Murph, "When I went back to the hotel that serves as the living quarters for the dig, I was confronted by Dr. Keller. She told me that I was being dismissed for defiling the sacred site of the tomb. She was angry and very disappointed in me. She wouldn't listen to anything I said. She told me to my flight out of the country would be the next morning, and she ordered me to pack my things. There weren't any witnesses other than Narmer and al-Said. My educational Visa has been revoked. My career is over… I went back to my room and cried."

Saleh's daughter reached up and hugged Carli. She stood up and kissed the girl lightly on her forehead. Setting her down, Carli nearly collapsed.

Murph raced over and cradled Carli in his arms. She looked so small and vulnerable. Her grief at the death of her dream was palpable, eating at her from within. Tears rolled down her face and onto his chest.

"Miss Chamoun." Saleh's voice was stern, commanding. "Those men chasing you weren't from immigration, inquiring about your Visa. Is there another reason for them to be hunting you?"

She pushed Murph away and wiped the tears with the back of her hand. Standing up at her full height, she lifted her chin and said, "When Dr. Narmer took the scrolls, he missed one that had rolled under a table."

"Do you know where it is?"

She reached down and pulled up the pant leg of her jeans. Taped to the inside of her calf was a plastic Zip-loc bag with a papyrus scroll inside.

Murph gasped, "Carli!"

Chapter 22

"What were you thinking?" Murph was beside himself.

"She did not think. Just do it — that is the American way, no?" Saleh seemed to be taking this all in stride.

Carli slumped back into the chair, with her head in her hands.

Now it was Murph's turn to pace around the room. "Maybe we can arrange to leave the scroll for them somewhere and get Carli out of the country. I have travel documents for her and the Gulfstream is still here. It might just work!"

"NO!" Carli stood up and set her jaw firmly. Murph stopped in his tracks. "I will not give in to pressure and slink out of the country. I'm going back to Saqqara to put the scroll back. You can go with me, or stay here, but don't get in my way."

Murph was still speechless. Saleh recovered faster. "I admire your courage, but they will certainly have secured the site. No matter how noble, it would be unwise to return to Saqqara."

"They may have security," Carli smiled defiantly, "but I'm the only one who knows the back way in. I found the secret passage when Narmer was out for a smoke, and I never told anyone. They aren't diligent enough to find it. Narmer and friends seemed more interested in closing up the dig than they were in learning anything."

Murph knew Carli well enough to know that when she set her mind to something, there was no changing it. He accepted defeat with as much grace as he could. "OK. I'm in. But let's plan this out this time. How about a little less of the 'just do it' motto."

"I agree," Saleh concurred. "I will make arrangements and prepare materials for us. I would suggest that the two of you get some sleep. It has been a long day, and I expect that it will be a longer night to come. It is unfortunate, but we must brave the tomb of the Pharaoh at night. Let us pray that the spirits are supportive of our efforts." He gave instructions to his children, and they led Murph and Carli to separate bedrooms.

Murph thought he would be too wound up to sleep, but he found that the soft cotton bedding and a gentle breeze proved the perfect combination. He was snoring as soon as his head hit the pillow. Saleh looked in on them both and was pleased that Carli was blissfully asleep as well. He busied himself around the house organizing for the night incursion into Saqqara. He let them rest for four hours, before rousing them for a light supper, expertly prepared for them by a concerned Ami.

The sun was lowering in the western sky as they said good-bye to the children, and received the blessing of Ami. The shadows grew long, and the sandstone buildings of Cairo glittered with a red and gold hue. It was a beautiful night, even romantic, but the three hardly noticed the scenery. They moved with a resolute purpose. Saleh had traded the black Mercedes for a dusty grey Land Rover that more suited their mission. The sun had set, and a sliver of moon was rising when they reached Saqqara. The searing heat of the desert had dissipated quickly with the loss of the sun. Murph and Carli shivered slightly, the chill in the breeze giving them a convenient excuse. It didn't do them any good to dwell on their fear. The bravado shown in Saleh's garden had faded quickly here in the dark desert. Carli felt very small facing the looming shadow of the Step Pyramid.

Saleh had retrieved Murph's luggage from the Marriott. After the nap, he had quickly showered and shaved. Feeling refreshed, he donned the dark jeans again, but paired them with a black long-sleeve, dri-fit warm-up and black cross trainers. His dark tan and hair completed the commando look. In the shadows, he faded into the dark, but it would be an uncomfortable ensemble when the sun came up in the morning. Carli sported a similar dark look, her jeans replaced by black athletic pants and a sweatshirt borrowed from Saleh's oldest daughter.

They had discussed the dangers of entering the tomb at night. Murph had insisted that Saleh stay with the car. As much trouble as he and Carli would be in if they were caught, the penalties would be more harsh on Saleh, a local helping out the foreigners raid the tomb of a pharaoh. Saleh had dropped them off at the edge of the Nile watershed. The trees gave them a brief amount of cover to consider their next move. They had over 300 yards of open sand to cover to reach the edge of the Saqqara complex.

They crouched down next to the road and surveyed the distance to the outer wall of the enclosure. Murph observed the rising moon and was glad that it would not be a bright, full one. "Time's wasting. We need to go."

Carli nodded, but before they set off she turned Murph around and reached into the backpack. This time it contained flashlights and a bolt cutter, among other things, but she passed them by to pull out the block O baseball cap again. "For good luck!" She winked and set the hat firmly on her head, the ponytail sticking out the back.

They had decided that a direct approach made the most sense.

There was no way to slink unseen across that much open sand, so they jogged at an easy pace up the hard packed sand used as a construction road. It felt good to run, shaking off some of the nervousness. They crossed the distance without any obvious alarm being raised and stopped to catch their breath in the shadow of the 30-foot enclosure wall. The main entrance to the Djoser complex was to the south, and the palace façade facing them contained 14 false doors. The Tura limestone had been carved to imitate bundles of reeds acting as pillars. It was a massive feat of design, and Murph would have enjoyed it, except that tonight the stone was cold and intimidating.

Murph looked up at the top, towering over them, but Carli grabbed his hand and pulled him to the right. They had approached the complex from the east, the Nile side. Carli knew that there was a functional door on the northeast corner of the complex. They found the door blocked by a chain link gate. Saleh had been right! Murph took the bolt cutter from the backpack and placed its blades on the loop of chain binding the gate closed. He glanced around, and seeing no guards, chopped the link. The metal parted easily, but the snap rang like a gunshot. With still no sign of movement around them, they opened the gate a crack and slid through as quietly as they could, closing the gate behind them.

They entered a narrow passageway and crouched down. Murph replaced the bolt cutters and took out two flashlights, giving one to Carli. She slipped hers into her pocket. He hooded his with his hand and switched it on. Panning the light around, they were in a limestone corridor with a close-fit brick floor. The walls and ceiling had been carved to look as though it was made from whole tree trunks. They moved quietly down the hall and passed through a massive stone portal. The ceiling rose up in the next chamber, as the pillars on either side were at least 40 feet high. Murph's flashlight beam wouldn't reach the top. He stood there with his mouth hanging open, marveling at the enormous scale of the structure.

"No time for sightseeing!" Carli hissed and pulled him forward, aiming his flashlight ahead as they ran through across the colonnade. At the end of the courtyard, there were eight carved stone columns, joined in pairs by huge limestone blocks. A staircase of pink limestone rose in front of them and Murph moved to climb.

"No, that leads up directly to the Pharaoh's burial chamber."

Carli couldn't help giving the guided tour. "It's beautiful, but we'll come back and see Djoser another day." She pointed him off to the right, where a narrow set of stairs led down, almost hidden behind another pillar carved to look like a shock of wheat. They descended into a labyrinth of tunnels. Where Murph was instantly lost, Carli moved with purpose, her sure-footed confidence making him feel better.

The tunnel ended in a small gallery. To their left, a wider passage way beckoned. It was of much finer construction than the labyrinth had been, ornate carvings in relief on the wall. To their right, the passage narrowed, formed of rougher limestone blocks. Murph started for the larger hallway.

"You do really want to see the Pharaoh's burial chamber!" Her relaxed smile eased his tension somewhat. "I told you I'd take you next time. Besides, his mummy is in the Cairo Museum. You've already seen him."

"Don't remind me!" He gave her hand a squeeze. She was in her element now. "Let's get this done."

"The entrance is just around the corner." She led him into the narrow passage. "The priests quarters are well built, but you can tell they weren't royalty. Look at the walls. Simple stone carvings, marking the occupants." They rounded another blind corner and reached an arched doorway.

"See." She waved at the hieroglyphics and took out her flashlight, shining it on pictograms in sequence. "The eye over the tusk symbolizes dentistry. There is the snake, and the crocodile is over here. You can get the point of the curse, even if you don't speak ancient Egyptian." Her smile lit up the hallway. This was her discovery, and she was proud to show it off. He hated to remind her that it was the middle of the night, and they were trespassing in a sacred tomb.

"Wait a minute," it dawned on Murph suddenly, and he dropped quickly to a hoarse whisper. "This is the front entrance. I thought you knew a secret passage?"

"I know where it goes out the back of the room, but I never went down it. I don't know where it ends."

"What?" Murph was speechless.

"But you never would have let me come if I had told you, right?"

"Caroline Chamoun! When we get out of here..."

She cut him off, "But we're here now, so we might as well go in." And she pushed back the plastic tarp covering the doorway and led him into the tomb of the dentists to the Pharaoh.

Chapter 23

The main chamber was as Carli had described, roughly 30 feet square. The ceiling was a lofty 12 feet or so. Murph panned his flashlight across the brightly painted figures on the walls. There was the dentist, Iy Mry, engaged in the daily life of a prominent Egyptian — scenes of slaughtering animals as sacrifice and reviewing his crops and land, as well as the obligatory images of him paying homage to Pharaoh. There was not much to be found here, as this was the part of the tomb that had been raided by thieves.

Carli led him to the far wall, where two other doorways led to small antechambers. Each doorway had lesser hieroglyphics than the main entrance, identifying Kem Msw and Sekhem Ka. The chambers looked more like closets to Murph, but Carli worked her way around a pillar and squeezed her small frame behind the stone, against the back wall. She pulled Murph along behind her. Even after he took the backpack off, he had to work to scrunch his tall frame under the low roof, without bending over and becoming wider. It was a tight fit.

"Only a midget would find this passage," he muttered under his breath.

"Watch the short jokes!" She elbowed him in the ribs, "Keep going. We're almost there!" Suddenly the walls opened into a 20-foot square mud brick room. The ceiling was low, but Murph could stretch out his arms over his head, his back popping with relief. *At least that bearded thug Omar Bengdara can't fit through there!*

"That feels better!" He looked around, but Carli was intently taking inventory of her archeological find.

"The scrolls are gone, but nothing else has been moved. Even my journal is still here." She picked up the bound leather book and stuffed it into the backpack.

The wall opposite the entrance had a white cloth tarp strung up with rope hiding it. "The hieroglyphics under the tarp tell a story that has me confused. That's why I came back."

The right side of the chamber was filled with stone jars, obviously for some sort of storage. Some were sealed, and some were apparently empty. The one that had contained the scrolls was lying on its side in the dust. Its lid had rolled away when Dr. Narmer had knocked it over in his haste to grab the scrolls. The left side of the room had a stonework bench built into the wall, with several bowls, metal vessels, and a short-bladed knife still resting on it. Everything was covered in the dust of centuries, and Murph was nervous to disturb it. He set down the backpack near the end of the workbench and pulled out latex gloves for both of them.

"Let's get this over with. Put the scroll in that vase lying on the floor, and I'll get the lid for it." He bent down and picked up the disc of heavy pottery.

"Just a second Murph. I need your help with this." She had taken her iPhone out and was powering up its camera. "Please hold back the tarp."

"We don't have time for this!" But there she stood, hands on her hips, and a look of defiance on her face. He shook his head and lifted up the cloth tarp while she ducked under it and began snapping images of the hieroglyphics. He held the beam of his flashlight on the wall to provide additional light.

Murph didn't notice the movement in the shadows behind him until the last moment. A form rose from behind the stack of jars, detached itself from the wall and stepped out swinging. He heard the whistle as the butt of a gun descended, and he turned slightly, but not quite quickly enough. He took a glancing blow behind his left ear. Everything went black, as he crumpled to the ground.

Chapter 24

Murph woke to a horrifying sound. The crisp smack of hand against flesh. His head throbbed, but he tried to open his eyes without moving. He lay face down in the shadows along the back wall of the chamber. The cloth tarp had been pulled down and part of it covered him. He must have kept his grip on it when he fell and tore it off the wall. His mouth was dry, filled with the sandstone dust from the floor. Another slap brought things into focus. In the middle of the room, Carli sat upright in a chair, her wrists bound behind her. As if creating a spotlight, an Arab in the dark robes of the Bedouin held a flashlight above and a bit behind her. Another backhand slap and her head snapped to the right, the ball cap flying off, skidding across the stone floor. Her assailant bent down into the light, his face inches from hers. Murph took in a crooked nose, narrow close-set eyes, wrinkled trousers and rumpled shirt — this had to be Tanen Narmer!

"Where is the scroll?" he hissed. "Where did you put it?" His spittle glittered in the intense light as it struck Carli in the face.

"It's in a hotel room." She lied defiantly. "Why do you care? You were never one to do any research work anyway?"

Another slap. "Do not lie to me!" He sniffed and cleared his throat with a snort. "We know you have it, and you must give it to me."

"Then what?" She was in poor position to bargain, but it was worth a try. "Will you let us leave Egypt?"

"You will take me to the scroll; then we will turn you over to the authorities. Do you know what Sharia law prescribes as punishment for thieves? No? You will learn soon enough, eh, Farhat?" The Bedouin guard gave a mirthless laugh.

Murph took stock of his situation. They seemed to have forgotten him for the moment. There was no other movement in the room, so he had to assume that Narmer and his guard dog Farhat were the only ones there in the middle of the night. They were enough trouble as it was. Something was poking Murph in the ribs. Without moving, he rocked slightly and determined it was the lid from the scroll jar. He must have fallen on it when he went down.

"Farhat... perhaps... we should take her to Dr. al-Said. He may prove more *persuasive*, although I am *so* much more *pleasant* to deal with." Narmer reached down and stroked her chin with his bony hand. Carli tried to pull away. "Still, we are alone here... and the night is young..."

Murph rose up and threw the stone lid like a Frisbee. His aim was true, hitting Farhat in the shoulder, deflecting up and glancing off his temple. He was stunned, dropped the flashlight and staggered back. Carli reacted immediately, rocking forward and rising up. The top of her head struck Narmer under the point of his chin, snapping his head back. He went down in a crumpled pile of khaki clothing. She swung around, using the chair tied to her back as a club and took the legs out from under Farhat, who collapsed next to Narmer.

Murph ran over to the workbench and quickly found what he was looking for. He grabbed the knife and ran toward Carli.

"Don't kill them!" She blocked his path, aware of the fire in his eyes.

He spun her around and cut loose the bonds holding her to the chair. "We've got to get out of here!" He took the knife and cut loose the other end of the rope holding the tarp to the wall. Murph then covered the slumped forms of Narmer and Farhat, taking the opportunity to punch Narmer once for good measure. He rolled them into a tangled ball as quickly as he could. Carli picked up the baseball cap and defiantly put it back on her head.

They both stopped and looked up, as they could hear voices in Arabic and the sounds of people rushing into the outer chamber. Without waiting for a translation, Murph tossed the knife in the backpack. That could come in handy! He gave the backpack to Carli and whispered urgently, "Where's that secret passage?"

She ran over to the end of the workbench and bent down. There was an area of bricks in the floor that made a round hole under the end of the stone tabletop.

Murph was incredulous. "That looks like some sort of a garbage chute!"

"What did you expect? The Cairo Metro?"

Murph threw up his hands in exasperation. He grabbed a loose brick on the floor and dropped it down the hole. It only seemed to fall a short distance before hitting bottom with a thud. The noises were growing louder. That made the decision so much easier. He dropped the backpack down and then lowered Carli into the hole.

"It's a passageway," she called up. "The drop is about 12 feet."

Farhat had begun to stir and was starting to try to free himself, shouting loudly. Murph scanned the table and grabbed the heaviest thing he could find. It was a solid metal cylinder about four inches in diameter, ten inches long. He ran over to the struggling form under the tarp and whacked him with the pipe. Farhat slumped and lay still. Murph took one last look around the room. He found his flashlight and pocketed it. He liked the feel of the heavy rod in his hand. It gave Murph a sense of security, so he kept it with him. He grabbed two of the stone jars and placed them to obscure the opening in the floor from the doorway. It wouldn't last long, but if they missed the escape route in the first glance, it might buy them an extra minute or two. It was the best he could do in a short amount of time. So much for all that planning. He lowered himself over the edge of the hole, hung by his fingertips to his full length, and dropped into the dark.

Chapter 25

Murph landed lightly on his feet, crouching down to absorb the shock. He bounced up, looking around for Carli. The passage ran in both directions. She stood at a crossroads about fifty feet from him, waving her flashlight. He sprinted to join her, and they ducked around the corner to the left. He took the backpack from her and put it on, cinching it tight so he could run.

"Do you have any idea where we are?" He was afraid of the answer.

"I'm not sure," she sighed. "They estimate that there are over two miles of tunnels under the complex at Saqqara."

"Then we have a long way to run. Let's trust to the Pharaohs, but we have to get moving."

"If my orientation is right, this passage should lead us deeper under the pyramid. I don't know of any exits toward the wall on this side, so I think we should go in."

"Run deeper under the pyramid?" Murph asked incredulously. "I guess that makes as much sense to me as anything else. Let's go!" Murph masked the light a bit, and they set off at a quick jog, moving deeper underground.

As they ran, Murph looked at Carli and tried to ask as casually as he could, "You've never been down here before, have you?"

"Murph... no one has been down here for four thousand years!"

Chapter 26

Hamid al-Said stormed into the chamber of Sekhem Ka like cold blast of wind. His two henchmen followed him. Again they were clad in black slacks and windbreakers. It appeared to be the uniform of the day for these thugs. Al-Said looked down his nose at the tarp covering the prostrate forms of Narmer and Farhat.

"Release them!" He spat out the words.

With some difficulty, Narmer was uncovered and rose to his feet on unstable legs. Farhat remained unconscious, but al-Said paid him no more attention than the broken chair. Tanen Narmer pulled his dirty handkerchief from his pocket and wiped the dust from his face. Hamid al-Said bent down and picked up the rope that had bound Carli's hands. He seemed to study the cut ends, noting that the fibers had not frayed, but been completely severed by a sharp blade. In one smooth motion, he whirled around and whipped Narmer across the cheek with the knotted end of the rope. The weasel fell to his knees, clutching his face as an ugly red welt sprang up instantly. He would carry that scar to his grave.

"Get up!" Narmer rose, but cowered back like a whipped dog. "How dare you let them get away? He is a dentist, not a Navy SEAL!"

Narmer started to protest, but Hamid cut him off. "Enough! They have entered the lower labyrinth. Take Ashraf and Razon... and find them!"

"Yes, Master. I will do my best"

"No! Results matter more than intentions! You must succeed. As you know, I do not tolerate failure well."

Narmer wiped away the trickle of blood from his cheek and hung his head in defeat. "Yes, Master." It was a whisper.

He followed the footprints in the dust to the hole in the floor. He called to his new assistants and they came over, rudely knocking the stone jars out of the way, shattering them as they fell onto the brick. Narmer began to protest but recognized the blank look on their faces. These men were hired muscle, and they didn't care about ancient history. He pointed for them to drop down and then for them to catch him. Ashraf and Razon jumped down, but they let Narmer fall without any help. He landed awkwardly and turned his ankle. Limping noticeably, he trailed the other two as they followed the footprints of their prey down the passageway.

Hamid al-Said withdrew a satellite phone from a pocket in his robes and calmly dialed. It was answered on the first ring, as always. "Omar… Narmer has failed. They have entered the lower labyrinth. They must not escape again." He snapped the phone shut and stalked from the chamber, stepping over Farhat, not caring whether he was alive or dead.

Chapter 27

Carli and Murph heard no sign of pursuit, but that didn't make their situation any better. They both knew the passageways had an exit years ago, but that was not necessarily still true today. As they ran, the construction had progressed from the rough mud brick to a more crafted limestone. Whenever they had been presented with a choice of tunnel, they chose the finer materials and craftsmanship, hoping it would gradually lead them to the Pharaoh's tomb and more recently excavated spaces.

They had kept up a steady pace for more than a half an hour before they stopped and drank from a water bottle in the backpack. The blow behind his ear had raised quite a lump. As they rested, Murph began to feel pain. *No doubt, Carli's facial bruises will start bothering her, too,* he thought. *Best to keep going now!*

"Let's get on with it," Murph said, once again shouldering the backpack. They set off at a brisk pace, as the water had done them some good. They ran with a clearer head and suddenly had their first bit of luck in a while. They turned right at a fork and found the limestone wall was inlaid with blue faience tile, imitating reed matting. Carli stopped and ran her fingers over the tile. She smiled. "This wall is part of the palace façade. We're near the funerary apartment!"

She led on now, picking up the pace, and the passageway opened up into another chamber. The walls were lined with marble columns, and the center of the room held a dais with a central throne. The reliefs on the walls were brightly colored and inlaid with gold. Murph was in awe of the size and opulence of the room. Carli pulled out her phone and began taking pictures of the throne and statuary in the room. Murph allowed it for a bit, but drew the line at taking photos of all the hieroglyphics on the walls.

"But, Murph, this is the funerary apartment. It exactly mimics the real palace, and tomb raiders have never touched it. This was the living palace for the royal ka. We are the first people to see it!"

"And, we'll be the last if we don't figure a way out of here!"

"Well, according to the construction records of Imhotep," she looked away again, seeing the papyrus in her mind, "on the east side of the chamber eleven shafts were constructed, leading to the store rooms. The twelfth led to a horizontal tunnel for the royal harem... but the existence of the harem is disputed by scholars."

Murph was already counting the shafts between the stone columns, running along the east wall. "Nine... Ten... Eleven... Twelve! This one is horizontal, here at the end of the room!"

Carli snapped a last picture and put away her iPhone. She took a minute to take in the whole picture, planning to draw it in her journal later. She came up behind Murph to find that he had reached a low wooden door, sitting down five steps below the level of the floor. The entrance was hidden in an alcove behind the last column in the room. It would have been easy to miss.

The door was locked, but the dry timber shattered when Murph slammed it with his foot beside the lock. He shoved open the door, and the beam of his flashlight showed a long straight tunnel. They both hit it at a dead run, secretly praying it would end somewhere above ground.

At the end of the lengthy passage, there was another wooden door, which Murph dispatched in the same way. They appeared to be in a smaller square building, and they found stairs going up. With great relief, they noticed the air was fresher with each level they climbed. Murph's legs were burning as they reached an open gallery. Carli jumped up at Murph, locking her arms around his neck, and he twirled her around. They could see the first grey predawn light filtering through the windows. Hugging her close, he whispered, "We're not out of this yet."

Murph put Carli down and crept up to the window, careful not to be seen as he raised his head up for a look. The step pyramid was in front of him, about a quarter of a mile away. They had come a long way, and the last tunnel had led under the outer wall of the Saqqara complex.

Murph sat back against the wall and described the scene to Carli. "We're outside of Saqqara, in a building well south of the pyramid."

She thought for a minute and then crawled up to look for herself. "The monastery." She was shocked. "The tunnel leads to the Amba Armiyas Monastery!"

Murph left her to ponder the significance of that connection. He had work to do. Pulling out the satellite phone, he contacted Saleh.

"Thank the Gods you are safe!"

"Yes, they have smiled on us so far. Narmer was waiting for us. We found a secret passage out. We are in the Monastery — Amba Army something"

"Amba Armiyas monastery. I will be there in five minutes. Be careful. Dawn is a dangerous time, even for the god Ra as he arises from the underworld. The forces of darkness are moving in this world."

"I feel the pressure. See you soon. We will be waiting as close to the road as possible."

Murph closed the phone, set it to vibrate, and placed it in his pocket. "Saleh is on his way. We need to get out of here and be ready to run for it. Somehow, I don't think we're in the clear yet."

Carli was looking out the window again. "I know how you feel. The stairs down are past that door, but we have to cross the terrace to get there. We'll be exposed if anyone is watching."

"There's only one way to find out! Let's get moving." Five minutes of resting, and Murph could feel his knees stiffening up. No time to worry about that now. He reached over and pulled Carli up off the floor. He gave her a quick peck on the forehead. "For luck!"

Chapter 28

Murph checked his watch. It was 5:05 a.m. They had been running and hiding all night. Saleh had checked yesterday, and sunrise would be at 5:13 a.m. The sun was still below the horizon, and in the half-light, the sand was cold and gray. Long, deep shadows dominated the landscape and were fading fast. The monastery appeared deserted, but the *adhan*, the Islamic call to prayer, would ring out from the *muezzin* standing in the minaret soon enough.

The only road into Amba Armiyas passed between the Step Pyramid and the monastery, running along the outer wall of the Saqqara complex. It then ran an irregular path through the sand and ended in a courtyard in front of the mosque. Murph and Carli would have to cross the terrace, descend the stairs, and then run between buildings to enter the courtyard. Murph studied the ground and planned their escape. A plume of dust on the horizon drew his attention… and that of anyone else looking, he was sure. A car was coming down the road at a high rate of speed. Murph couldn't be sure in the dim light, but he had to assume it was Saleh in the Land Rover. It was now or never.

"Cavalry's coming!" He led Carli to the door and tested the lock. It was open. "Whatever happens, just keep running!" Murph pulled the door back. The rusted hinges protested with a grinding creak, loud enough to wake the dead. Murph could imagine dozens of heads turning, eyes searching for the source of the sound. He shoved Carli out the door. "GO!"

They ran across the balcony and down the stone stairs, landing in a narrow alley between the buildings. As Murph had planned, they quickly reached the edge of the structures, which appeared to be a long abandoned dormitory complex. They stopped at the end of the building, crouching down in the deep shadows, surveying the scene. The courtyard opened before them, with the mosque on their left, its stone façade beginning to glow orange in the growing light. The far side of the courtyard was fifty yards away. The packed sand roadway passed through a narrow opening in a crumbling six-foot-high stone wall. Murph could see the plume of dust nearing them, weaving back and forth. The monastery remained quiet.

"Let's meet him at the gate. If he comes into the courtyard, it could be tough to get back out if there's trouble."

Carli nodded in agreement. The sun was just about to appear, the horizon a glowing rim of orange in front of them. The sky was increasingly blue, with the gray of night fading away. They burst from concealment with Carli in the lead. The sharp crack of a gun-shot shattered the calm, and the mud brick above Murph's head exploded, showering him with razor sharp particles of stone. He ducked instinctively, losing his balance as his foot slipped on the soft sand attempting to push off. He braced himself with his palms and kept going. "RUN!" Another shot, but no sign of where the bullet went this time. The crack of the gun was to his left.

Out of his peripheral vision, he saw Omar step out of the shadows in the doorway to the mosque. His hands were tucked calmly in his coat pockets, and he was smiling broadly again. Murph studied him as he ran, and noticed another gunman on one knee in the entrance. His arm was extended, holding a long-barreled pistol. Murph jinked left as the pistol flamed and barked. The sand burst near Murph's feet. In the flash, he saw that the gunman's eyes were covered with a hooded band. *Night vision goggles. These guys are serious!* Murph dodged again, trying to keep himself between the shooter and Carli as she ran.

We're not going to make it! He heard the roar of the Land Rover's engine, becoming ever louder as it came closer. He could almost feel the weight of the shooter's eyes on his back. *Any time now.* Just as it seemed that they would come up a couple of steps short, the rising sun cleared the wall. Murph was momentarily blinded, and the top of the wall became an indistinct blur of heat waves with a giant orange ball behind it.

If Murph had been startled by the sudden appearance of the dawn, it was nothing compared to the searing pain the shooter felt as sunlight flooded into the night vision goggles. The black-robed gunman screamed, dropped his pistol, ripped the goggles off, and rubbed his aching eyes. Omar Bengdara cursed, squinting after his prey as they ran straight into the rising sun. He reached behind his back and pulled the Glock 9-mm from its holster in his waistband. He began firing wildly, not really able to see, yet hoping to hit something.

Murph realized the gift they had been given. This won't last long. He lengthened his stride to catch up to Carli. Thinking Omar would guess the gate was his goal, he grabbed Carli's arm and guided her toward a low point in the wall where the top stones had crumbled. He sprinted the last 20 yards to the wall, and without asking her opinion, swept her up and threw her over it. "What the," she barely had time to exclaim, and then she was gone.

Murph stole a quick glance back. Bengdara had the pistol in his outstretched arms, feet spread apart, and it was aimed straight at him. He vaulted the stone wall, pulling up with his hands and rolling over the top on his back. Two more cracks of the pistol. The stone exploded inches from his head, and then he felt a burning pain across his stomach. He fell off the top of the wall, and landed in a heap, resting against the still cold, mud-brick wall.

Saleh raced up and turned the Land Rover, scattering crushed limestone everywhere. Murph struggled to get up. Carli pulled him up and dragged him to the SUV where Saleh pushed open the front door. Carli opened the back door, and Murph dove across the seat. Carli jumped up front, and Saleh mashed the accelerator to the floor. They sped away, even before the front door closed, leaving a rooster tail of dust and sand.

Chapter 29

Teddy Roosevelt had said, "There is nothing so exhilarating as being shot at and missed." Carli was bursting with the adrenalin of the moment, giddy with the excitement of the escape. The pain of her bruises and scrapes had not yet registered in her brain.

"What's the matter, Murph, did you twist your old knee again?" she teased.

He struggled to sit up and pulled a bloody hand from under his shirt. He studied the mix of red and brown mud filling in the creases in his palm. "No. I think it's a bit more than that, this time."

"Oh my God!" Her euphoria vanished. She squeezed between the seats and into the back.

Saleh peeked back for a second and then continued his frenetic driving. He knew they had to put as much distance between them and the pursuit as possible. "There is a first-aid kit in the back."

The Land Rover had reached the highway, and the ride had smoothed considerably as they raced toward Cairo. Carli had retrieved the first-aid kit and was proving to be a fair medic. She cleaned the wound and began to bandage it as best she could.

"It's not as bad as it looked at first," she reported. "The bullet grazed you, but it made about a four-inch long trench in the skin. It's superficial, but I know it hurts."

Saleh chuckled. "Then you shall have a nice scar… for the ladies," he pronounced knowingly.

"I was lucky, and God smiled upon us." Murph pushed himself up in the seat and kissed Carli. "Thanks!" He wiped the blood off his hands using some water and a towel.

Murph reached into his pocket and pulled out the satellite phone. He punched the number for Derek, hoping they would be up early. "We're not safe yet. We have escaped one problem, but old Omar doesn't strike me as one to give up easily."

The phone rang twice and then clicked. "*Air Apprentice*, how may we serve you?" Derek's voice was mocking, in spite of the early hour.

"Are you at the airport?" Murph demanded.

"What? No pleasantries? No 'How are you, Derek? How was your weekend, Derek? Did you sleep well?'"

"Derek!"

"Whoa! So, grumpy! I take it that things didn't go as planned with your little girlfriend, eh?"

"Derek, I've got a problem here! Are you at the hangar?"

"Yeah. We're here. We have to leave this morning and go home to get Dr. Farouk."

"Great! I need to get out of Egypt right away… and Carli, too!"

"Sorry to rain on your parade boss, but we're waiting on fuel, and it could be hours for them to get around to us here."

"How much gas do you have?"

"We could fly three to four hours, I guess. That would get us anywhere in the Med. What's the rush?"

"Derek, we're in trouble. I need to get out of Egypt within the hour, or we may not be able to get out at all. File a flight plan for wherever you can go. You can refuel there before going to Washington."

"I don't like it, but they did make you the boss! Do you have your ruby slippers on?"

Carli looked puzzled, but Murph finished the call. "Yes, and I'm clicking my heels together, but believe me, we're definitely not in Kansas anymore!"

"Well, I'll take you to Athens. That was our next stop anyway. Then, if you like, you're on your own!"

Murph shut the phone and looked up at Saleh. He had heard every word. "I will drive straight to the airport. I know the way well!" The Land Rover was flying down the road, entering the outskirts of Cairo. The lanes had been empty as they began, but were filling quickly. It was Monday morning, and Cairo was coming to life even at this early hour.

Carli and Murph filled Saleh in on their exploits of the night before, leaving out the part where she had not returned the scroll as planned. Murph had popped a couple of Advil, and the pain was starting to subside. The Sat phone buzzed, and Murph answered it.

Derek sounded concerned. "Departure is all set. They seem to be a bit edgy about the immediate departure. They don't like sudden changes. What's your ETA?"

Murph looked at Saleh, who held up both hands, fingers extended. "Ten minutes! And we'll be coming in hot!"

"Roger that!"

Murph and Carli made sure they were packed up, as the SUV raced along. Saleh had kept Murph's roller bag with them. Any attempt at small talk died quickly. Saleh gripped the wheel tightly, his attention focused on the traffic. Trying to avoid unnecessary attention, he forced himself to drive slowly onto the airport grounds approaching Terminal 5. After the sudden appearance of Omar this morning, Murph wasn't ready to see the lack of obvious pursuit as a good thing. They made it to the terminal without incident and pulled up behind the Gulfstream.

Chapter 30

Murph did not understand the hunt as well as Omar Bengdara. He was a Bedouin and knew the value of not tiring himself out. Let the prey run. If you know where it is going, then meet it at its lair. Omar had not raced after the fleeing Land Rover. He merely fired a few shots to get them running, then calmly opened his satellite phone.

The phone was answered after a few rings. "Speak," came the cool reply.

"Master, they have left Saqqara. Saleh has them. I expect they will go to the airport and attempt to leave on the Gulfstream. You can have their departure revoked, and I will have them trapped there."

The answer came with an icy chill. "That would lead to many questions. Would you like to explain to the party how you let them leave Saqqara with the scroll? No... I think not." The voice paused for a moment to think. "Assemble a team and meet me at the airport. I will deal with this myself. No more mistakes."

"Yes, Master." He took the rebuke without remorse.

"And, Omar, find our Dr. Narmer and give him my regards." The phone abruptly went silent.

Omar shut the phone and walked calmly back toward the monastery, replacing the spent magazine in his pistol with fresh ammunition.

Chapter 31

The clean hangar and gleaming airplane made Carli and Murph look all the more haggard. Dirty and scratched, with a scruffy growth of beard and a bloodstained shirt, Murph was a tattered version of the dashing young dentist that Derek and Ed had dropped off only a day ago.

"What the hell happened to you?" Derek was shocked. "Yesterday you left in a black Mercedes, and today you come back in a dusty Land Rover with... are those bullet holes in the back?"

Murph bent down and put his finger in one of two fresh round holes in the lift gate. He looked at his finger. *Hmm. 9mm, I know who that is.* "It's a long story!"

"It'd make a good movie, kind of like the Egyptian 'Hangover'... but you did get the girl!" He smiled a wolfish grin.

Murph introduced Carli to the pilots and then convinced them to get started. They had finished the pre-flight already, so they began to wind up the engines. Carli went over to Saleh first, while

Murph put his bag onto the plane.

"Thank you." She hugged him tightly. "I don't know how I can ever thank you enough!"

"Miss Chamoun, you have done more than you know for me and for Egypt. In time, you will be able to report your discoveries and we all will see the glory of the Pharaohs once again. Please be safe, and may the Gods be with you!"

Saleh turned to Murph and embraced him. The power of the clinch nearly took his breath away. "Dr. Murphy, do not believe that just because you have left Egypt that you are safe. Your enemies are powerful, and they have a long reach. But the Gods smile on you, for you have boldness in your heart. I am pleased I was able to help you."

"Saleh, I am honored to have you as a friend! Until we meet again!" They shook hands. Murph hurriedly led Carli into the G-550 and raised the stairs.

Murph leaned into the cockpit and reported, "All aboard. Let's get this puppy airborne."

Derek nodded, "When all the passengers are in their seats with seatbelts fastened and tray tables in fully upright and locked positions."

"Smart Ass!" Murph called and limped back to the galley as they began to taxi out. He looked at the Jameson longingly, but grabbed two water bottles. He opened one and gave it to Carli, then slumped into the seat next to her and belted himself. For now, they both were too stunned to talk.

I guess Omar gave up. Murph wanted to believe it, and there had been no signs of pursuit. *Time will tell, I guess.* Carli was sound asleep next to him. He felt the adrenalin ebbing away, and he closed his eyes as well.

Chapter 32

Within seconds of Murph and Carli going through the door of the plane, Saleh returned to the Land Rover and pulled out of the terminal as quickly as he could. He opened his satellite phone, reporting, "They are on the plane. They fly to Athens to refuel. She did not leave the scroll. I observed that it remains taped to her leg… Yes, Sir." He shut the phone and smiled as he drove slowly out of the airport, losing himself in the growing morning traffic.

Chapter 33

The pitch of the engines rose to a harsh whine, and the Gulfstream accelerated down the runway and into the brilliant blue sky. Its sleeping passengers rested, feeling free of the oppressive weight of Egypt. Their flight across the Mediterranean began without a bump, as Murph drifted through semi-consciousness. *It feels so good to be free. It was easy to clear the airport and get out of Egypt. We didn't even have to clear customs.*

We didn't clear customs! They let us go. It was too easy. Murph sat up with a start. Carli was sleeping peacefully, her features calm and her breathing deep and even. He covered her with a blanket and walked up to the cockpit. He buzzed, and Derek opened the door to the flight deck. He motioned for Derek to come back, and the pilot took off his headset and came into the main cabin.

"What's up?" He looked Murph over. "You look like Hell. You want to tell me what happened?"

"Bad shit going on with the dig. Local politics, but they think Carli knows something and they are out to get her. Pretty nasty guys, and they are playing for keeps. I just wanted to get her out safely and leave it all behind."

But who are they?" Derek was confused, and to be honest, it didn't make much sense to Murph either. It sure sounded crazy when he said it out loud!

"I don't know who *they* are. We had a run in with a couple of goons, one of whom is well connected with the ruling generals in Egypt." That part Murph knew was true. "When we left, did you get any trouble from the tower? Any resistance?"

"No, but I was worried that Customs would give us a problem, since I didn't see any paperwork on Carli. They denied our refueling request, but everything else went smooth as silk."

"Yeah, way too smooth." Murph paced around in the small space. "I smell a rat. They let us go, and I expect a warm reception when we land."

Derek agreed. "That would make the most sense. They know our flight plan."

Murph smacked his fist into his palm. "Then we have to change it up. Do something different." A plan was forming now, but it was just a wild idea. *Time to run with it.* It was all he had. "How much fuel do we have?"

"Not a whole lot. Why?"

"Change course! Take us to Rome!"

Derek thought a minute. "We should be able to get there, but then what?"

"Just get me to Rome, and I'll take it from there. I did a semester there when I was in college. I don't want you guys in any more trouble than you already are."

"*Now* you think about little ol' me." He smiled. "I'm in this all the way. I'll get you guys in to the executive airport near the Vatican. I've been there before, and it'll be easier than the main airport since they aren't expecting us and we don't have a reservation. After that, *may the Force be with you!*"

Murph grinned and gave Derek a big hug, drawling "I luv you, Man!"

"Get off me, you idiot! I've got work to do!" Derek turned back to the cockpit, shaking his head.

Murph stroked the stubble on his chin and felt the plane bank as they changed course for Italy. They had been running around blind. Being chased and shot at was getting on his nerves. It was time to get some answers and take control of the situation. *Knowledge is power... so think!*

Murph went to the galley and made himself a cup of coffee. The smell sharpened his senses, and he grabbed the backpack to get his computer. The bag was incredibly heavy, and he remembered the pipe he had brought along. Somehow, having a weapon had made him feel more secure. He took it out and marveled at its weight. It was bronze and obviously ancient.

Looking more closely, it wasn't a solid cylinder as he had at first thought. It had metal end pieces, and the shaft seemed to be made in two halves. One end had a shallow depression, like a cone that ended in an opening the size of a pencil. He was studying that end when it turned in his hands, shifting just a bit. The ends were caps! He worked the two ends off, and the cylinder opened like a book.

The outer casing of the pipe was bronze, but inside it was stone, and the open end connected with a row of shapes inside. *It's an investment, a mold for casting gold!* The shapes inside had been carved in wax and then burnt out. *The lost wax technique*, Murph suddenly realized. *And what are the shapes?* Murph nearly dropped the artifact. *This is a mold to cast nine gold teeth!*

Why would the dentist to the Pharaoh want to cast nine gold teeth? Maybe Carli had the answer to that one. He looked over at her, and she stirred slightly, changing positions and snuggling deeper in the blanket. *She can sleep a bit longer. She needs it.*

Murph got up and went to the bathroom. He decided to take some time to shower and shave. Feeling refreshed, he changed into a clean polo shirt and charcoal grey slacks, putting back on his comfortable loafers. He felt like a new man as he came out to find Carli awake and studying the contents of the backpack.

"Would you like some coffee?" he asked. "Cream and two sugars, as usual."

"You remember!"

He poured the coffee and gave her a steaming mug. She drank it eagerly. "The galley isn't really stocked well for this trip, but I still have a few granola bars." He tossed them onto the table and sat down across from her in one of the leather captain's chairs.

She thanked him for breakfast, took a quick bite and then showed him what had gotten her attention. "Did you really look at this knife?"

"I was too busy cutting your handcuffs off to study it."

"Oh, yeah! Thanks for that!" She handed the knife to him and pointed out how the blade was two separate pieces of metal that had been joined by a leather strap to the handle. "This is a psh-kef knife! Given where we found it, it may be the one used for Pharaoh himself. It's a monumental find. Look, the blades aren't corroded a bit after all this time, and they are incredibly sharp."

"I see that. While you were sleeping, I looked at the bronze pipe I used to lay out your friend Narmer. It's really an investment, you know, a mold used for casting gold. The form would make nine gold teeth. Banded in two arches, five on the top and four on the bottom. Does that make any sense to you?"

"THAT"S IT!" She jumped out of the chair and hugged him, nearly knocking Murph over.

Chapter 34

Carli ran to the backpack and pulled out her journal, flipping quickly to the last page of entries as she walked back. She set the journal on the table in front of Murph and pulled out her iPhone. She grabbed Murph's MacBook Pro and uploaded the photos she had taken in the tomb. It took a few moments, as she manipulated the images and magnified the part of the hieroglyphics she wanted. She placed the laptop in front of Murph and perched on the arm of his chair.

Carli ran her finger along the screen, indicating the symbols as she read. "This details the Opening of the Mouth Ritual for Djoser. It's pretty unremarkable, until we get here." She tapped the screen.

Murph was thinking how beautiful her fingers were. Her nails were carefully manicured, but kept short since she was always working with her hands at the dig. She always rubbed in lotion to keep them soft, in spite of all her time in the sand and dust. *Focus! Pay attention!* "Yes, I remember. We have to make the Pharaoh able to eat in the afterlife... Do you think he likes sushi?"

She elbowed him in the arm. "Can you be serious for a minute?" Her smile softened the blow, and she continued, "Djoser's death is recorded to have been sudden. In the main dig at Saqqara, there is a great deal written about the rise of Pharaoh and his accomplishments during his reign. He was a warrior king who conquered extensive territory and dramatically increased the wealth of Egypt. The records of his death and the succession in the kingdom after him are lost to time. There is some mention of a Queen, but her name is not known. It's as if the historical record, immediately after the death of Djoser, was intentionally erased. That's what makes the writings on the walls in the dentists' chamber so significant."

She stood up and began pacing, though there really wasn't much room to move in the small cabin of the Gulfstream. "The hieroglyphics on the wall detail the process of the Opening of the

Mouth Ritual performed for Djoser. My interpretation of the records shows a dispute among the dentists. Iy Mry, the chief dentist, performed the ritual as was the custom, but Pharaoh was missing several teeth... nine to be exact!" She grinned like the Cheshire cat! "The missing teeth should have been fabricated of gold and wired in place so Pharaoh would have a full set of teeth to eat with in the afterlife. There appears to have been something of a falling out between Iy Mry and Sekhem Ka, because during the ritual, Sekhem Ka disturbed the proceedings and stole the golden teeth before Iy Mry could place them in the mouth of the mummy. The records speak of a curse, damning Pharaoh to an eternity in limbo!"

The light was beginning to dawn for Murph. "So Djoser has been wandering around for thousands of years looking for his teeth?"

"Well, metaphorically speaking, yes. I'm sure that Iy Mry could not admit that Pharaoh's teeth had been stolen. That would have meant certain and immediate death for all the priests involved, beginning with him. The records in the main tomb of Pharaoh make no mention of anything out of the ordinary in Djoser's burial. I would have to guess that Iy Mry and his assistant priests acted like they had finished the ritual and that they intended to complete the ceremony after they recovered the missing gold. However, Pharaoh would not be able to cross over into the afterlife since he did not have all his teeth and the ritual was incomplete. The hieroglyphics in the dentists' chamber go on to say that once the teeth are replaced, then Pharaoh will return to life. Since Pharaoh cannot be at peace as long as his mouth is incomplete, upon the return of the gold teeth, he will return and wreak his vengeance on all who cursed him."

Murph couldn't help chuckling. "So let me get this straight. Thousands of years ago, a professional disagreement between two dentists led to an evil curse, and a Pharaoh is doomed to wander for all eternity because he doesn't have his gold teeth! And once he gets his teeth back, Djoser will return to get even."

"That's not the half of it!" Carli pulled up her pant leg and removed the zip-lock bag containing the scroll. "This says that Djoser was murdered... and one of the dentists did it!"

"What?"

"The hand-written notes here say that Pharaoh developed a toothache."

Carli went to the galley and got the first-aid kit. She removed a pair of latex gloves from the kit and put them on. She opened the plastic bag and carefully removed the scroll. She smoothed open the papyrus so they could both see it. She quickly photographed it with her phone.

Murph had no idea what many of the symbols meant, but he had seen the eye over the tusk symbol enough to know that meant dentist. One thing was perfectly clear. These were the carefully prepared clinical records of the dentist, indicating his diagnosis and description of treatment. A drawing in the left margin showed the lower jaw of a patient with swelling beside a molar. The next drawing indicated how the dentist had lanced the infection to drain it. Egyptian dentists knew that pain came from pressure building in the tooth and bone. They didn't know about bacteria, but they had come to a good conclusion that the pain would go away if the pressure were released.

Carli confirmed Murph's interpretation. "The dentist's notes state that Pharaoh's pain had been resolved by draining the infection. He removed the tooth and the dentist then reported that he expected the patient to recover fully. The next entry, however, indicates that another dentist treated Djoser, applying an arsenic paste to the extraction site."

Murph was able to add, "Because the poison seeped slowly through the wound into Pharaoh's body, his death would have been slow enough to have appeared natural."

Murph sat shaking his head thoughtfully as Carli carefully wrapped the scroll again and put it away. "You're holding the key to a five-thousand-year-old murder mystery. But it seems there are people who are very concerned that word of this doesn't get out now. Why do they care?"

"We do seem to have more questions than answers." She sat down heavily in a chair, the energy draining out of her.

"Well, I know the place to go to get answers." Murph got up and knelt in front of Carli. He held her hands and looked up at her. "We've got a mystery to solve, and we're going to Rome! Take a few minutes and splash some water on your face. We'll get some fresh clothes for you when we land."

She smiled weakly and went to freshen up.

96

Chapter 35

Carli felt much better, and Murph thought she looked radiant, even without any makeup. She had pulled her hair back and put on the ball cap again. She drank some orange juice from the galley and walked over to find Murph on his computer talking to someone on Facebook.

"Old girlfriend?" she teased, running her fingers through his hair.

"Hardly!" He smiled. "I played volleyball with a guy for a couple of years in high school, and he's playing now for a team in Rome. He's on his way to practice later, but he'll pick us up at the airport on his way."

"Chauffeur service. I like the way you travel, Murphy!"

The cockpit door opened and Derek walked back, shaking his head. "Good news and bad."

Murph shrugged. "Good news first, I guess."

"We're cleared into Rome. Should be on the ground in about 45 minutes."

"And the bad?"

"Your former employer is on his way in the other G-550. He won't get into Rome for a few hours, and we are not to let you leave the plane until he arrives."

"That doesn't sound good. I'm not ready to face Dr. Farouk yet. I have a few too many questions that I can't answer. "

Derek nodded. "I'm a pilot, not a cop. If he wants you detained, I'm not the guy to do it. However, Ed up there is more the company man than I am. He could be trouble for you."

Murph patted Derek on the shoulder. "Thanks for the heads up. I'll take over from here. The less you know, the better when Manny gets here. I owe you... Big!"

"Yes, you do!" Derek agreed and then became very serious. "Be careful. I'm worried about you. I don't know what's going on, but there's some bad shit about to go down. I can feel it!"

"Thanks, Man. Take care of yourself, too. For now, just land the plane, and stay in the cockpit."

As soon as Derek closed the door to the flight deck, Murph told Carli what had happened. They didn't have much time, so he had to work quickly. He had Carli carefully wrap the artifacts in cloth napkins from the galley and place them in the backpack. He collected a few more water bottles and snacks, as well as his toiletries and a change of underwear from his luggage. He put on a grey cotton sweater over a black open collared shirt. He found a windbreaker in the crew closet. It was sized for a female member of the flight crew, probably Tami, and was a good fit for Carli. It was black and had the logo of the Washington Center for Esthetic and Restorative Excellence on it. *How appropriate!* Even Carli smiled as she stowed it in the backpack. "Now I feel an official part of the team!" The backpack had become heavy, but it was all they could take with them.

Murph could see the glory of Rome out the windows as they made the final turns onto the approach to Ciampino Airport. He went over his plan with Carli. She took it with a grain of salt, but agreed with it since she didn't have any better ideas. The landing gear was coming out when Murph finished preparations, wrapping a fifth of Scotch in a bar towel and crouching in the coat closet just behind the cockpit door.

Ciampino Airport had opened in 1916 and is one of the oldest airports still in operation. It was Rome's main airport until Leonardo da Vinci-Fiumicino Airport opened in 1960. With low-cost carriers like Ryanair and EasyJet making Ciampino their destination of choice, passenger traffic had exploded recently. The Gulfstream had been granted landing clearance, but there was no space on the tarmac immediately available. It was Murph's good luck that they were diverted to an area of open taxiway off the end of one of the ancient hangars until the executive terminal had cleared.

The G-550 had braked to a stop, but the engines continued to idle when Carli popped the door and lowered the stairs, just as Murph had instructed her to do. As he had expected, when the open-hatch alarm sounded in the cockpit, Ed Salas had jumped up and opened the door. He immediately saw Carli poised to go down the stairs. As he rushed to stop her, he never saw Murph rise up behind him and swing the bottle. Even though it was wrapped in a bar towel, the Scotch made a thud as it struck Ed across the back of his head, and he went down, face first onto the carpet. He didn't get up, and Murph was immediately concerned that he had hit him too hard. Checking quickly, Murph was relieved to find that, although Ed was out cold, he was breathing. He swept up the body gently and laid him out on the couch. Murph opened the Scotch and splashed a generous amount on Ed's face and neck, loosening the collar on his uniform.

Derek had come out from behind the controls and was surveying the damage. "They teach you that in dental school?"

"I had some ROTC frat brothers in undergrad that liked to show off what they were learning," Murph admitted. "You should get the same treatment, otherwise Manny will be suspicious."

"I know," Derek cringed, "just make sure you don't leave any marks."

"Don't worry," Murph promised, "I'll spare your pretty face. Just enough to leave a good bruise!" Without waiting for any protests, Murph swung the bottle again and hit Derek above his right ear.

"Ouch! That hurt!" But a bump started to form as Derek rubbed it. He went back to the cockpit and sat in the left pilot's seat. He buckled, shut down the engines, and then slumped against the window. Murph thought it was a pretty convincing act of being unconscious, as if he had done this before. Derek gave a quick thumbs-up, and Murph backed out the door and joined Carli. They went down the stairs and ducked under the wing.

The shadow of the Gulfstream's tail extended to the edge of the hangar, so they quickly made their way to the security of the building and around the back. Their luck continued to hold, as the ancient chain link fence surrounding this corner of the airport had a rusted hole near the hangar. Obviously, they were not the first people to use this opening, so they didn't wait to celebrate their good fortune. Squeezing through the fence, they entered a low hedge and then passed onto Superstrada No. 7 around the airport. Murph had studied a map of Ciampino while on the plane and knew the right way to go.

Walking briskly, they soon covered the 300 yards to the Grande Raccordo Anulare (GRA), the Greater Ring Road that encircled Rome. Murph and Carli walked to a bus stop and calmly sat down. Having fled Egypt and now entered Italy illegally, their problems were continuing to mount. In spite of it all, they looked like a young couple enjoying the bright sunshine of a Roman holiday as their ride pulled up.

Murph had texted Pat Ansler before they had landed, and he was right on time. Carli was astonished to see the Fiat Panda pull up in front of them. The driver was grinning from ear to ear, waving frantically as he came to a stop. Carli was astounded as the microscopically small car opened and the gangly frame unwound from behind the wheel. All arms and legs, Pat was just under seven feet tall, with jet-black hair that stuck up wildly in all directions.

"Do you have any friends that are inconspicuous?" she asked casually.

"Nope!" Murph stood up to greet his friend, and they hugged, slapping each other on the back with gusto.

"Murph, it's great to see you!" He couldn't hide the fact that he was clearly thrilled. "And who's the *bella bambina*, your beautiful girl!"

"Pat, I'd like you to meet Carli!" Pat took her hand and kissed it, then kissed her on both cheeks and hugged her.

"OK. OK. That's enough. Turn off the gigolo stuff. This one's mine!"

Pat looked hurt. "You take the fun out of everything!"

Carli agreed. "He has a way of doing that."

"Hey!" Now it was Murph's turn to look crestfallen.

Pat grinned, "I like her already!"

Pat led Carli to the Fiat and opened the door, letting her get into the back seat. Murph got in as Pat folded himself behind the wheel again, and they accelerated onto the highway and headed for Rome.

Chapter 36

Murph breathed an audible sigh of relief, but still was looking around for signs of pursuit. Although he was trying to be as nonchalant as possible, Pat noticed his hyper-alertness and frowned.

"So… what brings you so suddenly to Rome? Last I knew you were still in D.C. That Apprentice show aired last over the weekend, and I know you lost to the girl in the final. You got screwed over by the way." Pat swerved around a truck and then back into the outside lane. "That taped months ago, I'm sure, so what have you been doing?" Pat looked Murph straight in the eyes. "And why are you looking around like you expect the bad guys from some Bond movie to show up?"

"It's a long story, and I really don't want to get you involved. I just needed a ride into Rome… and a couple of other favors."

"As you know, favors don't come cheap here in Italy. The price is information. It's really boring here, and I could use some excitement! So spill it!"

"OK. Here's the short form. Carli was working an archeological dig at a pyramid in Egypt. She made a discovery about a long-dead Pharaoh who may have been murdered. She called me and I came over to Cairo." Pat darted between slower cars again. Murph glanced into the back seat to see Carli hanging on for dear life, her eyes wide! "Since then, we have been on the run from some Arabs who want her back. We left Egypt in a hurry on the private jet of Dr. Farouk, and had to get into Italy without visas."

"You have been busy! Sounds like lots of fun!"

Pat stomped the accelerator to the floor, and the little Fiat jumped forward, just barely cutting in front of a vegetable truck and off the highway.

"Your driving is worse here than in the States!"

"Yeah, but they appreciate my talents more here. It's the Formula 1 culture!" He smiled broadly. "I'm saving up for a Ferrari."

"That'll make it better," Carli observed dryly from the back seat, her knuckles white as she gripped the seat.

Pat once again looked hurt. "So why do these Arabs care about a murder from thousands of years ago?"

"That's the part we can't figure out, but we didn't have the time to think about it much when they were shooting at us. I feel more in control here, where I know the city and can speak the language. I felt trapped in Egypt. Those guys were supposed to be well connected with hardliners in the government who have taken over control of Egypt since the fall of Murbarak.

"Who?"

"Don't you watch the news? Internet?"

"Not unless they have the sports scores!"

"Same old Pat!" Murph laughed. "Oh well, what I need now

is to change some dollars into Euros, and we need to get Carli some clothes. She left Egypt without any of her luggage."

"No problemo!" Pat cut a sharp right turn and entered a narrow cobblestone street. "I thought you were travelling rather light! I've got practice soon, but the Palazzetto dello Sport is in the Piazza Apollodoro. Nice shops there, but I'll run you by the bank first."

"You don't have any money either, as usual, right?"

"You know me too well." He turned around to Carli. "I never carry cash!"

"That's why I always got stuck with the bar bill," lamented Murph.

"Don't blame me… you always had it covered." He commented to Carli, "I'd stick with him if I were you. He takes good care of people!"

After a quick visit to an ATM, Murph felt much better with cash in his wallet. He hated to feel like he owed anyone. He always wanted to be in control of the situation, and that leadership was visible, whether or not he was trying. It was an ongoing joke with his friends that, no matter who was at the table or how many, whenever the waiter brought the check, it was always set down in front of Murph. It was so common now that, when the check was handed to Murph, everyone laughed! The server left the table shaking her head, wondering how she had missed the joke.

Pat drove quickly down the Via Guido Remi and into the Piazza Apollodoro. The ancient cobblestoned square was crowded with people, darting out of the way of the charging Fiat, as it dashed across the square and into the parking lot in front of the Palazzetto dello Sport.

In the middle of the Renaissance architecture of Rome, the Palazzetto dello Sport sat like some sort of alien spaceship that had landed in the middle of a traffic circle. Built for the 1960 Rome Olympics, its 3,500 seats rested under a prefabricated, ribbed concrete dome, braced by flying buttresses of gray concrete that stood out against red brick walls. It had been erected in 40 days and had all the charm of a warehouse. It was now the home for the volleyball matches of Roma Volley of the Italian Champions League, Pat's employer for the last two years.

Pat brought the Fiat screeching to a stop in a parking space on the circular driveway around the arena. As they got out, Carli stifled the urge to kiss the ground for their safe return, but she decided to be polite. "Thanks for the ride," she said as cheerfully as she could.

"Don't mention it!" Pat got his gym bag out of the hatch, and slung it over his shoulder. "I have to get some treatment on my bum shoulder before practice. Why don't you two take an hour and get your shopping done. Come in around six and I'll introduce you to the guys. Murph, you probably will recognize a couple of them." Americans playing in European leagues was not unusual and Murph had a number of former teammates scattered all throughout the continent. "Ciao!"

Pat walked into the arena without a backward glance. Carli just shook her head.

"He's crazy!"

"Yes," Murph agreed, "but you won't find a more loyal friend anywhere. We played club volleyball together in grade school and then in high school at Ignatius before he played for Loyola of Chicago. How many guys could you send a text after not seeing them for over four years and they would come straight to the airport to pick you up? No questions asked!"

"I'll say this for you, Michael Murphy, you have great friends, and those friendships are strong enough to last a lifetime!"

She held his hand in both of hers. Looking up at his face, a tear escaped her eye and rolled down her cheek. "After all, I called you in the middle of the night and you flew half-way around the world to get me. No questions asked…" Her voice broke on the last words.

He held her chin and wiped the tear away with his thumb. Murph pulled her close and she collapsed onto his chest. He could feel her relax as he kissed her lightly on the forehead and said, "Let's go get something pretty for you to wear and enjoy Rome. I have so much to show you."

Carli straightened up with a nod, and they walked off hand in hand across the cobblestones of the Piazza Apollodoro, looking every bit the loving couple on a Roman holiday.

Chapter 37

The Gulfstream G-550 turned off the end of the runway and taxied over to its mate sitting by the end of the hangar. The stationary plane was identical, except for the fact that it was surrounded by three police cars and a small horde of uniformed police combing the bushes behind the tail, their blue coats and trousers with a bright red stripe down the side made them impossible to miss. The G-550 had barely stopped, and the stairs were extending but not completely touching the ground, when Manny Farouk burst from the cabin. He went down the stairs two at a time, his face a mask, his lips drawn into a taut line. One of the uniformed Carabinieri blocked his way, extending a hand to his chest. Manny roughly swept the policeman's arm aside.

"Out of my way!"

"Signore! This is a crime scene. You cannot go in there."

"What crime? This is my plane and my crew. I will talk to them whenever I want."

The police captain was not used to being bullied. He pulled a notebook from his jacket pocket and a pen. "Your name, Signore?"

"Ask your Comandante Generale Beruni what happens to those who stand in the way of Manesh Farouk." He placed his forearm on the white sash and shoved the officer aside.

Capitano Abruzzo recognized true power when he saw it, so he decided discretion was the better course. He stepped back and called in on his radio for confirmation of his orders. It only took a minute, and the abrupt tone on the other end of the call changed his anger to dread. *I'm not paid enough for this*, Abruzzo thought. He called out sharply to his men, and they gave up their search and gathered by their black Alfa Romeo squad cars.

Abruzzo walked over to the open hatch of the plane and leaned his head up into the opening. "Signore Farouk! We will leave the aircraft to you. I will leave a few of my men if you have need of them. If not, we will be gone and not trouble you further."

Manny descended the stairs and faced Abruzzo, his anger fading. "Thank you for your offer, Capitano, but no further help will be necessary. This aircraft will be fueled immediately and it will depart. I will be spending a few days here in Rome, I believe. Thank you for your hospitality and for your care of my men. That will be all." And he turned on his heel and ascended the stairs.

Abruzzo closed his mouth and tried not to look as stunned as he felt. *I am Carabinieri, not meant to be dismissed.* But headquarters had been adamant, from the Comandante himself. *Do not interfere with Dr. Farouk.* He set his jaw and turned to his men. He barked at them, ordering them into the cars and back to work. They scattered like flies as he stalked to the passenger seat of his Alfa Romeo. He growled at his driver, and they set off back toward Rome.

Manny had found Ed Salas with an ice pack on the back of his head. Derek Whitman was in much better shape, although the knot over his ear was substantial. Both wounds would heal, but the tongue-lashing they were enduring now made the bruises seem like love taps.

Manny paced up and down the carpet between the seats. "You could not hold them on the plane? A dentist and a woman?"

Derek sat impassively and decided to take the punishment. Ed tried to make excuses, "They got the jump on us. We never saw it coming. Before I knew it, I was out cold!"

"SILENCE!" Manny cut him off with the wave of a hand, chopping the air crisply. "Do you know where they were going?"

Derek answered, "I didn't see them get out of the plane, but Dr. Murphy said he had been in Rome for a semester while in college and knew the city. He didn't share with me where he planned to go after we landed."

Manny considered this for a minute and could see that Derek was telling the truth. "Very well, I will have the aircraft refueled, and you will depart within the hour. You will go back to Cairo and sleep on the plane. I will contact you tomorrow. I have a cargo for you and then you will return to Washington." His voice turned icy, "And then we will meet again to consider your future." He left without another word, leaving Ed and Derek to twist in the wind.

Walking out of the Gulfstream, Manny waved over a member of the ground crew. In fluent Italian, he instructed that the planes both be fueled and readied for flight. He climbed into his airplane and stopped. He intentionally took a deep breath and exhaled, allowing the anger to escape.

He looked at Margaret, his assistant, in her usual perch with a laptop in front of her. She glanced up over the top rim of her glasses, which once again appeared ready to fall off the end of her nose.

Manny growled, "Whitmore and Salas know nothing. Murphy knocked them both out."

"I think you may have underestimated Michael. He seems much more resourceful than you thought." Margaret's assessment was calm and professional, as always.

"Time will tell. I have ordered them to fly to Cairo and await my orders. They can load the cargo tomorrow, and it will be in Washington by Wednesday. Make the arrangements!"

Margaret nodded and began typing. Manny walked back to the bar and poured a glass of Merlot. He contemplated the burgundy liquid as he rolled the glass in his hand. He savored the bouquet, sighed and drank.

"Where are they?"

Margaret's manicured nails clicked on the keyboard as she entered the commands. "Piazza Apollodoro. Currently stationary." She looked up at Manny. "What do you think he is going to do?"

"I'm not sure. I have studied his background. He was here at the Vatican for ten days while in high school and then did a quarter in Rome during undergraduate school. I believe he may have old friends here, but I do not know how close they are and of what value they will be to him."

"Do you think they suspect what is going on?" Margaret took off her glasses and chewed on the earpiece thoughtfully.

"Miss Chamoun has seen the hieroglyphics and was asking questions about the discrepancies in the ceremony. They have the bronze investment case, but I doubt they realize what they hold. They are clever, but they have no reason to suspect the danger they are in. We will pick them up and bring them back."

"They escaped Omar Bengdara. That is not a feat to be taken lightly."

"True enough, but as I have said, time will tell."

Margaret glanced down at her computer. "They are moving. They are crossing the piazza... heading toward the Palazzetto dello Sport?"

"Arrange for the team to meet me there." He finished his wine and stood, brushing off his tweed jacket and aligning the sharp crease in his black slacks. Assured that everything was perfect, he asked, "Is my driver here?"

"Yes, your car is just outside. Your immigration papers are stamped and ready for you." She handed him an envelope with his passport and visa. "Good luck."

"Yes, the hunt is about to begin, but it is almost too easy." Manny paused beside Margaret and looked at the map of Rome, as the red pushpin icon moved into the Palazzetto dello Sport. "The capability of GPS locators in phones is amazing." His laugh was bitter and without a trace of mirth, as he walked out of the Gulfstream and into the afternoon sun.

Chapter 38

Carli's simple style made shopping easy. It was a relaxing, fun break for them to wander the piazza, selecting the basics she needed to add to the jeans that were stowed in the backpack. She selected a bright green canvas shoulder bag and quickly filled it with necessities. Much to Murph's delight, the last boutique was perfect, and Carli virtually danced out of the dressing room in a burgundy sundress. She twirled in front of him, as he reached down and swept her up, swinging her around. The black Italian leather flats were as comfortable as they were stylish. She released the ponytail and added pearl clips to sweep back the hair from her eyes.

Laughing like kids, they settled down for a bite of dinner in a café. As the waiter brought Chianti and fresh bread with basil and garlic infused olive oil, they realized how long it had been since they had eaten. They ravenously devoured the bread, salad, and wonderfully light angel hair pasta with seafood in a white wine broth. It was much easier to think clearly with a full stomach. A plan was forming for Murph as they finished and headed back to the arena.

The sun was starting to set, turning the piazza golden. The buildings picked up the red and later purple hues. A hint of the rising moon showed in the east. All in all, it was the perfect end to a strange day. The sunrise in the shadow of the pyramid seemed like a surreal memory now.

They entered the Palazzetto dello Sport, and Murph could hear the familiar squeak of court shoes on wood and the smack of hands on leather volleyballs. It was like coming home.

Pat whistled to them and waved. They descended the long steps between the rows of bleachers to reach the floor, which was sunken below ground level. Carli's presence immediately generated the usual Italian whistles and catcalls. She blushed and sat in the front row, trying not to look too embarrassed. Murph walked onto the floor, as Pat introduced him to the coach and other players.

"Why, if it isn't the great Mike Murphy!"

Murph whirled around and was nearly tackled, ending up being lifted off the floor. "Jeremy!" Murph was genuinely stunned. "I didn't know you were over here. This is fantastic!"

Murph led Jeremy to meet Carli. "Carli, this is Jeremy Woodley. They say that white men can't jump, but they've never seen this guy! We played together at Ohio State."

Carli shook his hand and let Murph get back to his reunion. The coach, Alessandro Giacchino, blew his whistle. "Hey! We have a practice here. If you want to join in, we have need for a setter! Otherwise, butt out."

Jeremy took Murph's side. "He's the best setter in Ohio. I'll take him with me!" Pat joined them as well.

Murph slipped off his loafers, Jeremy tossed him a spare pair of court shoes, and Murph set for the hitting lines as practice resumed. It had been a while since Murph had played, but it felt good to be moving around again. His abdomen burned, which reminded him of their narrow escape. Had it only been this morning?

Murph was interrupted when Carli whistled and called his name. He looked up, and she gestured urgently toward the door. Murph did a double take, but there he was, Manny Farouk, with three steroid infused helpers, heads shaved and muscles bulging out of silk t-shirts that were several sizes too small.

"How did they find us?" Carli's voice shook with fear.

Murph shrugged. "Doesn't matter. Grab our stuff. We've gotta go!"

Carli shouldered the backpack and her bag, taking Murph's loafers as well. Murph looked at Jeremy and Pat. "Trouble!" He inclined his head at the three goons now coming down separate aisles to the floor. Manny stood near the door, simply supervising.

Pat looked up as the trap continued to close. "My car's out there, behind them. No way to get to it!"

Jeremy didn't bat an eye. "Come with me. Pat, you slow them down a bit."

"Right, but how?"

Murph realized he still had a ball in his hand. The nearest goon had moved onto the floor thirty feet behind them. In one smooth motion, Murph coiled and rotated, heaving the ball with lightning speed. The muscle-bound stalker had obviously never spent any time near a volleyball court and was caught by surprise. The leather ball struck him squarely on the forehead, snapping his neck back. He stumbled over the first row of bleachers and went down. Murph didn't stop to see if he got up. As they started to run, Murph saw the spare net coiled at his feet. He grabbed the net and threw it to Pat. "Catch some fish with this, will you?"

"Great idea!"

It was a race now. Carli and Jeremy were in the lead, with Murph charging to catch up, running up the aisle, taking the concrete steps three at a time. They could hear the shouting behind them. Murph stole a quick glance, and he saw Pat and several other players blocking the path of the goons with the spare net. It wouldn't hold up long, but it gave them enough time to reach the upper ring and dash out the door.

Jeremy led them along the building and pulled a motor scooter from the wall. He started the Vespa while he handed the two helmets to Murph and Carli. Murph quickly changed out of Jeremy's shoes as well. As they boarded the scooter, Jeremy said, "Good luck! Just text Pat and tell him where you left the Vespa. That was fun, let's do it again sometime!"

Murph gave him a quick hug and sped off through the parking lot, just as Manny and his three "assistants" came out of the arena. Murph smiled as he realized that one of the three was a bit wobbly. Their pursuers ran for the cars. Much to Murph's dismay, the lights on two dark sedans lit up, and the chase was on.

Murph chose the smallest alley he could find and raced down it on the scooter. He had the advantage of smaller size, but they knew the area better. He needed to think, not just run blindly.

Carli sat behind him, wearing the backpack and holding her bag. It was reassuring to feel her arms wrapped tight around his waist. They cut up and down alleys, hoping not to trap themselves in a blind one. Just when Murph thought he had lost them, the scooter came out into a piazza. A parked Alfa Romeo's lights popped on, nearly blinding Murph. He narrowly escaped by driving onto the sidewalk, scattering pedestrians like birds as he went, before racing into a park.

"They were waiting for us... but how? They seem to know where we are."

Carli had been thinking about that as well. "Did they give you anything that might have a GPS tracker in it? Watch, computer, phone?"

"That's it! The satellite phone! Margaret gave it to me before coming to Cairo. I could kiss you!"

Murph pulled off into a dark shadow behind a church and stopped the scooter. He took the backpack off Carli and pulled out the satellite phone. He was about to smash it, but Carli stopped his hand.

"I have a better idea. Let me have it, and you drive!"

"OK. You're the boss" and he sped off again.

They wove in and out of traffic, eventually ending up on the Viale Guissepe Mazzini. As they entered a traffic circle, Carli spotted what she wanted. "Get close to that bus!"

As the traffic slowed a bit, Murph maneuvered close behind the bus. The double decker tour bus had no passengers on the top level. Carli carefully lobbed the phone into the open upper deck, and they sped away in the opposite direction of the bus.

Trying to put as much distance between themselves and the bus without attracting attention, they went as far as the Musei Vaticani, then slowed down, and eventually pulled off at a café. Murph parked the Vespa and locked it in a visible spot in front of the museum, then texted Pat about the location of the scooter for Jeremy. He waited for a moment, hoping for a response, but there was none. There was nothing more they could do.

Choosing a café table back in the shadows, they stopped to think and plan, in the flickering light of a candle set in an empty Chianti bottle. It would have been romantic except for the fact that they had been chased all day.

"Murph, I'm scared. What are we going to do?"

"I have friends at the Vatican who should be able to help us figure this out. I know how to get in, but not until 7:00 a.m. We need a place to hide overnight, preferably where there are lots of people."

"That last group, the ones with your boss Manny... Omar wasn't with them."

"True. They didn't look Arab. Maybe they're local muscle. Mob connections?"

"I don't know. I just want to find someplace to hide and relax. But where can we go. It's late on a Monday night, and the café is closing."

She was right. The waitress was looking at them and the check she had placed in front of Murph some time ago. He pulled out his wallet and counted the correct amount for her latte and his espresso. No sooner had he set it down, than the server swooped in to pick it up.

"I guess we should take the hint and move on. Are you ready?"

Murph started to rise and pull back Carli's chair. "Wait a minute! What day did you say it is?"

Carli stared at him. "It's Monday night, silly. Why?"

Murph started grinning and then laughing. Carli thought he had finally lost it. "What's the matter?"

"Nothing!" He said, "I figured it out. It's Monday night! Are you ready for some football?"

And he grabbed her hand, leading her from the café. The weight of the world had been lifted because he knew just what to do. He started whistling as they walked, singing along to the Hank Williams, Jr. tune in his mind. "All my rowdy friends are here on Monday night!"

Chapter 39

It was past midnight when they walked down the narrow cobblestone alley and into the Piazza dei Quinti. The light of the half-moon glistened off the dome of St Peter's Basilica, looking down on them. They clearly had come within the shadow of the Vatican.

All was quiet though, and the streets were nearly deserted. Carli expected Murph to continue toward Vatican City, but he veered off to the opposite side of the piazza and into another narrow street, the Via Germanico. Carli was concerned, but Murph walked with a profound sense of purpose. She was surprised when he went up to a simple doorway, seeming very proud of himself.

"Here we are!" Murph waved his hand with a flourish, indicating the sign over the door.

"The Clevelander?" Carli was mystified.

Murph pushed open the door, and the quiet darkness was flooded with soft yellow light, and the sound of excited voices, that burst into a roar. Murph ushered Carli in, and as her eyes became accustomed to the light, she saw that The Clevelander was a bar – but not just any bar. The walls were filled with jerseys and pennants. The brown and orange of the Cleveland Browns, the red and navy of the Indians, wine and gold of the Cavaliers, and of course, the scarlet and gray of the Ohio State Buckeyes. The bar was packed with people tonight, many in Browns jerseys, all focused on the flat screen televisions over the bar.

"It's Monday Night Football. I finally remembered that the Browns are playing the Eagles tonight. With the time difference, they'll be up all night here. We can stay until morning, and no one will find us!"

"Leave it to you to find a sports bar in a time of need!" All she could do was smile and shake her head. "Well, we might as well get a beer!"

"My thoughts exactly!"

"And I suppose this isn't your first time at this bar..."

She didn't even get to finish the sentence when the bartender spotted them and bellowed, "Ha, Ha!" He was a bull of a man, short but solid. His forearms were as thick as Carli's thighs. His open collared shirt revealed thick black hair and a heavy chain ending in a gold crucifix.

"MURPH!" he boomed. Coming from behind the bar, he met Murph with a massive bear hug. "How's that pitiful flag football team of yours at Ignatius this year?"

"Still able to beat your Eagles" Murph patted him on the cheek and disengaged himself from the hug. He put his arm around Carli and pulled her forward. "I'd like you to meet Carli!"

His paw was so large it swallowed up Carli's as he shook her hand. "Any friend of Murph's is a friend of mine, especially the beautiful ones!"

Murph continued the introduction. "This is Rocco Meroni. His main failing is that he is a graduate of Cleveland St. Edward High School, but we Ignatius alumni are big hearted enough to forgive him that one."

Rocco bowed in mock appreciation. "You are so kind... and humble too!"

"Rocco came to Rome on a semester abroad from Ohio University, fell in love, and never left. The Clevelander is his little bit of home, and it was home for me when I was here."

"You two need a beer! And I've got work to do!" There was a group at the end of the bar gesturing aggressively at Rocco, waving empty glasses. "Aspettami! I'm coming... I'm coming already!"

Murph led Carli to a wood paneled booth near the bar, and they sat down on the red leather cushions. Murph made sure he was seated within easy sight of the door. He knew there was a back entrance past the restrooms, through the kitchen. They might need it, in a pinch.

Rocco came over and set down a foaming Guinness for Murph and a bottle of Miller Lite for Carli. He placed a bowl of peanuts and a bowl of pretzels between them and asked Carli how she was enjoying Rome. He told Murph he would be back when things quieted down later in the game. After halftime, since it was a pre-season game, the big name players were all gone and many of the fans were leaving. It was already 4:00 a.m., but Rocco at last had some free time.

Carli had curled up against the wall, using the backpack as a pillow, and was fast asleep. Rocco pulled a chair over, turned it backwards and eased his massive frame down with a heavy sigh. He crossed his arms over the back of the chair. "I'm not as young as I used to be. This middle of the night stuff has got to stop!"

"I know. I'm feeling it myself. It's been a long day."

"You look worn out. You OK?" Rocco, for his gruff exterior, was really concerned. "I saw you on that Apprentice thing. I was really proud of you, and I made sure that all my regulars knew I had taught you everything I know."

Murph laughed, and Rocco joined in as well. "But that's over now," Murph conceded.

"Yeah. So what brings you to Rome? Honeymoon?"

"No, not yet anyway."

Rocco pointed a stubby finger at Carli. "That one's a keeper. She looks like a strong one."

"She's tougher than I am." Murph lowered his voice a little. "I need to get into the Vatican tomorrow. My friends will help me once I'm in, but I have to get past the Swiss Guard. Do they still let the priests in at 7:00 a.m. for the morning masses?"

Rocco nodded. "That should work. And I won't ask why you guys are here and not in a nice five-star hotel. You're on the run from someone, and the less I know the better!"

"That's good policy."

"It works for me."

"But just so you know, " Murph felt obligated to explain something, "we didn't do anything wrong. Carli was working in Cairo on an archeological dig, and the government hardliners took offense to her findings. We left Egypt in a big hurry and Rome was the safest place I could think of."

Rocco thought for a minute. "That actually explains a lot. There was a mean looking Arab dude here earlier this afternoon looking for you. He had a couple of friends with him, and I know they were armed. I didn't tell them anything, since I hadn't seen you anyway."

"That's why you didn't seem surprised to see me! What did the Arab look like?"

"Tall and lean, dark skinned with coal black eyes. He had sharp, angled cheekbones and black hair slicked back. His main flunky was a bit shorter, about 5'8". He had a heavy black beard, lots of muscles and a couple of scars. Looked military, all business. Neither one of them showed any emotions at all. The tall one wanted me to call them if I saw you and *the girl*." He reached into his pocket. "He even gave me a card. How nice and polite!"

Rocco handed Murph the card.

Hamid al-Said, DMD
Regal Dental and Implantology Clinic
91 Mosaddak Street
Dokki, Cairo, Egypt

"Did you…"

"No, Murph, I wouldn't ever rat out an old friend, especially to the likes of those!" He spat. "But you be careful. Those guys were pros and cold as ice. I'll put out the word to my people to help you if they can. I've got connections, you know!"

"The Maf-"

"Don't even say it." Rocco cut him off. "But help will be there if you need it. Just be sure you don't. I don't like the looks of the people you're messing with. They mean business, and I know the type."

"Thanks, Rocco. We won't trouble you any longer. I don't want to put you in any danger."

"Ha! I spit in the face of danger!" Rocco flashed a big-toothed smile. "You stay as long as you need. You're safe here… safer than anywhere else in Rome!"

Rocco stood up and squeezed Murph's shoulder with his massive hand and then walked back behind the bar, looking tired.

Murph studied Carli, her small frame curled up on the bench, her breathing slow and even. "You're not sleeping are you?"

"Nope." Came the reply, and she sat up, running her fingers through her hair to straighten it.

"You heard?

"Every word." She set her elbows on the table, folded her hands, and rested her chin on them, looking into Murph's eyes. "So what's the plan, Stan?"

"For now, we rest a bit more. We need to be at the Palazzo Apostolico of the Vatican at 7:00 a.m., when I'll try to talk my way past the Swiss Guard to see Father Albers without an appointment."

"Did you know that Rocco had Mafia connections?"

"I suspected as much. Their business is about information, and Rocco is the best at listening and getting people to talk freely. He would be a valuable resource for them, and his lifestyle far exceeds the means of a humble barkeep. I'll introduce you to his wife someday!"

"I'd like that." Carli was quiet for a minute and then continued. "We need to get rid of these guys. We have a lot of things planned, but we need the time to enjoy them."

"We will… That I promise you!"

"I'll hold you to it!"

Chapter 40

The first light of dawn was creeping into the sky, banishing the mists from the pavement, when Rocco shuffled over to their table. The sound of two plates clinking onto the wooden top woke both Carli and Murph. Rubbing sleep from their eyes, they were surprised and very pleased to find golden omelets, with ham, cheese, red peppers and onions, toast, fresh jam, and crispy bacon. Steaming mugs of coffee came next, and Rocco brought his own plate, settling down with them. The bar was empty now, except for the busboy absentmindedly pushing a broom, gathering trash and dust in the corner.

"Best meal of the day. Eat up! I expect you'll have another long one." Rocco commented as he launched into his massive omelet.

They both thanked him for his hospitality and ate heartily. A full stomach did wonders for calming nerves and giving them the confidence they would need. Carli went to the restroom to freshen up, and Murph's carefully crafted mask of bravado slipped a bit.

"Realistically, what do you think our chances are of getting from here to the Vatican in one piece?"

Rocco chewed thoughtfully on a piece of bacon for a moment. "It's early, but you've got about eight blocks to cover. Our Arab goons don't seem to be the type to give up easily, so I'd place it at about fifty-fifty."

"That bad, eh."

"In Vegas, I'd take those odds. Besides, I've arranged a bit of help for you." Rocco took a big gulp of coffee and continued. "Some of my boys are here. It's not their fight, so they won't become directly involved. They may run some interference for you and buy you a bit more time. Once you're in the Vatican, you're on your own."

"Don't worry. I'll be safe in St. Peter's. It's the last sprint that worries me."

"One more thing." Rocco put down his mug and looked Murph straight in the eye. "The goons are bad enough, but the woman was the one that really gave me the chills."

Carli had walked up behind him. "Woman? You didn't mention her yesterday."

"I try not to give away too much information at one time. That stuff's too valuable. It's an old habit." Rocco shrugged and tried to look innocent. "Because you're family, you get this for free!"

"Thanks!" Murph had put up the face of confidence again, even though he was feeling more scared by the minute.

"While Hamid al-Said was trying to intimidate me with his bearded pit bull, I noticed her at the doorway. She didn't come in, as if she couldn't lower herself to come into a bar. She was tall, taller than me."

"Well, that wouldn't take much," Murph laughed, trying to break the tension.

Rocco pretended not to notice. "Probably five feet, ten inches or so, with long, straight black hair, hanging down onto her shoulders. She was painfully thin. I mean her cheekbones stood out, making her face look even longer and more angled. She had big eyes, dark black, angled up in the corners, with heavy black eyeliner and dark eye shadow — way too much makeup for me. She waved at Hamid with long, bony fingers and even longer nails, painted with dark polish. Her silk dress was tight fitting and black. She wore dark hose and knee-length shiny black leather boots. Her necklace was a huge gold choker, with some sort of giant turquoise stone. It was those eyes that were memorable — black holes that looked right through you. I've see a lot, believe me, but this woman is one to stay away from!"

Murph would file that away. "Thanks for the description. We haven't run into her before, and I hope we don't anytime soon."

He noticed that Carli looked shaken. *Maybe she met the tall woman before.* Murph decided he would ask her later, but for now, they had work to do. He looked at his watch. *It's 6:30. And we've got to be in St. Peter's Square before 7:00 a.m. for my plan to work.*

He tapped his watch and got up. "Hate to eat and run, literally, but we've got to go!" Murph shook Rocco's hand and gave him a hug.

The bear gripped Murph like a long-lost relative. "You be careful, and come back and see me again soon. I miss all your adventures!" He turned to Carli and gave her a giant hug as well.

"He'll take care of you," he whispered in her ear. "He's smarter than he looks." And he gave her a kiss on the cheek. "Next time stay for a while. I'll give you the grand tour. Rome is the Eternal City, and we won't stay up all night just sitting in this dingy bar."

Carli brushed away a tear. "I'll make sure we do. I wouldn't miss it for the world!"

Murph settled the backpack on his shoulders, and took Carli's hand as they walked to the door. With a squeeze, and a smile for confidence, he looked back at Rocco and gave him a wink. He touched two fingers to his brow and gave a casual salute. He pushed his shoulder into the wooden door and burst boldly into the street.

It would be a hot day later, but for now a light mist hung heavy on the air. The cobblestones were moist with dew, looking dark grey and foreboding. They looked quickly both ways, half expecting evil spirits to materialize out of the mist. Murph gathered his courage, and they set out walking briskly from the security of The Clevelander. They quickly left the narrow Via Germanico and turned onto the larger Via Fabio Massimo. There was no traffic this early in the morning, but the inhabitants of Rome were beginning to stir.

Murph was feeling more confident as their path widened, becoming the Via Terenzio. *Three blocks down, five more to go.* Two more bocks, and the grey shadow of the walls of the Castel Sant' Angelo darkened their view. A blacked out Alfa Romeo crossed their path and suddenly changed direction, speeding up as it went down the block, looking for a place to turn. It went out of sight, but Murph could hear its tires sliding on the wet pavement. He could feel the hairs on the back of his neck stand up.

"Run!" He pulled Carli by the hand as they raced up the slight grade. Another block and they could hear the Alfa Romeo screech behind them. A park, Piazza Amerigo Capponi, opened in front of them, and they sought safety in the trees. Traffic was prohibited from entering the park by stone pillars and barricades, so they ran as fast as they could under the green canopy. They heard the sedan brake to a stop and then heard the doors open and running footsteps charging after them.

"One more block!" Murph encouraged Carli as they ran. He stole a glance back and saw three men chasing them. Omar was in the center, with two others who looked familiar flanking him. They were once again wearing dark slacks and windbreaker jackets. *Is that some sort of uniform? It's not very original.* The goons were quick, but Murph and Carli were the better athletes and they were opening a bigger lead.

Murph was thrilled when they burst onto the Via della Conciliazione. It was four lanes wide, and the six-story, tan and yellow buildings were almost cheerful in the growing morning light. A few tour busses were moving about, and more pedestrians were walking, all heading in the same direction, drawn by the magnetic force of St. Peter's Basilica.

Murph tugged on Carli's arm, and they turned right, running in the pedestrian walkway, separated from the busses by a line of parked cars. The sandstone columns of the streetlights towered 30 feet overhead. Palm trees punctuated the passage, waving in the light breeze. Carli looked up and stopped. There in the distance, not more than 300 yards away, was St. Peter's Basilica. She had seen pictures of it on TV, but here, the sight took her breath away.

Murph had come this way every day for three months, but he never tired of this sight. He remembered the first time he entered St. Peter's Square from the Via della Conciliazione. He was always struck by the number of palm trees growing in Rome. Somehow, he never expected to see palms. It was a one-way street, a hundred feet wide, bordered by buildings and measured by the columns and palms. All the motion of the city flowed into the Vatican through here.

Sanctuary! Murph thought. It was more of a prayer.

It was ironic, he thought, that they had left Cairo, but now were running toward the Obelisco Vaticano, an Egyptian obelisk of red granite originally erected at Heliopolis by a pharaoh of the Fifth dynasty. It had been moved to Rome by Emperor Caligula and then was brought to St. Peter's Square by Pope Sixtux V in 1586. Bernini had utilized the Obelisco as the centerpiece of his piazza, and it made an obvious rallying point.

"Run for the obelisk in the center of the square. I'll meet you there." Murph shoved Carli in the back to move her on.

Murph turned to face Omar as he emerged from the same alleyway that Carli and he had exited moments before. There was that smile again, splitting the black beard that engulfed the bottom half of his face. Murph glanced left and right, looking for something to slow them down. A priest walking up the street near Murph caught his eye. He wore the usual white collar, but there was something that just didn't look right. He drew his hand out of his pocket and lifted his hat, nodding to Murph.

A street vendor, setting up his cart of religious trinkets, swung the cart suddenly, hitting Omar from the side and knocking him to the ground. One of the other henchmen ran over to help Omar up, but, with a crash, the contents of the cart spilled over onto them both, pinning them to the pavement. The third gunman drew a revolver from his pocket and ran over to his stricken comrades. A crowd was beginning to develop, and two uniformed policemen began to cross the street to investigate the commotion. The gun was quickly out of sight, and the goon backed away, melting into the crowd.

Murph looked at the priest again, who smiled and quietly said "Run, you fool!" So Murph turned on his heel and raced after Carli, quickly extending to his longer stride and catching her as they burst into St. Peter's Square.

Chapter 41

Entering into the square, Murph reached over to Carli and held her hand. He forced her to stop and then they began to walk slowly to the right, toward the Fontana Maderno, its waters spraying lightly into the white granite basin. The boundaries of the square were colossal Tuscan colonnades, four columns deep. Statues of the saints looked down from the ring high above. The sea of cobblestones was crossed with radiating lines of travertine, adding to the geometry of the elliptical Square.

"We're safe now. Rocco's boys took out Omar and friends." He held her hands in his and kissed her. "Take a deep breath, and relax. There is power here in the Vatican. I always can feel it. It is a peaceful place, where everything moves slowly in a measured way. In order to accomplish what I need to do, we must be very calm. Play along with my lead."

"OK, but why?" Carli was catching her breath, but really confused now.

"One of my former teachers is here and is now the head of the Vatican Library. He has a tremendous amount of influence and will help us... if I can get to him." Murph was scanning the growing crowd around them. "I don't have an appointment, so I need to con the Swiss Guard into calling him. They are not easy to convince!" Murph spotted what he was looking for. "Ahh, now that's who we need!"

Murph took Carli by the hand and walked over to a group of three priests, standing huddled around a map of the Vatican, one pointing a finger into the map, while another was gesturing at the steps to the Basilica.

As Murph approached, the tallest of the three was saying, "No. The entrance is over there, past the fountain." Murph was thankful they were speaking English.

"Father?" Murph came up to them. He chose the tallest, who appeared to be the oldest. "Are you looking for the entrance to the Palazzo Apostolico so that you can celebrate Morning Mass?"

"Why yes, young man." He looked relieved. "Can you help us?"

"I would be honored, Father. Just follow me!"

Murph led Carli, and now the three priests, as well, past the Fontana Maderno to the corner of the Square, just to the right of the steps into the Basilica. Between the last pillars of the Colonnato del Bernini, there was a narrow opening in the crowd control barriers. Murph confidently led his charges out of the light of St. Peter's Square, into the shadows, and up a short flight of stairs. At the top of the stairs was a simple doorway, flanked by two Swiss Guards in their renaissance uniforms of blue, red, orange, and yellow stripes, topped with a black beret. They looked coldly at the group, but Murph gestured to the three priests and mentioned that he was leading them to where they could say Morning Mass. His Italian was flawless, and the guards nodded. They said nothing, but one opened the door.

Murph wished he could explain to Carli that priests are required to celebrate Mass daily, and it is a goal of many of the Catholic clergy to one day say Mass at the Vatican. Each day between 7:00 a.m. and 8:00 a.m., priests could present themselves at the Vatican and be escorted to one of the small side chapels under St. Peter's. He knew that on any given day, it was possible to see priests from all over the world, saying Mass in any of hundreds of languages, perhaps even celebrating with a Cardinal or a future Pope.

Murph led them to the registration desk and introduced them to the registrar. Though no explanation was really necessary, as everyone here knew what they wanted, Murph smoothed the path for them.

"Thank you, young man," the older priest said, as the three were about to be led away by an altar boy, carrying a tray with the water, wine, and hosts that they would use to celebrate Mass.

Murph bowed slightly and shook their hands. "May you have a wonderful stay in Rome."

Once they had left, Murph turned back to the priest serving as the registrar today. He had to act quickly, as the Swiss Guard was opening the door, and moving to usher them out.

"Father, I would like to see Father Lawrence Albers. Could you contact him, please?"

Murph hoped that his appearance as a helpful young man would help his request land softly and be favorably received.

The registrar looked down his nose, past half glasses. His eyebrows narrowed. "Do you have an appointment?"

"Well, no, but I hoped you would be able to help me."

"Does he know you are coming?"

"No. He was a former teacher of mine when he was at Saint Ignatius in Cleveland… in Ohio… America."

The frown deepened and he took off his glasses. He deliberately withdrew a handkerchief from his pocket and rubbed the lenses. The priest sighed deeply and said, "I'm sorry. Father Albers is a very busy man, and I cannot be bothering him for everyone who wanders in here." He set down his glasses. "Walther!"

At that, the guard stepped in, and reached for Murph's arm.

"But," Murph protested, "I know that he will see me if you just call him."

Walther's grip tightened as Murph held his ground.

"I do not see how I can help you. As I have said, Father Albers has many responsibilities, and he is a very busy man."

Then a booming voice came from down the hallway behind Carli, on Murph's left. "He may be busy, but he'll make time for

Michael Patrick Murphy, I can promise you that!"

The guard released Murph's elbow, allowing him to turn and face his benefactor. The beaming smile that greeted him filled Murph with relief, and he laughed with joy. "Father Mahoney! I forgot you were here, too!"

"Yes, me boy. Everyone always remembers that self-important snob Albers, but forgets little old me." Father Brian Mahoney had been playing that "poor me" act since his time at Saint Ignatius High School. The Jesuit priests had sparred with each other for as long as anyone could remember, but in reality, they were the best of friends. Short and rotund, with a ruddy complexion and a big nose, Mahoney looked every bit the Irish country friar. Easy going and affable, he was quick to laugh and always ready with a joke. His arrival immediately dispelled the cold gloom in the room, replacing it with his bright, cheerful energy.

Father Mahoney shook hands and gave Murph a firm embrace. He patted Carli lightly on the cheek, "And welcome to you, my dear. The Vatican is an impressive place, but its beauty is cold and frozen as statues and paintings. It is a rare day when someone as beautiful as you graces us with your presence." Carli swept back the loose hairs from her face, suddenly feeling very aware of her bedraggled appearance after their hard run.

"Excuse me, Walther." Father Mahoney eased past the guard and stepped in front of the registration desk. "Father Porea, your obstinance is commendable, but no longer necessary. Please record the arrival of Michael Patrick Murphy of Cleveland, Ohio and Miss…" He raised his bushy eyebrows and looked at Murph.

"Caroline Chamoun of Columbus, Ohio."

"I will vouch for these two. Please call the office, and let Father Albers know that we are on our way up!"

"As you wish, Brian," he complied, his voice dripping with sarcasm. "It is always my pleasure to be of service."

Father Mahoney didn't spend time gloating in his success but quickly gathered Carli and Murph and ushered them down the marble tiled hallway from where he had come. The passage led back into the Basilica and across the opening into the main chapel. After passing the grand steps, he led them down a curving staircase and into the hushed silence of catacombs. They passed a group of nuns in shadows, quietly praying before a white marble sarcophagus.

The name of Pope John Paul II was clearly visible, carved into the stone and lit from above by a single floodlight. Murph had been here many times before, but as always, he was moved by the awareness of the presence of God. He stopped, bowed his head, and said a quick prayer asking for guidance. Making the sign of the cross, he hurried after Carli and the Irish priest.

At the end of the tunnels, they ascended five flights of stairs to the top level. Murph and Carli smiled to themselves as Father Mahoney wheezed and panted upon reaching the top. Murph made a show of bending down to remove an imaginary rock from his shoe, giving the priest the chance to catch his breath.

Mahoney appreciated the gesture. "You always know how to make an old man feel better. I suppose all those years of Jesuit education trained you well." He straightened his collar and tucked in his shirt. "Let's go and meet your mentor!"

Murph pulled Carli quickly aside. "Father Albers is very formal. He seems unapproachable and almost scary at first, but there is no one I would trust more to help us. He is a brilliant historian and was brought here four years ago to take over the Vatican library. That's unheard of for a non-Italian. With his help, I know we can figure this out."

Carli swallowed hard. She straightened and tried to be as tall as her five-foot frame would allow. She smoothed her dress and made herself as presentable as possible. Murph also tidi ed up as best he could, not knowing where to start when it came to explaining their predicament.

Father Mahoney looked them over. "Are we ready?" They nodded. "Well then, lets have at it." He led them the rest of the way down the hallway, his shoes squeaking on the polished marble. They came to a heavy cherry wood door, banded with metal. The brass nameplate proclaimed;

Rev. Lawrence Albers
Director
Bibliotheca Apostolica Vaticana

Father Mahoney stepped back and offered the door to Murph. "Feels like freshman year again, doesn't it?" he chuckled.

Murph nodded and stood tall. Taking the backpack off his shoulder, he held it at his side, down near the floor. He raised his hand and rapped crisply, twice, on the door.

"Enter!" came the deep muffled voice from beyond.

Murph reached down and opened the latch, pushing open the heavy weight of the door. Carli and Father Mahoney followed him inside, several steps behind. Murph set the backpack on the ground in front of Carli and looked across the room. It was a large space. At the end of the room, on his left-hand side, there was a massive mahogany conference table surrounded by 12 high-backed leather chairs. On his right, an imposing desk bisected the other end of the room. Two sets of French doors led out to a balcony. They stood open to the morning air, linen drapes swaying idly in the light breeze. With the light of the rising sun behind him, Father Lawrence Albers was a shadow rimmed in orange.

Murph blinked as his eyes fought to adjust after being in the dark hallways. "Father Albers? Thank you for seeing us."

"Michael, it is good to see you, but I did not expect to see such a *celebrity* darken my door again."

This wasn't starting out the way Murph had hoped. Carli bit her lip, concerned. Murph chose not to respond. He lowered his chin, but stood erect, bracing for the rebuke.

"I was very disappointed in you joining that ridiculous reality show — *The Dental Apprentice*!" he scoffed. "It was so beneath a person of your talents." Father Albers moved out of the light and approached Murph.

Where Mahoney was short and stocky, Albers was long and lean. His close-cropped hair was steel gray, which accented his parchment skin that looked so much like the books he supervised. His eyes were a penetrating blue and magnified by rimless spectacles, which sat low on his long, angled nose.

The librarian walked across the brocade carpeting until he stood before Murph and looked at him, their eyes level. "I watched the shows in fear for what would become of you."

The silence weighed heavy in the room. *"Esse quam videri,"* Father Albers intoned in his deep baritone.

Murph's eyes widened. "To be, rather than to seem to be! ... Marcus Tullius Cicero."

"Excellent, Michael. Your Latin remains perfect." He put his hands on Murph's shoulders. "Steak over sizzle... you behaved with dignity and class. Your actions were a superior reflection on your heritage and Jesuit education." He smiled broadly, warming the room. "I am most proud of you, my son!" And he gave the stunned Murph a warm embrace. "Welcome home!"

Father Mahoney closed the door and picked up the backpack placing it on the conference table, commenting under his breath to Carli as he walked by, "See... nothing to it. Had it in the bag all the time!"

Father Albers called for coffee and some scones, motioning them to the table. Father Mahoney was delighted, since he was never one to pass up the chance to eat. Father Albers seated himself at the head of the table, folded his arms, and fastened Murph with a penetrating stare.

"So, Michael, please tell us of your experiences. How did you come to return to the Vatican? And what assistance do you require of me?" He held up his hand to stop Murph from answering as their breakfast arrived. Albers accepted a cup of coffee from his steward and motioned him to leave. "Thank you, Bernardo. That will be all."

When they were alone again, the librarian continued. "This should be an interesting tale." He turned to Father Mahoney, as the priest took a generous bite of an orange scone. "Brian, were you aware that you admitted wanted fugitives into the inner Vatican today?"

Mahoney coughed and choked on his scone, taking a sip of coffee to regain his breath.

"I thought not!" Albers calmly sipped some coffee. "Moments ago, the Swiss Guard were informed by the Carabinieri to be on the lookout for two people matching your descriptions. By the grace of God, you had passed the checkpoint by that time, and were in the company of the good Father. I have been requested to detain you until they come to pick you up. It seems there is the matter of a murder in Egypt, and you are the prime suspects."

Murph and Carli both began to speak, but Father Albers held up his hand again, silencing them.

"We have plenty of time. You are safe here... for now... but this had better be an amazing story. Let us begin at the start."

Chapter 42

Hamid al-Said glared at the three accomplices, white-hot anger flaming behind his eyes. Omar stood impassively, his hands clasped behind his back. The other two, Kalam and Azad, shrank back from the tirade. Omar and Kalam were covered with dust and moisture from the street, where they had been toppled into the gutter by the "vendor'" and his cart. Azad was clean, but far from unscathed.

"How could you let them escape? May you and your descendants be cursed!"

They stood beneath the stone fortifications of the Castel sant Angelo, hidden by the shadows cast by the high walls. Hamid paced back and forth, then reached over toward Azad, prepared to strike. "And *you*, do nothing, even as your *friends* here are taken out by street vendors!"

"Patience." A chilling feminine voice interrupted, as she stepped forward out of the deepest shadows. "It is of no concern, and there is no point to dwell on lost opportunities. They have entered the Vatican, and in so doing, they have trapped themselves."

Hamid let the anger drain from him and agreed. "That is true. We have informed the Italian authorities, and they will do the work for us. When they arrest them, we can capture them and return to Cairo."

"The interloper and the dentist will return to us in due course, in spite of the incompetence that surrounds us." Her voice made even Omar's skin crawl. "They have served their purpose, and the wheels are turning. It is time to end this."

She walked over to Hamid and took his hand. "A drink in the bar at the Cavalieri will pass the time. We should hear from Capitano Abruzzo soon enough, now that we know they have gone into Vatican City."

He smiled an evil smile. Turning to Omar Bengdara, Hamid spoke with thinly veiled contempt, "Clean yourselves up and cover the exits to the Vatican, in case they run again."

As the couple departed down the pathway, her heels clicking on the cobblestones, Omar muttered to himself. "I liked things better in the army. We get to stand guard in the sun, while *they* sip champagne at a five-star hotel." *Like in the army, shit flows downhill.*

Omar began barking at his associates to "get moving," even kicking one. Then he disciplined his mind, willing it to focus on how to trap their quarry.

Chapter 43

Manny Farouk was toweling his hair dry, walking out of the marble bathroom of his suite when his phone chirped. He picked up the phone and saw that it was Margaret.

"Yes!"

"Manny, I have news from Saleh." She sounded far away, which she was since she had accompanied Derek and Ed on the Gulfstream back to Cairo. "Narmer is dead. His body was found floating in the Nile. He had a gash on his cheek, and his neck was broken."

Not the least surprised by this news, he walked out onto his balcony and surveyed the dome of St Peter's Basilica in the distance, the light growing ever brighter.

"A report was filed with the Carabinieri, naming Ms. Chamoun and Dr. Murphy as 'persons of interest' and requesting their return to Cairo for questioning."

"That is interesting. It means the others have lost their trail as well." Manny returned inside and tossed the towel on the bed. "There is only one place that Michael can go and be safe in Rome. He has taken her into the Vatican!"

"Most likely." Margaret continued sweetly. "They have to come out sometime. You can have your men watch the exits and take them."

"*I'll* see to that. *You* see to our cargo and return to Washington. I will join you there soon." He ended the call and dressed quickly. There was much work to be done, and little time!

Chapter 44

"Murder?" Murph was stunned. "Whose murder?"

Father Albers lifted the paper he had brought to the table and shifted his glasses. "This report from the Carabinieri indicates that a professor of Egyptology, Dr. Tanen Narmer, was found floating in the Nile River. According to an eyewitness, the two of you were the last people to see him alive. Because Narmer had accused Ms. Chamoun of academic fraud and theft of antiquities, they believe that could be the motive for his killing. The evidence is circumstantial, but a case has been made to have you extradited to Egypt.

At this point, Father Albers gave Carli a penetrating look and raised his left eyebrow. "And maybe there *is* sufficient cause... given what I suspect is in your backpack. It's remarkably heavy, don't you think?"

"It's not what you are thinking," Murph blustered. "I can explain!" Carli just buried her face in her hands and sobbed.

"Michael, my son, I believe you are innocent." The priest applied a calming tone to the rising tension. "Dr. Narmer's neck was broken, and that hardly seems your style! What we need to do is determine why these people want you so badly that they chase you across Rome and attempt to frame you for murder." He stood up and walked around the table. Placing his hand on Carli's shoulder, he made the sign of the cross and said a quiet prayer over her.

"Peace, my child. You are among friends. Michael has blessed me with his friendship for 12 years now, since he was a sophomore in high school. I may be a cranky old man, but he listens to me and has sought my guidance before. If you both tell us everything you know, I am sure we can make sense of this situation."

Father Albers went to his desk, picked up a laptop, and handed it to Father Mahoney. "Brian, if you will search for anything we need..."

"Pardon my old fashioned ways," he said to Murph and Carli, "but I think better with paper and a pen." He then removed an easel and large tablet of paper from the closet.

After setting up the flip chart, he sat on the edge of the table where he could take notes easily. "Now, Michael, you have taken my class. History is the discussion of the linear progress of events over time. It always works best to start at the beginning. Caroline, I believe this story begins with you."

She took a deep breath and wiped away the tears. Standing up, she began with her research. She found Father Albers, as a professor of the classics, to be well versed in Egyptian lore. She described her discovery of the antechamber behind the tombs of the dentists, and she showed them the photos of the hieroglyphics using Murph's computer. She and Murph proposed their theory that the drawings recorded the murder of the Pharaoh by one of the dentists.

While Mahoney shook his head in disbelief, Father Albers stood up and wrote on his flip chart:

Why would the dentist want to kill Pharaoh?
Why is this an issue today?

Speaking rapidly, alternating and finishing each other's sentences, they told of their flight from the Cairo museum and their break in at the pyramid. Carli detailed her abusive questioning at the hands of Narmer and their escape from Saqqara to the airport and then to Rome, and eventually the Vatican.

Father Mahoney was impressed. "Michael, you have made firm friends over the years, and you have made powerful enemies in the last week!

"But Father, the central question is why are these people my enemies? I thought I was on good terms with Dr. Farouk, until I was discharged from *The Dental Apprentice*. He did still send me to Cairo..." It was dawning on him now, "and he asked me to tell him what happened!"

Father Albers clapped his hands together. "Precisely! Hunters train their dogs to run into the brush to flush out the birds. For some reason, the opening of the dentists' tomb has set a sequence of events into motion."

"And I was sent to Cairo to flush Carli out of hiding, which I did, just like an idiot!"

"Yet, you proved to be too adept. You two were smarter than they thought and gathered the help of friends to escape all the way here, and I am positive you are carrying the keys to the riddle in that backpack."

Carli removed the scroll pouch, but did not take out the scroll. The image on the computer screen provided a clear record for her to translate. There was little doubt that Pharaoh had been poisoned by one of the dentists. The hieroglyphics contained the message of the curse.

Murph removed the investment from the backpack and disassembled it to show the negatives of the teeth that would be cast in gold. "There are nine reservoirs, in two rows. It would take quite a bit of gold to cast this." He reassembled the pipe and set it before them.

They all sat quietly thinking for a moment, and Mahoney was the first to speak.

"I think the curse is the key. As long as Pharaoh is not whole, the ceremony can't be finished, and he can't go into the afterlife in peace. He's in limbo. But, this isn't possible!"

Murph's eyes lit up. "But, what if Pharaoh wasn't the only one in limbo? What if others thought they were cursed by the ancient events?"

Carli caught on to what he was implying, but really didn't want to consider it. "You can't be serious — that descendents of the two dentists or others are struggling to lift the curse?"

Father Albers wrote this down at the top of another page on his chart. "Since we have no other plausible options yet, let us consider what would happen if this hypothesis were correct. As you said, Michael, it would take a great deal of gold to cast the nine teeth. In the hieroglyphics, Carli, can you see how the ceremony was disrupted?"

She returned to the image of the pictograms on the wall. "It's not completely clear, but after the curse was laid down, something was stolen! And the dentist ran from the room. The other priests searched for him, but could never find him! He must have taken the gold and has been hiding it for centuries."

Murph was rolling now. "So if someone collected all the gold, enough to make all nine teeth, they could cast them and complete the ritual. All they would need is the mummy. Once the ritual is completed, the curse is lifted! The mummy is at Saqqara, so maybe the excavation started the clock to his return!"

"No. NO!" Carli stopped him short. "Now you're thinking like Hollywood! The mummy was found years ago. Djoser is at the Museum of Antiquities in Cairo. You stood right next to his sarcophagus!"

She rubbed her eyes and thought. "But when the museum was vandalized during the uprising in Tahrir Square, the mummy was moved out of the sarcophagus and placed in the basement of the museum for safe keeping. The mummy would be more accessible now than it has been for centuries… What you're thinking, could it be possible?"

Father Albers set down the marker and folded his hands. "Let's look at the ceremony and the curse. In order to complete the ritual, one would need the mummy, gold to cast the teeth, and a priest, in this case the dentist, to perform the ceremony. Am I correct, Caroline?"

"Yes, Father, that would do it, but everyone has known where the mummy has been all along. What has delayed doing the ritual?"

"That is the crux of the initial question we posed. Why now?" Albers tapped the flip chart with his long finger.

"What if there was a certain gold that was required? Not just any metal, but the exact gold stolen when the ceremony was disrupted?' They were all surprised to hear this from Father Mahoney, thinking he had fallen asleep, as his chin had settled onto his chest, deep in thought. He smiled, "See… not just a pretty face!"

"If that were true," Murph thought aloud, "then when Sekhem Ka took the gold and ran, he would know they would come after him. He would need to find a place to stash the gold where it wouldn't be easily found, or he would need to keep it with him. But in Egypt, 5000 years ago, there wouldn't be many places to hide."

"Wait a minute." Father Albers tapped his finger to his temple and then repositioned his glasses. "Brian, let me see the computer." He took the laptop and began scanning his files for a document.

"Ah ha!" He opened a file with a click. "This is the diary of Tancred de Hauteville, a leader of the First Crusade. In 1097, he commanded a small force of knights at the Battle of Dorylaeum, in what is now Turkey. The main force of the army had been ambushed by Muslims and was in desperate straights. Tancred led his troops to bring reinforcements, and they successfully turned the tide, changing defeat into the first major victory of the Crusades."

Carli and Mahoney were both getting impatient. "But what does that have to do with the curse?"

"In due time!" The priest smiled sweetly. He truly enjoyed the slow unfolding of the story, which Murph knew well from the past. "Tancred writes of his party coming upon a strange scene as they rode near the river Thymbres. He describes a small party of Moors, dismounted and fighting trapped against the riverbank — and surrounded by a party of Turks. He finds this odd, because both groups are Muslim and the Moors are about to be overwhelmed.

Tancred's knights do not care to choose sides, since they believe they are at war with both groups, so they attack with the intent of killing all of them. The ferocity of the Crusader assault breaks up the Turks, killing many of them and the remnants of this group, including their leader, flee toward the mountains. Tancred's troops then move to finish off the handful of Moors that are left.

The leader of the Moors speaks French and pleads with Tancred to let them go. Tancred is in no mood for mercy or for wasting any more time, so he orders the Moors put to death. The Moors respond to the knights who are beginning to loot their pack animals by attacking with a renewed ferocity that surprises Tancred. In the packs are gold coins and jewelry, which provide Tancred with wealth and power that eventually lead to him being named Prince of Galilee. In spite of the plunder that falls into his hands, he writes that he is upset when the Moor commander shouts something about the Pharaoh's gold, grabs a heavy pack from his horse, and dives into the swollen river in full armor. He sinks like a stone and is never seen again. They cannot spare time to look for the body, and Tancred writes of his bitterness that he never possessed the *Pharaoh's gold.*"

Murph was considering this history, as Father Albers had taught him. "If he survived the river, a Moor would try to go to Spain and would want to get as far away from North Africa as possible. Given the commotion in travel at the time, it would have been relatively easy for him to disappear. If he were Sekhem Ka, he would be a priest and dentist. A priest of the old religion would have no place in Catholic Europe, but a dentist would be needed as a healer. Are there any mentions through history of a dark skinned dentist?"

Father Albers' smile broadened. "There is only one I can think of, but he is significant. Napoleon's dentist was a Pedro Tavira, and your father was the one who led me to him."

"My Dad, what has he got to do with this?"

"If you will remember, when you were a Junior at Ignatius and taking my AP European history class, you brought me a hand-written diary of Lieutenant Pierre Dumond, a French soldier of Napoleon's Grand Armee. A patient of your father's was going through his family papers when preparing to go into a nursing home. He brought the document to your dad to see if he had any ideas on where to donate the document. Sean can't read French, so he had you bring it to me to see if I had an interest in translating it. I found it fascinating and arranged with the patient to have it donated to the French Embassy when I finished with it."

"But how do Dumond and this Pedro Tavira connect to our story?"

Father Albers looked smug and sure of himself, the teacher leading the students down the path to a conclusion. "Lieutenant Dumond was assigned to guard the dentist, Tavira, while on a special mission in 1805. Tavira required a close personal guard because he was a Moor. Are you familiar with the term Austerlitz teeth?"

Carli and Mahoney shook their heads, and looked dumb-founded, but a glimmer of dawn began to break for Murph, growing in a rush. "Unbelievable! That would be perfect!"

Murph looked at Carli and Father Mahoney. "The Battle of Austerlitz in 1805 was one of Napoleon's greatest victories, where his French Grand Armee defeated the combined forces of the Russian and Austrian empires. After the battle, there were so many dead soldiers that teeth were extracted from the deceased and used in making dentures to replace missing teeth in patients all through-out Europe. There were so many teeth extracted at the battle site, that the dentures of the period were called *Austerlitz teeth*.

"A partial denture at that time would consist of extracted human teeth wired to a cast metal appliance. Pewter was used for the common people, but the rich could afford cast gold frame-works, and they fit much better! If you were a dentist and wanted to divide gold so no one could find it but you, this would be the ideal way! As the dentist to Napoleon's court, you would have access to the wealthy and powerful. Your denture services would be in high demand. You could hide the gold in plain sight. Just keep a list of patients and pick the gold back up when they die. It's positively brilliant!"

"There is more than that, Michael." Father Albers was calling up a document on his computer. When he had opened the file and scanned the writing for a minute, he tapped the screen with his finger.

"Here is the passage. Lieutenant Dumond discusses the task of removing teeth at Austerlitz because he found it very distasteful, and odd. It seems that Tavira was a rather imperious sort, who delighted in the fact that he was in charge of a detachment of French soldiers. Dumond was incensed that he must take orders from a foreigner, and a Moor at that. As they rode around the military hospitals after the battle, Dumond was aghast that Tavira desired only certain types of teeth, and that he searched extensively for perfect teeth, not marred in any way by decay or fractures. What shocked Dumond most was that Tavira did not take the teeth from the hundreds of rotting corpses, which the Lieutenant thought was bad enough. Tavira extracted the teeth himself only from soldiers who had recently died of their wounds. Dumond complains, here, about being assigned to chaperone a ghoul. He writes of going to confession as often as possible."

Murph could sense the pain of the French officer. "Does Dumond describe Tavira at all?"

"Yes, he writes of a handsome man, nearly as tall as himself, which would make Tavira somewhere around six feet tall. He was light skinned, for a Moor, with oily black hair and a broad white smile, the usage of which Dumond found creepy in today's parlance. The Moor was constantly making notes in a worn leatherbound book, which he closed immediately every time Dumond or anyone else came near. Dumond wondered about a suspiciously heavy pouch that Tavira always carried on his person. Dumond became bitter as time passed and resented Tavira for his power and apparent wealth. Dumond, a devout man, writes that he could not understand why a heathen should have such power in the court of his Emperor, but Dumond was fiercely loyal to Napoleon and did his duty exactly as ordered. Upon their return to Paris, Dumond was promoted by Napoleon and returned to his cavalry unit."

"What an amazing story!" Carli was stunned, and they all began talking among themselves.

"Ah, but there is one more thing." Father Albers held up his index finger for silence. "Dumond was injured in battle a few months later. He was knocked from his horse, and struck in the mouth by a rifle butt. He lost several teeth. When he returned to his home in Normandie to recuperate, he was visited by Tavira, who offered to make him a denture. Against his misgivings, he was convinced by his wife to have the teeth made. In thanks for his past service, the dentist made him a denture with a gold palate and four teeth wired to it. Dumond reports that it fit much better than he thought it would. Dumond returned to his unit and survived the remainder of the war, living out the rest of his exceptionally long life as a successful farmer." Albers paused for effect.

Murph couldn't resist and took the bait, "And then, Tavira visits him on his death bed and wants the denture back!"

"Precisely!" Father Albers was well pleased. "Dumond writes that it must have been Tavira's son who came to see him, as he looked the same as before, in spite of the years that had passed."

"That about settles it, then," Murph seemed convinced. "Once Tavira started hiding the gold, it would be logical for his lineage to continue the task. Someone, at some time would have to collect all of the gold in order to perform the ritual.

"Since it seems that the wheels are turning suddenly," Murph stood up and began to pace around the rug that occupied the center of the room, "someone may be working now to gather the gold, and that could leave a trail... Father Mahoney, I need to borrow that computer."

Murph began a search for suspicious deaths and dental problems. After filtering and refining the search, he discovered that the last surviving soldier who had been captured and led by the Japanese on the Bataan Death March was a dentist. He had lived to the extreme age of 97, but had finally succumbed, passing away in his sleep a month ago. The strange part of his tale was that there had been a break-in at the funeral home after the calling hours. The mortuary had been ransacked, but nothing significant seemed to be missing, except for the gold bridgework in the mouth of the poor dentist. Police were puzzled, but chalked the burglary up to petty thieves looking to make a quick buck selling the gold.

Carli took Murph's MacBook and continued on that vein. She found a police report about a small-time hood found in Washington, D.C. in a dumpster, with his neck broken. The coroner found a human denture held tightly in his hand, and his fingers were broken as if they had been bitten. The denture had a name printed on it for identification, Edwin Shafter! And the denture had a tooth broken out of it. When the police contacted the family, they confirmed that the Senator had a dentist put a gold molar in his denture years ago for good luck. After that, his political career had taken off. The family was understandably outraged, and the police were at a loss.

Murph looked over her shoulder and reported. "The body was found in a dumpster just off the National Mall, in John Marshall Place park. That's right near the Center for Restorative Excellence! And it was less than two weeks ago."

Not to be outdone, Father Mahoney had searched on Father Albers' desktop computer and now chimed in; "In this curious report, there is no death, but Christie's Auctions reported that an anonymous Middle Eastern bidder won the auction for the dentures of Winston Churchill. After a fierce bidding war, they went for an astronomical sum, more than ten times what the pre-auction esti-mate had been. They describe the dentures as a full set of upper and lower dentures, intact, with *gold molars* in the lower arch."

Murph smacked his fist into his palm. "That's it! It has to be! They're collecting the gold, but we still don't know who."

"Or what they want with us," Carli added somberly.

"Ah, Miss Caroline." Father Albers looked every bit the teacher again. "That is obvious. At first, it was *you* they wanted because of what you had discovered! Now it is *Michael* they want because of what he has accidentally taken. Without the investment to cast the teeth for the ritual, all the gold is worthless. They will hunt you down mercilessly until they have everything they need."

Murph nodded his head in agreement. "There appear to be two groups, Manny Farouk, whom I thought I knew, and this Hamid al-Said, whom I have to admit worries me more. His con-nection to Omar Bengdara is a big concern, as Omar is clearly a professional thug. We're not completely powerless, though."

"How so?" The worry was etched in Father Mahoney's face.

"We have something they want. Which gives us the ability to negotiate. Also, we have started to figure out what their plan is, so we need to stop running away and get ahead of them somehow. Sun Tsu said that first you need to know your enemy. Then you need to take charge of the situation."

Carli continued to search the Internet and got another hit. "I was looking into the fact that all of these people had led a long life and seemed to have accomplished something significant. There was a man in Germany just recently who was in his nineties when he died of an apparent heart attack. The odd thing was that he had apparently just had a tooth extracted. It appeared to have been a very difficult and violent surgery, but none of his family knew of him going to the dentist or talking about a tooth problem. The police found it suspicious but could not find conclusive evidence of a crime. He appeared to have collapsed in his study and was bleeding severely from his mouth. It happened just two weeks ago. His name was Willi Schultz."

"Where in Germany?" Murph was calling up a map on his computer.

"Nordlingen, a little town between Munich and Stuttgart."

"That's not far from here. I think we should go there and see what we can find out firsthand. I'm done running!"

Father Albers was impressed. "While I admire your bravado, there is still that little matter of the Italian police having a warrant out for your arrest. You are safe in the Vatican, for they have no jurisdiction here, but when you leave…"

Father Mahoney began to laugh. "But that's easy. Lawrence, you will provide them the way out!"

"How so?"

"Tomorrow, you leave for a visit to the Swiss archives in Zurich. You are taking several assistants with you. Who will notice two more members of the clergy in your party?" He reached for another scone, seeming very pleased with himself. "Michael, if we get you out of Italy and to Zurich, can you get to Nordlingen?"

"I believe that I have someone I can call there. When I studied at The Pankey Institute, a member of our class was from Zurich. We became friends, and he invited me to visit him in Zurich. It's time to take him up on his offer and see if he meant it!"

Father Albers took his flip chart notes and put them through the industrial sized paper shredder next to his desk. "Habit, I suppose." Then he began to tidy up. "It is settled then. We leave tomorrow after morning Mass."

"Yes, Father." Carli and Murph responded together.

"I have many details that require my attention before I leave. Brian, please see that Michael and Carli have anything they need today and then be sure that they have rooms in which to get a good night's sleep. I believe they will need it! ...Michael, this would be a good day to show Miss Chamoun the wonders of St. Peter's."

"With pleasure!" They packed up, and he took Carli's hand. The best place to start a tour on such a beautiful sunny day was to climb the dome and take in the gorgeous views from the top of the Basilica, with Rome spread out before them.

Chapter 45

Father Albers celebrated the morning Mass, with Father Mahoney assisting, in one of the small chapels in the catacombs under St. Peter's. Murph and Carli found the simplicity of the service in this setting to be a powerful experience. The party quickly prepared for departure, with Murph and Carli both donning the black cassocks of young initiates to the order. Carli wrapped her hair up into a biretta, the red square cap worn by members of the clergy. From a distance, she would pass for a young boy. The disguises would not hold to close scrutiny, so they were all a bit nervous, though they tried not to show it.

They boarded the blacked-out Mercedes SUV, with a driver and Father Albers in the front. Two young priests, who were Albers' assistants sat in the middle. Carli and Murph were relegated to the shadows of the third row of seats. The van headed quickly out of the gate, leaving behind the safety of the Vatican. Much to Murph's unease, he thought he saw Omar lurking in the crowd as the Mercedes sped by. His suspicions were confirmed when they came upon a hastily erected police checkpoint near the city limits of Rome.

The driver slowed as the SUV approached the barrier, a road

sign marked ALTO. Two Alfa Romeos angled together, causing the road to narrow. Several Carabinieri stood beside the cars, and one held out his white-gloved hand in the universal sign to stop.

Murph hurriedly scanned the crowd for Omar and was pleased not to see him, but his heart stopped when he saw the Carabinieri Captain talking to a tall Arab man with slicked-back, jet-black hair and a woman of regal bearing, with long straight hair the color of ink. She looked up, and Murph could feel her eyes trying to penetrate the tinted windows of the Mercedes.

He motioned to Carli. "Is that Hamid al-Said and friend?"

She gulped and managed a hoarse "Yes."

Father Albers nodded to indicate that he had heard as well, but he did not look back. He lowered his window as the Carabinieri officer walked over.

"Good morning, Father. What brings you out so early in the day?"

"Ah, Capitano… Abruzzo, is it not? How good to see you!"

"Why Father, how kind of you to remember my name." The Carabinieri Captain was shocked. They had met only once, when preparing the security for an exhibit of Vatican treasures outside the Holy See. But Father Albers was a man who knew it was important to never forget a face.

"I always remember good Catholics who have served Italy and us in the Vatican well. I trust you and your children are well."

"Yes, Father. Thank you for asking." Abruzzo looked ill at ease. "Father, I hate to question you, but there is the matter of fugitives who were seen heading into the Vatican. I believe my office sent you a fax concerning them yesterday."

"Yes, Capitano. I saw that information. Terrible business, murder! The world is so violent these days."

"Father, I must ask you. Where are you going today?"

"My assistants and I are making a scheduled trip to Zurich to consult with the Archives there. We are planning a joint show of artifacts and manuscripts in the next few months. This is a planning meeting, much like our meeting to arrange security last year."

"How many people are with you, Father?"

"My driver, four assistants, and myself."

Abruzzo leaned in and looked back. The priests smiled. Murph nodded as well, though hidden by shadows, and Carli's head was down, as if she were sleeping. He leaned back on his heels and hesitated. He knew he should conduct a thorough search, but he hated to offend the priest.

Sensing his indecision, the woman with Hamid shouted in a shrill tone, "Make them get out, you idiot!"

That did it. That made three days in a row of being bullied by foreigners! Not today! He was tired of being pushed around by these Muslims. "Thank you, Father. I will not hold you up anymore from you business. Enjoy your trip to Zurich, and have a safe return."

"Thank you, Capitano. I will remember you and your family in my prayers."

Abruzzo waved them on, through the checkpoint and returned to face the Egyptians. While the woman was seething, coiled, waiting to strike, Hamid was calm. He placed his hand on her arm. "Banthaira, there will be a time for that."

He faced Abruzzo. "Capitano, I find your behavior unacceptable. Yet I do not have the power to change it. Rest assured that your superiors will hear from me." He turned on his heel and walked back to their waiting car.

Hamid opened the door for Banthaira and then got in himself. He looked up at Omar, sitting in the front passenger seat. "Well?"

Omar set down the infrared microphone he had been aiming on the Mercedes SUV and removed his headphones. "They travel to Zurich."

"Then so shall we." He tapped the driver on the shoulder. "Go!"

Chapter 46

Manny Farouk was confident. His contacts in the Vatican had confirmed that Carli and Murph had reached the Vatican safely. His informants also reported that the couple had left the next day with a party traveling to Zurich, but the contacts did not know Murph's and Carli's ultimate destination.

Manny considered his options and decided that, rather than chase his prey, he would wait for them to come to him. He reasoned they would be smart enough to want to return to Washington at some point. He ordered his people to follow them and determine where they were going. Manny was to receive regular reports on their activities, but no attempt was to be made to stop them.

Feeling he had attended to all the details he could, Manny boarded the Gulfstream and headed back to Washington, D.C. In due time, his apprentice would seek him out. Of that he was sure.

Chapter 47

Traveling with papers bearing the Vatican seal, Father Albers and his party easily crossed the border into Switzerland. Murph had searched out his contact the day before and was pleased to find that his office was in the central part of Zurich. He had discussed with Father Albers that they did not want to put the priest or his mission in any danger, so they would be dropped off quietly in Zurich and make their way to visit the dentist on foot. The Mercedes slid smoothly down the Freiestrasse and turned into an alley, coming to a stop in the shadows.

Murph and Carli had removed their cassocks and were once again in their familiar traveling clothes. Both had slept well and taken a much-needed shower. They looked primed and ready for the next phase of the adventure. Murph had planned for their exit to be quick, but Father Albers motioned for them to wait. Both priests got out of the Mercedes, while the driver kept an anxious watch.

Father Albers extended his hands and placed them on their shoulders. "Michael, my son, may the Lord bless you and watch over you both. May He give courage, strength, and clear vision in your task…"

Father Mahoney interrupted, "and may He bring you back safely to us… because I really want to know what happens!"

Murph and Carli both laughed. "Amen to that!"

Father Albers removed his glasses and massaged his tired eyes. He regarded Murph carefully. "Michael, this is an important quest. There are ancient powers in motion here. You have been trained well by our Order. In everything you do, remember *Ad majorem Dei gloriam*."

"For the greater glory of God!" Murph translated for Carli. "It's the motto of the Jesuits."

"I believe that the two of you have the ability to avert a great evil. Our thoughts and prayers go with you."

"Thank you, Father. We will do our best." With nothing more they could say, they turned and raced off down the alley.

Father Mahoney waved after them. Father Albers made the sign of the cross over their backs as they ran. Losing sight of them, as they rounded the corner at the end, the priests returned to the Mercedes, Father Mahoney shaking his head sadly.

Chapter 48

According to Murph's GoogleMaps survey, the alley they had selected opened into the Steinweis Platz. Across the square was the Kinderspital Zurich, the children's hospital. Their target was in the next block. Murph scanned the busy street carefully, but nothing stood out as unusual for a Wednesday afternoon. They tried to walk with the flow and pace of the other pedestrians, attempting to draw as little attention to themselves as possible. It was tough to do, as Murph was significantly taller than average and Carli was petite and stunningly beautiful with her auburn hair now loose and blowing in the breeze.

They crossed the Ilgenstrasse and came upon a modern office building of five floors. Entering the lobby, they found the name Murph wanted and got on the elevator for the top floor. Getting so close to the goal, Murph had failed to notice the BMW motorcycle lingering across the street, the rider sitting quietly. His matte black helmet had the visor smoked, so they could not see his eyes follow them into the building. As they ascended the elevator, he snapped open his cell phone and reported.

Murph led Carli to the door labeled Dr. Klaus Janzen, Zahnarzt (Dentist). *I sure hope this works,* he thought to himself, and he opened the door. They entered a modern reception area, beautifully appointed in black leather furniture and white marble flooring and counters. The walls were a rich, warm gray. The receptionist was a perky blonde in her twenties, whose head popped up immediately when they came in.

"Guten tag! Wie gehts mit einen?" Seeing Murph's blank expression as he struggled to translate, she shifted immediately, "Auf English? Of course!"

He nodded and managed a weak "Thank you!"

"Vait a minute," she stood up and came around the desk, "You are Docktor Murphy! I recognize you from *The Dental Apprentice* on television. Docktor Klaus is always talking about you. He is so proud of knowing you! He tells everyone!"

"Well, I'm glad to have attended a class with him as well."

"Oh, let me tell him you are here! He vill be so happy! Just vait here!" and she raced off down the hall toward the sound of the dental drill in the distance.

Carli was looking at the beautiful black and white photography that graced the walls of the reception room, when the noises stopped suddenly. "Vat! Here in my glinic?"

Murph had to laugh. Klaus always pronounced it "glinic." No matter how much Murph tried to help him during their time together in the esthetics class at The Pankey Institute, that word wouldn't change. His English was excellent, but every day Klaus asked, "Do you think we will go to the glinic today?" After a while, they both couldn't stop laughing, and their classmates wondered what was up with the inside joke. Murph was laughing now, and Carli looked at him suspiciously, having clearly seen nothing funny!

"Murph!" Klaus burst from the hallway into the lobby. "Ach! How have you been?" Klaus Janzen was about ten years older than Murph, showing more wrinkles around his eyes. His tan showed his love of the beach and the sun. His hair thinning slightly, he had taken to having it replanted. Murph thought, the new growth was coming in well. His octagonal glasses were rimless, with polished metal sides, clearly the latest in fashion. Under his long white lab coat, his Cavalli crocodile-print silk shirt was open at the collar. He swept in and embraced Murph in a back-pounding hug.

Carli relaxed a bit. This was going better than she expected.

Maybe it would work out after all. Murph introduced Carli, and Klaus snapped to attention, every bit the gentleman, and kissed the back of her hand.

"Katrina! Please make my friends welcome. I have to finish with this patient, but she is my last for the day. Have some wine and cheese, and make yourselves comfortable." He led them into a conference room with a round tabletop of black marble and a plush, white Berber rug. He offered them the leather chairs to relax in, and then his staff was quick to come in and introduce themselves. They all seemed to regard Murph as quite the celebrity and peppered him with questions about *The Dental Apprentice*. There were plenty of questions for Carli on American fashion and pop culture as well.

Murph excused himself and made his way to the treatment room. "Klaus, may I come in and observe you at work?"

"I would be honored to have such an esteemed guest!" Klaus said with a laugh. He introduced Murph to his patient. Somehow Murph wasn't surprised to discover that Klaus was placing porcelain veneers on the 21-year-old blonde model, who would be competing for Miss Switzerland in the next year. The dentistry and the patient were stunning.

After complementing her and Klaus about the beautiful smile, as she left, Murph clapped Klaus on the back. "Just as I expected, the finest dentist in the world!"

Klaus put his arm around Murph. "Nein, only in all Europe!" He laughed, "You have America all sown up, my friend." They walked down the hall and found Carli chatting away with the ladies. "Enough, all of you, you vill badger her to death!"

His staff laughed off the rebuke and left to tend to the tasks to close up the office. Klaus closed the conference room door and sat down opposite the two Americans. "I'm always pleased to have guests, but the fact that you came unannounced would lead me to think that this is not a social call. Yes?"

Murph became serious as well. "You did say that if I ever needed anything, I should ask…"

Klaus smiled. "Indeed I did! So how can I help?"

As succinctly as possible, Murph and Carli explained their situation. It seemed even more outlandish when they laid it out on the table. Murph feared the worst — that his friend would call him crazy and throw them out.

Much to both of their amazement, Klaus listened to the tale, tapped his fingers together, and jumped up. "Vell then, it is like one of your American movies! You know I love adventure, so even if this is all just verruckt, crazy as you say, then it will be fun to be on the chase together." He walked around the room, thinking aloud. "And if you are right, what a story to tell mein kinder!"

Klaus went to his office to hang up his lab coat and pick up his briefcase. They said goodbye to the staff, with kisses for all, and he told his staff not to call him tomorrow. It was his day off anyway, but he would not be answering any emergencies.

He led them down the elevator to the parking deck below ground and to his waiting car, a gleaming black Porsche Panamera Turbo. Klaus beamed like a proud father. "Now you will be treated to the finest in German engineering. Buckle up! All it understands is speed."

They settled into the buttery soft black leather as Klaus fired up the turbo and reveled in the roar. Murph looked at Carli in the back seat as she tightened the strap on her belt, looking anxiously out the darkly tinted windows. With a squeal of tires, Klaus weaved out of the parking deck and burst onto an alley into the late afternoon sun. Their exit was from the back of the building, and the dark watchman on the motorcycle was left sitting in front of the building, wondering why they never came out.

Klaus had called home while he sped through the streets of Zurich and out into the countryside. If his wife was annoyed at his sudden arrival with houseguests, she hid it well. Erica Janzen could not have been a more pleasant and responsive hostess. Where Klaus was all flash and style, she had a simple, timeless beauty — dark hair and eyes, with an easy grace and class that came with her background in the Swiss aristocracy. She welcomed Murph and Carli to their estate and made them feel instantly at ease. They were shown to a sumptuous guest bedroom and allowed to freshen up before dinner.

After small talk and a fabulous meal, Klaus poured an excellent cognac for them, and they retired to the library, settling in high-backed leather chairs around a fire.

Murph laid out the basics of his plan. "We need to get across the border into Germany and to Nordlingen. I hope to learn something there about the mystery surrounding the death of Willi Schultz and his missing tooth."

Klaus had done some research before dinner and broached the subject with his wife. "It is about a four-hour drive, maybe a bit less in the Porsche!" He smiled slyly.

"Klaus!" Erica scolded him lightly. "We will accompany you, of course!"

Carli protested. "But we couldn't impose on you..."

"Nonsense!" Erica made the decision sound final. "I will not let Klaus have all the fun by himself. He left me behind when he went to America to that Pankey place, and I told him I would not be forgotten again. He says he did nothing but talk teeth for a week, but I just cannot believe that is possible."

Murph started to defend his friend, but he quickly realized that it was a battle he had better stay out of. "When we get there, my German is poor so…"

"Ha! You make me laugh! Your German is like a child. You would not be able to order wiener schnitzel and a bier!" Klaus smiled broadly. "We are, as you Americans say, 'way ahead of you!'"

Erica smiled sweetly and took several papers out of a file folder. "While you were washing up, I did some research. The house where the man died is for sale, but as you would imagine, there has not been much interest yet. Tomorrow, while we are driving, I will call the realtor and arrange for us to see the house."

Carli agreed. "That's an excellent idea! That would be a perfect place to start."

Klaus clapped his hands together, "It's all settled then. Tomorrow we begin the great adventure!"

Erica thought that their youngest daughter, now away at the Universite de Geneve, might have some clothes that would fit Carli, so they went off to see if they could expand her very limited wardrobe. Murph and Klaus sat by the fire and laughed about their time together in Miami for the Pankey Esthetic Dentistry course, and they caught up on what had happened in the years that had passed since then. It was late when they went to bed. They had an early start planned, and the morning would come quickly upon them.

Chapter 49

Klaus and Murph were comfortably chatting and completely unaware of the presence of the darkly clad man hiding in the bushes under the window. He clicked open his cell phone, and in clipped Arabic, he confirmed to Omar Bengdara that he had found his quarry.

Earlier that day, as the afternoon had worn on, the rider had become tired of waiting outside the building. He had realized that Murph and Carli must have left by another exit. Entering the lobby, it had taken only a few seconds to determine the building contained only three dental offices. He had identified the home addresses of the dentists and visited each in turn. Sadly for him, the Janzen home was his third, but his persistence had been rewarded because Omar had seemed pleased, or at least less irritated, when the scout, Abir Sharif, had given him the good news.

As a prize for his excellent work, Abir was required to stand watch outside the home and to report in when the group was on the move again. It was going to be a long night, but he was used to hardship, given his years in the Egyptian Special Forces. With his motorcycle carefully concealed in the woods nearby, he settled down against the stone wall of the house, hidden by the shrubbery to wait until dawn.

Omar closed his phone and reported to Hamid and Banthaira that the dentist and his girlfriend had been discovered, and the trace had been set for the morning. Omar returned to his room in the hotel, having been dismissed from the suite occupied by his employers. He did not resent the arrangement. He had given years of service in the military and understood the chain of command. He took orders well, never questioning, and carrying them out with ruthless efficiency. It was the way of his world, simple and definite, and he preferred it that way. He slept soundly until the morning.

Hamid al-Said had intended to sleep, but he found that it eluded him. There was something he was missing, and it lingered around the edges of his consciousness. He could not grasp it, but he knew it was there. He could easily capture Murphy and the girl, and he could take back the vessel with the investment. He knew that Banthaira would be happy to torture them and learn everything they knew, but he wasn't sure that it would give him what he was seeking. He decided to wait and to follow them, hoping they would blunder into something that would make everything clear.

He had waited so long for this moment… maybe it would be only a little longer before everything fell into place. Making his decision, he fell into a restless sleep and dreamed of chasing ghosts and then finding that the ghosts were chasing him. He awoke tired and shaken, like he had not felt in many years. Something was shifting in the sands!

Banthaira, for her part, slept little, but this was nothing new. She remained aloof, with steely resolve. Her temper was difficult to control, and the edge of her wrath was something that all her servants feared. No matter their station in life, they all were her servants, after all, and she tolerated their shortcomings and weaknesses poorly. If only she could do things herself, it would be much easier, but that simply would not do for a person of her position. Even Hamid, though he was her lover, was merely a tool for her larger plans. She had realized that it was in her best interest to have him believe that he was in charge, but she knew that she was the true power. She fingered the scarab amulet of gold and turquoise at her throat. Yes, it would soon all be over, her years of planning finally coming to pass. Just a few more moves and the game would end forever, and she would be the winner. This she knew to be true.

Chapter 50

Murph awoke rested and comfortable, Carli nestled in the crook of his arm. They slept soundly until the barking dog alarm he used on his iPhone woke them. He reached over and turned it off. She rolled over, face down into the pillow and moaned about wanting a few more minutes. He ruffled her hair and kissed her lightly as she lifted her head. "Places to go, things to do!"

Murph padded into the bathroom and turned on the shower. He shaved and they got ready quickly, coming down to breakfast. Murph had decided on wearing his dark charcoal slacks and pastel blue silk polo shirt, under his well-used, pale gray, cotton Lacoste sweater. His luggage was limited, so it was the slacks or the jeans, and for today, playing the American couple going to see a house in Germany, the slacks and polo shirt seemed more appropriate. Carli looked delightful in crisp black linen slacks and a lavender tank and sweater set belonging to Kristin Janzen — who hopefully wouldn't mind her mother giving them away while she was at school.

Klaus was prepared, and Erica was working in the kitchen. Carli quickly offered to help, as the two of them had become fast friends. In mere minutes, a fine breakfast of eggs, ham, whole grain toast and jam was prepared. Klaus had proudly managed the coffee, and they all sat down for a good meal. They reviewed the plan again, and Murph and Klaus packed the car with a cooler of drinks and snacks, as if they were on holiday. Klaus drove the Porsche, with Murph riding shotgun. Carli and Erica happily sat in the back seat. They sped out the drive and onto the winding road, heading for the German border.

They missed the grey-clad rider stretching out the kinks in his back. He climbed on his BMW motorcycle and kept a respectful distance behind them. He reported in every thirty minutes with a position update. As it became clear that this was not a pleasure drive through the Alps, Hamid and his entourage prepared to follow.

The Porsche passed easily across the border, and Abir informed Omar of their path. Closing his phone, Omar dutifully reported to Hamid, "They have crossed the border into Germany. Their route leads between Stuttgart and Munich. Possibly toward the city of Ulm. Abir is trailing them at a safe distance. They do not seem aware of his presence. He will continue to report as their destination becomes more apparent."

Hamid thought for a moment. "I know where they are going. They are proceeding to Nordlingen. We need to get there as quickly as possible. See to it." He raised the window separating the seats of the Mercedes limo, closing himself off from Omar and the driver. He sat back in the seat, folding his hands in front of his face, tapping his fingers together nervously.

I know where they are going, he thought to himself, *but how do THEY know? They cannot possibly understand. We must get there.* He smacked his fist onto the seat. *I need to take them now!*

Banthaira simply smiled. Lacking any warmth at all, her

smile was an evil disfigurement of her face. As if reading his thoughts, she said, "We will catch them… and then they will tell us everything we want to know." She turned away, took out a file, and smoothed her polished nails to a razor sharp point.

Chapter 51

The countryside of southern Germany had been beautiful as the Porsche sped along, and they were excited when they pulled into the Marktplatz in Nordlingen, arriving at the Kaiserhof Hotel Sonne. There, they found Lilli Utsch, the realtor, waiting for them in the lobby. She had chosen this quaint site, because the dark wood floors and bar were warm and inviting, evoking the Bavarian charm of the region. She was determined to make as positive an impression as possible. She hoped they did not know about the house's recent history, as she knew the mysterious death of its owner would make the house difficult to sell.

As soon as they entered, Lilli greeted Klaus and Erica warmly, welcoming them to Nordlingen.

Klaus took control of the situation, and shifted to English to introduce his friends, "Lilli, I would like to introduce Carli and Doctor… "

"Michael Murphy!" She interrupted him, giggling like a schoolgirl in spite of herself, instantly recognizing Murph. She shook his hand and couldn't stop herself, standing up on her toes and wrapping her arms around his neck, kissing him on the cheek. "I loved you on *The Dental Apprentice*! I was sad when you didn't win, but I'm so glad that you are coming to Germany. Can I be your first patient?"

"Hello!" Carli was frowning, arms crossed. Klaus and Erica tried hard not to laugh. "It was better in Egypt," Carli observed dryly, "There no one had television, and it was easier to get around without *Dr. Apprentice* here always making a scene."

Lilli recovered her composure, "Oh, I am sorry. I just got carried away." She waved to the barmaid. "Let's sit down and go over the property before I take you there." She motioned Murph to a table and sat next to him, leaving Carli on the other side with the Janzens. Murph looked up at Carli, trapped, and shrugged. Carli tried to look irritated but just smiled and sat down. Frothing steins of local beer were brought over with huge soft pretzels, and Lilli went through her sales pitch. This area would be perfect for such an esteemed American dentist to establish practice. After a few minutes and a little beer, Murph was warming to the idea. Then Carli kicked him in the shin under the table, and he remembered the task at hand.

"Lilli, can you tell me something about the owner of the house?"

Lilli tried not to frown, but she knew this was the tricky part. She wasn't sure how much they knew, and it wouldn't help her to give away any more than she had to. " He was a successful businessman here. His company made toys. The stuffed animals, especially the bears, were prized and collected all around the world."

Carli pushed her a bit. "I see that the house is being sold by his estate. How long ago did he pass away?"

"A couple of months ago, I'm afraid. He was very old."

"Oh yes." Carli continued. "I seem to remember reading something about that. There were questions surrounding the nature of his passing, I think."

"Yes," Lilli was forced to admit. "Apparently, he passed away of a heart attack. The police were called in to make sure it was from natural causes, and they didn't find evidence of any crime," she lied smoothly. "His sons want to sell the house quickly since they do not live out here in the country. I think you will like the price."

Murph could sense tension building between the two women. "Lilli, that sounds great. Can we see the house?"

Lilli assured him that if he didn't love it, she had several other homes to show them. They left the Kaiserhof and went back outside into the bright sunshine. Lilli offered to drive Murph in her BMW while Klaus followed.

As they started the Porsche, Klaus couldn't help noting, "I think she is trying to sell more than a house!"

"And the TV star's head is getting too big to fit in this car."

"Well, it could be a brilliant plan. If he keeps the St. Pauli girl occupied, we can search the house more effectively."

"It had better be a plan, for his sake!"

"Oh Carli, " Erica patted her arm to reassure her, "I've seen the way he looks at you."

Lilli had pulled into the driveway, so Klaus parked the Porsche in the street and they got out. Lilli was walking Murph up the brick walk, laughing and tossing her hair.

"Sheesh!" Carli snorted, and Klaus burst out laughing. Erica elbowed him in the stomach, which shut him up.

They walked up the flagstone driveway, admiring the series of carefully trimmed topiary in ornamental red clay pots that flanked the drive. Opening the front door, Lilli left them standing in the foyer as she went to turn on the lights and open the curtains, brightening the house. Both Murph and Carli smiled. They liked it immediately. It was just the kind of warm, cheerful home they would want... but that wasn't the point today.

Klaus looked at Murph and asked quietly, "Just what are we looking for while we are here?"

Murph shrugged, "I don't really know... anything Egyptian or looking like something relating to the Pharaoh's gold... or anything from his dentist? It's a long shot anyway, but it's worth a try. I'll try to keep Lilli occupied so you can search."

Carli, still frowning, asked, "Why don't you have her show you the bedroom?"

Before Murph could protest, Lilli came back.

With another toss of her hair, Lilli beckoned them down the hallway. "The home is a center hall colonial. In the front of the house, here, is the sitting room with a study in the back. The kitchen is to the left with the dining room to the front of that side of the house. There are four bedrooms upstairs. Why don't we start there?"

As Lilli led Murph up the stairs, Klaus and Erica couldn't stop laughing. Carli mocked her in a falsetto voice, *"Why don't we start upstairs? Nya, nya nya!"*

Klaus noticed that Lilli didn't seem to care that the three weren't following. "I think we should look in the study."

Carli agreed. "They probably have cleaned everything, but we need to be sure. The report on the Internet implied that he died in there."

They left Erica at the base of the stairs as a lookout, and went into the study. It was a fairly large room, with two tall windows open to the garden in back. The heavy curtains had been pulled back, and the room was flooded with the afternoon sun. Walking around a leather sofa, they found a coffee table with magazines spread on its top and two tufted leather armchairs on either side. A Persian rug anchored the grouping. Carli noticed that the stain on the oak floor was darker right around the edges of the rug.

"Look here!" She knelt down and touched the floor near the rug. "This is a new rug, and it's slightly smaller than the old one. The stain has lightened in the sun over the years, and this area was covered before. I wonder if the old carpet was removed because of the blood on it?"

"That would make sense if he died here." Klaus went over to the bookcase and scanned the titles. "The owner was well read. This is an excellent library."

Carli went to the orderly and functional desk, where she observed a decanter of cognac, glasses, pen, pencils, and photographs of his family. As an old-school Prussian gentleman, there was no computer on the desktop. Instead, his leather bound calendar sat in the center. The day planner showed a week at a time and stood open to the week he had passed away. Klaus translated the calendar notations for Carli, and they learned that the gentleman had attended a festival in his honor on the morning of his death. Not wanting to touch anything, Carli took a pencil from the cup and used it to turn the pages of the calendar. When the page turned and uncovered the current week, she stopped and gasped.

An engraved invitation lay between the pages. Wilhelm Schultz had been invited as a guest of honor to the *Ring of Gold*. The event was to be held at the Willard Hotel in Washington, D.C. The date had been circled in the calendar. It was clear he had planned to go.

"Klaus, today is Thursday, right?"

"Yes, Carli, and that invitation is for this Saturday!"

"Look at the RSVP address! It's from the Washington Center for Esthetic and Restorative Excellence!"

By his furrowed brow, she knew Klaus was concerned. "Dr. Farouk!"

Erica coughed from the hallway. "They are coming down!"

she whispered harshly.

Carli hesitated only for a moment and then used the pencil to slide the invitation out of the book to where she could reach it without touching the desk. She picked up the invitation, turned the calendar back to where they had started, and pocketed the invitation and pencil in her bag. They hurried out of the study and ducked down the hall.

As Lilli and Murph came down the stairs, the three acted like they had been coming back from the kitchen. Murph raised an eyebrow and asked, "What do you think?"

Carli wrinkled her nose and tried to sound snotty, "I don't think it's big enough. We need more room for our guests. You know full well they'll be coming over all the time from the States. I've seen enough. Let's go!"

She led off toward the front door at a brisk pace, with Erica and Klaus quickly behind her. Murph shrugged his shoulders and mouthed to Lilli, "*She's the boss.*"

They stopped briefly on the front porch as Lilli locked the doors. Carli continued her spoiled brat act. "If we are coming to Germany, I want to be in a bigger city than this. Klaus, let's leave the countryside tonight, have some fun, and continue looking in a city tomorrow morning. You know how I like the urban nightlife!"

Lilli bit her lip as Carli led the little party to the Porsche. "Michael, let me give you my card, so you can call me." *When you get rid of that bitch, she implied with her eyes.* "I have it in my car."

Murph called to Carli that he would be over in a minute, and walked Lilli to the BMW. Lilli reached in and took a business card from her portfolio. She wrote her personal number on the back and gave it to Murph. As he was about to escape, she grabbed him and kissed him. He pushed her away and staggered back in surprise. He bumped into one of the topiaries, and when he knocked it over, he was surprised that it was so light.

"MURPH!" Carli's shout was urgent. His head snapped around, expecting her fury, but he realized that it wasn't anger but fear. Carli was pointing at a black Mercedes limo barreling down the street toward them, and they both realized they had seen it before.

Murph raised his right hand, index finger pointing upwards, and made a rapid rotating motion.

It was the international sign to "crank it up" and Klaus caught on instantly, unlocking the doors and starting the engine. Murph quickly thanked a confused Lilli for her help and promised to call. He bent down to stand up the topiary, and then all hell broke loose.

Hidden in the hedge separating the house and its neighbor, Abir Sharif had been sitting on his motorcycle, watching the developing scene. He had been ordered by Omar to observe and take no action. When Omar arrived, he wanted to personally capture the Americans.

When Abir realized that his quarry had recognized the approaching Mercedes and that Omar would not make it in time, Abir revved his engine and moved in to stop the Porsche.

The sound of the motorcycle startled Murph, and he saw Abir burst through the hedge, a blur heading for the Porsche. Adrenalin rushed through his body as Murph saw the black-helmeted rider pull a handgun from the small of his back and aim it at Carli.

Murph's grip tightened on the trunk of the topiary, and he swung it with the strength of an Olympic hammer thrower. Luckily, his timing was perfect, and the clay pot struck Abir square in the chest. The riderless motorcycle continued across the lawn and fell on its side before reaching the street.

Abir's body had crashed onto the brick walkway with such force that it bounced like a rag doll onto the grass. From where he stood, it was clear to Murph that Abir was likely unconscious with multiple injuries. *He is out of the chase,* Murph thought as he ran for the Porsche, glancing at the prone rider to see if he was still breathing. Thankfully, he was.

Murph jumped into the passenger seat as Klaus hit the accelerator. The forward momentum of the car caused the car door to slam shut. Murph gave Lilli a smile and a wave as they sped away. Standing open-mouthed like a statue, Lilli raised her hand to wave back and remained staring as the Mercedes limo raced past, its tires screaming on the pavement.

Lilli knew enough to pack up and get away as quickly as possible. There was a man unconscious on the lawn, and he had a gun. She wanted no part of being there when he woke up. She threw her things into the BMW and drove away as fast as she could, shaking her head all the way. She decided to drop that listing immediately. There was definitely something wrong with that house!

Chapter 52

Carli shouted above the Porsche's roar, "They knew we were there! That guy on the motorcycle was waiting for us to come out!"

Murph was securing his seat belt and generating a road map on his iPhone. "I think we left the house sooner than expected — before they could completely set the trap." He was trying to sound calm, but his heart was racing. "Klaus, get on the Autobahn as soon as possible. I hope the Porsche can outrun that Mercedes limo."

Klaus was grinning like crazy man! "Outrun and out corner. Just watch me!" And he sent the Porsche around a tight corner, its tires screaming louder than Carli and Erica in the back seat.

As they weaved through the residential neighborhood leaving Nordlingen, the Porsche gained ground with every turn. Klaus was as masterful a driver as he had boasted. They entered the Autobahn like a rocket, with about a half-kilometer lead on the Mercedes. Looking back, Murph was delighted to see the flashing blue lights of a German police car intercepting the limo. Unable to see what happened, Murph urged Klaus to keep moving quickly, but not to be so conspicuous now. They had entered the nearest ramp without much thought to their direction so Murph was working quickly to identify their location and possible places to go and hide. They were driving southeast, toward Augsburg, and continuing in that direction would take them to Munich. In the third largest city in Germany, their options for obscurity would increase.

There was no sign of pursuit, but that had not proven to be a sign of safety in the past. They continued at as high a speed as was practical and made excellent time to Munich. They arrived in the ancient city in the late afternoon and merged into the press of rush hour traffic. Murph sat quietly planning. He and Carli were in a trouble of their own making, but now his friends were at risk.

Murph suggested they park the Porsche in a parking garage near the Marienplatz. The bustling center of downtown was alive with people hurrying home after work or arriving for the evening. They came out of the garage onto the square just before 5:00 p.m., and were surrounded by a crowd that was obviously waiting for something significant. At precisely five o'clock they realized why. Much to their delight, the Glockenspiel struck the time, and the figures came out to perform the Schafferltanz, or cooper's dance, as they had three times a day since 1517.

The dance had originally been performed to celebrate the end of the plague, and now Murph and company had something of their own to celebrate. As the bright tones of the carillon bells pealed and the playful colored figures moved, the tension of their flight from Nordlingen burst like a bubble. Murph laughed and hugged Carli, then Erica and Klaus. They all relaxed for a moment and reveled in the experience, standing amid the Gothic architecture, surrounded by tourists and their video cameras.

"Munich is famous for its breweries and the Weissbier," Murph said, craning his neck around. "I need a beer!"

Murph led them through the crowd, towards a building in the distance that proclaimed HOTEL in large blue letters over the door. The setting sun was turning its tan stucco exterior a pale pink color, making the five-story structure easy to spot. "That looks promising, except for the fact that it's pink."

"The Platzl Hotel is tan, " Klaus observed, "but I agree that it makes a good choice. You have excellent taste… for an American!" Klaus slapped him on the back, and they entered the hotel.

The warm and inviting lobby led way to the hotel's Ayingers Tavern, specializing in draught beer from wooden kegs. Klaus and Murph left Erica and Carli at a small table and went off in search of the local brew. They returned shortly with tankards dripping with foam and a bowl of soft pretzels.

"Now I can think better!" Murph concluded happily, raising his mug and announcing "Prosit!"

Klaus raised a mug as well. "To your health!" And they all drank heartily.

Murph asked Carli for the invitation she had taken from Willi Schultz's desk. "There's no doubt that this came from The Center in Washington, and that Manny Farouk is deeply involved. Carli and I have to get back there before Saturday night. That's going to be a tall order, given that it's Thursday evening now."

Carli was feeling a bit free from the beer, so she challenged Murph. "That should be your specialty." They all looked at her.

"Well, you seem to be able to find a friend to help you whenever you need one! I think if I dropped you in the middle of Africa, you'd find an Irish pub and know someone drinking there!"

"There's not much chance of me finding a friend here!" Murph was still laughing when two hands, bearing long fingers and beautifully manicured red nails reached around his neck and tightened across his chest.

Chapter 53

Flowing red hair cascaded down Murph's shoulder as she bit him on the ear and purred, "Michael Murphy, what a pleasant surprise finding you here!"

Klaus looked admiringly over and down the long legs tightly wrapped in skinny jeans, ending in red stiletto heels. Murph glanced up at the face, freckles sprinkling across the small nose and cheeks. He rose quickly and turned, giving his assailant a quick embrace.

Murph laughed, "You certainly know how to make an entrance!" Carli and Erica sat with their mouths open, beer mugs half way to the table. Murph's surprise friend stood nearly as tall as he did, making her almost six feet tall. Her Kelly green silk top was skin tight and sequined, set off by her bright cherry red lipstick and finger nail polish. Realizing that his companions were completely stunned, Murph smiled and said, "May I present Maeve Corrigan. We've know each other since high school."

Carli recovered quickly. "I've seen you before! In a picture... you were Murph's..."

"Prom date, yeah, that's right! We dated his senior year. I played volleyball for St. Joe's."

"Then she went and got all political on me!" Murph shook his head. "I ran into her again last year in D.C. She was campaigning for that guy who was running for Senator from Ohio. Maeve got me to help with his campaign since he was an Ignatius grad."

Carli's brows narrowed, "Tell me more about running into her in Washington!"

Klaus opened his mouth to save Murph, but Erica kicked him under the table.

"No, it's not like that. Maeve needed calls made to Ignatius alumni to get support, and I made them for her. She's dating another guy. His name was… Justin, right?"

A voice behind Murph broke in, "Justin Dirkson!" He was an inch shorter than Maeve, with black hair and a thin moustache. He stepped between Murph and Maeve, putting his arm around her waist, protecting his turf.

Murph smiled broadly and shook Justin's hand with enthusiasm. "Hey, Man! Good to see you!" He thought, *not a moment too soon either. That was close!* "Justin is another Cleveland guy, on the staff of Senator… Borlon, right."

Maeve was enjoying this a bit too much, "Yes… the junior Senator from Ohio… and a Democrat, much to Murph's dismay unfortunately."

"Maeve and I never did agree politically, so we didn't talk about it much." Murph conceded. "As a dentist, and planning to run my own business, I guess I just became a conservative Republican. I do like Senator Borlon though. He is a practical, moderate Democrat, and he is doing a good job for the people of Ohio, as much as I can tell." Murph moved around to face Maeve and Justin, standing next to Carli. He rested his arm on her shoulder, and she leaned into his hip, just enough for Maeve to notice.

Murph felt a bit more in control of the situation, and Klaus grinned. Erica kicked him again. Murph asked Maeve, "So what brings you to the middle of Germany on a Thursday night?"

She laughed. "Do you read the newspapers — perhaps, *Washington Post, New York Times, CNN, Yahoo News*?"

Murph shrugged. "I've been a bit busy lately. Enlighten me!"

"You're impossible! The G-20 summit was here in Munich, dummy! Senator Borlon is here as part of the U.S. delegation. I'm his chief of staff, and Justin is also part of the senator's team. The meetings ended today. We fly home tomorrow, so this is our first, and only night to relax and enjoy the town."

"Excellent!" Murph squeezed Carli's shoulder. "How are you getting back to D.C.?"

"We leave on the Congressional charter flight at 9:00 a.m. Why?"

"Is there any chance Carli and I could get on that flight?"

Justin's smile vanished, but Maeve continued without pausing, "I suppose so… why?"

Carli started to open her mouth, but Murph cut her off. "Well, after I didn't win *The Dental Apprentice*, they offered me a part on another reality show. It's kind of like *The Amazing Race*. I've been sent around the world, but I have to get back to the U.S. secretly. There are hidden cameras on us now, so don't look shocked. I really just need to get out of Germany and to the States as fast as I can." Lying didn't come easily for him, but he tried to sound as convincing as he could. The beer helped a bit, but he couldn't tell if Maeve was buying it. Justin didn't trust Murph anyway, so this was pushing him over the edge.

"I didn't figure you for a reality show junkie." Maeve seemed disappointed.

"Well, that fifteen minutes of fame thing... you know?" Murph shrugged.

"I guess. It's just that I thought you had higher goals than that." Maeve frowned.

Justin was quick to jump on that, "I guess people change. Even the best of us don't reach our potential." He smirked, "If that dentistry thing isn't working out well, you have to find work where you can!"

Murph wanted to slug him right there, but kept playing the part. "If I can get back first, the prize is a half million dollars. It's like a big scavenger hunt!" He looked into her eyes. "Can you help me?"

Maeve thought a minute, then her shoulders slumped, "I guess so. The Senator will have to make the final decision, but meet us at the corporate terminal at eight o'clock and I'll put in a good word for you." She seemed defeated.

Justin piped in, "Good to see you, Man! Gotta run. We'll see you in the morning!" He guided Maeve back into the crowd toward the bar.

They watched them move away, Justin reaching up to say something into her ear. Murph lost sight of them, which was just as well, as he could see Justin laughing. Murph moved back to his seat, and sat down, looking glum.

"That was beautifully done." Klaus regarded him with respect. "Hard on the ego, but well done."

Murph smiled sadly. "If it gets us home, it was worth it." Carli studied him carefully, and smiled.

Murph drained his beer with a gulp, set down the tankard and managed a wan smile. "Klaus, you and Erica need to go home. I don't think they know who you are. Hamid al-Said and his people may be watching for the Porsche for a few days, so you may want to rent a car."

Klaus thought a moment and agreed. "I can leave the Porsche here for a while and return home in a rental. Where will you go until tomorrow?"

"I doubt there are rooms available with the summit in town, but I can check. If not, we can stay here in the bar. It won't be our first time sitting up all night in a bar together!"

Carli took his hand and squeezed. "He's such a fun date! That's why I love him!"

Leaving the girls, Klaus and Murph left the table and went out into the lobby, where it was quieter. Klaus made a call and arranged for a car. There was a rental location only two blocks away.

Murph was surprised to find that the Platzl Hotel did have one small room available, which he booked for an exorbitant rate. The desk clerk, Werner, seemed to infer that Murph had met a girl in the bar and wanted the room quickly. Murph didn't try to dispel that notion, as it would serve as a convenient excuse. *No need to lie. Just let people go where they want to go and believe what they want to believe.*

Murph tipped the desk clerk for his effort and was given a sly wink along with his room key. Murph thanked him and winked back, tossing the key in the air and catching it with his other hand. He walked away whistling. Werner followed at a distance and nodded approvingly when he saw Carli. As he went back to his desk, he thought, *definitely worth the price*!

Returning to the bar, Klaus told them that he had arranged for a car immediately. Murph also laid out his plans. They would take a taxi to the airport in the morning and hopefully return to D.C.

Erica asked what his plans were when they got back to Washington.

Carli waited for Murph, cocking her head to one side, curious herself to hear the plan.

"I suppose we'll make it up as we go, just like everything else." That didn't seem to satisfy anyone. "OK, I think we need to go to that reception, just to see who shows up!"

Klaus thought that over. "Yes, I think that would be a good place to start. Let us know what happens!"

"I will. I will also let you know when it is safe and then you can return to get the Porsche. I've grown very fond of it and want to see it back safely in your hands." Murph stood up and embraced Klaus warmly, then Erica. Carli got a hug from Klaus, and then she and Erica held each other for a long time.

"I will pray for you." Erica was in tears. "You two must come back and see us when you have more time."

Carli agreed, holding Erica by both wrists. "We will be back. I promise." Her eyes were moist as well.

Erica and Klaus went through the revolving door and out into the night. Murph carefully looked around, but didn't see anyone suspicious lurking around the building or in the lobby. He led Carli to the elevator and nodded at Werner as they passed. The clerk flashed a wicked smile.

Their room was small, but comfortable. They ordered a light supper from room service and settled in for the night. Although they were exhausted, sleep was slow to come.

As Carli snuggled against Murph, she asked him, "Are you going to continue that lie about *The Amazing Race* tomorrow?"

"I don't know," he admitted. "If Maeve is there, I have to keep it up. But if I can talk to Senator Borlon alone, I'll tell him the truth and see what happens. I don't feel good lying, and I'm not very good at it."

"Just see that you don't get better with practice!"

He kissed her lightly on the forehead. That was all the conversation they needed.

Chapter 54

Friday dawned bright and early. Murph and Carli were up and ready to go. Both knew without talking about it that this was an important day. Once they got out of Europe and back to America, things would get easier. They also had a plan now and felt the confidence that came from understanding more about what needed to be done. While they weren't completely sure what Saturday would bring, it was clear where they needed to be and what they had to do. It all hinged on Murph's ability to talk their way onto that plane! A commercial airliner would never do, due to terrorist surveillance and metal detectors, thanks to the archaeological treasures they were carrying.

After an excellent breakfast, they walked the short distance to the Hauptbahnhof, the main railway station. It took the train 45 minutes to reach the Franz Josef Strauss International Airport, but they had allowed plenty of time. They were waiting when the motorcade arrived with the political dignitaries. Maeve was easy to spot, given her height and flaming red hair. Justin, as expected, was hovering close, as Maeve introduced Murph and Carli to Senator Borlon. She quickly excused herself to tend to the other details of boarding the plane, leaving them alone in the terminal.

Murph began rapidly to make his case. "Senator Borlon, thank you for meeting with us, and listening to our request. "

At 42, Brooks Borlon was exceptionally young for a senator. His bright blonde hair was tufted on his head, slightly windblown on his run in from the limo to the terminal. It was part of the charm that got him elected. He never looked perfect, just relaxed, like one of the regular people he represented. His piercing blue eyes danced playfully from Murph to Carli. "I know, Maeve told me. She thinks very highly of you, you know. And I have learned to trust her judgment implicitly."

Murph looked down at his shoes, wrinkled his toes, took a deep breath and looked the Senator in the eyes. "I lied to Maeve last night in order to get her to agree to let us see you. I want to tell you the truth."

The Senator smiled. "I thought that story sounded fishy. So as one Ignatius Wildcat to another, tell me what's really going on."

Murph and Carli proceeded to tell him everything, including their need to get to the Willard Hotel on Saturday to unravel the mystery that people seemed willing to kill for.

Senator Borlon whistled through his teeth. "That's so preposterous that it has to be true. No one in his right mind would make that up!" He tapped his chin with his finger. Glancing up, they all saw Maeve coming their way across the terminal. She was walking with purpose, her heels clicking on the tile. Time was short.

Murph thought, *It's now or never. Does he believe me? Is the truth compelling enough?*

The Senator had always been decisive. It was his greatest strength, though sometimes it cut both ways as well. "Michael, your story rings true, if completely far fetched. Ignatius men forever — that's our motto! Now let's get on this plane and get you back to Washington." He burst into a smile and shook Murph's hand with a grip of iron. "When this is over, call me. We'll have a drink, and you can tell me *the rest of the story*. For now, your *Amazing Race* tale is good enough."

Maeve had arrived and looked to the Senator for instructions. "Put these two in the back of the plane. Don't just stand there.

Time's wasting!" He moved off, leaving Maeve, Carli, and Murph standing dumbfounded.

Maeve seemed surprised. "Well, I'll be..."

Carli finished, "We'll all be going to Washington now!" She firmly took Murph's hand and they followed the Senator out the door and across the tarmac to the waiting chartered 757. Maeve trailed behind, still shaking her head.

Murph and Carli tried to draw as little attention as possible. They moved to the back of the plane, selecting the second to last row. Murph crossed to the window seat to be less visible, even though he preferred an aisle to fit his 6'2" frame.

They had almost escaped notice when a NBC TV reporter across the aisle looked up from her Blackberry. "Hey! You're the guy from *The Dental Apprentice*! Mike Murphy, right!" She said it a bit too loudly, and the entire back half of the plane turned around.

"Guilty!" Murph managed a smile and a wave. He recognized her from the evening news. Although still young at 30, Sarah Wainright was one of their senior political correspondents, cute but also very smart. She had a bright future and her star was on the rise. Covering the G-20 had been a feather in her cap.

The rear of the plane was filled with reporters, so they followed her lead, being very aware of pop culture news. He received the usual, "Loved you on the show!" "Great job in Alaska!" "Really thought you should have won!"

He said thanks and was polite, but was evasive on what he was doing in Germany. Murph then gave the turned heads a knowing smile and said in a loud, fast rush, "CIA business — black ops — need to know — if I told you I'd have to kill you." Everyone laughed and settled down as the flight attendants ordered them to fasten seatbelts and turn off their cell phones.

Sarah took the last minute to tweet, then shut down her Blackberry as the plane began to roll out. Murph and Carli settled in, happy to be going home.

Simultaneously in Washington and Germany, iPhones chimed. Both Manny Farouk and Hamid el-Said examined their screens. Their searches had struck gold. The twitter feed glowed up at them.

**Murphy, the Dentist Apprentice is on my flight
back to DC. He's cuter in person than on TV. Don't
know who's with him, but she's a lucky girl. Wish I
were sitting with him!**

The shouts went up immediately:
  "Margaret!"
  "Banthaira! Omar!"
  "We have them now!"

Chapter 55

Gaining six hours by flying west, the charter landed just before 11:00 a.m. at Reagan National Airport. Since they were traveling with only the backpack and Carli's shoulder bag, clearing customs was quick and painless. The U.S. Customs Agents hardly paid them any attention, focusing instead on the larger luggage and greater possibilities of finding undeclared items. Murph tried not to look too happy, as he was concerned about how he would explain the bronze tube in his backpack, and the psh-kef knife tucked in his sock, outside his right ankle.

Murph and Carli said thanks to Senator Borlon, and promised again to meet for a drink soon. Maeve was nowhere to be found, so Murph considered that a lost cause. They hurried out of the terminal and into the mid-day sun. It was another beautiful late summer day in the nation's capital, and Murph easily hailed a cab. He felt very relaxed, for he was home again.

The cabbie looked at Murph for a destination. Murph opened his mouth to give his home address and then shut it immediately, realizing that would be a bad idea. "JW Marriott on Pennsylvania Avenue," he blurted out. Carli's head snapped around surprised. The cab raced off toward the city, angling to cross the Potomac River.

Murph settled back into the seat and pulled Carli close. "My condo will probably be watched. Going there will be something Manny would expect, and he knows the address." He spoke softly so the cabbie couldn't hear clearly over the engine but didn't whisper, which would have made the driver suspicious, and more likely to eavesdrop.

Carli nodded. "Sounds good, but the JW?"

"First thing that came to mind." Murph could only shrug and smile, "But it'll work out well. It's a large, busy hotel on 14th Street, across from the Willard InterContinental. The shopping mall at the National Press Club is right there, and we do need a change of wardrobe. "

"I can't argue with that. This is your town, after all."

"And it's about time I treated you to a fine dinner. You've certainly earned it!"

"We've both earned it, but I *am* getting really hungry!"

The taxi dropped them off at the JW Marriott, and Murph was pleased to find that there was a room available for the weekend. After settling in, they showered and opened the curtains, taking in the view of the south lawn of the White House. With the grit and grime from travel removed, they felt refreshed. One thing had been gnawing at Murph for a while, so he picked up his iPhone and dialed Derek Whitmore. He put the phone down on the table so Carli could hear as well.

"Murph?"

"How's our favorite pilot doing?"

"Man, are you OK?"

"Yeah, why? Is everything good with you?"

"I'm cool, but there sure has been some weird shit going on since you left in Rome!"

Carli couldn't wait, "What do you mean?"

"Hi, Carli! I'm glad to hear your voice! You two had me worried!" Derek sounded nervous, without the usual bravado. "You hit me on the head, then left. Then Manny Farouk arrived with Margaret. Dr. Farouk went all ape-shit and read us the riot act. Man, I thought I was fired and was going to have to walk home!"

"Sorry, Derek. I never meant for you to get into hot water."

"No problem, Mon!" Derek slipped into a mock Jamaican accent. He seemed to be relaxing. "Manny calmed down, then sent us back to Cairo. That was the last place I wanted to go! That's when it got strange."

"What do you mean?"

"We landed and took on cargo. Your friend Saleh met the

plane and supervised the loading of a casket. He never said who the dead body was, but there was talk about some archeologist, a Dr. Narmer, who had been found floating dead in the Nile River."

Murph looked at Carli, and she had turned white. She had forgotten about Narmer in all of the running. The memories of her ordeal came flooding back, and he could tell she was shaken. Murph moved closer to her and held her close. "Do you think the body was Narmer?"

"No way to tell. But that's not the weird part!"
"What else?"

Derek whistled, "Saleh had been beat up! His clothes were all dirty, and he was bruised around his head and face. I think he had cigarette burns on the inside of his forearms. It looked like he had been interrogated hard. But who would want to torture him? And why?"

"I don't have any idea." The lying was getting easier, Murph admitted sadly to himself.

"And Saleh brought his whole family with him when we left Cairo for DC."

For some reason that made Murph and Carli feel better. "I'm glad of that. Where did they go when you got back to Washington?"

"No clue! Margaret met the plane and they unloaded everyone and put the casket into a hearse. That's the last I saw of anyone. Ed and I have been stuck here at Reagan since. We're under orders to be ready to leave with 15 minutes notice so we have to sleep in shifts. It's a real pain in the ass!"

Murph smiled to himself. *That's Derek, not happy unless he's complaining about something!* "That's why you make the big bucks!"

"Shit!"

"Hey Derek, one more question. A few months ago, you flew Manny to Germany, right?"

"Yeah! It was around the first of May, why?"

"Where did you go?"

"It was strange. Dr. Farouk was the only passenger. We landed in a small city called Augsburg. He was gone for the day and then came back to the plane. Seemed really happy about something. Then we made a short flight to Paris. We stopped overnight, and when he came back to the airport in the morning to come home, he was mad as hell — seemed to be in a big hurry — really agitated and irritable. He's usually a cold fish, not one to talk much, but he kept badgering us about how much longer the trip was going to take. When we landed, he barely let the Gulfstream stop rolling when he tore off the plane. Why?"

"No special reason. I'm just trying to put all the pieces together in this, and nothing makes much sense."

"Well, if you do, let me know. This is just too weird for words!"

Murph had heard enough. "Derek, when I get back to Washington, I'll give you a call and buy you a beer!"

"You owe me a lot more than that. You hit me in the head, remember!"

"Yeah, I remember. You be careful!"

"Hey, that's me. The soul of caution! You watch your back, too!" The phone clicked off.

Murph squeezed Carli's shoulder and stood up. Pacing seemed to help him think. "We know a lot of *what*, but very little *why*!"

Carli was forced to agree. "Manny flew to Augsburg, so he probably went to see Willi Schultz in Nordlingen. That's how the invitation got there, and why Willi would have agreed to go."

"Yeah. Manny can be a very persuasive guy. But why would Willi be invited, and what kind of gathering is it tomorrow at the Willard?"

"I'm worried about Saleh!"

Murph nodded. "Me too. If he was tortured, the only thing he knew that anyone would have wanted was what we were up to and where we were going. Saleh is connected to Manny, which is bad, but my instincts tell me that Saleh is a good guy."

"I agree. He's on our side. I can feel it!"

"Does your women's intuition give you any idea who the body is?"

"No, but I don't think it's Narmer. It wouldn't make sense for Manny to bring that slime ball to Washington."

"I agree. But we've got a lot of questions to answer... and we've got to stay hidden until we can safely expose what they're up to! If we only knew what exactly they are up to..."

"And it feels like we are running out of time." Carli walked over and buried her head in Murph's chest. He held her close for a minute.

"Then we need to keep moving. We're not going to figure it out staying here. Let's go shopping!"

Carli looked up and laughed. Murph thought it was the most beautiful sound. "That's ridiculous!" she said. "But it makes as much sense as anything else… so let's go!"

They hid their treasures in the hotel room safe and left arm in arm for the mall.

Chapter 56

Murph and Carli looked like the typical young couple out for the afternoon in Washington. They entered the National Press Club and then passed into the mall area. The aroma of food drew them into the food court, reminding them how hungry they were. They shared a quick turkey pesto sandwich at the deli before turning their attention to the sorry state of their clothing. A visit to J. Crew proved successful one-stop shopping, as Carli found a tank and light cotton sweater with a poppy hue that complemented her auburn hair. Murph selected dark stretch chinos and an eggplant colored cotton pullover, with a gray shirt underneath. They collected jeans, athletic gear, underwear, makeup, and toiletries, before heading back to the Marriott, feeling much better prepared.

As they neared the exit to the mall, another couple passed in front of them, entering a stationery shop. The young girl pointed out the invitations to her fiancé, and it was clear they were planning their wedding.

Carli gave Murph's elbow a squeeze. "Aren't they cute!"

He smiled, "Yes, it does look like fun!" Then his smile vanished. "Wait a minute!"

Murph led Carli over to the table display in the doorway. "Look!" He pointed to a red leather-bound journal, next to a pile of invitations. "We're going about this the wrong way!" He took her hand and raced back to their room.

Murph sat Carli down in the plush chair and paced excitedly

around the room. His mind was racing as he had a felt glimmer of understanding, and he was trying to hold it together before it faded away.

She stared at him expectantly. "Will you stand still? You're making me dizzy!" She waited as patiently as she could for him get his thoughts together. When he began to smile, she knew it was time. "So, enlighten me!"

Murph started slowly, but the words began to spill out faster as he went. "As fascinating as it would be to see who shows up at the reception at the Willard InterContinental tomorrow, that really doesn't help us much. We won't know who they are, and we will be easy to spot."

"That's true. You're no master of disguise, and it's hard to make you less tall!"

"But since all the action is at the Willard, it makes a fantastic diversion!"

"What do you have in mind?" Carli was beginning to warm to the idea. She had never been high on the direct approach of charging into the reception without the slightest idea of what was going on.

"I saw the book in the stationery shop! If you have to track the gold over all this time, the journal must still exist. The binder that Dumond mentioned, or its current form, must be somewhere. Manny never let it out of his sight so there's only one logical place where he would keep it…"

"The Center for Esthetic and Restorative Excellence."

"Precisely!" Murph was beaming. "It has to be in Manny's office. I've been in there twice before — when I asked permission to leave to come get you and also on the day I was eliminated from *The Dental Apprentice*. It's full of Egyptian artifacts, but I never really took the time to study any of it."

Carli went to open the safe. "Then it's time you did it now."

"What?" Murph had been rolling along, but now he was confused.

"Everything on the *The Dental Apprentice* was taped for TV, silly." She pulled out Murph's computer and launched the Internet. "I'm sure that episode is online, on Hulu.com. Let's check it out!"

"You're a genius!" He reached around her as she sat at the table and kissed her on the neck.

It took a couple of minutes, but Carli found it. There he was, standing before Manny's desk, being chastised for his decisions, and fired from the show. Murph had never watched any of the shows before. He hated seeing himself on TV, since all he saw were the flaws — things he would like to do differently. He frowned as he saw himself squirming under Manny's interrogation.

"Just concentrate on the walls! You look great, and everyone thought you did fine!" She patted his hand supportively.

"There!" Carli hit pause, as the camera panned from Murph to Manny. "On the wall behind him. That statue is a replica of the one in the Cairo museum! Except without the broken nose!"

Murph spotted it now, especially since her finger was pointing to it. "That's our favorite Pharaoh, Djoser, isn't it?"

"Very good!" She released the video to play on. Manny stood up and walked around the desk to shake Murph's hand goodbye.

"Wait!" He called, and she stopped the video again. "It's blurry, but that looks like a set of dentures in a glass case." Murph pointed them out. "I can't tell, but they shine like they're made of metal, maybe gold."

The scene in Manny's office ended quickly, but they had seen enough.

"You're right, Murph. We need to get in there!"

"And tomorrow's the day to do it." Murph felt the best he had in days. *I love it when a plan comes together!* "I promised you dinner, so let's get changed and celebrate!"

"Last meal for the condemned…" Carli observed dryly as she closed the computer.

"Way to kill the mood, Chamoun!" But nothing could wipe the smile from his face.

Chapter 57

Jet lag finally caught up with them, and they fell asleep on the bed until the setting sun crept lower in the window, its bright orange beam traversing the pillow and hitting Murph in the eyes. He awoke with a start and sat up suddenly, not really knowing where he was. That woke Carli up, and she regarded him, rubbing her tired eyes.

"It's Friday, and we're in Washington, D.C."

She nodded. "Sounds about right."

"I promised to take you out for a fabulous dinner?"

"That's the way I remember it!"

"And all the people chasing us was just a bad dream?"

"Sadly, no… unless we have been having the same nightmare for the last week."

"Crap! I was hoping." Murph stood up, scratching his head and stretching, pressing his palms to the ceiling. "Let's go have dinner, and we can plan our breaking and entering expedition for tomorrow."

"You do know how to show a girl a good time!"

"You started this, remember?" He teased, "I was just minding my own business here in D.C.!"

She pushed out her lower lip, making a pouting frown. "Well, you didn't have to come!"

He bent down and scooped her up off the bed, twirled her around once, and held her close. "I wouldn't miss this for all the money in the world. You're stuck with me!"

Carli kissed him deeply, "Perfect!"

They changed quickly, Murph into dark dress jeans and a charcoal and black plaid shirt. Carli was stunningly simple, in her new skinny jeans and a sunny yellow top. She grabbed a camel tan short trench coat in case the evening was cold, and they left the Marriott behind.

Murph told the cabbie "Martin's Tavern, Wisconsin Ave, in Georgetown!" As usual, the driver said little besides a grunt and rocketed off into the traffic.

Carli glanced over at Murph. "Another Irish bar?"

"Of course! But this one has the best food in D.C., and great atmosphere. You'll love it!"

"I know I will!" She nestled under his arm and watched the evening lights sparkle as they moved through the monuments of Washington. "I haven't been here since my eighth grade trip!"

"I've always loved Washington but I appreciate it even more since I've lived here for a year. No matter what, I always see something new. When we have more time, I'll show you everything."

"I'd like that." She felt relaxed and at peace. "You know,

lately we've listed enough things we want to do to last a lifetime."

"Sounds like a perfect plan. We need to finish this, so we can enjoy it together."

The cab pulled up to Martin's and they got out. The Tavern had been there since 1933 and had been frequented by Presidents, movie stars, world travelers, and locals who loved its warm, friendly atmosphere. Billy, the owner, greeted Murph like a friend and regular, which he was. Murph introduced Carli, and Billy regarded her approvingly. He led them to a secluded booth beyond the bar. The dark wood and faint smell of cigar smoke lent an air of history to the place. Many a big political compromise had been forged at these tables, over whiskey and beer.

"I know what you'll be having," Billy smiled at Murph, "but for the lovely lady?"

"A glass of chardonnay, a crisp California one if you have it!" Carli smiled and nodded. *Exactly right!*

Billy turned. "I have just the thing. Suzanna will be your server. I'll get this started for you."

He returned quickly, delivering the white wine for Carli and a stiff pour of Jameson on the rocks for Murph. "It's good to see you Murph. Glad to have you back!"

Murph regarded the golden liquid in his glass then raised it toward Carli. "To us!"

She touched her glass to his with a light clink and tasted the wine. "Perfect!" *Oh dear, that word again – the perfect guy, the perfect plan, the perfect wine — I could get used to this!* Carli couldn't help but smile at Michael.

They enjoyed an excellent salad and the house specialty of sautéed seasoned crab cakes and mushrooms. It was obvious that Murph had many friends here, as a constant stream of people came over to say Hi and wish him well. Even Billy found time to bring over a chair and chat for a few minutes. Dessert was a splurge. They shared a warm brownie, with golden vanilla ice cream and hot fudge. They finished stuffed and contented.

"We need to walk some of this off!"

Carli agreed, so Murph paid for their meal, along with a generous tip for Suzanna, and they shook hands all around as they left. Murph hailed a cab and had them dropped at the World War II Memorial, in the middle of the National Mall, in the shadow of the

Washington Monument. They walked slowly around.

Murph always loved the monuments at night, with the light of the fountains sparkling in the dancing water. A giant bronze moon, nearly full, was rising in the east, and he led her that way down the Mall. The heat of the day had dissipated into the cool of evening. As they strolled down the stone path in front of the Smithsonian Castle and then the Air and Space Museum, Murph wanted the night to last forever, and Carli seemed content.

However, as much as he was enjoying the evening, he had come there with a purpose. Turning across the Mall, he led her up behind the sprawling stone shadow of the National Gallery of Art. They strolled through the Sculpture Garden and out onto Constitution Avenue, facing the National Archives.

Murph studied the Archives building and pointed it out as the residence of the Declaration of Independence, while guiding Carli further east. They dodged the late Friday traffic, fairly light given the hour, and crossed Pennsylvania Avenue at the Canadian Embassy.

This was familiar ground for Murph. He followed his regular running path through John Marshall Place Park. He stopped Carli in the shadow of a maple tree fronting C Street NW. He was carefully examining the three story stone building nestled in the trees across the side street.

"That's the Center for Excellence isn't it?" she whispered, even though no one was around to hear.

Murph just nodded. The building was completely dark, except for light filtering through the edges of the blinds in the first floor corner office that Murph knew belonged to Manny Farouk. Murph took Carli's hand and crossed the street, trying to appear nonchalant. As they reached the far sidewalk, they could just see around the building into the parking lot behind.

"Do you recognize any of the cars?" She had a bad feeling about this. There were only two.

Murph whispered, "The Aston Martin convertible belongs to Dr. Farouk. The other one is a dark SUV. Could be a Land Rover or Mercedes. Unfortunately I have a hunch who prefers that style!"

Carli shivered.

As they began to walk toward the building to get a better look, the back door of the Center opened, flooding the area with a pool of light. Murph pulled Carli down into the hedge, and they both peered through the shrubbery.

Three men and a woman came out of the building. Though they couldn't see any faces, they knew their silhouettes immediately. Carli involuntarily gasped then steadied herself. The leader was a man with an athletic build. He had a tall and erect posture. A tall slender woman, wearing high heels, followed him. The third man was shorter and thick, like a fire-plug. Even though he was facing away, Murph recognized the heavy black beard that covered the bottom half of his face, and he could feel the smile.

As if he could sense their presence, Omar Bengdara stopped in his tracks and scanned the surroundings. The fourth man closed the door and then ran to unlock the car while Hamid cursed at him for being too slow. Omar continued his thorough search, then made his way to the SUV and climbed into the passenger seat. Darkness had returned with the closure of the rear door of the Center. The engine roared to life, and the SUV jumped forward from its parking space toward the exit.

Murph realized with horror *if they turn west on C Street, they'll see us!* He grabbed Carli and pushed her up against the trunk of another maple tree, wrapping his arms around her and kissing her. Her arms automatically went behind his neck. He moved with not a second to spare.

The SUV, another Mercedes, charged out of the lot and around the corner behind them, without slowing for the stop sign. Omar saw the couple embracing in the shadow of the tree. He produced a vicious grin. *Lucky bastard,* he thought, as they disappeared into the night.

Murph started to relax, but Carli held on. "Don't stop. I like the aggressive protector thing!"

"That was too close! We need to get back to the hotel."

Carli held his hand, swinging their arms as they began to walk. "I know, but I just wish tonight didn't have to end."

"Me too. Let's enjoy tonight. Tomorrow's a big day. Tonight can be just for us."

He raised his arm and she snuggled under his shoulder and put her arm around his waist as he held her shoulder. They strolled smiling back up Pennsylvania Avenue to Freedom Plaza and into the JW Marriott, looking to all like they hadn't a care in the world.

Chapter 58

Manny Farouk awoke early on Saturday. This was the day he had planned for years. Everything needed to be perfect. He showered and dressed in his habitual tailored jacket, black silk shirt, and dark slacks. He met Margaret, looking lovely in a plum wrap dress and heels, and inquired about the plans for the thousandth time.

Everything is fine, she reassured him again. Just follow the script, and things would take care of themselves. They left early for the Willard InterContinental, arriving at 1:00 p.m. The reception was scheduled for four, but Manny felt the need to oversee the final preparations. Margaret had to work to keep him from driving the hotel staff completely crazy. She ended up enticing him into the bar with a large glass of a fine Merlot to calm him down.

Murph and Carli had not set an alarm, choosing to sleep in if possible. They woke up rested, feeling like they had finally shed the effects of jet lag. They went back to the shopping mall, outfitting themselves for running, with shoes, pants, and dri-fit shirts. Murph was thinking that they would attract less attention on the National Mall if they looked like runners. Carli wasn't so sure, but it felt good to be dressed casually, and she really wanted to run. Exercise always made her feel good.

Leaving the Marriott at three in the afternoon, they took a leisurely jog through the National Mall that brought them to the Center for Esthetic and Restorative Excellence thirty minutes later. They surveyed the building. The parking lot was empty, and everything appeared quiet.

Murph looked Carli in the eyes, "It's not too late to back out. We can just give them the investment and the scroll, and then walk away."

"I don't think it's that simple." As she said it, he knew she was right; they had considered this before. "Besides, I didn't come this far to just run away. Let's see it through!"

"That's my girl!" He kissed her on the forehead. "For luck!"

Jogging across C Street, this time they entered the parking lot and went to the back entrance. Murph removed his ID card from his wallet. "I hope they haven't deactivated my ID."

"It will make for a quick burglary, if they did!"

Murph slid the magnetic strip in the card reader, and the lock made a satisfying click. "Last chance…"

Carli shook her head. Murph pulled open the door, and they entered the hallway. Murph led her quickly past the ground floor exam and consultation rooms. He stopped to reach into an exam room and pulled two pairs of latex gloves, large for him and small for her. He continued into the main reception area and then selected the corridor to Manny's office. They entered the small waiting area, usually guarded by Margaret. Murph knew she had a button to release the door lock to Manny's private office. With Carli standing by, Murph searched the desk and found the button under the desktop, to the left of her chair.

"Aha!" He pressed the button with a flourish… but nothing happened.

Carli frowned. "That would have been too easy, I guess."

Murph bent down and studied the button. Where it should have been illuminated, it was dark. The system was inactive. Murph stood up and went over to the door, then back out into the corridor, working his way back along the outside of the common wall to the private office. He found the other door at the back, behind where Manny's desk would be. There was a number pad next to the door lock, its red light blinking like a challenge.

"I was with Manny once when he deactivated the alarm. I'm not sure, but I think I know what the code is. He could have changed it, or I could get it wrong and set off the alarm."

"No way to know until you try. Besides, that's why we're wearing running shoes!" Her smile gave him confidence. "Give it your best shot!"

Murph closed his eyes and tried to see the spot when Manny keyed the code. He could hear it, *Dee-Dee-Dee-Dah*. He remembered that Manny's hand covered the bottom half of the pad, but Murph could still see the top numbers. It was a chance worth taking.

Murph keyed 5-5-5-9 — *Dee-Dee-Dee-Dah* — it sounded right. They both waited, no alarms sounded, but Murph could hear his heartbeat in his head. The red light went out. He started to step back, and Carli turned to run. Then the green light brightened, and the door clicked.

Carli reached over and squeezed his bicep. "Nicely done! We're in!"

Murph pulled the door toward them, and they entered the inner office of Dr. Manesh Farouk.

Chapter 59

Even though Carli had seen the room on *The Dental Apprentice* video, it took her breath away. The obsidian desktop was supported by obelisk shaped legs, which she immediately realized mimicked the architecture at Saqqara. Murph could see the resemblance now that he had been to Egypt. Carli was drawn to the statue of Djoser. Standing over four feet tall, it was carved of obsidian, as well, and was an exceptional likeness of the original they had seen at the Cairo Museum.

Murph was drawn to the dentures in the glass case on the bookshelf. He examined them closely. Gold palate and denture base with natural teeth wired in. They were one piece, hinged in the back and with springs, so the upper and lower would force against the jaws. The owner would have to work to keep his mouth closed with these in place.

"Carli! I've seen these before." She came over quickly. "These are George Washington's dentures — the ones that were stolen from the Smithsonian when they were moved during the Bicentennial! I have a photo in my dental history trivia lecture I do for the kids."

"I think you're right, but that's not why we're here. You can turn in the thief later." A section of hieroglyphics was reproduced on the wall. She went over and began to study it.

"Here, let me take a picture of that, and you can decipher it later." Murph took out his iPhone and shot several images. "We need to find the journal."

Carli suggested they concentrate on the desk. Each took a side of the drawers, and with gloved hands, they dig through the papers. Carli found it first.

"I've got it!" She pulled out a brown leather pouch, rolled then tied with string. She untied the string and smoothed it out on the desktop. Breathless with anticipation, she opened the cover.

The initial entries were in hieroglyphics and then shifted to Latin. Murph was rusty, but he had to thank his teachers at St. Ignatius for insisting he learn the dead language well. It progressed to a section of French, which Carli was able to translate, and the final pages were in English.

Murph and Carli read mesmerized by the history unfolded before them. The journal detailed the distribution of the gold over time — names, dates, places, and events. Each page began a thread, the tale of each parcel of the Pharaoh's Gold.

They read of Saint Nicasius, a knight Hospitaller of the Crusades. He was a Christian martyr, beheaded by Saladin after his capture at the Battle of Hattin in 1187. His entry ended with a red X.

"That gold must have been lost," Murph wondered aloud after he had translated the Latin for Carli.

"That seems to be what it means. Here's another." Carli turned the page and pointed to another red X on the bottom. This page was in French. "Another part of the gold was lost with the death of the Frankish knight Roland, who commanded the rear guard for Charlamagne at Roncesvalles in 788. Both he and St. Nicasius would have been killed by Muslim warriors."

The next page told of a large parcel of gold that passed through France in the Middle Ages. Carli was moving her finger along the text as she translated, but Murph got ahead of her, blurting out "George Washington!"

She finished the page and confirmed, "Yes, oh impatient one, if those dentures over there are President Washington's, then that is Pharaoh's gold. And a large part of it!"

The next page had an X in the middle of the page that appeared to have been crossed out. This ingot also came to America and was lost with General Custer at Little Big Horn. The text continued after the X, describing how the gold had been recovered. It had been placed in the 1930's with a Dr. Browne Pearson.

"How have I heard that name?" Carli stopped reading and looked up at Murph.

"He was the dentist who was the last survivor of the Bataan Death March." Carli's eyes widened as he reminded her. "We read about it on the Internet. The funeral home was burglarized, and his gold bridgework was taken. His family said that he called them his lucky teeth."

"I guess now we know why!"

"But who got the gold? The journal doesn't say!"

Carli turned another page. "Let's keep going. This is amazing!"

A parcel ended with Senator Edwin Shafter, and the red X again told bitterly of its loss.

Another page traced gold to Willi Schultz, with a molar crown placed in 1933. The red X was recent and covered over a pencil notation. Murph read it aloud. "Willard."

Another thread listed the current owner as Colonel Robert Anderson, an Airborne Ranger stationed at Fort Bragg. His note also had Willard as an ending in pencil.

That was the key! They quickly scanned the next few pages, finding four more pencil notations for Willard, including the rapper Bada$$.

Murph laughed aloud. "I guess his Grill is Pharaoh's Gold. I'm sure Djoser would be rolling in his grave if he knew that!"

"Don't even joke about that!" Carli hissed angrily. "This is serious." She turned the page.

The next parcel ended with Winston Churchill. The journal announced in bold script that the gold had been recovered from his denture.

Another thread wound through European history, the precious metal reassigned from one person to another, this time ending with... Mary Kay Steinmiller of Coral Gables Florida.

Murph and Carli just stared at each other.

Murph was the first to break the silence. "I guess I always knew, deep in my heart, but it still seems shocking to see it written there."

"Your final task on *The Dental Apprentice* was placing Pharaoh's Gold!" All she could do was whistle softly. "You're part of the chain of history."

Murph read further, revealing that the next ingot was assigned to Brent Hathaway. No address for Mr. Hathaway, but the journal listed Claire Summerville of Washington, D.C. as the contact. "The final task for both of us was crowns of Pharaoh's gold. How ironic.

I thought I was going to Cairo to see what you were up to, and in reality, I was already involved!"

"Strange, isn't it? The way things work out sometimes?" Carli turned the page, and there were no more entries. They stood there staring at the blank page, aged ivory parchment open on the black desktop.

Their reverie was broken by the sound of sirens. Faint at first, but growing in intensity. They looked at each other in panic. There was no sign of an alarm having gone off, but the insistent wailing was clearly heading their way.

Carli quickly photographed the pages of the journal on Murph's phone, then closed and tied the cord. She replaced the volume in the desk drawer and looked around quickly to straighten up.

Murph grabbed a handful of Kleenex from a box on the desk and reached in the glass case, grabbing George Washington's dentures. He wrapped them in tissue and stuck them in his pocket.

"What are you doing?" Carli was aghast.

"I know they don't belong here! I'll find a way to get them back to the Smithsonian."

"You're crazy!" but she ran to the door and out in the hall.

Murph stopped at the door and armed the security system again. He caught up with her, and they ran to the lobby. Murph figured that the secrecy was useless now, so he intended to go out the front door. They entered the main reception area and headed for the glass double doors to the steps.

A black Mercedes SUV careened past and turned into the parking lot. Murph grabbed Carli's arm and yanked her back from the tinted glass doors, leading her through a side door into a stairwell. They raced up two flights and entered the clinic Murph knew so well from the *Drillings* during the TV show. The back window looked out over the parking lot. Murph knew the tinted glass worked as a one-way mirror, which let them watch Hamid, Banthaira, and Omar jump out of the car and run to the back door.

They made no attempt to hide their intent. Speed seemed to be their highest priority. Omar carried a shotgun and blasted the lock. He jerked open the door, and in they came.

Murph pulled Carli away from the window. Her hands were like ice. He took her into the secured room for the CT scanner and closed the door. If they had guns, there was little he could do. He still carried the psh-kef knife in his sock, feeling somehow more secure with its presence, but it wasn't much of a defense against guns.

They could hear the burglars noisily banging on the door to Manny's office. The shotgun blast sounded again, then the building alarm began to blare.

"The sirens!" Murph thought aloud.

"What??"

"The sirens from the police coming here... they died away. They were going someplace else."

They heard a crash from below and the sound of something very heavy falling over. Then, there was no noise other than the building alarm, wailing for help. Suddenly, they heard the squeal of tires and raced to the window, just in time to see the Mercedes shoot out of the parking lot.

Murph and Carli were alone again in the Center, so they flew down the stairs and returned to the carnage that was Manny's once immaculate office. It had been professionally ransacked, the statuary knocked down and the desk overturned. Carli looked in the drawer, confirming what she knew she would find. "The journal's gone!" Tears of anger formed in her eyes.

"We've got to get out of here! The alarm will bring the cops, and we need to be far away first."

Carli wiped away the bitter tears with the back of her hand.

"We'll get it back." Murph was determined. "But we have work to do first."

Carli nodded, a resolve developing in her. "Let's roll!"

They ran down the hall and out the open back door, not pausing to examine the blasted lock. They ran quickly south, onto the National Mall, intending to lose themselves in the Saturday crowd.

Instead, they found the Mall in a panic, people milling around, or streaming to the Metro subway stations. They stopped a mother and her teenage kids, asking what was wrong. Murph and Carli could feel fear in the air.

"There's been a shooting at the Willard Hotel. An army officer was killed, and some other people were hurt. They think it's terrorists! We've got to get out of here!"

As calmly as he could, Murph explained where the Metro

183

station was and which train they should take to their hotel. The mom thanked him and hurried off, keeping a close eye on her kids.

Carli used her iPhone to look for the news feed. "There's not much here, but the AP confirms an attack at the Willard InterContinental. There were at least three fatalities, one of which was an army officer. The assailants wore black masks and got away in all the commotion. The rapper BadA$$ was hit in the mouth. The injured mostly had gunshot wounds, though apparently at least one was stabbed with a knife."

"Oh, my God!" Murph pulled Carli close. "al-Said is forcibly gathering all the remaining gold right now!"

"And he has the journal, the list of where it all has been hidden!"

"Mary Kay Steinmiller! She's in trouble and doesn't know a thing."

"Neither does your other apprentice, Claire. And they'll go there first!"

Murph grabbed his phone from his pocket. "Carli, you're right!" He pulled up Claire Summerville from his contacts and hit dial. "Come on! Pick up!"

He shouted when voicemail picked up. "Claire, this is Dr. Mike Murphy! Call me immediately! If you're out, don't go home. If you're home and screening calls, don't answer your door! I'm being chased, and you may be in danger. Call me back right away!"

Carli was worried, biting her lower lip. "Do you know where she lives?"

"Absolutely! She's still at the condo *The Dental Apprentice* cast used, until she buys a place in D.C. We can be there in 25 minutes if we run. There's no way we could get a cab now."

They took off at a runner's pace, only the prize wasn't a blue ribbon. They didn't want to think about what would happen if they didn't make it in time.

Chapter 60

Fueled by adrenalin, it took less than twenty minutes to reach the condo. Murph was encouraged not to see the black SUV in the drive, but his heart sank when he saw that the front door had been blasted off its hinges. Racing inside, they found Claire Summerville sprawled on the floor in the kitchen, bruised and battered. She was bleeding profusely from cuts on her arms and had a nasty bump on her head. Murph grabbed a dishtowel and tried to stop the bleeding, as blood was pooling red-brown on the sandy travertine floor.

Her eyes fluttered open, and she grabbed Murph's hand. He looked down at her helpless form and tried to reassure her. "You'll be OK. Just lay there and relax." Carli grabbed the house phone and called 911, requesting paramedics immediately. She was told politely that it was really busy now, with the terrorist attack and all, and that Claire would have to wait her turn.

Murph applied a tourniquet and seemed to be getting a hold on the bleeding of her arm, but Claire seemed to be fading. She opened her eyes again and held Murph's hand. "Who were they? The big guy with the beard held me while the woman kept asking me who my patient was? I couldn't figure out what she wanted. She kept getting more angry and crazy, yelling at me! I couldn't think. Did she mean my Board exam patients or the people I saw this week?"

Murph patted her hand. "Save your strength."

But she continued, "It finally dawned on me she meant my *Apprentice* patient. As soon as I told her Brent Hathaway in Arlington, he threw me away against the cabinets, and I landed down here. They just walked out and left." She was crying softly now. "I think my back is broken. I can't move. It's so cold in here."

Murph gently pushed his hand under her back and realized she had massive internal bleeding, pooling now in her back. He looked over at Carli and shook his head side to side, ever so slightly. Carli slid back, out of Clair's sight and silently began to cry.

Murph held Claire's hand tightly and comforted her, talking until she gradually became silent and slipped away. The paramedics never came, and Murph had no way to move or treat her.

He knelt and folded her hands, placing them in her lap. He gently closed her eyelids and made the sign of the Cross over her face, praying quietly for God to accept her soul in heaven.

He looked up. "All she ever wanted to be was on *The Bachelor*!" His voice caught, and then broke. He shed a few tears.

Knowing they couldn't afford to stay here and get embroiled in the investigation, Murph got up and used another towel to wash any traces of blood off of Carli and himself. They ran out the door and back out toward a busy street corner.

Murph hailed a passing cab and instructed the driver to get as close to the JW Marriott as he could. They had to run the last three blocks, but it made their cover look more legitimate when they were sweaty coming into the lobby. They acted like they hadn't heard anything about the terrorists, but then they took the opportunity to say they were leaving immediately.

They ran up to the room, changed back to their traveling attire, loaded the backpack, and escaped the Marriott. Murph again got a cab and had them delivered two blocks away from his apartment in Georgetown. They approached cautiously, but there was no sign of anything amiss.

He didn't want to stay long. Quickly packing a cooler with water and grabbing a box of granola bars, he took all the cash he had stashed there. Grabbing the car keys, he loaded his 2009 Ford Mustang, keeping the cooler and food in easy reach behind his seat. Carli got in, and Murph started the engine with a roar. The car was Dark Highland Green, the signature color of Steve McQueen's Mustang from the movie *Bullitt*. He knew it would be as fast, but the chase was on. It was now a race against time, and he had to find Mary Kay first. He owed her that, and it drove him. They sped out of Washington and headed straight south for Miami.

Murph knew that the Egyptian killers would have a private jet at their disposal. He did not have that luxury anymore. By the time they could have booked a commercial flight, the earliest they could have arrived in Miami would have been late Sunday. Buying a ticket on the way to the airport was also the way to assure close scrutiny by the TSA, and there was no way they could get a

10-inch bronze pipe and the psh-kef knife past security. It was a good thing that Murph loved to get out on the open road and drive. It was their only option!

Hamid may have been able to fly faster than Murph could drive, but the young dentist still had a few tricks in his bag. He keyed his cell phone, and the Ford's female voice politely asked what he wanted to do.

"Call Dad!"

The phone rang three times. A cheerful voice answered, "Yello!"

"Hey Dad!"

"Michael! Great to hear your voice... Sounds like you're in the car. What's up?"

"There's too much to tell now, but I need a favor quick, and I'll tell you the details later."

"Sure! What can I do for you?"

"Well, I'm with Carli..."

"Excellent! Of all the girls you've dated, your Mom and I like Carli the best. She's special!"

"Dad!"

Carli giggled, then said loudly, "Hey, Dr. Murphy!"

"Uh-oh! Hi Carli! I didn't know you were on the line as well."

"It's OK, Dr. Murphy. I miss you and Mrs. Murphy too."

Murph cut them off. "We'll have a big reunion later, but for now, about that favor!"

"OK. OK. What do you need?"

"I know that courses at the Institute run from Sunday through Thursday. Can you find out who is teaching the course that starts tomorrow?"

"At Pankey? Sure, why?"

"Find out who the faculty are and call me back, then I'll tell you why? OK?"

"OK. I'll call you back in five minutes." The phone clicked off, and the radio began again.

Carli was still smiling. "You know you're going to have to tell him the story. You two are so much alike!"

"We are not!" he protested, but she just laughed all the more.

It was early Saturday evening so the traffic was light, and

they continued to make excellent time on the interstate. It took only three minutes before the phone rang.

"Yes?"

"You're in luck! It's a TMJ therapy class. Faculty is George Platt and Mike Rogers."

"Texas Mike?"

"Yes, from Dallas, how do you know him?"

"Mike Rogers was one of the people who taught the Esthetics class I took there last year. We got along really well."

"These two are my best friends. What do you need?"

"I promised to tell you, so here's the story. I don't want to tell you too much on a cell phone, so please don't ask any questions." Murph gave him the basic details up to now, leaving out the most recent violent events in Washington.

"Your Mom saw the reports of the attack in D.C. and was worried. She was going to call you to make sure you were OK. Was the attack related to this?"

"I'd rather not say." *OK, now they know. Why did I say that?*

There was silence on the other end for a moment before his dad asked. "What can my Pankey friends do to help?"

"I need a safe place to meet with my patient and remove the crown. Once it's out of her mouth, I think she'll be out of danger."

"I'll call George and explain things to him. Let me text you the cell phone number for Mike. Since he knows you, you can call him on your way."

"Dad, I may not get there fast enough to beat them to her. If I called Bert, do you think he would go pick her up and take her to the Institute?"

"I'm sure he would! He's that kind of guy. I have his cell number. I'll text it to you as well."

"Thanks. Tell Mom I love her!"

"I will. You two be careful!"

"We will." Carli's sweet voice made everything OK. "We'll see you soon!"

Murph clicked off the phone, continuing to drive aggressively as the sunset turned the sky from blue to orange to purple. The green Mustang became black with the onset of night.

Chapter 61

"Carli, can you look up Mary Kay Steinmiller in Coral Gables? See if you can get an address."

It took her less than two minutes on the iPad to have her street address and a MapQuest right to her door.

"You know that if I can find it, so can Omar!" Her voice sounded defeated.

"I know. We won't get there fast enough. That's why I need Bert's help."

"Who is Bert?"

"Humberto Garza," Murph explained, "was the jack-of-all-trades for the Institute. If anyone needed anything, faculty or students, he would move heaven and earth to make it happen." Bert was easy going and gregarious. A New York native, who relocated to south Florida, he and Murph began talking baseball one morning over Cuban coffee. A spirited debate ensued concerning his beloved Yankees and Murph's Cleveland Indians. They had become friends over his week at the Institute, and Bert had told Murph the proverbial "If there's ever anything you need, just call me." Well, it was time to make the call!

Bert answered the phone on the first ring. Since the Yankees had just clinched another Eastern Division Title with a win over the hated Red Sox, Bert was sure Murph was calling to congratulate him and concede that, for another year, the Yankees were in the playoffs and the Indians were out.

"How 'bout them Yankees!"

"Yes, Bert. Another great year for you guys! And the Indians get to say 'wait 'till next year'."

"Aw, the Tribe did better than everyone thought, but not as good as the Yankees!"

"They'll be tough to beat in the playoffs, but we can talk baseball later. I need a favor!"

"Anything for you, Doc! What is it?"

"I'm on my way down to Miami now, but I'm driving this time. Did you see *The Dental Apprentice* on TV?"

"Every show! You were great, but you sure got the shaft at the end. I don't understand why Dr. Farouk did that to you after you did the right thing to help that lady!"

"Well, there's a lot more to it than they showed on TV. In fact, I'm coming down to fix things for my patient." *How can I explain this quickly enough to Bert?* "The gold in her crown was very rare and old. There are people who want to take it from her, and I need to get it first. Believe me, this is a matter of life and death!

"Bert, this is dangerous. It's a really bad gang that wants this particular gold. They'll stop at nothing to get it. If I remove it, they'll next be looking for me and I'll have to figure the way to get it to the right authorities, but at least she will be out of harm's way."

"Doc, if you're in, then so am I. We gotta stick together and help her!"

"Thanks, Man! Here's what I need… " Murph proceeded to give Bert Mary Kay's address in Coral Gables. Bert agreed to pick her up first thing in the morning and take her to the Institute until Murph could get there. The Mustang was a dark blur racing through the Carolina night, but it would be at least 11:00 a.m. before he completed the eleven-hundred-mile drive.

Chapter 62

Hamid al-Said was pleased. He sat in the back seat of the Mercedes SUV, enjoying the scent of the new leather. With the door open, he could hear Banthaira shouting angrily into her cell phone. Having concluded their business in Arlington, they had driven directly to Reagan National Airport. They found that the crew of their leased Lear jet had gone home for the night. Banthaira, for all her screaming, was finding them unable to return to work, as the crew had exceeded their duty day according to the FAA rules. The Lear was not going anywhere until the morning, and no amount of berating the pilot would change that.

It is no matter, Hamid thought. *We will go to Miami in the morning. We are close! So very close!* He turned a glass vial in his hand, the golden crown sliding from one side to the other. *The gold is so beautiful, even with the bloodstains on it…*

Chapter 63

Murph stifled a yawn. It was still early. The moon was beginning to rise, maybe a sliver short of full, but shimmering, casting a ghostly light on the landscape. Two more calls to make, then he could just concentrate on driving.

He disconnected the phone from the hands-free speakers and dialed the number Mary Kay had given him at the end of her appointment. He wanted his voice to sound as normal as possible, not like he was driving 80 miles an hour on the interstate.

"Hello?" came the voice on the other end of the line. She sounded wide awake. Murph was glad she hadn't gone to sleep early.

"Hi, Ms. Steinmiller! It's Dr. Murphy!" He tried to sound happy, light and breezy. He glanced over at Carli and she shrugged, mouthing a silent good luck.

"Well, I'll be. How are you, young man? You certainly didn't get what you deserved from that mean boss of yours."

"I wondered if you had watched the show."

"Every episode! My friends and I just love you. We were rooting for you all the way!"

"Thanks for the support! How is that tooth feeling?"

"I'm glad you asked. I wanted to call you and tell you that it feels fine. In fact, I've never felt better in my life! I've got so much energy. I feel like I could live forever!"

"I'm so glad you feel so good, but that's why I'm calling. I need to take that crown off and put on a new one. There is something wrong with the gold." He didn't want to lie, but it was just too complex to explain over the phone. "It won't hold up, and I need to change it."

"That's strange."

"I know. I'll explain it all when I get there. I'm coming down to Miami now, and I can see you tomorrow morning. I will have a friend of mine, who works for The Pankey Institute pick you up and take you there. I'll see you in the clinic and explain everything. The Institute is in Key Biscayne, so it's only about 20 minutes from your home."

"That will be fine. I was going to church at eight. Can your driver pick me up after that?"

"I will have Bert pick you up at 9:30." He described Bert for her so that she would be comfortable with the arrangements. "Thank you for meeting with me tomorrow. I don't have much time in Miami before I have to be back in Washington."

"All of this reality TV is very strange. Are you going to be done with this soon?"

"Oh, yes! This will be the last thing I do with *The Dental Apprentice*!" He was sure of that! "Have a good night, and I'll see you in the morning."

Murph ended the call and drove on in silence for a minute. "Mary Kay is so willing to help, but I can tell that this doesn't make any sense to her." He looked at Carli. "Who am I kidding? This doesn't make any sense to me either. I'm asking her to take this on blind faith!"

"She trusts you! Everyone trusts you. That's why we can do this!"

"Then I can't afford to screw up. Too many people are depending on me now."

Murph dialed Bert again to update him on Mary Kay and to tell him what he had told her. It was imperative that Bert act as natural as possible. He wanted Mary Kay to be relaxed when they were removing the gold and placing the temporary crown. It wouldn't do to have her think anyone's life was in danger, especially if she were the one at risk.

Chapter 64

Murph keyed the phone again, making his last call of the night. "Mike Rogers."

"Hey, Dr. Rogers, it's Mike Murphy!"

"Hello, Mike. I'm glad you called. I just talked to your Dad, and I have to tell you that Sean isn't making any sense! Just what the hell is going on here?"

"Do you have time to talk now?"

"Sure. I'm in the faculty condo with George, so I'll put the phone on speaker and you can tell us both at the same time."

"Hey, Dr. Platt. My Dad has told me so much about you. I'm really glad you two are there this class. This is really tough to explain, but bear with me, and I'll start from the beginning."

The two dentists sat in stunned silence as Murph told of their experiences, in Cairo, Rome, Zurich, Germany and then Washington. When he finished, Murph was worried that he had lost the connection somehow. The silence was deafening.

"So, Bert will be bringing your *Apprentice* patient to the Institute in the morning." Dr. Platt was the first to speak. "And you want us to do what exactly?"

"She has a full gold crown on her lower right first molar. It needs to be removed and a temporary crown put in its place. The sooner this happens the better for my patient."

"That's easy enough." Texas Mike concluded. "But is this Pharaoh's Gold so important that the Egyptians would come down to Miami to get it?"

"I'm not going to lie to you. It's so vital that they have killed for it." There was that dead silence again. "When Mary Kay arrives, at least take the crown off; it's on with temporary cement. I'm driving as fast as I can, but I won't be there until around eleven. I know you have students coming in but keep the doors locked as much as possible, and if people come looking for me and demanding the crown, give it to them and then get yourselves and Mary Kay out of there!"

"We can hold the fort down until you arrive." Both voices agreed. "Just take care of yourselves on the way in!"

"We're moving as fast as we can safely. See you in the morning!"

Murph hung up the phone and bumped up the cruise control a bit more. It was going to be a long night.

Carli had been studying the news feed from today on the iPad. Sadly, the reports were grim.

"I don't want to get you down, but… "

"It's OK, " Murph forced a smile, "I'm stressed enough as it is, so let me have it!"

"The police are confused. They have what they see are unrelated events. Their biggest concern is what they believe is a terrorist attack on the Willard Hotel. Since it is less than a block from the White House, the Secret Service and Homeland Security are involved. Even the FBI has people investigating." She read from the AP wire report:

"A group of armed suspects attacked a private gathering at the Willard InterContinental. While their initial intent seemed to be to cause commotion and fear, the attack turned deadly. The terrorists entered the hotel conference room and disturbed a dinner reception hosted by Dr. Manesh Farouk, the celebrity dentist who hosted The Dental Apprentice on TV. Several guests were assaulted, including the Rapper BadA$$, who was struck in the mouth. One of the guests at the event was Colonel Robert Anderson, an Army Ranger, recently retuned from Afghanistan. When Col. Anderson attempted to protect one of the other guests, the terrorists opened fire, killing Col. Anderson and two other people. Dr. Farouk sustained wounds, as did five other people, including two injured as the armed assailants fled the hotel. D.C. police continue the search for a woman and several men. Conflicting witness reports place the number of suspects at as little as four to as many as nine."

Murph sighed deeply. "Three dead and six wounded. This is spiraling out of control. They're getting desperate!"

"And more dangerous!" Carli was right. "There are two other stories here. Separately, the news reports on the death of *Apprentice* winner Dr. Claire Summerville, the victim of an apparent burglary at her condo. Police have no suspects in Claire's death."

"They're too busy with the Willard to connect the dots on this one, but they'll make the connection soon enough. What else is there?"

"The last story is really buried, but the body of a Brent Hathaway was found on the porch of his home in Arlington. The police believe he was killed as he returned home after being at the theater."

"That's Claire's patient. Does the report say anything about him missing a tooth?"

"No, but if there is a bit of good news here, it is that he was apparently killed around 10:00 p.m."

"God rest his soul! By coming home late, he bought us some

time."

Carli could feel the agony of the decision still weighing on Murph. "You did the right thing by leaving immediately. We couldn't have helped him, and we have a chance to save Mary Kay and to stop them!"

"I know, but condemning a man I've never met... "

"We can try to call the police and get help, but I just don't see them believing any of this!"

Murph swallowed hard. He needed to keep up his resolve. "I know. We're in this alone." He thought of Mary Kay and then the words of Mother Theresa, "If you cannot save a hundred people, then just save one."

He didn't realize he had said it aloud. "What's that?" Carli wondered.

"The words of Mother Theresa."

"It sounds like a prayer, and it's a good one for what we are trying to do."

"We've come this far! Let's finish it!"

Chapter 65

The Florida sun had risen, bright and golden on a new day. Murph shifted in the leather seat and scratched the stubble of a beard on his chin. Carli was leaning on his shoulder, fast asleep. She had stayed awake through the night, keeping him alert. After they had stopped for gas and coffee at dawn, she had drifted off, and Murph let her go. She needed the rest. It was going to be a long day.

His phone buzzed, vibrating on silent, and he answered quickly. Bert sounded wide awake — *probably the Cuban coffee!*

"Good morning, Doc! How are you?"

"Tired of driving, but I'm almost there!"

"Good. I just wanted to let you know that I have Ms. Steinmiller, and we are on our way to the Institute."

"Bert, that's great! Thanks so much. I talked to the faculty yesterday, and they are expecting you."

"My pleasure! I like this lady. She's feisty!"

Murph had to laugh. "I know. I think that's why *The Dental Apprentice* producers chose her. Tell her I'll be there soon."

"Drive carefully... I'll have the Cuban coffee waiting for you!"

"Thanks Bert. I'm going to need it!"

It was a beautiful morning in south Florida. Murph and Carli roared down I-95 — the final stretch run. They passed the port of Miami on their left, cruise ships docked with passengers disembarking from their relaxing week in the Caribbean. But there was no relaxing for them yet. Just past downtown, Murph angled off the highway and onto the Rickenbacker Causeway toward The Pankey Institute. The causeway was a five-mile ribbon of concrete connecting a chain of small islands in Biscayne Bay. The Institute was on Key Biscayne, the final island in the chain and the site of a quiet community.

The view from the Rickenbacker Causeway was majestic, with blue water and white sand lining the path. As he sped along the last miles, he could hear the soundtrack to Miami Vice in his head. That was Miami — beautiful and dangerous — a crossroads of cultures — the gateway to the Caribbean and South America, yet filled with travelers from Europe and Asia. Anything could happen here, and no one looked out of place.

This morning, everything seemed at peace. Sunny and warm, the radio had predicted 89 degrees for the high, without a chance of rain. The causeway narrowed to become Crandon Boulevard, and they entered Key Biscayne.

The first major building upon entering the Key was The Pankey Institute, started in 1972 in honor of the world-class dentist and educator Dr. Lindsey Pankey, Sr. Since that time, the Institute had provided a place for advanced continuing education, where dentists could explore the meaning of excellence and renew their commitment to practicing the finest dentistry possible.

The four-story, Bahamas-style education center stood at the entrance to the gateway to the village. Its pale green walls and white trim looked perfectly at home on the island, and its lush tropical landscaping provided an oasis from the world. Murph turned the Mustang into the palm tree lined driveway and cruised around the back of the Institute to park under the north side of the building.

He backed in, leaving the car ready for a quick get-away. He turned off the ignition with a sigh of relief. "We made it, and I don't see any suspicious vehicles," he said, tussling the back of Carli's hair. They got out and stretched eagerly. Murph was pleased when the kinks in his back released with a satisfying pop. The Mustang was comfortable to drive, but bending his tall frame into anything for that long was tough.

"Welcome to The Pankey Institute!"

Carli was surveying the grounds. "Last time you were here, you met me at the airport, and we went on the cruise." She sighed, "Seems like such a long time ago!"

"Memory lane will have to wait. Let's get going."

Murph led Carli to the front and up the steps to a large brass double door. As he had hoped, it was locked. He buzzed, and Bert quickly let them in. Bert gave Murph a giant bro-hug, and they exchanged a few pleasantries in Spanish. Murph's Spanish was clumsy, far from fluent but passable. Bert always laughed, but appreciated that Murph tried to use his native tongue.

Murph introduced Carli to Bert, and they crossed the green marble floor and up the grand marble steps into the main lobby. It was Sunday, so none of the regular staff were at the large reception counter. Carli took in the warm cherry woodwork and pale flan-colored fabric wallcovering.

Murph had called Mike Rogers earlier and knew the current class was using the large laboratory and lecture hall on this, the main floor. He looked at his watch — 10:51 — great time! It had to be close to the land speed record from D.C. "Come on, I can hear their voices."

Down the short hallway, Murph led Carli through the first floor lab. Each lab station was set up for a student. The mannequin head was attached, and all the instruments were laid out for the day's lab exercise. For a full class of 26 students, the lab benches were set up in five rows of six stations. The theater operatory was in the front of the building, next to the lab.

Murph introduced Carli to the two faculty members: "Texas" Mike Rogers, outgoing and funny with a razor sharp wit, and George Platt, the smooth talking southerner from Arkansas. *Dad always said George was the idea guy.*

George explained that they had decided to fill-in the resident

197

Chairman of the Education Department about what was going on. He had provided them with access to his private operatory, where they could lock the door. Patient release papers for Ms. Steinmiller to sign prior to treatment were waiting in the operatory. He had even escorted the students to an early lunch so George and Mike could fabricate her provisional crown and seat it. His only proviso was that he expected their famous Pankey alumnus, Dr. Mike Murphy, to say hello to all the students and chat about *The Dental Apprentice*, when they returned from lunch. Ms. Steinmiller had been very agreeable, trusting Murph's colleagues. George had already removed the gold and replaced it with a temporary crown that Mike had skillfully made for her.

Murph left Carli with Bert and his colleagues and went in to see Mary Kay. She looked tired, but was happy to see him.

"Ms. Steinmiller, it's great to see you! How are you feeling?"

"Dr. Murphy, I'm so glad you're here! They have all taken great care of me and been so nice, but it's wonderful to see a familiar friendly face."

"How is it going?"

"They already took that crown out and made me a nice temporary until the new crown comes back from the lab. They said the tooth looks super, but I feel really run down. It must be all the stress in rushing here."

"That can happen sometimes. When we get worried about something, our bodies produce adrenalin and once the stress is over and the adrenalin is used up, we feel really tired. I'm sure you will feel like yourself very soon."

"I hope so. They said I was done and that Bert could take me home just as soon as you saw me. It's a treat to see you again."

Even though Murph knew the work done by the faculty would be flawless, he put on gloves and examined her mouth. It put her at ease and allowed him to praise his colleagues for their excellent work.

"That looks fantastic," he said as he took off his gloves and washed his hands. "Let's go see your other docs. I want to confirm the lab arrangements for your new crown with them, and then we'll take you home." Murph patted her on the shoulder and took off her bib.

"When am I going to see you again?"

"When the crown is back from the lab, maybe in a couple of weeks, they will call, and then I will arrange to come see you. You are a very special patient to me!"

"Dr. Murphy, I'd travel half-way across the country to keep you as my dentist." Her eyes were sincere. She meant it!

Murph escorted Mary Kay into the lab, introduced her to Carli, and seated her in the closest chair so they could talk. Mary Kay was obviously delighted to meet Dr. Murphy's girlfriend. She could sense the connection between the two and liked her immediately. Mary Kay found Carli very easy to talk to. Mary Kay wanted to know all about Carli, and they chatted away.

Murph turned to his colleagues. "Perfect work, gentlemen!"

Mike Rogers pretended to look hurt. "You expected anything less?" George rolled his eyes. "I mean this is Pankey faculty we're talking about!"

"Do you have the gold crown?" Murph asked quietly.

"Got it right here!" Texas Mike held up a pill bottle and made it rattle by shaking it side to side.

"Excellent!" Murph held up his hand, and Mike tossed it to him. As he caught it with a clink, Murph looked down and saw the crown. He marveled at the anatomy he had carefully carved and cast into it. It was some of his best work.

"Very well done, especially for a young guy without much experience in waxing and casting gold." George Platt had removed the crown, and he had seen how nicely it fit and functioned in her mouth.

"My Dad taught me a lot, practicing in his lab and doing his lab work. I wish I could work with him more, but there's no burning opportunity back in Cleveland."

Texas Mike drawled, "It's hard to keep them down on the farm, after they've seen Par-ree!"

"Something like that. I've just come to like the bright lights, big city thing, but time will tell where I go from here." He wrapped his fingers around the bottle and went to put the crown in his pocket.

"Such touching sentiments!" A voice like ice cut through the air, and their attention was drawn instantly to the doorway. "Do not bother putting that away. I'll be taking it now!"

Chapter 66

Murph fumbled the vial, and it dropped onto the lab bench, spinning like a top until coming to rest on the gray Formica top. "But how???"

Hamid al-Said walked into the lab, casually holding a 9mm pistol in his left hand. "When you make secret plans by telephone, it would be wise to remember that old people often write things down next to the phone… so they will remember."

Mary Kay gasped as Hamid waved a hand-written page, torn from a flowered note pad. They could all clearly see written in her large, flowing hand:

Bert
Pankey Institute
9:30 am

"Well, that answers that question! Do we all go out for Cuban coffee now and talk about it?" Murph was talking as he hastily scanned the room, looking for options.

The lab was a 40-foot square open room. Five lab benches crossed it, leaving aisles in between, obstructed by the rolling dental stools for the students to sit on while working. The benches were of desk height, around 32 inches off the floor, but the dental lights on swinging arms and computer monitors in front of each station provided a significant visual barrier up to almost five feet high. Panoramic glass windows covered the outside wall, only one floor above the parking lot, but Murph knew these were hurricane proof glass, and not a viable exit, even with only a 15-foot drop to the ground below.

There were only two entrances to the lab. Hamid stood in the main pathway to the front entrance, the way Murph and Carli had entered just a few minutes before. On the opposite end of the lab, the doorway opened to Masters Hall, the main lecture room. Murph believed this was the path to safety, as there was a back way out of the Institute that would be open to them… if they could reach it.

The main obstacle was the ever-smiling face of Omar Bengdara, standing with his arms crossed in the open door to Masters Hall. Even though he appeared unarmed, Murph expected a weapon to appear when it was required. Omar seemed to be the type to be prepared. That left Banthaira un-accounted for, and usually they had a driver.

Murph motioned for his band of followers to get behind him. George shepherded Mary Kay, and Texas Mike shielded Carli as they moved away from Hamid and the entrance, closer to the windows and the aisle created by the ends of the lab benches. Bert stayed low, against the bench, and put his hand on one of the wheeled chairs. The perimeter of the room was occupied by work surfaces, sinks, and mechanical equipment; bench lathes, cast grinders and steam cleaners for melting wax.

Hamid and Omar both began walking purposefully into the room. "Dr Murphy. I grow tired of all this useless conversation. You will hand over the gold crown now!"

"And if I do, no one gets hurt and you will leave?"

"Now why would I agree to that? I hold all the cards"

"And you aren't afraid to use them." Murph was certain they were all dead unless he could think of something — and fast! "We know about the attack on the Willard!"

"Stupid Army fool. No one needed to get hurt, but he insisted on playing the hero."

"I was with Claire Summerville when she died after you questioned her. You know, she would have gladly told you everything you wanted to know if you had just asked her the right question! Did her patient, Brent Hathaway, have to die too?"

"All of this was unnecessary. If people would just do what I tell them!"

"Where is your girlfriend? She seems to be the one with the temper. While you seem to be reasonable, she strikes me as the type to leave no loose ends behind."

Omar chuckled once, in spite of himself, but Murph noticed it out of the corner of his eye. *So that's it. She's the really dangerous one! That knowledge could be useful.*

"Banthaira and Faraj are making sure that we are not disturbed. She is convincing your incoming class of students to return to their lunch. Faraj will deal with the police should you be stupid enough to try to summon them."

Murph looked down at the vial with the gold tooth on the counter top. Sitting next to it was a metal bur block, holding dental drill bits for the afternoon's lab exercise. It was about the same size as the pill bottle with the crown in it. He reached down and scooped up both items in his hand, fairly certain that Hamid's view of his hands was blocked. Murph stepped back to the bench in front of the windows. He could feel the heat of a steam cleaner on his back. He moved Carli to his left, closer to the exit door on the far end of the lab. Texas Mike and George were to his right, with Mary Kay in between them. Omar had walked into the lab and was now at the other end of the aisle between the lab benches, directly facing Murph.

Omar still had not drawn his pistol. He knew Murph was unarmed, and he didn't think the dentist was dangerous. But Murph did seem to be surprisingly calm. There was no hint of panic.

Scanning around the room again, Murph noticed the entrance to the supply storeroom in the corner of the lab. It was just five steps beyond the faculty dentists. The small closet was not an exit, but it did have a heavy door. He needed to have as few people in harm's way as possible. Very quietly, he said "George, Mike, take Mary Kay and Bert into the storeroom… now."

Texas Mike nodded, put his arm around Mary Kay, and ran. He was half carrying her with him. George followed with Bert, covering their rear. After their sudden first step, they were hidden by the obstructions on the top of the lab bench. Hamid fired off a hasty shot, hitting a computer monitor. It exploded, sending shards of glass onto the floor.

Omar charged down the aisle straight at Murph, shoving aside the dental chairs like an angry bull. Hamid moved past the lab bench, to get a clear shot at his escaping prisoners, but they reached the safety of the storage closet and slammed the door. Murph could hear the crash of metal shelving, as his friends barricaded the door as best they could.

Murph shoved Carli down the aisle, toward the open doorway at the far end of the room. Looking up at the approaching Omar, Murph hurled the bur block past Hamid at the other door. Both Omar and Hamid followed its flight, as they assumed it was the vial with the crown. Hamid turned to follow the block as it landed and went skittering down the tile hallway. Omar hesitated slightly and then continued bearing down on Murph.

The momentary distraction gave Murph his chance. He reached behind him and grasped the handle of the steam cleaner. It was basically a clothes steamer, connected by rubber tubing to a spray nozzle. It provided the high-pressure steam that was used to melt wax off of dental models in order to clean them. Murph crouched down, as if he planned to meet Omar's charge like a wrestler.

At the last minute, Murph brought around his hand, holding the nozzle. Omar's eyes widened, as he realized his mistake. Murph squeezed the trigger and sent a blast of steam the short distance between them. Bengdara screamed and fell to the floor, his hands clutching his scalded face.

Murph grabbed his backpack and put his hand in the middle of Carli's back, propelling the stunned woman in front of him. They neared the door to the darkened Masters Hall as Hamid shouted from the other side of the lab, "Get them. He still has the crown!"

Carli stumbled into the lecture hall first. After the lab, which was bathed in sunlight, the darkened lecture room made vision difficult. Murph felt more than saw a shadow to his left, and he drove his shoulder into it, like a linebacker making a tackle. There was a satisfying "OOF" as the air went out of what Murph assumed was Faraj. Murph maintained contact with the body, pushing it hard into one of the desktops in the room. Murph felt a crunch, and the body went limp. His gun fell to the floor, and Murph picked up the pistol, rolling off of his target and standing to face the doorway.

Murph could see Hamid silhouetted in the doorway, and he raised the pistol. "Stop, or I'll shoot!" It sounded so silly, even as he said it.

"Oh, I think not!" Hamid flicked on the lights, and Murph could see Carli firmly in the grasp of the much taller Banthaira. She held a fistful of Carli's hair in her right hand and a long-bladed, gold-handled knife was pressed against her neck. Banthaira's lips were a thin line across her face. Her eyes burned at Murph.

"You have something I need, and I have something you

want." Hamid summarized the situation. "It is time we ended this, because both of us know you will not shoot. Omar!" Bengdara entered the room. His eyes and forehead were red, but the beard had shielded much of his face.

Hamid looked coldly at Murph. "You will give me the crown and the bronze investment you have in your pack. Get them out now, or you will get Miss Chamoun back a piece at a time… and it would be a shame to mar that pretty face."

Murph hesitated, but Banthaira tightened her grip, and a trickle of blood began to flow from the point of the knife, just under her jaw. The corners of Carli's eyes tightened with the pain, but she refused to give Banthaira the satisfaction of a scream.

Murph pulled the vial out of his pants' pocket and then removed the investment from his pack. He set them on the desktop to his left and stepped back a foot. He held the gun on Hamid. Try as he might, he didn't look very convincing.

At Hamid's command, Omar moved over and picked up the vial. He examined it and verified it contained the crown. Nodding, he tossed it to al-Said, who caught it and held it up to the light, smiling in triumph.

Omar picked up the bronze pipe and looked at Murph. "Next time you threaten someone with a gun, remember to take off the safety!" Omar swung the pipe with deadly force in a roundhouse move at Murph's head. A bit too late, Murph recognized the attack and began to duck, rolling to his left. The investment connected with the back of Murph's head solidly enough to give Omar a satisfying crunch. He hit the floor hard, face down, and stayed there.

Carli screamed, and Banthaira laughed a demented, evil laugh.

Hamid simply pocketed the vial with the crown and led them off. Banthaira's heels clicking on the tile floor as she dragged the sobbing Carli, at knifepoint, along with her.

Chapter 67

A few minutes before all hell broke loose, the Chairman of Education had returned to the Institute with the 26 dentists taking the course. When Banthaira had stopped them in the lobby, he quickly surmised the situation and told the students something was wrong in the lab. Making up the excuse of a water line break, he sent the dentists back to the condos with plans to meet in the Faculty Condo at two o'clock for a Case Presentation.

The Chairman herded them out the door and waited to make sure they all headed south toward the Pankey condos. He used the landscaping to shield himself from view and hurried along the building. Upon reaching the southeast corner, he unlocked the back stairwell door and crept up the steps. He prayed he wasn't too late to help the others.

Chapter 68

Murph's quick reactions had not completely avoided the blow to his head, but the quick dive he had perfected during his volleyball career had reduced some of the downward force. He hit the ground dazed but not completely out. He wisely stayed down, hearing them go down the marble stairs and then the audible security beeps from the front doors opening.

He popped up quickly. His vision blurred, and he nearly blacked out. Steadying himself on the desk, he reached up and felt the knot growing on the back of his head. *No more sudden moves!* He was weaving a bit as he made his way to the door that lead to the back hall and his original goal, the stairwell at the rear of the Institute.

Just then, the Chairman appeared in the doorway, a bit breathless, with a look of grave concern on his face. He reached out to grab Murph's shoulders, steadying him.

"Murph, are you OK?" The Chairman could see blood on the

collar of Murph's shirt and the large bruise behind his head.

"Sorry, chief! There's a big mess in the lab. They've got Carli!"

Before the Chairman could stop him, Murph broke away and dashed down the back stairs and out the door to the parking lot, the pounding in his head increasing with every step. Murph wasn't sure what he would do when he caught them, but he knew he needed to help Carli. He would have to make it up as he went. *That's all I've been doing lately anyway,* he thought bitterly.

Murph ran around the back of the building to the north side where he had parked the Mustang, close to the exit. A black SUV was at the open gate and about to race up Crandon Boulevard toward the causeway. He had to get to it! He broke into a full run across the parking lot.

From the laboratory window, Mike and George could see the man crouching behind the Mustang. They waved at Murph to warn him, but he was oblivious to them and the danger. Powerless to help, they watched an assailant fly at Murph from behind and throw a cloth over Murph's mouth and nose.

Murph struggled briefly but soon collapsed in the arms of his attacker. A white cargo van pulled up. Its door opened, and Murph was loaded inside, backpack and all. The attacker, a firmly built man with a dark complexion, got in the van and closed the door. Then, the van sped north, in the wake of the SUV.

The Chairman had run to the front of the building just in time see the white van. He barely had time to note the license plate number as the driver cleared the gate and headed toward Miami.

Mike Rogers called 911 to report the break-in. The Chairman met up with the three dentists in the lab, and they all went to the front entrance to meet the police.

The Chairman quickly summed things up. "Murph's famous now, so the police will know who he is. We'll tell them he's been abducted."

George agreed. "Keep it simple. We can give them a description of the attackers and their vehicles. There's only one road off this island and the causeway is long one. If we give them the urgent facts fast, there's a chance..."

Just then, sirens blaring, a police car came up the front drive. The Key Biscayne Fire Department emergency team parked immediately behind, and two more police cars parked on Crandon Boulevard, one of these blocking the exit from the Institute. The property was secured within seconds!

As the police stepped out, hands on their holsters, the Chairman shouted, "Dr. Murphy from *The Dental Apprentice* show… he's been abducted! They drove off in a white van, and I've got the license number!"

The lead police officer rolled his eyes and looked at his partner, shaking his head. "OK, Doc." He chuckled, "Where's the leak in the laughing gas tank?"

Chapter 69

Omar Bengdara stuffed a handkerchief in Carli's mouth and tied the ends behind her head. He bound her wrists and ankles with duct tape and carried her like a sack of potatoes onto the Lear jet, dumping her unceremoniously into a padded chair while she glared at him. He patted her on the cheek and sat in the matching chair across the aisle from her, buckling in for take-off.

Hamid and Banthaira sat further forward as the jet rolled out and took off. Carli had no way of knowing their destination. She pretended to fall asleep, but remained hard at work, listening for any information.

As the jet leveled off, Hamid and Banthaira came back a bit to the table in the center of the cabin. Hamid opened a briefcase and removed a series of glass vials, lining them up on the table. Carli could tell they held pieces of gold. Some were large lumps of melted down gold, but some were clearly shaped like teeth. *The recently collected gold crowns,* she thought. Carli tried not to think of the faces of the dead who had once owned those crowns. It was a gruesome collection, amassed over time, beginning centuries ago with a striking number of acquisitions made in the last week alone. Banthaira surveyed the situation arrayed before her but did not participate directly in the accounting.

Hamid removed a leather bound folder from his briefcase. He untied the thong and opened the pages. Carli recognized the journal immediately. Hamid checked off the names of the carriers of the gold prostheses against the vials in front of him. He seemed to be making some calculation.

Banthaira hissed at him, "Well? Is it enough?"

"I cannot be sure without weighing it accurately. But I am afraid that we are still short of the required amount. We are still missing the gold from the dentures of Winston Churchill and George Washington. That is a sizeable amount, especially Washington's denture. Without it, I am afraid there isn't enough."

Banthaira flew into a rage, screaming in a language which even the fluent Carli had trouble following. She went over and grabbed Carli by the shoulders, shaking her and raising her hand to strike.

"Wait!" Hamid halted her arm. "We still have a hostage. When we land, I will contact Manesh directly and see if we can strike a deal. He may be ready to be done with this as well."

Her anger passed slowly, but Banthaira walked to the front of the Lear again. She sat down and stared off into space, not speaking for the duration of the flight.

Hamid completed his entries in a ledger and replaced the gold vials carefully in the aluminum briefcase. He poured himself a large snifter of brandy and sat, alone with his thoughts, looking out the window.

Omar was snoring peacefully across from Carli. His red cheeks and forehead beginning to blister and peel.

Carli tried to shift to a more comfortable position, but found it impossible. Gradually, she fell asleep, tormented by dreams of being chased through the pyramid. She awoke in a cold sweat, as the Lear began its descent.

Chapter 70

Derek Whitman was lounging in a folding chair, enjoying the sun next to the Gulfstream 550. He heard the van coming and packed up his gear as the white truck pulled up. Manny Farouk got out of the driver's seat, looking out of character in a ball cap and t-shirt. He walked over to Derek.

"Time to go. One more passenger this trip."

Manny climbed the stairs to the cabin as the rear door of the van opened. Margaret jumped out, in shorts, halter-top, and flip-flops. She helped Saleh out, as he had a heavy load. Derek was shocked to see Murph's unconscious body draped over Saleh's shoulders in a fireman's carry.

"What the hell?"

Saleh cut him off. "No questions. Just fly!"

They all boarded the plane, closed the cabin door, and taxied off, leaving the van standing in the middle of the tarmac.

As the Gulfstream moved to the runway, Murph's body was placed on the sofa and restrained by a seatbelt. Saleh lightly tied his hands and ankles with twist ties.

Manny looked at Saleh and pointed to Murph. "Search him!"

Saleh frowned. "You know as well as I do, he is unarmed."

"Yes, but as Bengdara found out, unarmed is not necessarily safe."

"It is his mind that makes him dangerous, not any weapon. I can search him if you like, but it will be a waste of time!"

Manny gave up. "Suit yourself. He is your responsibility anyway."

They all buckled in and roared down the runway into the sky.

Murph awoke with his head pounding and a ringing in his ears. He was lying on his side. *That ringing isn't in my ears. It's jet engine noise. I'm on a plane.* He tried to raise his head, but a wave of nausea crashed over him and he nearly vomited. He moved his arms and realized his wrists were bound. So were his ankles.

"Slowly, my friend!" The deep baritone voice was reassuring and very familiar. "Let me release you. I don't want you to hurt yourself." Strong hands held his legs then arms as a razor knife cut the plastic ties.

Murph's eyes were having a tough time focusing, but he looked long into the face. Finally it dawned on Murph. "Saleh?"

"At your service!" He smiled broadly. "You have come a long way since we last parted. You have accomplished some amazing things, not the least of which has been staying alive. Besting Omar Bengdara is no small feat."

"Carli!" Murph jumped out of the couch and staggered to his

209

feet. Saleh caught him and eased him back into a sitting position. "They have Carli!" Murph's voice was a strangled cry.

"I know. We are going now to try to do something about that!"

"They will not harm her." Manny Farouk swiveled his chair around to look at Murph. "She is a valuable hostage. They need her, and Hamid knows it." Manny smiled a sad smile.

"Dr. Farouk, I ought to… " Murph lunged forward, his fist pulled back. Saleh easily intercepted the attempt and dumped Murph back into his seat.

"Michael, do not judge me too harshly, at least until this story is at its end. You have discovered a great deal since we last met, but there is more yet to play out."

Manny poured Murph a generous portion of Jameson as a peace offering and filled his own glass as well. With Murph glaring at him, Manny sat back down and continued, "You were correct in deciding that the Pharaoh's Gold was placed in many people's mouths over the years. Hamid al-Said and his lover Banthaira have been attempting to collect all the gold, and now they have nearly enough. However, they lack two parcels, and these together constitute a significant amount of the total gold."

He had changed back into his normal dressy attire, khaki slacks and a silk Tommy Bahama shirt. Manny reached into his pocket and removed a small glass bottle. "This vial contains the gold from …"

"The denture of Winston Churchill." Murph filled in the blank.

"Excellent! I knew you had talent." Manny nodded approvingly. "The other parcel Hamid failed to possess is …"

"George Washington's denture, stolen from the Smithsonian during the Bicentennial!"

"Yes. The largest piece of them all." Manny folded his hands in his lap and began tapping his index fingertips together. "But the denture is no longer lost. It is, in fact… in your pocket, is it not?"

"Yes," Murph conceded the point.

"Well, that impulse to save the denture — that little theft, taking it from my office, may be the thing that saves us all!"

"What do you mean?"

"Simply put. Without the gold that is in Washington's denture, Hamid does not have enough to cast the prosthesis needed to replace the mummy's teeth. Without the teeth, he cannot complete the ceremony, animate the mummy and lift the curse!"

Murph whistled through his teeth. "So, it's all true!"

"Yes, indeed it is. After five thousand years, the tale is nearly at its end." Manny looked off into the distance, his eyes losing focus. "When we land, I expect Hamid to call me. He will try to trade Carli's life for the gold he needs. I will arrange for us all to meet, and you will have to decide what to do."

"What do you mean?"

Manny sighed. "You hold the largest single piece of Pharaoh's Gold. It is the key to the curse. He holds the life of the woman you love. When you see what is at stake, you must decide what is most important. All will become clear in time. For now, you must rest while we complete our return to Washington, D.C. You took quite a bump on the head, and the chloroform used to subdue you leaves a nasty headache. You'll need a clear mind soon — rest."

Manny turned his chair around again, having said all he had intended. Murph thought, *I wish that bump on the head had awakened me from a bad dream. If only this was all a bad dream. He could feel the denture, biting into his leg where it sat in his pocket. Nope, this is all real. Very real!*

Chapter 71

No sooner had the Learjet's wheels touched the runway than Banthaira powered up her cell phone. Her conversation began quietly in Arabic, but soon escalated into frenzied shouting, which Carli had no trouble following this time.

"We will leave immediately after refueling. The full moon peaks tonight, so we must work quickly. Prepare everything for the ceremony!"

Carli looked over at Hamid, who was following Banthaira's phone conversation intently.

"What do you mean? No, it is not missing. We moved it to the basement during the rioting! Search, you fools! Search! He must be found!"

Hamid looked very concerned.

After agonizing minutes of silence, Banthaira screamed and threw the phone across the cabin. It hit the bulkhead and shattered into pieces, scattering across the floor.

The Lear rolled up to the hangar and shut down. The whine of the engines disappeared, and an eerie silence enveloped the plane. No one dared speak.

Hamid al-Said rose from his seat and took out his phone. He selected a number from his contacts and made the call. He put the phone on speaker, laying it on the table in front of him and sat down. He waited quietly while the phone dialed, but Banthaira glared at the ringing object with contempt.

"Hello, my old friend!" Came the voice on the phone. Carli stifled a gasp as she recognized Manny Farouk. "I have been expecting your call."

Hamid took a deep breath and slowly let it out between clenched teeth, calming himself. "I am returning to Egypt immediately. You should join me. We have business to attend to there, you and I."

"Much as I would dearly love to see our home again, that would be a terrible waste of time and aviation fuel, I'm afraid." The disembodied voice was deadly calm.

"You seem so sure of yourself, when I hold all the cards!" Hamid hissed, his anger beginning to rise.

"Once again, my friend, your rash actions fail to take into account all of the facts. You wish to remove the curse. Indeed, nothing would please me more, but I believe that you are lacking several of the key pieces for the procedure."

"I have the gold and the investment. And I have the girl. I will return to Cairo and complete the ceremony, thus breaking the curse."

"You have the investment, but you lack enough of the gold to cast the prosthesis! Did you not do the calculations?" Manny chided, seeming to imply that this was not the first time that Hamid had paid little attention to details.

"I have done the calculations!" Hamid spat out the words. "You will give me the remaining gold!"

"But the gold is not mine to give you. Did you not realize that Dr. Murphy had Washington's denture in his pocket? It was there right in front of you all the time!" he taunted.

Hamid swore!

"It is no matter. I have Dr. Murphy with me. You can ask him yourself and see if he will trade you the denture... for Ms. Chamoun, perhaps?"

"You do not set the terms, servant! I am the master!"

Manny ignored the insult. "Are you planning the ceremony at the Cairo museum, or back at Saqqara?"

"We have moved the mummy to Saqqara and are preparing. Time is short!"

"Indeed it is. This is the night of the full moon of the fall solstice. We cannot wait." Manny sounded confident. "Are you *sure* the mummy is at Saqqara?"

Hamid cursed again.

Manny laughed. "It is alright. As it has always been, I have prepared everything. The Pharaoh is safe. I had his mummy moved from Cairo a week ago. The House of Gold has been readied for the ceremony. Tonight, we shall finish this together, as we began so long ago. I am sure you know where to meet me here in Washington. Bring the gold you have collected and Ms. Chamoun, unharmed!"

Hamid was struggling to regain control of the situation. "I am pleased that you have made all the arrangements. I will come when I am ready."

"You have until one hour before midnight, so that everything can be made ready. Do not be late!" and the phone went dead.

Hamid sat staring at the silent BlackBerry on the tabletop. Banthaira seethed. Omar was reserved and silent. Carli smiled around the gag. Hamid noticed and waved a cautionary finger her way. "You should not be so smug! The mummy will be mine to command!"

Carli smiled and flashed her middle finger at him. Omar reached over, smacking her with the back of his hand. It left a red welt on her cheek.

"Enough!" Banthaira shrieked. "We shall get off this infernal plane and go to the city. Now that we are so close, I will not be denied!" She bent down, putting her face inches from Carli, and whispered, "You shall see the awesome power at my disposal, and you will quake with fear. This I promise you. Laugh now, for your hours are numbered!"

She stood up and motioned for them to follow. "Come. Destiny awaits."

Chapter 72

Manny Farouk pressed the button and ended the call. The limo driving them from the airport rolled smoothly across the pavement. Murph, Saleh, and Margaret had heard every word. He sat back in his chair, folding his hands in his lap. He looked at Murph, scanning his eyes for understanding.

"Let me be sure I understand things." Murph began. "You are going to perform the ceremony on the mummy of Djoser here tonight. It is the full moon, and you will be attempting to complete a ceremony that was disrupted over four thousand years ago! All that remains is for you to cast the gold teeth and place them in the mouth of the mummy?"

"Mostly correct. I expect that *you* will be casting the gold prosthesis. Hamid will not permit me to leave his sight with all the gold, and he will not suffer to do it himself. He finds that sort of task beneath his *exalted* status."

Murph was stunned. "And you stole the mummy from the Cairo Museum of Antiquities?

When the Gulfstream left Cairo, its passengers were Margaret, Saleh and his family, and the mummy of Djoser! How did you manage that? Carli told me that the mummy was moved from its sarcophagus on the second floor of the museum to the museum basement in order to keep it safe during the Tahrir riots, but Carli thought this actually would make the mummy more accessible than it had been in centuries."

"Quite right. You both are amazingly well informed and perceptive." He nodded approvingly. "Hamid moved the mummy with the help of his allies. It made it easier for him to accomplish what he intended, but it also improved my chances. He forgets that I also have contacts within Egypt, though the power of my people has waned of late." He looked at Saleh, who nodded sadly. "I expect that Banthaira has not reacted well to the discovery that the body in the temporary sarcophagus is that of Tanen Narmer. I would have loved to see her face when she heard the news." He closed his eyes, savoring the imagined screams. He cringed and then shook his head. "Then again, perhaps not."

The limo turned past the Pentagon and crossed the Potomac River. The obelisk that was the Washington Monument gleamed in the golden light of the setting sun.

"Hamid will expect that you are my prisoner and that you will do my bidding as my apprentice. Margaret has made all the preparations for the ceremony."

"Am I correct in thinking the House of Gold is in the basement of the Center for Esthetic and Restorative Excellence?"

"A wise conclusion. The casting facilities are in the lab on that level. You are familiar with them from your final task."

"Yes. I remember the facilities." The mention of the Apprentice reminded Murph of Claire, and he darkened for a minute. "Are you aware that Dr. Summerville is dead?"

"Yes. I was deeply saddened, but I was comforted to know that you were with her at the end. The brutality to which Hamid and Banthaira have descended shocks me, even after all this time." He fixed Murph in his gaze. "They are very close to the power they have sought for thousands of years. It would be well for you to remember that they will stop at nothing and let nothing stand in their way tonight. That makes them supremely dangerous. You must harden you resolve and have no mercy. They will have no mercy when it comes to you — or Carli."

"I've had enough of them! It will be good to end this."

"You have no idea. I have planned this night for four thousand years." He sighed. Murph thought Farouk looked suddenly old and tired as he said, "The darkness comes before the dawn."

They arrived at the Center and parked quietly at the rear of the building. They all sat quietly for a moment, absorbed in their thoughts. Margaret released the locks and opened the door. Her voice calmly urged them to action. "Come. We must prepare. There is still much to do!"

Chapter 73

Margaret led the group into the Center and down the hallway to Manny's office. The desk was overturned and glass cases smashed. Trash littered the floor. The golden wall relief of the hieroglyphics had been repositioned and stood against the wall. Dr. Farouk passed the artwork, lightly caressing it with his hand. He pressed a panel on the wall, and a segment of the paneling opened, exposing a safe. He dialed the combination and opened the safe's door. He removed another of the glass vials and shook it to verify its contents. A lower denture, with gold crowns on the molars, clinked back and forth.

"Come! We must extract the gold."

He led Murph to the elevator, and they descended to the lab. Margaret and Saleh went off to continue preparations, while Manny and Murph went to the lab bench, next to the equipment for casting. Murph withdrew Washington's dentures from his pocket, dusting them clean. As Manny removed the teeth from Churchill's denture, Murph used pliers and a drill to remove the carved ivory teeth from Washington's prosthesis. They wiped the Pharaoh's gold with disinfectant and placed each denture's piece in a separate glass jar.

Murph handed his jar to Manny, but Manny refused to accept it. "This is yours to control. It is a huge bargaining chip. You must use it to its best advantage. I will use the other one for the same purpose."

"Thank you." Murph considered Manny Farouk, looking deeply at his face. "Thank you for allowing me to be your apprentice. Whatever happens, it has been an exciting time for me."

"You are no longer my apprentice. Remember that! What you will become is up to you. I have merely given you the opportunity — an opportunity four thousand years in the making."

Margaret came back into the lab, looking anxiously at her watch. "It's time. We must hurry!"

Manny nodded and led Murph out the back of the lab, down another hallway, away from the elevator up to the surface. As they left the lab, Murph noticed that this passage was made of natural stone and lit with torches attached to the wall. As they descended, there was less and less evidence of modern materials. At the base of the passage was a wooden door with an iron clasp and hinges.

Manny rapped on the door, and it opened from within. Saleh held open the door for them.

Margaret stepped back and took Murph's hand. "This is as far as I dare go. It is forbidden for me to proceed." She squeezed his hand and kissed him on the cheek. "Trust yourself," she whispered, "and good luck!"

Murph followed Manny through the doorway and heard it shut behind him with a metallic clank. *I'm in this all the way now!* He thought.

Saleh led them to a small group of chambers off the main hall. Each contained a stone basin of steaming water. The scent of perfume was in the air.

"We must purify ourselves for the ceremony. As a dentist, you are a priest of Ptah. You must disrobe and bathe. Soaps and lotion have been provided. Hair is impure in the eyes of the Gods, so we must shave — head and body."

Murph scratched his head. "Everything?"

"You must shave off all hair. Then perfume yourself, and dress in the robes provided." Manny gestured at the white linen tunic and loincloth on pegs in the wall. A leopard skin hung there as well. "When you have finished, come out, and Saleh will make sure everything is in order. I have my own preparations to complete."

He left Murph alone with his thoughts. *I've come this far. I need to see it through.* He bathed and shaved, finding the straight razor incredibly sharp. The lotion reduced the burning sensation, and the perfumed oil left him glistening, with a faint golden sparkle. Putting on the loincloth and then the tunic over top, he admired his reflection in the mirror. *Carli will be in for a surprise. But I have to play the part in order to get her back.*

Murph still had the psh-kef knife in his sock, and he hated to part with the security that the blade gave him. It balanced well in his hand, the wooden handle filling his palm and the leather straps binding the blades together. It was not long, maybe eight inches, looking like an ancient wood chisel. He scanned around the room and found two lengths of leather thong. He tied them around his thigh, holding the knife suspended blade up, just above his left knee.

Murph examined the leopard skin and found it to be a drape for his back. The forelegs ended in gold clasps, so he placed the pelt on his shoulders and fastened the clasps. The leopard's legs crossed in front of Murph's chest, while the body covered his back, the legs and tail dangling down behind his legs. A gold mesh belt with a turquoise clasp completed the ensemble.

If I didn't feel this is life and death, I'd just have to laugh. I look like Mr. Clean in fur! He turned in front of the mirror, the torchlight dancing on his oiled, bald head. *This would be an award-winning Halloween costume!*

"Doctor Murphy, are you ready?" Saleh's booming bass voice brought him back to reality.

"Yes!" Murph had been thinking about this evening for a while now. He had decided that projecting confidence was the best course of action, regardless of how scared he was. For Carli's sake, he had to control the situation as much as possible. His last confrontation with Hamid and Omar had confirmed that being bold and unpredictable was the correct path! He took a deep breath, stood tall, and stepped out into the hallway to meet his fate.

Chapter 74

Manny Farouk smiled broadly up at the face of the taller Mike Murphy. "You are truly a priest of Ptah." Manny was similarly attired and also now devoid of his customary tightly combed black hair. He extended his arm and shook Murph's hand firmly. "I feel I owe you a formal introduction. The time for secrets has passed... I am Sekhem Ka!"

Murph stood silently, feeling the power of the moment, and sensing with dread the motion of colossal events in the background.

"I was trained by Hesi-Ri. I am the private dentist and priest to Pharaoh, Djoser the Mighty. I have protected him for four thousand years. But my time in service is almost at an end. Although it has been an adventure, I am sorely tired."

Murph reached out and clasped the man he knew best as Manny on the shoulder. "I have read your writings on diagnosis and treatment. They set the standard for the profession. I am in your debt, but let's finish this. It is time for you to rest!" Manny smiled at the compliment but said not a word. The time had come, and he was ready.

Saleh led them down the torchlight passage to a large chamber. Murph recognized immediately the significance of the gilt coating on the walls. They descended six steps to the floor of the chamber, allowing Murph to survey the scene.

The center of the chamber was dominated by a mound of white sand. Murph stopped in his tracks. Lying on his back on the sand was the mummy of Djoser. His head had been unwrapped, but the grey linen bandages still covered the remainder of the mummy. His skin was ashen gray, with his eyes sunken into their sockets. Much of the flesh had rotted away, leaving a skeletal visage. His head had been shaved bald, as was the custom. His mouth was open and his head rolled back off the sand, making him look as if he were sleeping.

Another mound of sand had been built next to the Pharaoh. A limestone table sat as an altar before the head of the mummy. On it were several gold bowls, some filled with water and perfume, one was empty.

Another stone table was in front of Murph as he reached the bottom of the stairs. He noticed vials of oil and colored pigments, incense, linen cloths of white, red, green, and blue, and a single feather. He tried to remember what Carli had said about the Opening of the Mouth ceremony. *An ostrich feather!* He could hear her voice now. *An ostrich feather is presented as a symbol of Maat, patron of truth and order, indicating that the natural order had been restored by allowing the mummy to journey to the afterlife and be reborn.*

There was a commotion in the distance, then a clattering of hooves on stone. Saleh emerged from a side doorway, leading a bull on a chain, with the iron ring through its nose. He bound the bull to a stake in the floor, and after a moment of defiant snorting, the animal lay down quietly on a pile of straw. *If you knew what was coming,* Murph thought, *you wouldn't be so compliant.* Murph could see the sword belted at Saleh's waist, and he had a good idea that it wasn't going to end well for the bull. He was hoping that he wouldn't share a similar fate.

Looking back, to Murph's left, he saw the obsidian statue of Djoser mounted on a limestone altar, standing by itself in front of a small alcove. He grinned. *Just like the one at the museum, except that the nose isn't broken.* That's what he had told Carli about it when he recalled seeing it in Manny's office. Now the statue was here, looking down that nose at Murph. Seated in all his regal bearing — headdress, long wig of hair, right arm across his chest, holding a scepter, left arm in his lap, hand on his knee — his face was impassive, mouth a straight line over the square "Pharaoh" beard, and the eyes were dark, hooded deep in shadow by prominent brows.

The room was illuminated by large bronze braziers along the walls and one central fire pit between the sand mounds and Djoser's statue. The fire pit was a giant limestone circle, lined with bronze and filled with burning wood and charcoal. Manny took the bowl of incense from the table and tossed a generous spoonful onto the main fire. The flames burst higher, showering sparks, and then settled down to a green tinted flame.

Manny moved to stand in the center of the room, near the head of Djoser. Saleh loitered near the bull and fingered the grip on the sword. Murph, sensing what was coming, drifted to the opposite side of the room, finding some comfort in being near the statue of Djoser.

A gong sounded in the distance. The latch on the door from which Murph had entered opened, and the gong sounded again. Murph thought, *Showtime!*

Chapter 75

Hamid el-Said entered first, now completely shaved like Murph and Manny. He also wore the leopard skin over a white linen tunic; however, his neck was encircled with a golden choker. A golden band surrounded his head, holding a tail of sky blue cloth covering the back of his neck. He walked down the stairs slowly, his head erect, his nose up as if the scent displeased him.

The door swept open to its fullest, slamming against the wall. Banthaira stepped through the threshold and stopped, surveying the scene. She was regal — breathtakingly beautiful, but cold and forbidding. Her raven black hair hung long and straight over her bare shoulders. Her gown of crisp white linen was held at her breast by golden clasps. An amulet of turquoise in the shape of a scarab was suspended with gold banding around her neck. Her gown ended with gold banding at mid thigh, and her anklets were of gold and precious gemstones. Her bare feet made no sound as she descended the steps.

She glared at Murph. Her eyes were painted with iridescent green lids, and black dye lined her eyebrows and covered her lashes. Her lips, reddened with henna, were drawn in a taut line. She raised her left arm and repositioned her gold bracelet, in the shape of a serpent, tightly on her forearm. She snapped her fingers, then placed her hands on her hips, waiting impatiently.

Omar Bengdara, attired like Saleh in a simple, rough cotton tunic, had not shaved. His bushy beard still enveloped the lower half of his face, with the full black eyebrows dividing the red, peeling skin of his cheeks from his forehead. Murph couldn't concentrate on him, as he only had eyes for Omar's captive.

Omar's hand was locked on Carli's arm as he dragged her into the room. She defiantly shook off his grip, but made no move to run. She examined the chamber and wasn't surprised to find everything set just as she had envisioned it would be. She nodded at Manny, who smiled at her approval. Carli suddenly realized that the tall, muscular priest staring at her with his mouth open was Murph. Her face lit up as she grinned, inclining her head slightly to one side, and winked.

To Murph, she was a vision of loveliness. Where Banthaira was icy and terrifying, Carli radiated warmth and energy. Her skin glistened with a golden sparkle. She wore a wispy white dress, draped tightly over her frame. The kalasiris, as it was called, extended to her calf, and her bare feet were adorned with anklets of gold, fashioned in a grapevine pattern. Her biceps were gripped tightly by golden serpents, and her auburn curls were pulled back from her face by a gold tiara, holding a turquoise stone centered in her forehead. Where Banthaira's eyes were painted a harsh, bright green and black, Carli's were painted a smoky blue and purple. The heavy dye on Banthaira's brows and lashes was absent from Carli's.

Carli smiled broadly, and Murph's heart melted.

Carli floated down the stairs and quickly made to run to Murph, but Omar jumped to the floor and blocked her path, regaining his vice grip on her arm. Murph began to rush to her aid, but Banthaira held up her hand. "Stop!" she commanded.

The gong sounded again, and the door closed behind them with a thud.

Hamid stepped forward to the edge of the fire pit, opposite Manny, and pronounced in a loud voice, "I am Iy Mry! High Priest of Ptah! I come to complete the ritual over Pharaoh. It has been delayed for too long!" He folded his arms over his chest and glared at Farouk.

Manny opened his arms, palms up, looking up at the ceiling. A black stain from the smoke was growing on the golden tiles. "I am Sekhem Ka, Priest of Ptah. We are here to attend Pharaoh, assisting him to join the North Stars. It is just and proper that we do this!"

Iy Mry motioned to Omar. Banthaira came over and grasped Carli, her glossy black fingernails digging into her arm. Carli winced, but stood proudly, her head held high. Omar went back out the door and returned with a briefcase. He set it down before Iy and opened the lid. The gold teeth glistened in the glass vials as the firelight flickered and danced on them. He surveyed Murph. "Have you brought Washington's gold?"

"I have the gold from George Washington, as well as Winston Churchill. Release Carli and I will give you the gold!"

Iy laughed. "I fail to see how you are in any position to bargain. Give me the gold now, and let us get on with the ceremony."

Unfortunately, Murph could see that he was right. His only hope lay in disrupting the ceremony, much as Sekhem Ka had done 4,500 years ago. Murph selected the vials of gold from the altar in front of the statue of Djoser and carried them to Iy. He placed the gold down and stepped back.

Sekhem Ka nodded, pronouncing, "It has been over four thousand years since this gold was together in one place. This is a grand reunion. May Maat, the God of Order and Justice, be pleased!" He closed his arms, clapping his palms sharply together once.

The room shuddered, the tremor rumbling for a moment, and the flames erupted to twice their height, returning to normal, as suddenly as they had flared.

Iy Mry pointed at Manny. "Sekhem Ka. My servant! " He spat out the words with contempt. "Collect the gold and cast the prosthesis for Pharaoh! I shall prepare the body!"

Sekhem Ka bowed and reached for the case.

"No!" Murph interrupted, his voice cutting the air. "He has done enough! I shall cast the gold!"

Iy Mry choked a cold, mirthless laugh. "So, priest, you now have a servant of your own to do your bidding!"

Manny shook his head. "He is not my apprentice. I fired him weeks ago. He acts on his own, often contrary to my wishes. I have no control over him now, and truly I never had."

Murph never stopped moving, stepping in front of Hamid and collecting the briefcase, the bronze tube that was the investment, and all the vials. "I will return when I have finished. I know you will wait for me here!" His sly smile irked Hamid, as he had intended. *Need to get them angry and distracted.* Murph quickly climbed the stairs and went out the door. As he walked down the corridor to the lab, he thought he heard the gong sound again.

Chapter 76

Senator Brooks Borlon hated using the tunnel from the Russell Senate Office Building on a nice night like this one. He much preferred the short walk across the street to the Capital. It gave him time to think. That was especially valuable tonight, as he had a major address to the Senate. The energy bill under consideration was a significant piece of legislation, and he was its primary sponsor. It fell to the young Senator to champion its passage in this late night session. He was ready, he knew, but the sight of the full moon rising gave him pause. *A lucky omen*, he thought. As he climbed the steps to the Capital entrance, he felt the tremor and was shocked to see the trees and streetlights swaying.

At first he thought he had imagined it, but Maeve was questioning, "Senator, did you feel that?"

"Yes," He tried to sound confident. "Only a slight tremor. On we go, Maeve. Big things to do tonight!" He ran up the final steps two at a time, but a feeling of dread was creeping into the edges of his mind. He looked down at his watch — 11:15 p.m. *Why does the Senate have to do everything at the last minute now? Nothing good happens this late.* He tried to shake off the feeling, but he entered the Capital with a deep feeling of foreboding.

Chapter 77

Murph exhaled and tried to breathe normally as he strode up the hallway and into the lab. It felt like he had been holding his breath for hours, but challenging Hamid had given him a few free moments to think.

Murph always enjoyed lab work. The quiet peace of working with wax or gold helped him to organize his thoughts. He quickly went to work on the lab bench, setting out the bronze investment. He made sure the opening was clear of any dust or obstructions, so that the molten gold would flow easily into the mold. He placed the investment into the oven to pre-heat it, keeping the gold from setting too quickly. He opened the containers for the gold, setting them aside in easy reach. He placed a four-inch diameter steel basin in the cradle, which supported its rounded base up off the bench top. He donned fireproof gloves and readied the tongs. Taking the bronze tube out of the oven, he placed the investment, so that he could easily tip the basin and guide the molten gold into the mold.

With everything in place, Murph lit the torch. He debated and then chose the gold from Washington's denture first. It was spotlessly clean, shining in his hand. He placed the metal in the steel basin and touched the flame to it. As he moved the torch around, the tongue of flame flared against the solid gold, and the gold began to lose its oxidized surface. Gradually, the metal softened and then began to liquefy. The golden liquid pooled and then pulled together, like a raindrop, into a glittering semicircular ball.

Murph selected the Churchill gold next, placing it on the side of the basin. He treated that gold ingot to the same loving care and was rewarded when it formed a drop and then rolled down the side of the basin. It struck the first blob of molten gold, bumping into it. The surface tension of the two drops broke down, and the two merged into one larger drop. Murph was vaguely aware of a slight tremor as the droplets joined into one.

Taking a crown this time, Murph noticed the gold appeared red, probably from the blood, as it had been forcibly taken from its owner. Murph tried to clean off the gold with alcohol and then acetone, but the bloody residue could not be removed. He was forced to melt the gold as it was.

This smaller chunk melted faster and retained a deeper red hue. When the droplets merged this time, there was no denying the rumble beneath his feet. After the next crown, the tremor caused the glass vials to clink together. Murph could feel the power building as the gold was reunited, but he had no choice but to continue. He grabbed another crown in his tongs and watched as the flames licked at it, blood red deep within.

Chapter 78

The tremor was mild and would not have caused him to wake up but for the sudden startling of hundreds of pigeons into flight outside his window. Father Albers looked at his watch and realized it was nearly 6:00 a.m. and not yet sunrise. *What could have caused such commotion in the birds?* They usually sat quietly on the tile roof of the Vatican until the sun came up.

There it was again. He felt the tremor that time, and the birds spooked again. *Something is wrong. Very wrong!* Father Albers got out of bed quickly and put on his robe and slippers. He dialed the phone, and Father Mahoney answered on the first ring.

"Brian, do you feel it?"

"Yes. I can't escape it — the sense of dread!"

"Something very old and powerful is coming into the world. I feel a great evil afoot. I think Michael is in danger!"

Another tremor struck the Vatican, stronger this time. There was a crash of breaking glass, then shouting in the courtyard.

"Brian, join me in the chapel immediately! We must pray!"

Chapter 79

Murph was down to the last three crowns. The collected gold roiled like an angry ocean, deep red under the shiny golden surface. As this molten crown joined the mass, the quake nearly knocked Murph off his stool. He stood up and shoved the stool aside with his hip. He moved on to the next crown. *Quickly, this cannot wait!* The elevator bell rang, and the doors opened. *Now what?* A sniffle indicated the car wasn't empty, and Margaret carefully peaked her head out. Murph looked up at her, lifting the torch off the gold momentarily.

"Oh, Michael. You're here!" She ran into the room and over to the lab bench. She looked into the basin, regarded the swirling mass of molten gold, and recoiled, shivering uncontrollably.

"Margaret, it's OK. I almost have all the gold combined, then I can cast the teeth and end this." He smiled to reassure her.

"Michael, everything is crazy up there!" Murph studied her more closely. Her face was white and drawn, though her eyes were red and puffy. It was clear she had been crying. "Manny said goodbye and told me to go home, but I couldn't leave. I tried to watch TV to wait it out here, but the news is all full of everyone going crazy."

"What?" Murph frowned.

"Since you began down here, the full moon has turned blood red, and the earthquakes are increasing. There is panic in the streets. People are posting on their blogs that the apocalypse is coming. The 'blood red moon' is a sign of the end of days. With each tremor, more people take to the streets of Washington, frantically running, but they don't know where to go. It's horrible!"

At that, Murph had completed melting another gold tooth, and it joined the mass of metal, touching off another quake, this one stronger and longer than the one before.

Margaret sobbed, leaning her head on Murph's shoulder. "Manny said goodbye like he knew he wasn't coming back. I just know I've seen him for the last time, but it may not matter if Hamid completes the ceremony and controls the mummy. I promised I wouldn't cry, but I'm such a failure."

"You are not! It is a scary night, but we'll be OK. Manny is a brilliant guy, and I trust his judgment. This will be fine." He hoped he sounded more convincing than he felt.

"Actually, it's Manny who trusts you. He is counting on you to accomplish what he was never able to do!" She leaned over and kissed him lightly on the cheek. "I believe in you as well. I always have."

Murph smiled in thanks, not having any words to express his gratitude for the vote of confidence when he needed it most. He lifted the second last crown into the basin and began to heat it.

Margaret studied the basin and the roaring flame, losing herself in the gold. "It is out of our hands now. That's what he said!" She sighed deeply. "I'll leave you now and go upstairs to continue my vigil. I won't leave until it's over." She squeezed Murph on the arm and walked to the elevator. She punched the button for up, and the chime sounded, opening the door.

"Margaret?" Murph called to her and she stopped in the doorway. "I don't think I ever learned your last name?"

"Why, it's Farouk! What did you think?" She smiled, and the elevator door slid quietly closed, leaving Murph alone with his task.

Chapter 80

Ead Abdel-reheem, newly appointed Minister of State for Antiquities, arrived early at the Egyptian Museum of Antiquities in Cairo. He needed to determine the truth in the conflicting reports he was being given concerning the presence of a dead body in the Museum. There were hundreds of dead bodies in the museum, of course, but all of them had been deceased for thousands of years. The current concern was the presence of a week-old crime victim, found in a sarcophagus. As sensational as this was, the truly embarrassing thing for Ead was that the mummy who should have been in the sarcophagus was missing.

So far, he had been able to keep these events a secret, but bad news, he knew, could not be kept silent forever. Rushing to the museum at 6:00 a.m., he hoped he could conduct his own search prior to anyone else arriving – and without interruption or further inquiry. A short, rotund little man, he scratched his balding head and pushed his heavy glasses back up on the bridge of his nose. He fumbled with his keys, his haste making him clumsier than normal.

He finally unlocked the private entrance in the rear of the building and was shuffling briskly toward the mummy, when the tremors started. Dust began falling from the ceiling, creating a fine mist that was making vision difficult. The museum relied on its skylights for much of its illumination, and as the sun had not fully risen, a dim light filled the building.

Ead rounded a corner. When the final, severe tremor struck, he dodged sharply to his right, catching his foot on a case filled with amphorae, and fell to the ground. He looked up in horror, as the statue of Djoser toppled over, narrowly missing him and tipping face down onto the marble floor. The dust cloud expanded rapidly. Momentarily blinded, the curator rolled over and found himself staring into the face of the Pharaoh, nose shattered and neck broken. He jerked back in terror and ran from the building, screaming,

Chapter 81

Murph melted the last crown and prepared for it to join the swirling mass of gold. He held on to the bench as the final piece of gold was reunited. The building shook, and the tremor abated only slightly when all the gold had formed one blob. Murph heated the metal until it was white hot and then poured it into the open mouth of the bronze investment. The mold devoured the molten gold, drinking in every drop. He prayed the gold would flow freely and not form any voids that would mar the casting.

He used the tongs to grab the burning investment and immerse it in the sink, which he had filled with cold water. The bronze tube hissed as it struck the water. Murph imagined, given the sound, that a snake would rise out of the water. It bubbled angrily, but cooled.

Murph removed the investment and unscrewed the end caps on the bronze tube. He opened the sides of the investment with a lab knife, exposing the casting. The oxidized gold appeared dark and dull, but there were no voids. There were nine teeth, chained in two rows — five and four, just as he had envisioned when he first examined the investment on the plane flight that now seemed so long ago.

He cleaned off the dust from the metal and used the steam jet to wash the prosthesis. He polished the gold, and it achieved a deep luster almost immediately. It was a high grade of gold, extremely pure and very soft. It bent easily in his hands, which would allow it to be molded to fit the mouth of the Pharaoh. Even though Murph had been sure to clean the crowns before melting them, he could swear that the highly polished gold had a blood red hue, deep within the metal. The gold teeth for Pharaoh were beautiful, yet frightening to behold. *There is an awesome, terrible power within this gold that truly has been tainted with blood.*

Murph's task was done so he gathered the golden teeth and carried them with respect in the cupped palms of his hands, starting at a steady pace down the long corridor to the House of Gold.

Chapter 82

Senator Borlon had barely begun, when the tremors became impossible to ignore. The chandelier in the chamber swayed from side to side, threatening him as he stood at the podium to address his colleagues. The evacuation began in a panic, and Maeve pulled him out the side entrance to the chamber.

Others spilled out onto the Capital steps. The swaying of the building had alarmed them, and now they were terrified by the scene unfolding before them.

The rising full moon had changed from ghostly white to a deep blood red. Midnight was passing, and a new day was beginning, but Twitter and Facebook posting exploded with pictures of the moon. TV networks were frantically trying to put their experts on camera to explain how a blood red moon occurs... and how it is perfectly normal. But Google searches for "blood red moon" all spoke of a prophecy for the "end of days." It seemed to the people of Washington that the apocalypse was upon them. In homes and apartments, people huddled in fear. In the streets, the frantic race to escape the city was on.

Senator Borlon put his arm around the frightened Maeve Corrigan. There was no need to panic, he assured her. He had a feeling that Murph was involved in this and that they were all in good hands. *Ignatius Men Forever!* He prayed he was right. He called his wife back in Ohio, and told her, together with Maeve, the full details of Murph's elaborate story. It was as good a way as any to pass the time. There was nowhere to run.

Chapter 83

Murph arrived at the sealed wooden door to the House of Gold. He held the Pharaoh's dental prosthesis in his hands. He had arrived at a critical moment, but still had not formed any kind of plan. The more he thought about it, he didn't really know enough to plan. He would have to follow in the footsteps of his forefathers. *We're Americans; we don't plan.* He realized that the essence of his strategy had always been to act boldly, charging ahead. *JUST DO IT!*

He reached for the handle to release the latch, taking a deep breath and steeling his resolve. Suddenly, there was a loud roar of pain, a snort and then a crash. Murph shoved open the door, to see the bull down on the straw, bleeding to death from a wound in its neck. Saleh had opened the chest and was handing the bloody heart, still beating, to Manny Farouk.

Manny took the heart and presented it to the mummy, holding it high in the air, cupped in his hands. Hamid grabbed the heart from Manny and placed it on the stone altar before the mummy. They had used the golden bowls of water to wash and purify the mummy, especially the mouth. *Pharaoh should be purified with water from the Nile, both the Upper and Lower Egypt, poured out of golden bowls.* Carli had described the ritual in detail when translating the hieroglyphics. Murph remembered it well.

A bull is butchered and the heart is presented to the mummy.

Its foreleg is severed and pointed toward the deceased. The foreleg of the bull is a symbol of great strength, the leg serving as a conduit to focus the transfer of the life force of the bull to the mummy. Murph could see Saleh carving the right leg out of the bull and passing it to Manny. He laid the leg on a golden shield, placed on the floor, and carefully aimed the leg at the mummy. The blood from the animal flowed freely across the floor, leading to a drain, which had been covered by the shield. The blood moved like a river from the bull to the shield, extending toward the sand bier that supported the Pharaoh's remains.

The priests perform the ritual to bring about the transformation and free the ka and ba, body and soul, from the mummy, allowing them to roam the world. Hamid and Manny were chanting in their ancient tongue, lost in their own world from thousands of years ago.

It was then that Murph noticed that the other sand mound was no longer empty. Carli was chained to the bier, her arms held out, spread eagle. Banthaira stood over her, supervising the dripping of blood from a cut on her bound wrist into a golden dish. Carli was pale and lifeless.

"CARLI" Murph's voice boomed across the chamber, stopping the proceedings. He jumped down the steps to the floor and ran toward her, still cradling the gold teeth in his palms.

"Murph!" She cried weakly and opened her eyes, a tired smile crossing her face. "I'm OK... If you give them what they want, she says she will release me."

He turned to face Hamid and instinctively passed both sets of gold teeth to his left hand, lightly closing his fingers around them. "I have completed the task, and the prostheses are ready! Release Carli, and I will give them to you."

Hamid eyed him coldly. "I am Iy Mry, High Priest of Ptah. You are nothing!"

Omar Bengdara sprang from the shadow of the stairs behind Murph, clasping his forearm across Murph's throat, closing a vise with his other arm behind Murph's neck. Gasping for breath, Murph was forced to his knees by the weight of the larger, stronger man.

"Kneel, and I will take what I want from you, and give nothing in return!" Hamid calmly crossed to Murph and took the golden teeth from his hand.

Murph struggled, to no avail, so he relaxed and spoke as soon as he could breathe, "I have studied the Opening of the Mouth Ritual, but I don't remember anything about human sacrifice!"

Hamid stopped and turned back to Murph. "This is the new technique. I think you will find it has a much more exciting ending!"

Hamid al-Said held the two gold bands, supporting the teeth, high in the air. He studied them in the firelight, the deep golden hue, tinged with red, sparkling in the flickering light. "You have done well. These are finely crafted. Sekhem Ka has taught you well!"

"He is far more talented than you!" Murph asserted boldly.

"We shall see!" Hamid took the band of lower teeth and smoothly bent the soft metal in his fingers. Gold of this high content, virtually pure, would never be used in the mouth of a living person, since it was far too soft and malleable. It was perfect for this task, however, and Hamid gently molded the prosthesis into place. It replaced the four missing lower teeth perfectly. Hamid spread his hands and arms wide as he stepped back, and he turned around as if he planned to take a bow, looking for the applause of the crowd. He reached for the upper prosthesis and turned back to the mummy.

"So, Hamid!" Murph taunted, trying to buy more time, "Do you want to raise the mummy and take over the world? Do you get to control the army of the dead or something?"

Hamid stopped and turned to regard Murph in an icy stare. Laughing, he mocked him. "You watch too many movies! No, you simpleton, I want to kill Djoser and keep on living as I am. Over the centuries, I have commanded armies, and the world has come to me! The curse has been a blessing!" He smiled expansively and then pointed a long finger at Manny. "This servant has cursed himself. I have lived a life of riches and power, while he has scrambled and scuttled like a rat, hiding his precious pieces of golden cheese from me." Manny's face reddened, as Hamid continued, "My star is in its ascendency again. This is the new dawn of my power! When I kill the mummy, I will possess my queen!"

Banthaira had moved over to stand beside him, as he offered the golden teeth up to the fire, and intoned the spell. He placed the prosthesis in the upper jaw and molded it to fit the maxilla. The five teeth missing in the upper jaw were replaced seamlessly. Hamid closed the mouth of the mummy, squeezing its teeth together. The fires leaped, and there was a clap of thunder.

Hamid stood back and turned with his back to the mummy, facing Murph and Manny. "It is done! I am master of the mummy. I am Iy Mry, High Priest of Ptah! Sekhem Ka, you have failed!"

Chapter 84

A massive bolt of lightning and a rumbling clap of thunder split the sky. The moon shone blood red, rising ever higher in the sky. Birds screamed and flew around in circles. Dogs barked, wolves howled, and the power went out in Washington, plunging the city into darkness, lit only by the blood red moon.

In Cairo, the tremor shifted the sands around the pyramid at Saqqara. The final thunderclap was followed by the crash of limestone, as the false doors along the colonnade around the palace collapsed. The pyramid now was open to the world, and the spirit of the pharaoh had free access to the entire complex. Horrified guards ran from the area as angry clouds of sand swirled up, blocking out the blue sky and the rising sun. Though it was dawn, the darkness of night had returned.

Chapter 85

Hamid stood, basking in the glory of his moment. "For nearly five thousand years, I have waited to savor this moment! The time is mine!"

The mummy groaned and growled, beginning to stir slightly in its wrappings.

"See, the creature animates. Now is the time!"

Hamid turned and approached the bier as the mummy opened its eyes. "Banthaira! Give me the knife and I will end this!"

She advanced next to him and extended the gold-handled

blade. As Hamid reached for the knife, she spun and slashed his neck with the blade. A look of disbelief crossed his face, his eyes opening wide. He grabbed his throat, blood spurting between his fingers, splattering the mummy. He staggered but managed to stay erect.

"You have finished the task, O Great High Priest," she shrieked the title with contempt, "the task you failed at so long ago. You have such small dreams, you little man! I am in control. I always have been." She reached out her hand and pushed him in the chest. Hamid collapsed into a sitting position, looking up at her with awe. "You do *MY* bidding. I have been cursed to be burdened with you for five thousand years. The kingdom was *MINE*. I designed it, and then you ruined my carefully laid plans with your bumbling."

Banthaira lifted her foot and placed her toes on his forehead. She shoved, and he fell over backwards, his black eyes open, but staring blindly at the ceiling.

"I am Banthaira, Queen of Egypt, whose name has been lost to history, but all will know me now! Awake, my Pharaoh and regain your rightful place." She took the bowl of blood from under Carli's wrist back to the mummy. She opened its mouth and poured in the red liquid. "Arise, and command your army. The world is ours!"

The roar echoed in the chamber, rattling the walls. The sound carried throughout Washington. Something terrible had awakened in the city, and the people shook with fear.

The mummy rolled off the sand bier and stood between Banthaira and Carli. Stretching its arms, it rose to its full height of six feet. The sight was awesome and terrible, and beyond belief.

Banthaira reached out her hand and took its arm. "Welcome, my Pharaoh to your new kingdom. Leave behind the underworld, dawn is coming, and it is our time to rule."

Manny rushed forward and lifted the bull's heart off the altar, presenting it to Pharaoh. "Greetings, my King, but you do not belong here. Your place is ever with the North Stars — those that never set — constant in the night sky. We will help you pass on through, as is proper."

Pharaoh rubbed his chin, rotting flesh coming off in a clump. "I know you! You cared for me, when I was ill, but I died in spite of your feeble efforts."

"Yes, Pharaoh. You had a condition with which I could not contend. You were being poisoned!"

"By whom? Who presumed to murder Pharaoh?"

Manny indicated the prone body of Hamid, lifeless on the floor. "He was the one. Your High Priest conspired to place arsenic paste in your abscessed tooth. The poison entered your body, and you succumbed in the end."

"He is dead, so I will deal with him in the underworld. Why did you summon me here? I wish to pass on to the afterlife. I have endured too much for thousands of years. Why do you keep me here against my will?"

"My King," Manny pleaded, "your presence here alters the natural order of the universe. You belong in the afterlife, not with the living. Maat is displeased. We must complete the ritual and send you along, balancing the world."

Pharaoh roared again, clenching his fist and shaking it violently at Manny Farouk. "What do I care for Maat? Complete the ritual then, and leave me in peace!"

Banthaira laughed, a high-pitched cackle. "But he cannot! The High Priest is dead! And the servant killed him!" She lunged at Manny, who pushed her back. "You are doomed to stay here, in this time!"

Manny protested, but the mummy swept past Banthaira and grabbed Manny by the throat. Pharaoh lifted Manny up off his feet and shook him. "Priest, if you cannot help me, then you shall join your High Priest. I have no use for you!" He flung Manny across the chamber, his body striking the wall with the crunch of breaking bone. Manny collapsed to the floor and lay still.

The mummy turned to Banthaira, "My priests are dead. If I must remain here, then I shall return to my kingdom and rule as Pharaoh."

"Yes, my Pharaoh!" She demurred. "I shall lead you and take you there. Once we return to Saqqara, your followers will rise up to support you. It is a long and perilous journey. We need the help of your army on the way. Call them forth!"

Carli, pinned on her back, strained to look over at Murph. He mouthed, "What does she mean?" But Carli could only shake her head. "I don't know!"

Banthaira stepped back and collected the golden bowl containing Carli's blood. She took it to the prone form of Hamid, and poured the liquid into his mouth. The mummy chanted quietly. The chant rose in volume as he raised his left arm, palm up, to the sky. The body of Hamid rose and stood upright, its eyes staring blankly in the distance. Banthaira cackled again, and Carli screamed.

Pharaoh smiled broadly, gold teeth flashing in the firelight. "Complete the sacrifice! Then we shall take back my kingdom!"

Banthaira set down the small golden bowl and picked up a much larger basin. She moved menacingly toward Carli, raising the blood-stained knife high in the air. The mummy stalked his prize as well, reaching Carli's prone form. She shied away in horror, but the chains bound her arms and feet. The Pharaoh held her down by her neck with his left hand, while he snapped the chains with his right. He lifted Carli's writhing body up. He held her around the waist and pulled her head back, exposing her throat for Banthaira. The Queen placed the gold basin against the glistening skin on Carli's neck and drew back the knife.

Murph had been forced down on one knee by the weight of Bengdara on his back. He had shifted into a crouch, using his hand to support him off the floor, kneeling on his right leg. His left leg jutted forward, holding his weight. Seeing the danger, he shouted "NOOO!" almost without thinking. He reached under the hem of his tunic, his right hand easily finding the psh-kef knife tied to his left thigh. Grabbing the handle, he pulled and the blade of the knife parted the leather thongs like butter. He began to rise up and could immediately feel Omar tense and push down against him.

Murph extended his right leg back and dropped down suddenly, tucking his right shoulder under and turning, using Omar's own strength against him. Bengdara's weight, combined with his downward pressure, toppled him over Murph's shoulder. Omar let go of Murph's neck as he crashed to the stone floor. As he had done thousands of times diving after a ball on the volleyball court, Murph rolled completely over and popped immediately to his feet. He lunged, extending his right arm, burying the psh-kef blade into Omar's chest. Not stopping to see its effect, Murph withdrew the knife and shoved the Egyptian to the ground, driving into him with his shoulder as he ran past.

Murph's only thought was to reach Carli before Banthaira

could strike. The Pharaoh seemed somehow amused, standing there, feet spread apart, holding Carli and waiting. But Banthaira was stunned at the sudden escape of the dentist. She hesitated a moment, which gave him the chance he needed.

Murph sprinted three long strides and was almost there. Then his foot caught on the base of the statue of Djoser, and he tripped, crashing into the stone altar in front of the sand mounds. He bounced up instantly. *Stupid statue. What is it doing here anyway?* He pushed himself off the altar and stopped, the light of revelation bursting in his head.

The Statue! The proper ritual is about the Statue! Not the Mummy! He looked down at the knife in his hand, blood dripping off the blade. It was really two blades, bound together. *Meteoric Iron!*

Murph held the knife high. He managed a booming voice of command, calling out, "I hold the psh-kef knife — made with God's Iron of Upper and Lower Egypt — the metal of Heaven."

Banthaira froze. "No! It cannot be! The ntjrwy was lost to history, thousands of years ago!"

"Many things that were lost have been found today!" Murph smiled at her. "I am Michael, priest of Ptah. Pharaoh, your journey is at an end. Your trials in the underworld are over." Murph was working quickly, trying to remember everything he could about the Opening of the Mouth Ritual. He had Pharaoh's attention now, but he must keep it.

"As Osiris was dismembered and then reborn as he was before, you have wandered for more than four thousand years. Tonight you are whole again. It was I who cast the gold and made your teeth! Now that you are complete, I will finish the ritual and set your ka and ba free to roam the world. Then you shall cross into the afterlife."

The mummy closed its eyes and whispered, "Yes!"

Murph searched his memory for Carli's voice. *Tell me the words from THE BOOK OF THE DEAD!* As he remembered her words from the night in Saleh's garden, Murph repeated loudly for all to hear. "My mouth is opened by Ptah. The bonds that gag me have been loosed by my god. My lips have been parted by Ptah with the psh-kef with which he has parted the mouths of the Gods."

Murph advanced to the front of the statue. *I remember this part!* He was sure of it. He looked at Carli with a smile of reassurance.

"O Osiris King, I split open your mouth for you — with the God's iron of Upper and Lower Egypt!" He touched the psh-kef knife to the lips of the statue. To his amazement, when the blade contacted the obsidian, it penetrated the stone. Air rushed past his face, and an audible pshhh filled the room.

The mummy let out a breath, "Ahhhhhh" and released Carli. She fell to the floor, gasping for breath. Djoser stood still, folding his arms across his chest, watching. The animated form of Hamid collapsed where he stood and did not move again.

Banthaira shrieked and charged at Murph. He grabbed her hand and stopped the golden blade from piercing his heart. The force of her attack was pushing him back, and he tripped over the steps up from the chamber floor. He fell back on the ground, and Banthaira swooped over him in triumph.

Carli got up, looking around frantically. Grabbing the only weapon she could see, she took the bull's foreleg and swung it over her head like a club. She struck Banthaira between her shoulders, driving her over Murph's prone form, and sending the Queen sprawling into the wall.

Carli extended an arm and pulled Murph up. "We must finish the ritual! You've gotten control of the mummy for now, but that will be only temporary unless we complete the ceremony."

"I don't remember any more. What do I do?"

"Light the incense and take the ostrich feather!"

Murph took a bowl of the incense and sprinkled a handful of the fragrant material on the fire in the central brazier. The flames flashed blue, and the pungent smoke filled the room. The mummy inhaled and drank deeply of the aroma.

Murph lifted the ostrich feather, and Carli softly led him to repeat, "This feather of the ostrich honors the presence of Maat. The natural order has been restored. Pharaoh will pass to the afterlife, and the force of his presence is removed from this place. Pharaoh has journeyed through the underworld and will be reborn with the dawn."

Carli was working quickly now. She anointed the statue with oils and painted the face of the statue with green and black eye paint. She dressed the statue in white linen, adorned with green, blue and red. Carli told Murph, and he announced to Djoser, that the red cloths would protect Pharaoh from his enemies, the blue would hide his face so that he would not be known by those who would do him harm, and the green would ensure his good health!

Pharaoh nodded his assent and smiled. He rose and turned to lie down on the packed sand bier.

A sharp pain burned in Murph's left shoulder, and he whipped around to find that Banthaira had driven the knife deep into his back, striking his shoulder blade. He flung her off him, the knife remaining buried to the golden hilt. She jumped up, reaching her claws for his eyes. Carli intercepted her, again wielding the bull's leg.

Swinging it like a baseball bat, Carli struck Banthaira across the jaw, sending her reeling. The Queen came within reach of Pharaoh, and he grabbed her. Pulling her close, Djoser considered her face, looking deeply into her eyes. She shook her head from side to side slowly, then increasing in pace.

"I understand now!" Djoser seemed sad, but determined. He had made his decision.

Banthaira screamed. "Nooooo" but it was choked off. Djoser held her head and neck, lovingly kissing her on the forehead, then tightened his grip. He twisted his hands, breaking her neck in one sudden motion. He cradled her lifeless body and carried it to the white sand mound. He laid her gently on the bier, folding her hands in her lap. Djoser returned to his bier, nodded to Murph and spoke, "Thank you, my priest! I am free to rest at last." To Murph and Carli, the words came from all around them, more in their minds. Djoser had indeed crossed into the afterlife. He was nowhere and everywhere all at once.

Djoser lay down on his back and folded his arms. He closed his mouth and eyes, and was gone.

The fires burned down, and the room became silent. Murph took the ostrich feather, tickled Carli on the nose and placed it in her hair. Laughing, she leaned against him, but he stumbled and fell to the floor.

Chapter 86

Carli knelt down and realized that Murph was bleeding. She had forgotten that the knife was still lodged in his shoulder. Saleh came over and helped remove the knife, binding Murph's shoulder with part of Hamid's tunic. Carli then sat with Murph on the floor, holding him to her, planning to never let him go.

Saleh examined the unconscious Omar Bengdara. He had lost a great deal of blood, but he was alive. Saleh bandaged his wound with more of the tunic.

Murph gathered some strength and, with Carli's help, went to Manny, finding his body broken. His neck had snapped when he struck the wall. His face appeared peaceful, even smiling. With his right hand, Murph closed Manny's eyes and arranged the body in a more comfortable position.

"He sleeps peacefully now. His work is done — Pharaoh has passed on."

"Yes," Murph whispered and then prayed silently, kneeling next to the body of the man who had become his friend.

Chapter 87

On the steps of the Capital, Senator Borlon looked up as a cloud passed in front of the moon. The night had been clear, so the sudden disappearance of the red moon was a welcome sight. As the cloud passed on, the moon reappeared, full, white, and beautiful! The panic ceased. People stopped to gaze at the moon. A cheer went up. Strangers were hugging each other and crying. It felt as if the weight of the world had been removed, and their spirits soared. Hardened politicians broke down and sobbed.

The pigeons settled again onto the clay tiles, and the winds died down. Deep in the catacombs of the Vatican, the priests could feel the change. They didn't need to see the angry clouds dispersing, nor the calming of the birds. In their hearts, they knew that a great evil had been thwarted and order returned to the world. Father Albers raised his voice in praise, and they gave thanks.

The sandstorm abated, leaving piles of white sand redistributed in new places. The cloud passed from the sun, and the blazing heat of day returned. Everything was as it had been for five thousand years and would continue to be. The land of the Pharaohs stood still again, statues in silent repose, guarding their secrets.

Chapter 88

With the disappearance of the blood red moon, Washington, D.C. rejoiced. Margaret did not. She raced down to the basement in fear, knowing what she was likely to find. But she had to see for herself.

She left the elevator and ran down the hallway to the chamber. She entered the House of Gold and was struck dumb by the scene. Blood and bodies littered the floor. She slowly came down the steps, and Murph got up and caught her, holding her with his good arm.

Margaret spotted Manny's body against the wall, arranged peacefully on the floor. "Is he?"

Murph nodded, but couldn't speak.

Margaret ran to him, kneeled down, and cradled his head in her lap. She had expected this and thought she had prepared herself. She wept openly, tears streaming down her face and dropping on Manny's forehead.

Murph and Carli went to her, and they supported her in her grief. There were no words, so they all knelt silently. Time no longer mattered. There was peace again in the city.

Chapter 89

Murph helped Saleh move the wounded Omar to the lobby of the Center. Murph began to call 911, but he was stopped by Saleh. "Too many questions we cannot answer!" Saleh warned. He made a phone call, and within minutes, a private ambulance arrived. Omar Bengdara was taken away quietly. The physician and his team examined Murph, and pronounced him extremely lucky. They dressed his shoulder and bound it tightly. They cleaned the wound on Carli's wrist and applied a few sutures and a dressing. With any luck, he thought, the scar wouldn't be too bad. It was on the inside of her arm, nothing an attractive new bracelet wouldn't fix!

At dawn, Saleh and Murph carried the body of Manny Farouk to the elevator and took it up, as Margaret made arrangements for his remains to be readied for the funeral. Without ceremony, Saleh had thrown the body of Hamid al-Said into the fire. He dusted off his hands, glad to be done with him.

Murph led the exhausted Carli out, locking the doors. They all left the Center. There was so much to do, but today was not the day. They were totally exhausted and in pain. They headed for Murph's condo. Despite the apparent buzz throughout the city after the events of the night, all they wanted was a quiet day of rest. Soon they were both asleep, Murph cradling Carli in his arm, no dreams interrupting the silence.

Chapter 90

Murph stood on the tarmac, hunched against the cold wind, his left arm still in a sling. A light rain was falling as he watched the coffin loaded onto the Gulfstream. *Time for you to go home, Pharaoh! It has been a long journey!*

Saleh saw to the security of the casket and came over to join Murph.

"It is nearly done!" The Egyptian waved at the waiting limo. The door opened, and a frail figure was helped out and over toward the jet. He looked drawn and had clearly lost weight, but the bearded face of Omar Bengdara would always be easy for Murph to recognize.

"I am pleased you are recovering," Murph offered.

"I am well enough to go home where I belong. I invite you to return with me, but it would be unwise for you or Miss

Chamoun to ever visit Cairo again." Though weak, his voice conveyed the malice in his heart.

Murph shuddered. "I shall try to remain safely here. I have seen enough of Egypt to last a lifetime."

Omar turned to walk away, but Murph's final comment stopped him in his tracks. "The Egyptian government claimed you are an assistant to the Ambassador here. You may have gained diplomatic immunity, Omar, but we know who you are. The video cameras in the Apprentice house captured the torture and murder of Claire Summerville. Currently, the U.S. government is not officially acknowledging that anything happened, but if you ever return to America, you will be arrested and tried for her murder. I will see to that personally… this I promise you!"

They locked eyes for a moment, and then Omar shrugged his shoulders dismissively. "So be it." He walked to the plane and disappeared up the stairs.

After Omar boarded the jet, Murph regarded Saleh.

"I never suspected that you were the former Head of the Egyptian State Security Police."

"Dr. Farouk had many ties to the old government. It is good that I am able to smooth the transfer here. Omar will return and say nothing. He would be viewed as a failure, and that is unacceptable to him. They will blame Hamid al-Said, which is good, for you. I will be able to clear your names, and close the investigation on the suicide of Tanen Narmer. I would, however, agree with Omar. You should not come to Cairo while the current government wields power."

"Then this will have to be goodbye, my friend!"

Murph embraced Saleh heartily and then smiled, raising his good arm. Carli opened the car door and trotted over, giving Saleh a hug as well.

"I'm sad you're leaving so soon," she said sweetly.

"It is necessary. I have many details to arrange." Saleh regarded them with a smile. "Everything is as we had discussed. I will return the mummy of Djoser to its rightful place at the Cairo Museum of Antiquities. Banthaira's body and the Pharaoh's ka statue remain here."

Carli nodded. "I have been offered the task of creating an exhibit at the Smithsonian's National Museum of Natural History.

We will display the statue, the investment and psh-kef knife, as well as the scroll and wall relief of hieroglyphics from Manny's office."

"That is a good job for you!"

"I will be able to complete my Ph.D. thesis here. Dr. Keller understands the truth now and has transferred me to a mentor on the faculty at Georgetown University. My initial translation of the hieroglyphics is fascinating. I think that Dr. Farouk, or Sekhem Ka, drew them as a journal to tell his story. Banthaira had planned to murder Djoser and take over the throne. She convinced her lover, Iy Mry, to poison the pharaoh. In advance, she had removed all rivals. Anyone with claim to the throne was eliminated. She was ruthless and successfully manipulated Iy Mry to get what she wanted."

Murph agreed. "It was a clever plan."

"Too clever, it seems." Carli continued. "When Sekhem Ka disrupted the ceremony, and cursed them, all four were suspended in limbo, including the pharaoh. Pharaoh existed in the shadow world of death. The other three passed through time among the living — involved in daily events, but never aging. Banthaira had been too successful at eliminating her rivals. When Pharaoh died and then Banthaira fled, her disappearance caused a leadership vacuum in the kingdom. There was no clear successor to the throne. After significant infighting, a new Pharaoh emerged. He had her name stricken from all records, and she was lost to history. Now the whole sordid tale can be told."

Murph chuckled. "It reads like fiction, but it will be an amazing exhibit!"

Saleh's face darkened a bit. "And what will happen to Margaret?"

Murph smiled. "That's right, you won't have heard. She has been made the Director of the Washington Center for Esthetic and Restorative Excellence! I never considered anyone else for the job. She's a natural!"

Saleh looked puzzled.

Carli burst in, "Dr. Farouk's will left the Center to Murph. He is the new President and chief dentist. With all the exposure, business is booming!"

Murph glanced down at his shoes, uncomfortable with the praise. "I'm too young and new at this to know everything, so I've enlisted help. My dad and several of his Pankey colleagues are going to come in several times a year as consultants to help me, and to use the Center for teaching graduate dentists here, as well as in Key Biscayne. I'm looking forward to learning something new every day!"

"Dr. Farouk would be proud. You are truly a worthy successor to his legacy." Saleh bowed slightly. "What are you planning to do now?"

Murph regarded the Gulfstream. "We are having dinner tonight with a good friend, who is a Senator from Ohio. Then, there is so much to do here! Carli has the exhibit opening in a few months, but I can't treat patients with a bad shoulder. I think we'll go for a trip! We promised friends in Rome and Switzerland that we would return to spend some time with them." With an ironic smile he added, "Washington can be so boring, you know!"

Saleh smiled and shook his head. He embraced Murph warmly and walked to the Gulfstream, as the engines began to whine.

Murph put his arm around Carli and held her close. She nestled against his body and rested her cheek on his chest. After running constantly for two weeks, it felt good to both of them to just to stand still. They watched the jet taxi out with the Washington Monument standing tall in the background.

Murph looked down at Carli. "I'm hungry. I know this great sushi place in Miami. Let's go for dinner!"

Carli stared at him in wide-eyed disbelief.

"What?" He grinned. "My car is still in Key Biscayne, and I want to bring the Mustang back."

"You're impossible!" She punched him lightly, in his good shoulder. "What am I going to do with you?"

Murph bent down and kissed her lightly on the forehead. "You'll have a long drive to figure it out!"

Laughing, they turned and walked, hand in hand, back to the hangar as the Gulfstream lifted off and banked east, taking the Pharaoh home at last.

Inside the Life of a Dentist

Patients expect us to be the best at whatever we do, and they deserve our best effort. A general dentist today has a variety of tools in the toolbox to solve any patient problem. A broad base of graduate and postgraduate training allows us to be competent and confident in recommending the full scope of available options for each patient's special circumstances.

Recently, I completed the first phase of a case for the mother of a large family. After a long time seeing to her children, it was her turn to take care of herself. For financial reasons, we had to go slowly, and it took over a year to complete the first phase. The final seating of five crowns with some composite fillings gave her the front of her smile back, if only in the upper teeth. It certainly wasn't an extreme makeover, but what I came to realize was that I had given her dignity and self confidence back as well.

I placed the crowns, gave her a mirror, and she cried. Then we all cried. She has not stopped smiling since, and neither have I. This case has become one of an ever increasing number that I keep in my memory bank, to open up and savor when I need a smile, or a little lift to keep going in a tough day. As these are my people, I have reminders of the smiles around me all the time; at church or at the ball field, at school, or in the grocery store.

Each year there is a local town fair called the Fairview Fun Fest. As I walk in the parade or down the midway, people wave and say "Hi, Doc!" When he was young, my son, Mike, would ask, "Why do they call you Doc?" Jokingly, I used to tell him that it was because they forgot my first name! Now I know that it is because they are my people, and I am their dentist.

Keep smiling!
Matthew J. Messina, D.D.S.
docmessina@cox.net